HOLDING YOU

Holding You

by Jewel E. Ann

For my mom,
who first recognized the author in me.

PROLOGUE

*"Where you used to be, there is a hole in the world, which
I find myself constantly walking around in the daytime,
and falling in at night. I miss you like hell."*

~Edna St. Vincent Millay

*W*HY IS MY *heart still beating? My body is numb and it's the
only thought floating through my mind. I'm dead, yet my
heart still beats.*

"Ma'am? Is there someone we can call, family or friends?"

*Th-thump, th-thump, th-thump. It's the sound of limbo. My
soul is desperate to leave my body but it doesn't know where to go.
Th-thump, th-thump, th-thump. It's the last drops of water before
the well runs dry. It's the last seconds on the clock before the bomb
ignites. It's the final moment before being sucked into the abyss.*

*"Ma'am, we're going to take you to the hospital and have you
examined. You've inhaled a lot of smoke and we may need a chest
x-ray and some blood tests."*

Th-thump, th-thump, th-thump ... total darkness.

CHAPTER ONE

"Here's all you have to know about men and women:
women are crazy, men are stupid. And the main reason
women are crazy is that men are stupid."

~George Carlin

L EAVING THE MIDWEST was my goal. I craved oceans and
mountains. So when I got my big chance to make my
escape, I loaded up the moving truck and said goodbye to
Chicago and hello to … Milwaukee. My mom, God rest her
soul, was right when she said, "Mother knows best," and
"Bloom where you're planted."

Milwaukee was magnificent in the spring. I loved living by
the water. It wasn't the Atlantic or Pacific, but Lake Michigan
wasn't a shabby body of water. The majestic view never failed
to amaze me. Living so close to the water was symbolic of my
state of being—always teetering on the edge of drowning, a
swaying pull from both directions.

I was a thirty-one-year-old orphan.

Love without fear.

Life without death. After all—I was already dead.

Being a self-proclaimed free spirit, I never missed an opportunity to stop and smell the roses, or the lilacs in the spring. I
had all the time in the world—no need to rush. My weathered
sneakers tracked the familiar path along the Milwaukee shore

of Lake Michigan to the vacant one-way street in front of my business.

Lilacs.

God, I loved the smell of lilacs. Halting in the quiet street to soak up the last bit of sun before stepping into the shadow of the building, I closed my eyes. The crisp spring air seduced me. I raised my arms up like angel wings, tilted my head back to feel the glorious sun bathe my face, and inhaled a slow deep breath, relishing the exquisite fragrance.

A horrifying clash of sounds punched the air from my lungs, jerking me back to reality.

"ADDY, WATCH OUT!"

A car's horn, screeching tires, a familiar voice.

The essence of lilac still filled my nose. A tingling chill washed across my skin, my vision hazed from the sun, the salty taste of blood filled my mouth, and shouting voices vibrated through my ears.

"Adler Sage Brecken what are you doing?" Mac squealed in a winded panic.

My best friend's face came into focus. Green eyes narrowed at me, brows furrowed behind a wispy curtain of windblown strawberry blond locks. Her mouth twisted into a grimace. It was never a good sign when she used my full name. I released my bloodied lip from the death grip of my front teeth.

Through the deafening whoosh of blood in my ears, I registered a deep, angry voice coming toward me. I held up my finger to silence Mac and tilted my head in the direction of the voice. Although clearly agitated, it was laced with a hint of Spanish accent.

Did I just hear someone call me a spaced-out, seventies throwback, pot-smoking, dumb blonde? What the hell?

In slow motion, my peripheral vision picked up a pair of men's black leather, designer shoes, just a few feet from me. Directly in front of me was a white SUV with the words *Range Rover* in chrome.

Turning to my right, I homed in on a white linen, button-down shirt that exposed the top of well-defined chest muscles wrapped in the perfect shade of olive skin. My gaze trailed north, capturing a strong, sharp jaw line, ruddy lips pursed in a formidable line, a Roman-sculpted nose, reflective brown eyes framed with thick lashes, and a full head of rebellious black hair.

Well done, God.

As if I had all the time in the world, I finished my sight-seeing tour by working my way back down Michelangelo's clothed version of David to those shoes that presumably cost more than most people's monthly rent.

"Hello? What the hell is your deal?" 'David' growled between clenched teeth.

"She's just got a lot on her plate today, sir, sorry for the scare. You're good. She's good. Everyone is good. Come on, Addy." Mac huddled me to her side, looking over her shoulder at the almost-accident while leading me toward the sidewalk.

I jerked away from her grip and crossed over into 'David's' personal space. My squinted eyes darted up to his, demanding his attention.

"First, I was not spaced-out," *I call it meditation,* "second, my style is organic and earthy, not seventies throwback," *maybe modern hippy,* "third, I don't smoke pot," *anymore,* "and finally, I may be blonde, but I am NOT dumb!"

What was that new smell?

A new fragrance overpowered the lilacs—an unwelcome

aphrodisiac. It had to be some ridiculously expensive cologne made from thousands of poisonous chemicals, and I cringed just thinking about the headache I would get from the toxic cocktail. However, in that moment, I wanted nothing more than to inhale it like a drug and live off the high. Everything about David was a heady combination. *Especially that damn sexy accent.*

"Well, I about ran your organic, earthy, smart-mouthed, blonde pigtailed, sexy ass over, Pippi." Each perfectly-accented word tumbled from lips molded into an arrogant smirk.

"You're supposed to yield to pedestrians in the crosswalk, you egotistical, reckless maniac!" A second later, my emotions regressed just long enough for my brain to catch up.

Sexy ass?

His eyebrows peaked as he gripped both of my arms and turned me around. "The cross walk is about fifteen yards that way, Pippi. Maybe you should think about using it next time to practice your role as Maria in the Sound of Music."

Shit, shit, double shit!

THE MORNING SUN reflected off the lake on one side and my brick building stood on the other. Sure enough, the stoplight was another half a block up the street.

"Let's go, Mac, we're going to be late." I tilted my chin up, threw my shoulders back, and walked to my café, with its recessed entry framed by two large arched windows, green awnings, and *Sage Leaf Café* in white with a light green sage leaf as the accent on *café*. After sneaking a quick glance back to look for Mac, I noticed Mr. Tall Dark and Hot as Hell slipping on his sunglasses while pulling away from the curb in his feed-a-small-country-for-a-day SUV. A rush of relief washed over my body. That was until Mac walked through the door and donned her Cheshire Cat grin.

"OMG, LMFAO, Maria in the Sound of Music, did you catch that? That *is* what you looked like out there and the Pippi comment …"

"Yeah, yeah, I get it, whatever. And what's with all the acronyms? What are you, twelve?" I grumbled over my shoulder, walking toward the kitchen while flipping my braided pigtails over my shoulders.

MY SMALL BUT growing business was closed because we landed a great catering gig at Zen Garden, Milwaukee's newest "green" hotel. We were the only all-vegan café in Milwaukee. The morning's unexpected events put us a bit behind. Thankfully, I padded our schedule with an extra hour.

Lizzy McDonald, one of my most loyal patrons, was part of the hotel's management team. She oversaw accommodations for VIP requests. Some financial guru from Chicago was holding a meeting there with local land developers and a few bigwig city officials, to talk about expanding green business trends in Milwaukee. Nothing said eco-friendly like a catered vegan lunch.

"So, Addy, want to talk about what just happened outside?" Mac asked, not making any attempt to hide her devilish grin. Her personality was as wild and untamed as the red curls that escaped her messy bun to tease her face.

"No, I want to finish packing all this food and bag the fresh garnishing herbs so we stay on schedule … anyway, there is nothing to discuss," I mumbled, keeping my eyes focused on my busy hands.

Mackenzie "Mac" had been my best friend since college. Her twiggy figure had at least three inches on my five-foot, six-inch, somewhat curvy stature. We met our freshman year at a peaceful protest in front of the University of Chicago's Student Union. There were over two hundred protesters there that day demanding the school source their meat from small local farms instead of large factory farms. It was friendship at first sight. I wore a "Runs on Veggies" T-shirt and she wore a "What the Kale?!?" tank top. Of course we were not in support of meat consumption from any farm, but rather a step in the right direction. Our make-love-not-war brains believed the logical step after local farms was veganism—us and less than one percent of the population.

Twelve years later we were still two peas in a pod, two kale leaves from the same plant. Our relationship was deep-rooted and forthright. We kept no secrets from one another, therefore lying to her was like lying to myself.

"I guess it must have been my imagination that the fine physical specimen you were inches away from in the street had your panties drenched and nipples at full attention, huh?"

"Oh my gosh, Mac! He about ran me over. I could have died this morning and you're trying to turn this into some smut novel you like to read!"

"WE ... some smut novel *we* like to read. Don't act like you don't have your iPad library filled with every smut novel published in the last ten years. That's why you don't date, you know no man will ever satisfy you like sex-script."

"First, I don't read *that* much, and second, you know that's not why I don't date. Just get the rest of those bags and let's go," I narrowed my eyes at her with an *end of conversation* finality, lips quivering to hide my grin.

OUR SMALL CREW arrived at Zen Garden Suites by eleven forty-five. With the help of a few hotel staff, we had everything unloaded and into the kitchen by noon. Lunch for twenty was to be served in a small conference room with floor-to-ceiling windows overlooking Lake Michigan.

I oversaw my staff plating the mixed garden-greens salad with pickled beets, asparagus, and ginger-fig dressing, while Mac assembled the roasted vegetable sandwiches. The hotel serving staff distributed the cucumber-mint water and raw juice spritzers while Lizzy McDonald paid a visit to the kitchen.

"Listen up, everyone. Here are the rules of the luncheon."

Rules of the luncheon? What the hell?

"Mr. Jamison requests the hotel staff serve the meal and tend to any needs of the guests. After dessert is served, Addy will be invited to the front of the room where Mr. Jamison will shake hands with you, publicly thanking you for the meal, and posing for a few photos."

The old Addy would have blown a gasket, insisting the Sage Leaf Café staff serve the meal that *we* prepared. It was a real testament to my growth that I willingly allowed my staff to be hidden in the kitchen until Mr. High Society Jamison decided it was socially acceptable to make a token appearance at the end of the meal. The new Addy practiced yoga, meditation, and control. I smiled and nodded at Lizzy in agreement.

More like submission.

"Rules?" Mac whispered.

"Just go with it," I said through gritted teeth. "Flying under the radar will allow me more time to add the coconut cream and raspberries to the raw cheesecake."

"At least you dressed for the photo op." She smirked.

I looked down at my dirty apron covering my café logo T-shirt and wrap skirt. "Shit."

"I've got the cheesecake. Go." Mac shooed me out of the kitchen.

Stealing a quick minute I didn't have, I made my way to the ladies' lounge to freshen up.

I tore out my ponytail holder, letting my hair fall down my back as I finger-combed the tangles with little success.

I braided my unruly bangs and clipped them off to the side, then pinched my cheeks to add color to my makeup-less face.

Sweat.

I wadded some paper towels and shoved them in my armpits for a few seconds. Some days the no-antiperspirant thing bit me in the ass. My deodorant was good. I didn't smell, but man did I sweat. The good news? My pores weren't clogged. The bad news? The pits of my shirt were drenched. *Lovely.*

Mac found me on my way back to the kitchen. "Addy, they're serving dessert. Lizzy said Mr. Jamison is ready for you."

Deep breath ... I am peaceful, I am strong.

I made my way to the double doors of the conference room.

Deep breath ... I am peaceful, I am strong.

I pulled on the door to the right but it didn't budge, so I pulled the door to the left. No luck.

What is this, a top secret meeting? What's with the locked doors?

Deciding I didn't care if I received any recognition for the catering, I turned and leaned back on the doors to wait for someone to come out. Before I could catch the weight of my body, I found myself falling into the conference room and landing flat on my ass. I closed my eyes. *Push, Addy, not pull, you idiot.*

Deep breath ... I am peaceful, I am strong.

Just when I thought my seven years of bad luck were over, the proverbial black cat crossed my path again.

"Well, well, you are just an accident waiting to happen, Pippi," an all too familiar deep voice filled my ears.

Breathe dammit ... peaceful ... strong ... peaceful ... strong.

It was an unwelcome moment of déjà vu as my eyes made the journey up Michelangelo's sculpture for the second time that day. My face flushed under his cocky but damn-if-it-wasn't-still-sexy smirk. He offered his hand.

These feet have pounded too many miles of pavement and these arms have held countless inversion poses. I will NOT be needing help up, thank you very much!

"Addy? Are you all right?" Lizzy whispered, sharing my nervous embarrassment. "Mr. Jamison is ready for you."

After righting my clothing and pulling the stray hair away from my face, I once again threw my shoulders back, tilted my chin up, and walked toward the front of the room and away from David.

Mr. Jamison started his introduction. "I'd like to introduce the chef and owner of Sage Leaf Café, Ms. Adler Brecken."

I let the warm response calm my nerves while I told myself that most people were, in all likelihood, too busy chatting to have noticed my grand entrance.

"Ms. Brecken, you've outdone yourself with this superb lunch. I hope to visit your restaurant the next time I'm in Milwaukee," Mr. Jamison boasted with the cheesiest fake smile I'd ever seen. It matched his fake tan and complimented his weak handshake, stiff comb-over, and, large, overfed figure.

He had perhaps been a football linebacker in high school or maybe even college. However, money, lack of exercise, and a taste of the "finer" things gave him the classic indulgent lifestyle appearance. I didn't bet a single penny that I'd ever see him in my café.

While the photographers finished, I fixed my gaze to the back of the room. Mr. Smug Ass (he'd been rechristened after this latest humiliation) leaned against the back doors with his muscular arms crossed over his broad chest and one leg casually crossed over the other at his ankle.

Was he undressing me with his eyes?

Jesus, Addy, where did that come from?

Or was he just bored with the whole 'giving credit where credit is due' spiel? Why did he rub me the wrong way?

Maybe because I was frustrated with myself for imagining him rubbing me in another way. *ADDY, get a grip!*

In a desperate attempt to exude confidence in my stride, I carefully navigated to the conference room exit. Why was he there? Cocky arrogance oozed from him as he stood by two other guys who looked like some form of security or body-guards. They were dressed in black suits, but Mr. Smug-Ass-slash-Smirky-Face wore the same semi-casual attire he had on that morning. The absence of a camera or notepad suggested he was not part of the press, and everything about him screamed money. *And sex.*

He blocked my exit, and with each approaching step I prayed he would move, but he didn't. His indifferent expression and his self-assured posture said he owned the place, and worse than that, his look said he owned *me.*

Deep breath ... I am peaceful, I am strong.

"Excuse me, please," I whispered, disappointed in myself

for not mustering more of a voice.

I kept my head down with a stoic face.

"By all means, let me get the door for you, Miss Brecken, although I think odds are you've figured it out by now." His voice dripped with sarcasm.

Once I made it through the door and past the parameter of his panty-dropping aura, I sucked in a deep breath, attempting to cool my inflamed body.

"Oh, Miss Brecken?"

All vocal abilities failed me, which was very uncharacteristic. I looked up at him with raised eyebrows, relinquishing a barely-detectable nod.

"I think maybe we got off on the wrong foot this morning. However, I've come to find your presence very … stimulating." The corners of his mouth slowly turned up into a grin.

"Good God … uh, I mean, good day, Mr. um?"

Shit shit, double shit!

"Cohen, Quinten Cohen." A smile that reached his eyes graced his perfect face and I had to get the hell out of there.

CHAPTER TWO

"Sometimes I wonder if men and women really suit
each other. Perhaps they should live next door and just
visit now and then."

~Katharine Hepburn

EARLY MAY IN Milwaukee that year was a gift, as the
unseasonably warm spring weather continued. The sun
and the sounds of seagulls rained peace all around me. My "off
day" three weeks earlier with the dark and dangerous Mr.
Cohen sent my nerves into a tailspin, shaking my well-
rehearsed carefree persona.

Mac was onto me when I tried to brush it off as nerves
from nearly being crushed by an SUV. It was absurd to even
try that excuse with Mac—the one person who knew there was
not a cell in my body that feared death. Losing nearly every
reason to live had that effect on a person.

Rounding the last curve of the path, I accepted Mother
Nature's invitation to spend more time outside that morning.
A mature maple tree skirted with lush green grass made the
perfect spot to do some yoga in the park.

Quenching my thirst with a big swig of water, I removed
my runners and socks. The cool touch of the shaded grass
under my feet grounded me. My limbered body easily flowed
through several Sun Salutations. On my last Down Dog I

spotted an upside down figure a few feet away.

Casually leaning against the massive maple trunk with one arm crossing his chest and the other resting at a ninety degree angle, holding a Starbucks cup inches from full rosy lips, stood Mr. Cohen. I closed my eyes with an inhale and finished my sequence ending in Mountain Pose. Turning toward the tree, my lips curled up into a smile.

"Mr. Cohen."

In a most calculated and sexy motion, he straightened and closed the distance between us so much so that I had to lift my head to meet his eyes. A vanilla coffee aroma filled my nose as his free hand tugged one of my braided pigtails. "Pippi."

Thank God I was already flushed, sweating, and out of breath, because his proximity kept my thermostat stuck in the red. His eyes trailed up my body, pausing at my lips. He delivered a lopsided smirk. I snapped my jaw shut. Even outdoors his arrogance suffocated me. *Or his sexiness sucked all the air from the atmosphere.* No, definitely the former.

BREAKING THE TRANCE, I stepped back and bent down to grab my water. A long swig allowed me to catch my breath and buy a few extra seconds to formulate a comeback. "You live near here, or is this just your new stalking ground?"

"You think I look like a stalker?" He tilted his head to the side.

"I think you act like a stalker."

"I was just observing the yoga class." He shrugged.

"I'm the only one doing yoga. It's not a class, which means you were not observing but rather stalking. I have to say it's a little creepy." I grabbed my socks, shoved my bare feet into my runners and began walking, keeping my eyes firmly fixed ahead of me.

"What if I told you I was just admiring the scenery?"

"Even more creepy," I called over my shoulder while crossing the street to my building.

I lived in a loft above my café, but with stalker-guy shadowing me, I refrained from using the direct entrance behind the building. Instead, I swerved toward my café. We weren't open yet, but I knew Jake, who'd worked for me almost three years, was in the kitchen cleaning and slicing food for the day.

Banging on the door, I hoped he would hear me. I didn't have my keys since my other loft entrance only required a security code.

"Most women would insist on a shower after exercising and before going to work, but just as I suspected, you are not like most women." He hovered inches behind me and so close to my ear for that last part I could feel the heat of his breath down my neck.

Deep breath ... I am peaceful, I am strong.

My eyes flew open when I heard the door unlatch. Saved by Jake!

"Hey, Addy, having your smoothie before your shower this morning? Must have been an intense workout."

"Uh, yes ... smoothie first," I mumbled while hurrying in past Jake.

"Great, I'll juice you a shot of wheatgrass that's ready to go in the back. Is your friend having anything?"

"My friend?"

In the rush of anxiety that propelled me through the door, I failed to notice Mr. Cohen follow me inside, uninvited. Jake locked the door behind us.

Mr. Cohen perched his unwelcome, stalking ass on a

barstool at the juice bar. My eyes narrowed at him. I didn't want to like the tight-fitting charcoal T-shirt that hugged every one of his sculpted muscles or the white cargo shorts that hung low on his hips. Even his feet were sexy, clad in flip flops propped up on the lower rung of the stool.

Could feet even be sexy?

As he bounced his legs, I caught myself taking in the flexing motion of his calf muscles for a little too long.

Jake cleared his throat.

My gaze cut to Mr. Arrogant. "Jake, this is Mr. Cohen and he's not my friend. In fact, I don't think he noticed our hours. I'm sure if he wants something he can come back once we're open."

"Jake, please, call me Quinn. And Addy is being a little modest about us. We're definitely *friends,* so I'll have what she's having, please."

Jake started to smile but it quickly faded when he glanced at the scowl on my face. It was a shame. My twenty-two-year-old employee had a ruggedly-sexy smile to match his tatted Hulk body that looked ready to bust out of his café T-shirt. He was my apprentice by day and an underground fighter by night.

"So ..." Jake pointed toward the kitchen "...I'll be right back with the wheatgrass shots."

I nodded, feeling defeated that Mr. Cohen got his way.

"Wow, Mr. Cohen—"

"Quinn."

"*Quinn*, I'm trying to figure out the 'definitely friends' part." I kept my eyes on him as I tossed fresh fruit and pitted dates into the blender. With raised eyebrows and a soft, close-lipped smile, I waited for an explanation.

He seemed to ignore me, his eyes inspecting every inch of my café. The spacious interior had high ceilings with contemporary brushed-steel fans and dark, wood-stained LED pendant lamps. The crisp white walls were tastefully decorated with environmental posters and quotes such as: "Let food be thy medicine and medicine be thy food – Hippocrates"; "Nature does not hurry yet, everything is accomplished – Lao Tzu"; and "Environmentalism is about Right vs Wrong, not Right vs Left – Rustle the Leaf".

Square tables made from dark-stained, reclaimed wood with brushed steel pedestals filled the middle. The chairs were salvaged from another restaurant that went out of business. We painted the wood light green and they looked brand new. Each table had a living centerpiece of either herbs or wheatgrass, growing in a cubed glass container.

"I've seen your eyes peruse my body, more than once..." his eyes focused back on me "... and I'd say what's going on in your pretty little head crosses the line of *friends* by a few lengths of a football field. But since I have no wish to embarrass you in front of your employee, I thought I'd downplay it."

Cocky ass...

How could one person make me so damn mad?

I gritted my teeth, glaring at him as I flipped on the switch to the blender. Before I had time to react, the fruity concoction flew everywhere. It took me a moment in the fruit barrage to gather my senses enough to switch it off.

The first thing I spied was the lid still on the counter. *Brilliant.*

Then I wiped my face and surveyed the mess. Not only was I covered in smoothie, Quinn had taken his fair share of the collateral damage too. The look on his smoothie-covered face was complete consternation as he sat stiff as a board, holding his fruit-splattered arms out to the side.

"Oops, I assumed you wanted your smoothie to go." I smiled sweetly before breaking out into a fit of laughter.

Wetting my pants was a real possibility if I didn't rein it in a little. Quinn gave me a curious look, indubitably questioning my sanity, but then something resembling a smile started to pull at the corners of his mouth.

"Oh my gosh! I'm so sorry, but you should see the look on your face," I couldn't stop laughing.

"Shit," Quinn whispered, trying to hold back his full, pearly-white grin, as he wiped his face and arms with napkins. "Goddamn, woman, you are truly a walking disaster."

"That she is," Jake agreed as he walked out with a tray of wheatgrass shots and orange wedges, shaking his head and sporting his own shit-eating grin. "I got this. Bottoms up with your shots and then go get yourselves cleaned up."

Still dripping with smoothie, I held up my shot glass in salute, downed it, sucked the juice of the orange wedge, and flashed Quinn my first genuine smile. He pressed his lips together and raised a skeptical brow. Maybe it was his first time doing wheatgrass shots.

He hesitated for a moment not moving his eyes from mine. I couldn't ease his apprehension by telling him it would taste like nectar from the gods. Wheatgrass could range from tart to sweet, but there was no other way to describe its taste other than grassy.

A moment later his face softened. "Cheers." He saluted then downed his shot with a grimace. I shoved the orange wedge in his mouth, my fingers grazing his lips as my tongue traced my own.

"Jake, I'm going to take Quinn upstairs to clean up." My eyes didn't leave Quinn's.

"Got it, Addy."

The door to my loft was back near the kitchen. I entered the lock security code and turned to inspect Quinn a few steps behind. He crept along, being careful not to let any more of the smoothie drip. Taking complete inventory of the damage I did to him, I was relieved to see that his shorts were unscathed and a clean shirt would do the trick.

When we reached my loft I headed straight to the linen closet to get two bath towels. He took it, not looking at me. Just like downstairs, he didn't hide his thorough perusal of my place. My loft was my sanctuary. The view of the lake was nothing short of stunning when the iridescent reflection of the sun shimmered across the surface like dancing diamonds.

Every detail, from the building materials to the interior design, was feng shui'd. I spent many months checking the architectural salvage store for the perfect pieces to show up. Framed mirrors to dressers, coffee tables to coat trees, I was always in search of something that told me a story.

Since I'd become so busy with my café I had to sweet talk Conner, the assistant manager, into calling me whenever pieces of possible interest came in. Conner was a muscle-bound, heavily inked, sex-on-legs guy, roughly ten years my junior— much like Jake—who had a bit of a crush on me and a definite appetite for my gourmet vegan cuisine. As long as I showed up wearing something sexy and carrying a brown bag of food, I was in like Flynn.

"I have one bathroom and it's through there, so you can go ahead and get cleaned up while I grab you a new shirt."

Quinn sauntered closer to me. I struggled to keep my

breathing steady as he traced his finger from my cheek to the corner of my mouth. He placed his finger in his mouth and rolled his tongue over it lapping up the fruity liquid.

"There's not a part of your body that isn't dripping with smoothie. I do believe you should clean up first. I'll just take my shirt off and wait."

I forced a hard swallow. In one swift motion he removed his shirt and set it in the kitchen sink. No fat. The guy had no fat, just sex appeal—maybe too much sex appeal.

When he turned toward me the air in my lungs evaporated. He was a perfect anatomy model, with every muscle being well-defined but not too bulky. Years of yoga gave my muscles definition, but maintaining a body like his had to be a full-time job. What kind of person had time to look perfect?

Presentable. I went for presentable.

My full-time job was food. I loved food and I exercised for my health, and to keep my ass squeezed into my jeans. Quinn exercised to look like *that*—perfect.

Damn him!

He raised his eyebrows. Yes, I stared. I was supposed to shower, but I didn't. I just stared.

"Wo—wow," I stuttered.

"Excuse me?"

"Nothing," I whispered, a little breathless.

Before he had a chance to respond, gravity brought me back to Earth and I made a dash for refuge in the bathroom.

After making it to safety, my back collapsed against the door and I struggled to keep myself from sliding to the floor. Blood drained from my head, engorging my breasts and swelling my sex. A blubbering, googly-eyed idiot took over my body. Someone needed to shut her down before all dignity evaporated.

Deep breath ... I am peaceful, I am strong. That was my mantra. It kept me focused, calm, and alive in the face of adversity.

Allowing Quinn to wander my loft unattended for too long was not a good idea, so I took a shower in record-breaking time, even with a quick shave of my armpits and legs. Wrapped up in my towel, I slipped through the back sliding door of the bathroom that connected to my walk-in closet, snagging the essentials: panties, bra, green capris, and a white café tank. A fast comb through my tangled hair and I was done.

Quinn stood by my large windows overlooking the lake. His back was glorious. Yes, it deserved fame and honor—a sight of beauty. That assessment stayed locked in my mind with all other tongue-twisted, teenaged-girl descriptions of the man who tried to kill me with his gas-guzzler. That was something I needed to remember. I almost took my last breath as human roadkill beneath his fancy-pants SUV.

His hands were shoved in his pockets, tugging down his cargos and exposing the gray waistband of his briefs.

"Jaw-dropping view, huh?" his deep gritty voice echoed.

How did he know I was in the room and staring at him?

"I was just ..."

"The lake, you have a beautiful view of the lake." A fine smirk played across his face as he turned to witness my blushing skin.

"Yes, the lake, it's amazing. I'm done, the bathroom is all yours. I'll get you a shirt while you clean up."

"Thanks, Addy." He made a quick inspection of me before leaving me to pant like a dog.

Lack of sex was the most plausible explanation for my flustered behavior. As soon as I heard the water running I scrambled to my bedroom and dug out a plain navy T-shirt that seemed large enough to fit Quinn. I had a whole drawer dedicated to freebie tees I received at different expos and trade shows; most of the time I used them as back-up nightshirts.

The warm breeze dried my damp hair while I waited on my deck for Quinn. When I sensed his presence I took a moment to imagine him looking at me the way I had at him. My body hoped so, but my brain didn't. I turned and gasped at the sight of him in nothing but his cargos and wet black hair, a few rivulets of water still melting down his torso.

Adonis may have been the Greek god of beauty and desire, but Quinn was unmistakably a Latin sex god. Refusing to feed his oversized ego with any more panting and drooling, I tossed him the shirt and cleared my throat.

"This should fit."

He caught it, and without even looking at it, slipped it over his head, easing it the rest of the way down, no doubt putting on a show for me.

"How long have you been a vegan?"

His question was typical and in the realm of answers I was willing to share.

"Twelve years. I saw a documentary on slaughter houses and I could no longer physically or mentally handle consuming meat. I was a bit of a tree hugger anyway and veganism is great for the environment so it was a no-brainer. But please … no judgment. It's just how I choose to take care of my body. It's not a cult and we don't all throw red paint on fur coats."

I slipped on my flip-flops and headed back down to the café. "You coming?" The Q & A ended with my well-rehearsed spiel. My life wasn't an open book. It was more of a locked vault buried at the bottom of the ocean. But food ... food I would talk about.

"I'm sorry again about your shirt. I'll get it washed and maybe you can stop in and pick it up sometime. I'll have it behind the counter in case I'm not here." I hoped I wouldn't be there; nothing about Quinn was good for me.

"Thanks, and I'll return your loaner as well." He tugged at the shirt I gave him.

I nodded. Quinn smiled and headed toward the door. Too busy shamelessly checking out his rear, I failed to notice the back of the T-shirt. Jake nudged me with his elbow, bringing me out of my trance. It was the T-shirt I received at the Raw Food Expo. The back of the shirt read: *RAW girls taste better.*

"Quinn!"

"Yes?" He stopped at the door and turned.

"The shirt ... uh it's ... it's yours, just keep it." Demonstrating commendable restraint, I managed to keep my grin polite, but Jake raced to the kitchen, snorting in uncontrolled laughter.

"Thanks, but don't think you're getting out of seeing me again." And with that, he left.

"He's either going to be so pissed with embarrassment that you'll never see him again, or ... he's going to knock down your door with a raging hard-on, demanding to find out if raw girls really do taste better." Jake laughed, buckled over, hand fisted at his mouth.

"Jake! God, you are so crude."

"I'm just a guy, Addy."

"Then guys are animals with a one-track mind."

"I won't argue with your assessment. You're smart and sexy."

"Flattering the old boss will get you nowhere, young Jake."

"Except next Saturday off to take Jessica boating, right?"

"Yeah, yeah, except that. Now get to work."

Jake was a flirt since day one, but I knew he was harmless and smitten with his girlfriend, Jessica.

IT HAD BEEN five days since Quinn walked out of the café, not that I was counting, but I had a hunch I wouldn't see him again. The T-shirt incident was not at all intentional—I thought of it as a happy accident—but five days later and no contact from him, I knew it was the "pissed with embarrassment" scenario. While I was on my way to the market, Mac called me.

"Hey Mac, 'sup?"

"Eighty degrees and gorgeous, that's what's up. Thought you'd come sailing with me and Evan today."

"Hmm, fifth-wheel invite and I'm on my way to market anyway. Thanks, but I'll pass."

"Adler Sage, don't you dare give me that fifth-wheel crap. Evan and I are married, not teenagers dating. It's just an afternoon sailing on a yacht that's yours anyway."

"Stop, Mac, you know what's mine is yours and I'm serious about needing to go to the market."

"One hour, Addy, drop off the food with Jake and get your ass down to the marina. *No* is not an option."

Mac had a gift for always getting her way. She also had a way of making me think that it was my idea in the first place.

"Fine, but tell Evan I'm only along for the ride. You two are in charge of sailing today. I'm not in the mood to ferry the love birds around the lake."

"Yadda, yadda. One hour, Addy. Bye."

I pulled into the marina with five minutes to spare. Tossing my bag over my shoulder and slipping on my aviator sunglasses, I strolled down the ramp to my majestic, one-hundred-foot CIM Maxi 88. It was quite the sight for any sailor's eyes.

As I rounded the corner I brushed my fingers over my lips, seeing *The Sage* elegantly scripted on the side. It was still hard to swallow the lump in my throat and blink back the stinging moisture in the corners of my eyes that was always there when I came aboard.

"Addy on time, it's a miracle—"

Mac stopped short when I ran a finger under my glasses to wipe my eyes. "Oh, sweetie, why do you do this to yourself? You should just sell it and find something that doesn't hold so many bad memories."

"Mac, you know I can't sell it. Besides, the memories hurt because the moments were so fragile and cherished. They weren't bad memories." *Deep breath ... I am peaceful, I am strong.* "Now enough with memory lane. Tell Captain Evan I'm ready to set sail."

No words, just a warm embrace and a knowing look were all she gave me.

"Evan, baby, let's do this!" Mac yelled.

Evan was a perfect complement to Mac's personality. She was a complete spitfire and he was as laid-back as they came. His short, bulky, body-builder frame contrasted her twiggy appearance. Where she was fair, he was golden brown. He looked nothing like the typical white-collar professional. They complemented each other in every way.

The warm breeze, bright sky, and gentle lull of the lake made the afternoon perfect. I found such serenity in sailing.

The wind through my hair and the sun bathing my skin was a beautiful evanescence of a world that didn't matter.

"Addy, check out that yacht! It rivals *The Sage* in luxury yachts that look too nice for Lake Michigan."

"Jeez, Mac, you act like cruising Lake Michigan is slumming. We have our own yachting association, for goodness sakes."

She knew I was a yacht enthusiast, so after a few minutes I couldn't resist. "Fine, hand me the binoculars. Let's have a look."

"I'm just saying, certain yachts like yours and that one scream coast of Italy, not Lake Michigan."

I tried to focus in while it was still a good two hundred yards away. "Sweet... looks custom built," I hummed in admiration.

On the upper deck were two young kids, maybe five and seven, drinking what appeared to be juice boxes. A tall, slender woman with long, dark hair joined them, attempting to corral her hair with a silk scarf.

Moving the binoculars a fraction, the backside of a tall man with broad shoulders, swarthy skin, and dark hair came into focus. He turned and I stumbled backward, flustered as though we made eye contact, which was ridiculous since I was the only one with binoculars.

"Quinn," I whispered.

"What's that, Addy?" Mac questioned.

"It's Quinn, and what appears to be his *wife* and *two kids*."

"Shut the fuck up. Are you serious?"

"Remind me to give your mouth a good washing before we have kids," Evan added while shaking his head.

"Oh you love my dirty mouth," Mac deposited a deep wet

kiss on his mouth.

"Well, that explains why I haven't seen him since the smoothie disaster. I'm amazed Cleopatra didn't cut off his nuts and bury them in my shirt."

"A shame. That was organic cotton, wasn't it, Addy?"

"Yeah, it was," I laughed, but part of me felt punched in the gut.

Why the let down? I'd seen Quinn three times: the first he insulted me after almost running me over, the second time I fell on my ass in the most embarrassing fashion, and the third time I drenched him in flying smoothie, like the walking disaster I was.

But each time I'd been with him, I'd felt something other than the constant beat of my heart marking time. I tried to convince myself he was just a sexy distraction, which he was, but there was something else. The man flirted with me. He stalked me. Single Quinn was sexy and alluring. Married Quinn was scum of the worst kind.

Pathetic-piece-of-shit cheater.

"Kind of quiet, Addy. Ready to head in?" Evan asked as he applied more sun lotion to Mac's shoulders.

"Earth to Addy. Did you hear Evan?"

I nodded and put the binoculars back. I knew Mac was onto me but she wouldn't have brought it up in front of Evan, which was good because I didn't know what I would have said anyway.

CHAPTER THREE

"Love is the answer, but while you are waiting for the
answer, sex raises some pretty good questions."

~Woody Allen

"*A*DDY, *ADDY? CAN you see me? It's me, Mac. No, stop, you
have to leave your oxygen mask on for a few more hours
while they monitor you.*" Sniffle, sniffle. "*I'm sorry sweetie,
they're ... they're,*" sniffle, sniffle, "*They didn't make it, they're
gone.*"

Th-thump. Th-thump. Th-thump ...

EAGER TO EXPERIENCE the beautiful essence of Lake Michigan
at sunrise, I woke up at five every morning, except Sunday, and
took a thirty-minute jog on the lake path. Then in my east
facing sunroom, I flowed through an hour of yoga and fifteen
minutes of meditation, followed by hot tea, a shower, then
down to my café for wheatgrass shots, a green smoothie, and to
open up shop.

Self-pity liked to rear its ugly head in the evening. I kept
busy concocting new recipes, updating the café's website and or
social media pages, or reading. The closest thing I had to a
social life was live performance nights at the café on Fridays
and Saturdays. We stayed open until 11:00 p.m. and usually

ended up with only standing room by ten. The patrons varied in age from early twenties to late fifties, depending on the night's entertainment.

By TEN O'CLOCK Saturday night after the "Quinn incident," we had a packed house with Super Moon, a popular local band, playing a great mix of alternative music. Jake, as I promised the week before, had the day off. The two new part-time girls I hired the month before busted their butts serving the customers while Mac worked her magic behind the juice bar.

Once the food requests slowed down, I grabbed an order pad and helped Mac. After tugging on my pigtails to tighten them a bit, I looked for a pen from under the counter.

"What can I get ya?" I asked the next customer in line, without glancing up.

"Green Goddess, *in a cup* this time, please."

Quinn.

Deep Breath … I am peaceful, I am strong.

"Anything else, sir?"

"Yes, I think you're holding a T-shirt for me somewhere behind the counter."

"Sorry, sir, I wasn't sure who that old thing belonged to so I donated it to a refugee family."

"You what?! That was a two hundred and fifty dollar shirt," he gritted between his teeth.

"Sorry, looked like a Target special to me."

He placed both hands on the counter and leaned in closer. "Have I done something wrong? Because last I knew *I* was the one wearing the '*RAW girls taste better*' shirt to the market, bank, AND for the big reveal … to lunch with some buddies."

"Well, sounds like a good thing it was drawn to your attention before your *wife* saw it. Here's your drink. Next!"

I willed myself to stay strong. When he leaned into the counter my body started to perspire from the seductive scent of his woodsy, probably chemical-laden, cologne.

"Wife? What the hell are you talking about?"

"DON'T! Don't you dare give me that line of shit." I pointed a stiff finger at him.

"Addy, uh why don't you take this someplace else? The girls and I will close up. You're kinda making a scene." Mac pushed me toward my loft door.

"You're right, Mac, I'm done. Make sure Mr. Cohen pays for his drink and finds his way out."

I punched in my code and took the stairs two at a time. When I got to the top I felt a large hand grip my arm, turning me around. I couldn't believe Mac let him follow me. *Traitor.*

"What do you want? Is this about your stupid shirt? I'll buy you a new one, whatever, just leave! You have a family, what the hell is wrong with you? Go. Home!" I went to pull my arm away but he yanked my other one as well and pushed me against the wall. My breaths came so fast and heavy I could have passed out, if it hadn't been for the adrenaline running through my shaky body.

"First, I don't give a fuck about the shirt! Second, I don't have a wife and—"

"I saw you, her, them ... your kids." I huffed. "On. Your. Yacht!"

He searched my eyes, but looked through them into someplace deeper, someplace he wasn't invited. I didn't see it, I *felt* it and I didn't like it. The feeling made me nervous and scared. The unwelcome vulnerability shook me to the core.

"Alexis is my sister." He moved his mouth to my ear without making contact and whispered, "And those were her kids."

He loosened his grip on my wrists and feathered his fingers up my arms, leaving a trail of goosebumps in their wake. Cradling my jaw in his hands, he grazed his lips and nose across my cheek from my ear to my lips. He pulled back and rested his forehead on mine as he breathed out. "My God, you're so beautiful." Those simple words sounded like a plea and if his assessment of my beauty somehow pained him.

I closed my eyes and felt his thumb brush my bottom lip. My breath remained hostage in my chest. Gliding his mouth back to my ear, he sucked my earlobe into his mouth and grazed it with his teeth. Releasing it, he whispered, "Goodnight, Addy."

Paralyzed, all I could do was watch him walk down the stairs. The door slammed shut. I sucked in a shaky breath and melted down the wall, resting my arms and head on my bent knees.

Ho-ly shit!

THE NEXT MORNING brought little clarity to the out-of-body experience from the previous night. While sipping my Rooibos tea, my phone chimed with a text from Mac.

What did you do to Quinn last night?

Not following?

He came back down, grabbed his smoothie, winked at me, and tossed a Ben Franklin by the register b4 walking out ... must have done something for that kind of tip!

WTF? He left a $100 tip?!

Yep, oh and did I mention the huge smile he was wearing?

Ugh ... not what u r thinking, call u later!

You'd better!!!

As I walked into the kitchen to get more tea, my door buzzed.

"Yes?" I answered into the intercom.

"Delivery for Miss Brecken."

I peeked out the back window. A black Bentley was parked in front of the steps and a gentleman, possibly in his late fifties, wearing a black suit, held a box wrapped with a sheer bow and floral embellishment.

"One minute."

Scurrying around my loft, I slipped on yoga capris and a sweatshirt over my white tank and pink boyshort panties, then I opened the door.

"Miss Brecken?"

"Yes."

He nodded and handed me the box.

"Sunday delivery, huh? What company do you work for that sends their driver out in a two hundred thousand dollar vehicle?"

He rewarded me with a small but warm smile. "I work for Mr. Cohen."

Note to self: spend more time finding out about Quinn's business ventures and less time drooling over his body.

"Well, thank you, sir, have a nice day."

"Miss, I've been instructed to wait for a response."

Signing for a package was normal, waiting for a response ... not so normal. I squinted, but he simply nodded toward the package. I removed the lavender roses. Untying the sheer bow, I read the lettering on the dark brown box: *Allison's Gourmet*

Vegan Truffles. Under the lid was a hand written note.

Dinner 7:00 p.m. tonight?

Quinn

Wow, no pressure with Mr. Suit waiting for an answer. I decided to stall. Removing the protective cover I offered him a truffle.

"No, thank you, Miss."

"Oh come on, it will speed up my response. Please?"

He reluctantly took one and plopped the whole thing into his mouth. I, on the other hand, bit it in half and predictably ended up with a creamy fruit filling dripping down my shirt.

"Oh, crap!" I laughed, wiping my chin, while trying to chew with my mouth closed.

Mr. Suit struggled to hold back a smile.

"Oh my God, these are so good, right?"

He nodded.

"That answers that. You can tell Mr. Cohen my response is ... yes."

"Very well, Miss Brecken, seven o'clock it is. Mr. Cohen said to wear something nice."

I smiled.

Nice?

I wasn't sure how to interpret that, but I had all day to figure it out.

IT WAS ALMOST six-thirty as I second—more like tenth—guessed my choice of attire. The winner was a basic, black halter dress with a bodice that accentuated my 34B-cup chest and a flared skirt that fell an inch above my knee. A plunge back revealed ample skin, which I initially covered with a sheer wrap then decided to ditch at the last minute.

The truth? I wasn't looking for a relationship. Sex—I needed sex. Could a woman use a guy for sex without being a whore or offering her heart? History put the odds of success in my favor. Thirty-one and single—I could do whatever the hell I wanted. Even if I hadn't done *it* in a while.

As I buckled the wide black strap of my four inch, wedge, open-toed Stella McCartney shoes around my ankle, the door buzzed.

Stepping out the door, I expected to see Mr. Suit waiting by the black Bentley, but the man at the bottom of my stairs dressed in a platinum suit, pinstriped shirt, black tie, and sexy, perfect white smile was none other than my seductive new acquaintance.

"Quinn," I breathed, but just barely to myself. A mixed cocktail of emotions warred in my head: guilt, fear, anxiety, lust, desire, and need. The kind of need that was a physical craving. A craving to touch and be touched. Steadying my shaky legs, I took my first step, a step that felt like a gigantic leap.

He watched me ease my way down the stairs and everything in me screamed to run back inside, shut the door, and move to a remote village in China. My body, being the ultimate traitor, continued forward, pulled by something resembling a magnetic force.

I grinned as his eyes moved like honey over my body. He didn't try to hide his pleasure one bit.

"Cat got your tongue, Mr. Cohen?"

He gave me a slight nod while wetting his lip. "I wanted to take you to dinner but what you're wearing implies we should head back up those stairs."

Flirting was a game I knew well: bashful smiles, stolen glances, a giggle. Quinn didn't flirt. He fucked me with his eyes. A calm, calculated predator, stalking his nervous prey.

"Your uh ... driver, chauffeur, whatever, said to dress *nice*."

"Mmm, yes, well, I have to confess I had you pegged for *nice* being a sundress with flip flops. This..." he walked in a complete circle around me then shook his head, and held his breath for a moment "...this is distracting."

"Well, enough ogling, eyes up here, big guy."

"Big guy, huh? We haven't even gotten to that part of the evening yet, but I can assure you, I won't disappoint."

"You're presumptuous."

"Not at all. You're full of too many surprises."

"Speaking of surprises, are we dumpster diving for dinner or was I supposed to pack a granola bar? I don't see your car anywhere but we can take mine."

"No need to drive." He offered his arm and I willingly accepted it. We walked to the front of the building and crossed the street to the lakefront.

I stopped as the pier came into view. A sheer, round tent with gold Chinese lanterns enveloped a single, candlelit table, and two white, fabric-wrapped chairs waited at the end of the wood-planked dock. I was in shock, but my heart knew better than to show it.

"Oh jeez, same old 'private dinner on the pier' date. You'd think guys these days would try to be a little more original."

Quinn dropped his shoulders, head shaking. "Gonna make me work for every inch, aren't you?"

I looked up at him through my black-painted lashes and gave him my best innocent smile. After we made our way down to the tent, Quinn seated me in my chair then feathered his index finger up my bare back to my halter tie. He took a shaky breath and exhaled with a moan as I felt his mouth ghost across the hair behind my ear, releasing a seductive whisper. "So distracting."

It was about seventy degrees with a light breeze, and I couldn't blame the shiver that vibrated my whole body on the cool evening.

I'm in way over my head.

He took his seat just as a server appeared out of nowhere with two glasses of water garnished with spiraled lemons and a bottle of red wine.

"Merlot, Miss?"

"Thank you."

The server gestured the offer to Quinn, but he gave a slight shake of his head while keeping his eyes locked on mine.

"Are you ready for your salads?"

"Give us a few minutes."

"Very well, Sir."

"You don't like red wine?" I asked.

"I don't drink alcohol."

"Then why did you have the server offer it?"

"I thought you might enjoy some wine."

"What made you think that?"

He shook his head and let out a light laugh. "Just a shot in the dark, Addy, that's all it was."

"Are you an alcoholic?" I didn't mean to pry. It just seemed like the next logical question.

"No."

"So ... why then?"

"Are you originally from Milwaukee?" he countered.

"I take it we're done discussing your reasons for abstaining from drinking?"

"Correct." His eyes pierced mine and his face tensed.

After a few seconds of silence I swallowed my defeated pride that came from feeling chastised for prying into his personal life. I gave him a slow nod in acceptance and fixed my eyes on my wine glass. I decided to be grateful the whole bottle was mine because I needed some liquid courage to make it through the evening.

I broke the awkward silence. "I'm not from Milwaukee. I'm from Chicago, born and raised."

It was sex. We didn't have to divulge our darkest secrets. At least I'd hoped it would be sex.

Quinn's face relaxed and I again recognized the face that greeted me just minutes earlier.

"What brought you to Milwaukee?"

My pathetic attempt to rebel and leave the Midwest.

My mother told me to bloom where I was planted, so the first chance I got, I rebelled and moved to Milwaukee. I sucked at rebelling. I also sucked at telling the whole truth. My fragile heart lacked the luxury of honesty.

"I wanted to stay on the lake and near a larger populous that could support a vegan café without the extreme chaos of Chicago." It sounded ridiculous, even to me, but I thought he'd let it fly for the moment. In a way, it was the truth, and it was much more mature than the rebel explanation.

"So is your family still in Chicago?"

"I'm an only child and my parents are dead." God, I hated myself for sounding so callous, but *dead* said I'm fine and *died* invited too much sympathy that I didn't want. I hoped the food would arrive soon. That line of questioning required a lot of wine, so I had to get some food in my stomach.

Quinn looked pained, but not like he shared mine; it looked like his own. "Addy, I'm—"

"It's fine." I gave him a tight-lipped smile.

"How'd they die?"

I thought he'd take the hint. Most people did.

"Are *you* originally from Milwaukee?"

He gave me a knowing, close-lipped smile that matched mine, while he fiddled with his napkin on the table.

"Well played, Addy."

I batted my eyelashes at him over the rim of my wine glass and took another sip.

Saved by romaine, our salads arrived and I was pleased to see they were void of cheese, meat, and eggs. Ironically, some guys didn't connect the dots that the owner of a vegan café would most likely be a vegan. But Quinn remembered because he was not just "some guy."

As I tried to stab the appropriate amount of lettuce to fit in my mouth without dripping vinegar on my dress, Quinn dabbed his mouth with his napkin and cleared his throat.

"Let's try a different approach; what would you like to tell me about yourself?"

My soul is injured. My heart is shattered but won't stop beating. You see the person I want to be, not who I am. I don't fear death. I fear the pieces of my heart could be further shattered and it will still keep beating.

"I love good food, yoga, and sailing. I despise chemicals, war, and Styrofoam. When I'm not donating food and insanely expensive T-shirts to refugees, I walk dogs at the local shelter. I have an appreciation for all genres of music, but my heart belongs to classic rock. I can play any instrument, but my favorite is the piano. I floss every day and belong to the Milwaukee Hooping Club, however, I am the sole member. I've driven the same car for 10 years; she's a red Toyota Prius and her name is Karma. I was identified as having photographic memory at an early age, but the more precise term is Eidetic, 'adjective pertaining to or constituting visual impressions recalled vividly and readily reproducible with great accuracy.' Oh, and I rank dark chocolate on the same level as oxygen as being imperative to my existence, so kudos to you for the truffles."

Quinn leaned back in his chair with his chin resting on his steepled fingers. The look on his face was unreadable, but after a thoughtful silence he spoke.

"Why do I get the sense you've just told me everything and nothing about yourself all at the same time? But the most disturbing part for me is I don't know what hooping is or if I should feel privileged or frightened to be sitting with the lone member of such an exclusive club."

It may have been my third glass of wine or that I genuinely enjoyed Quinn's company and our playful banter, but I couldn't wipe the smile from my face, and his reflected the same sentiments.

"Hula hooping." I giggled. Okay, it was the wine, because I laughed often but my true giggle came out when I got a wee bit inebriated.

"Hula hooping? Sounds sexy."

"Oh yeah, real sexy, ranks up there with pole dancing. In fact, I was wavering between the two but hooping won over because my pole wouldn't fit in the back of Karma." I giggled again.

Oh my God, I have got to lay off the wine. How embarrassing!

The server brought our dinner and offered to open another bottle of wine, but Quinn shook his head and waved him away before my impaired brain had time to formulate an answer.

"Okay, Quinten ..." I somehow managed to stretch his two syllable name into three. "Quid pro quo, what's your thirty-second summary?"

The intensity in his eyes burned into me, exposing a vulnerability that came only with my altered state. I squeezed my legs together to ward off the unwelcome pressure in the pit of my stomach and the hypersensitivity in my girly parts. He broke into his signature half-grin, like he knew precisely what he did to me.

"I am the oldest of three. My mother is from Spain; my father is from Brazil. However, I was born and raised in New York. I studied business and finance at Dartmouth, but I've always been good with numbers and investment intuition. I like extreme sports and I'm a self-professed adrenaline junkie. I've traveled the world, more than once, and when I'm not seeking adventure or traveling for business, I reside in New York. I'm not a vegan, but I eat well to keep fit and I, too, love good food. I enjoy beautiful women but my longest relationship lasted six weeks. *And* ... I rarely get side-tracked in places like Milwaukee."

"You're side-tracked?"

"Completely." His gaze fell to my lips.

I said nothing but slowly mouthed *wow!* At a complete loss of what to do or say, I scooted back in my chair and stood.

"Where are you going?" Quinn stood, reaching for my arm.

Stupid, stupid, stupid.

I should have stopped at one glass of wine and while I wasn't drunk, I had trouble expressing what I felt.

No, Addy, don't feel, think.

So I thought about smacking the smug SOB in the face, running like hell, or dragging his ass back to my loft. Maybe Addy the giver would be Addy the receiver for one night—fuck his brains out, then kick his ass to the curb before he had time to fasten his pants. A devilish grin pulled at my lips when I thought of the player getting played.

I used my other hand to remove his grip from my arm, then laced our fingers together. Without a word I pulled him toward my loft. His narrowed eyes held uncertainty, yet he followed me without question.

When we reached my loft, I left the lights off but the blinds were up and the street lights provided some illumination. Quinn tracked my every move as I sat on the arm of my sofa and removed my shoes.

"Addy ... we don't have to—"

"Shut up."

His eyes widened and so did mine. I said those words, but not in a voice I recognized. Quinn did that to me, or years without the touch of man did that to me ... it's possible the alcohol played a part too.

Whatever it was, I didn't want it to end. I just *needed* something physical, emotionless, mind-blowing. I grabbed his jacket and ripped it off his broad shoulders. His tie soon followed and my shaky hands made the buttons of his shirt a bigger challenge than I expected.

Impatient that the distraction of my fumbling hands would make me lose my nerve, I pulled at his shirt until the next two buttons popped off. He grabbed my wrists, halting my motions. I pushed up on my toes and crashed my lips to his, begging him to just let it happen.

My heart raced like the wings of a humming bird, making every movement even more frantic and desperate. He released my wrists and cupped my face, deepening our kiss. Our tongues met and explored each other in an erotic dance. My fidgety hands tugged at the button to his pants, but he broke our kiss and pulled back.

"Addy, slow down." He breathed hard.

That wasn't what I wanted to hear. Slowing down gave my brain too much time to rethink my intentions. I just wanted to take Quinn on my terms: fast, hard, and *unattached*.

"No." I finished unzipping his pants and gripped the waistband to pull them down.

Quinn grabbed my wrists again and held them at my chest, this time with more force. "Addy, stop!"

I froze, feeling rejected, embarrassed, and confused. The uneven tempo of our breaths permeated the silence. I sensed his dark eyes burning into me, but I refused to look at him. He stole my moment and I just wanted him to leave.

"Look at me." His voice was softer but still demanding.

If I looked at him he would see right through me, to a part of myself that I was not sharing with him or anyone—ever. All I could do was stare down at his hands holding my arms.

"I can't ... I can't look at you." My voice shook, my body rigid, and tears threatened my eyes. We were silent for what felt like an eternity.

"Then don't. Just close your eyes. Don't think, just feel ... with your body, not your heart. Close your eyes, just for tonight, just for this moment, and just ... *feel*."

His words were but a whisper, a command, a promise. He offered me one night and maybe that was all I wanted. Maybe I just needed to be touched in a way I hadn't been in years. So I did, I closed my eyes and just *felt*.

Quinn released my wrists and moved my hands back to his chest. The feel of his skin beneath my hands soothed me. With steadier fingers, I finished unbuttoning his shirt and eased it off his shoulders. My touch ghosted across his broad shoulders and down his chest, exploring and tracing every chiseled muscle.

He stood still, his only movement the rise and fall of his chest, as though he knew what I needed and offered it to me without reservation. Appreciating the firm definition of his back as I inched my fingertips to his waist, I slipped my hand under the band of his briefs without hesitation and kneaded his firm butt. He shifted just enough that I felt his erection press against my abdomen. My lips whispered kisses over his chest and stopped to taste his nipple with the tip of my tongue. That was his undoing.

Quinn's breath caught and he moved his hands up my bare back with enough pressure to tell me he was tense and fighting his own battle to take it slow. He pulled the ties of my halter, letting the top of my dress fall. The fabric pooled at the top of my breasts, and the only thing holding it on my body was the contact of my chest to his stomach. He cupped my face with both hands and ran his thumb across my bottom lip. I flicked my tongue out to lick it then drew the tip of it in my mouth, sucking and biting before releasing it.

He moved both hands down my neck and over my chest, drifting to the top of my breasts. Pausing for a second before sliding them down the rest of my body, he pushed at the fabric until nothing held it up and it fell to the floor at my feet. My heart pounded in my chest but I felt it pulsing between my legs as well.

"Oh God," I moaned, tilting my head up and arching my

back, pushing my breasts further into his grasp.

His mouth captured mine, absorbing my moan, his tongue deep in my mouth mimicking the motion of his thumbs stimulating my nipples. Everything below my waist liquified. I moved one of my hands from his backside, keeping it on the inside of his boxer briefs until I held his full, hard length in my hand. The moment I touched him he broke our kiss again.

"Fuuuck ... Addy ..."

I did that to him and that knowledge intensified my eagerness.

He pushed himself into my hand until he couldn't take it anymore.

"God, you've got to stop, I'm going to lose it."

He pulled my hand out and grabbed the other one, wrapping both around his neck. In one swift movement, he gripped my legs and pulled me up to him. As I wrapped my legs around his waist, he started a new assault on my mouth with his tongue, while walking us to my bedroom.

The pulsing of his length, pushing at my entrance, separated only by the lace of my panties, obliterated all coherent thoughts. One goal: Quinn inside of me ASAP! My legs clenched around his waist as my heels dug into his firm ass. It was simple. I was starving for sex and hungry for him.

"Quinn—" I panted.

He laid me on my bed and had to peel me off him. I was so desperate I could have self-combusted.

He stood.

I panted.

Pathetic?

Absolutely.

Did I care?

Not one damn bit.

He removed the rest of his clothes. I changed my mind; Quinn surpassed Michelangelo's David. How was it possible for a human to look so perfect? Every part of his anatomy was hard, defined, sculpted, and flawless.

I would deal with his excessive perfection later—after I took full advantage of it.

His eyes found mine and he whispered, "Close your eyes and remember, tonight just *feel.*"

So I did. I closed my eyes and surrendered my body, telling my heart to disappear, just for one night. Sex. It was just sex.

His hands moved along my feet then drifted up my legs, his hot breath at my core, his lips ghosting across my lace panties. Hooking his fingers along the top, he pulled them at a painfully slow pace down my legs. The leisurely ascent of his mouth back up my legs, sucking, licking, and nibbling at my hypersensitive skin, nearly sent me over the edge.

My knees trembled, but then his hands were on me, steadying them for a moment before spreading them wider. The rush of cool air sent a whole new flood of sensations to my sensitive flesh. His lips continued to burn a path up my inner thighs. My nerves were frayed, leaving me desperate to find some balance, some control. I reached for his head and started fisting and pulling his thick dark hair. He released a deep, guttural groan that made me yank it even harder.

I wasn't a virgin, but Quinn's mouth was the first to touch me *there.* He paused, his hot breath so close to my core I didn't know if he was breathing in my scent or trying to read my signals. My hands clenched his hair, one hand pushed him away, the other pulled him closer. Right versus wrong. Need versus want.

"Addy, just *feel*," he breathed and then ... he was *there*.

"Oh God!" I cried.

It was impossible to hold back. My hips jerked off the bed the moment his tongue penetrated my folds. With one hand on my hip he pushed me back down on the bed while the other traveled up my stomach, reaching for my breast, kneading it at first then pinching my nipple. What felt like pain for an instant turned into a lightning sensation straight to my sex, causing me to uncontrollably buck my hips uncontrollably again. His tongue retreated.

No!

Before my protest found its voice, his finger slipped into me, and I moaned in desperation. It was wrong for any woman to go this long without sex.

"Ah, Quinn, I'm going to ... ah ..." I was engorged, vibrating, and ready to burst. I couldn't take it anymore.

"Let it go. Feel it, all of it." He moved his thumb and circled my clitoris once and I exploded.

I yelled his name in a mix of pleasure and embarrassment. What he did felt so wrong and yet so very, very right.

The most incredible orgasm left me hovering above the earth. I couldn't even formulate a coherent thought. "Fuck ... me—" I breathed in satisfaction, once again hearing foreign words come out of my mouth.

What is he doing to me?

He cut me off with a deep kiss, plunging his tongue into my mouth. Then he trailed kisses across my face and whispered in my ear, "That's the plan."

It dawned on me. That was just the beginning, an appetizer in the most literal sense.

He removed his fingers and spread my wetness around.

Hovering over me, with his weight on his elbows and his hands tangled in my hair, he lowered his mouth to my neck. I gripped his firm arms as he sucked every inch of my throat, earlobe, and then back to my mouth. When his tongue collided with mine and our kiss deepened, I felt so possessed by him, I could have orgasmed again just by that sensation alone.

His erection rubbed against my leg, a promise of more. My fingers grazed down his muscle-strained back to his firm butt contracting and releasing. I brought my hand around and grasped him, using my thumb to rub circles over the wet tip of his cock then stroking the entire length.

"Fuck, Addy, you're killing me."

He kneeled in front of me and I opened my eyes just as he rolled on a condom.

"Over." He signaled, circling his finger.

I hesitated for a moment. My experience with sex was missionary position and only missionary. I swallowed back my apprehension and rolled onto my stomach.

"Knees up."

I brought my knees under me, spread in child's pose. Quinn bent over the back of me and licked a hot, wet trail up my back. His chin brushed my shoulder then his teeth made claim to my skin.

"Hold on to the top of the bed and don't let go."

For the love of all things sane, why do I need to hold onto something?

"Do it," he demanded again in a calm but firm voice.

I extended my arms above my head and gripped the wrought iron railing.

He rubbed the pads of his fingers over the ends of my nipples; the touch was so soft, but the sensation caused an almost painful throb between my legs. A short pause later, he touched my nipples again until my core was engorged again and dripping.

God, I was dripping!

"It's too much, Quinn, I can't—"

"Patience, baby."

He stopped his gentle caressing of my nipples and gripped my hip with one hand while he guided his length to my entrance with the other.

"Close your eyes, Addy."

I felt him plunge into me so hard I almost orgasmed just from the deep impact.

"Ah, you feel fucking amazing!" he growled.

He paused just long enough to let me acclimate to his invasion. Then he started moving, slow and deep at first, then his pace picked up, steadying me with one hand on my hip and the other hand rhythmically squeezing and releasing my breast.

"Harder," I pleaded.

Whose needy, wanton voice is that?

"Not yet." He pushed me to the edge, and my body was desperate for release. I couldn't find the friction I wanted and with every thrust he hit the spot that kept me on the edge without sending me over.

Touch me, please!

The sensation was so intense it was almost painful. His response was to thrust faster and harder. I could feel his body tensing and his breathing reached a staccato, but I couldn't wait. I let go of the rail with one hand to reach between my legs. The intensity of the moment robbed me of all shame as I tried to touch myself to release the agonizing buildup, but Quinn grabbed my hand.

"No, I'm your only pleasure. Don't. Touch. Yourself." His voice was a mix of anger and greed.

I moved my hand back to the railing in defeat and let out a small whimper, wondering if anyone had ever died from delayed gratification. If not, I would be the first.

Just before actual tears escaped, he massaged my clit with two fingers, sending an orgasm ripping through my body, devouring all my senses.

I moaned in pleasure and jerked my hips into his hand, and that was all it took for Quinn to find his own release.

"Addy ..." he groaned out in a strained voice.

He gave one more hard thrust, circling and grinding into me, milking every last bit of his own orgasm.

I released my hands and fell into a postcoital coma. Sex 101 with a true master, another checkmark on my bucket list.

THE HYDRAULIC SCREECH of the trash truck behind the building brought me out of the best sleep I'd had in years. Snuggled on my side, I blinked open my eyes and read my zen clock: 6:45 a.m.

So much for my run this morning.

A sly grin crept up my face as I rolled over to deal with the naked sex god from the night before. Stretching my arms above my head and arching my back, I shifted my naked body toward the middle of my bed.

Empty, huh?

Tying my robe, I walked to the bathroom. A dull ache settled between my legs. I answered it with a grimace, but memories of the night before replayed in my head and my face settled into a smile. I couldn't remember the last time my girly parts received a workout like that. Yes, I could—never.

The bathroom was empty. I checked the great room and glanced out to my deck.

"Quinn?"

No answer. Then I noticed a piece of paper on my kitchen counter with a pen on top like a paperweight.

Addy,

Thanks for last night. It was fun!

Take care,

Quinn

No. Fucking. Way!

Livid, lurid, angry, savage, and furious all failed to describe how monumentally pissed off I was at that moment.

Thanks for last night. It was fun! FUN?

Work was not an option. I grabbed my phone and messaged Mac.

Not working today. You're in charge. Keep Jake in line and tell him not to scare off the new girls.

Not waiting for a reply, I jumped in the shower and washed the essence of Quinten fucking Cohen off my body. After dressing, I stripped my bed and tossed everything in the washer.

Note to self: get a new bed ASAP.

That vintage, wrought iron bed would forever trigger the images of Quinn telling me to hold on.

An hour later Mac banged on my door. No big surprise, I never skipped work. I buzzed her in, closed my eyes, and chanted my mantra while she made her way up.

Deep breath … I am peaceful, I am strong.

"Hey, woman, you not feeling well today?"

"You could say that."

"Wanna talk about it?"

"No."

"Too bad, it wasn't really a question. Sit and spill."

I took a deep breath and quickly exhaled through my nose.

"I did something I shouldn't have done."

"You ate meat?"

I rewarded her attempt to relieve the tension with a half-grin and an eye roll. "No, I had sex."

"With a guy?" She brought her hand to her mouth, eyes wide.

"Yes, with a guy. What the hell, Mac?"

"Hey, can't blame me for asking. We both know you haven't been with anyone since ..." she trailed off without finishing because we both knew what she meant.

"I just ... I don't know what got into me."

"Hmm, just a wild guess but I'm thinking it was Mr. Sexy Ass Cohen, and if I may say so, well done, Addy. I'm sure you are the envy of every heterosexual female with a pulse. I'm sure the list of women who would kill to have Quinn *in them* goes on for infinity."

"Jeez, Mac, I'm sure Evan would love to hear you talking like this."

"Evan and I are married, not dead."

"Such a cliché."

"Maybe, but it's true. So what's the problem? Was he trying to work his magic on you with a wee little wand? Did he forget to pleasure you? Call out some other girl's name?"

"No, no, and no. I don't know how to say this without feeling like I'm disrespecting ..." Memories of my past surfaced like a road block.

Mac held my hands in hers. "Addy, Malcolm was my brother and I loved him dearly, but I'm not under any illusion that he was perfect, and you can't compare every man you meet to him. It's not fair to them or you."

She was right, but discussing this with her was still not easy. "It was just physical, Mac, but ... it was the most sensual and erotic night of my life. Quinn did things to me that I've never experienced, ever. At times I felt like I was outside of my own body, watching it happen to someone else. It was as if we were reenacting a scene from one of my romance novels. Malcolm and I had good sex but it was always, I don't know, textbook."

An awkward silence settled over us for a moment, and I couldn't muster the courage to look at her. It felt like stomping on her brother's grave, tarnishing his memory.

Finally, without warning, she burst into a fit of laughter. I darted my eyes to hers and squinted.

"Oh my gosh, Addy, I can't believe it. My brother was a missionary man?"

My jaw unhinged. She was laughing at my sex life with her brother.

"I should've known. I mean, we were raised in such a strict Baptist family, and I was the rebel, but not Malcolm. He was the pleaser child. Apparently that didn't spill over into your bed. You poor thing, did you ever even have an orgasm with him?"

"Mackenzie! I am not having this conversation with you." I had to be twenty different shades of red.

"I'm sorry, I'm not trying to embarrass you. Well, maybe I am." She winked. "I just assumed since you both were so young and in love that you would have been animals in bed."

"Can we drop it now?"

"Yes, yes, sorry. Let's get back to Quinn. I guess I don't see the problem. You're single, he is too, as you discovered. There's an undeniable attraction, he's apparently a god in bed, so …?"

"The problem is this…" I handed her Quinn's note "…This is what I found on my counter this morning."

"Oh, shit."

"I know, right?"

"You have to call his dumb ass on this one and let him know you will not be treated like some one-night stand floozie."

"I can't."

"You can and you will."

"No, I mean, I can't. I don't have his number and I don't know where he lives, other than in New York. And to be honest … it *was* a one-night stand. I didn't want—I don't want anything more than … sex." I grimaced. Looking at my friend—in all rights my sister—and confessing my newfound inner slut was difficult.

"But you're pissed."

"Yes. I know … it sounds stupid. I just wanted a proper goodbye, not a goddamn note that makes me feel like some clinger. It's as if he was afraid I wouldn't let him go if he stayed to say goodbye."

"In all fairness, I bet he's had his fair share of clingers … and let's be honest, how many women are okay with one-night stands? Did you discuss the terms of your sexual encounter before it happened?"

I laughed. "No."

"And he lives in New York?"

I nodded.

"What was he doing in Milwaukee?"

"I'm not sure, maybe something to do with work."

"You don't *know*? How can you not know? How many times did you see him, three? Four? And this never came up? What the hell did you talk about?"

I cringed, picking at my fingernails. Looking at the situation under the light of Mac's questions, I wondered if maybe I got what I deserved.

"I think he may be connected somehow to Mr. Jamison," I murmured in a weak voice.

"Mr. Jamison? The financial dipshit from Chicago that spoke at the Zen Garden?"

I nodded.

"Why do you think that?"

"Quinn was there, in the back of the room. We exchanged a few words."

"You exchanged a few words, huh?" Mac nodded her head but I knew she was internally shaking it in disbelief.

"I don't suppose those words included, 'Hey, what an odd coincidence, what are you doing here?'"

"Nope." I wrinkled my nose.

"Well, my dearest friend, I guess you'd better hope you did something to him last night that brings him back begging for more."

"Not likely and … and … I don't want anything more."

"Just a proper goodbye."

"Yes."

"A hand shake. No more sex."

"Well…" I grinned "…I wouldn't exactly turn it down." I shook my head. "But that's not the point. I don't care how good the sex is, his lack of manners is unforgivable. No … no I wouldn't have seconds if he offered … which I doubt that he would."

"Oh jeez, Addy, you are so oblivious to just how hot and sexy you are. I've watched men ogle you for years, even with your pathetic attempts to look ordinary and unappealing, pigtail girl."

"Hey, I like my pigtails."

"Yeah, well, men do too, but not for the reason you think."

"What's that supposed to mean?"

She released an exasperated sigh. "Nothing. So what makes you so sure Quinn won't be back?"

"When we were at dinner last night he said he 'enjoys beautiful women' but his longest relationship only lasted six weeks."

"And yet, you still ended up in bed with him?"

"Ugh, I know!" I threw myself back onto the couch and pulled a pillow over my face. "Because I just wanted to use him for sex!"

"And you did."

"Yes, but he left me … not the other way around. So he used me."

"I don't think it would have made much sense for you to leave your own place."

I laughed—hard. It was all I could do. The ridiculousness of the situation flashed in neon. I could have sex without falling in love, that was easy. But my female genes didn't allow me to have it without any emotions. I was pissed over a stupid note.

"Well, look at it this way, you have some great visuals for lonely nights with Mr. Dilly Doe."

I heaved the pillow at her. "Shut up!" We both laughed.

"Seriously, Addy, what are you going to do about him?"

I thought for a moment. "Nothing. Absolutely nothing."

CHAPTER FOUR

"After about 20 years of marriage, I'm finally starting to
scratch the surface of that one [what women want].
And I think the answer lies somewhere between
conversation and chocolate."

~Mel Gibson

S IX WEEKS LATER, summer in Milwaukee hit full swing. The
lake became destination central, and Sage Leaf Café was
busy every day. We had black iron café tables and chairs set up
under the front awnings, with wheatgrass centerpieces. I set a
big bowl of water on the sidewalk for the four-legged friends
that were out on those steamy days. The owners were usually as
grateful as the pooches.

I immersed myself in work, sort of. I loved creating new
recipes for my customers, so it might have been a stretch to call
it work. Mac and Evan dragged me out sailing at least one day
a week. I didn't know why I ever resisted. I loved the peaceful
escape of being out on the water. The sun on my face and the
whip of the wind through my ears was my connection to
everything greater than myself. I felt significantly insignificant,
as if my presence in the world, albeit small, was still necessary.

My time with Quinn felt that way too. A one-night stand
was insignificant, but the fact that he was the first sexual
encounter I'd had since Malcolm was very significant. It was

the equivalent of swimming in a tank of sharks with an open wound. The chances of survival … slim. My personal life had been horrifically shattered. Dinner outside of my café was a risk, but sex was jumping into the shark tank with my arm already severed. Yet, I survived.

Significantly insignificant.

Mac's parents celebrated their fortieth wedding anniversary in Chicago that weekend, so we went "home" for a few days. It was bittersweet going back to what I thought of as my 'previous life', but I was a stronger person, and Mac assured me her parents wanted to see me.

It had been a while since I'd seen them … and by a while I mean not since Malcolm died. I severed ties with everyone and everything connected to that life, except Mac. Not that I didn't try, but she was persistent, to put it mildly. She followed a strict hug-em-into-submission code.

After Malcolm's funeral, I decided to take a year off from life. I packed my bags, went to the airport, and randomly picked a starting destination. I called it the Adler Brecken leave-me-the-hell-alone tour.

Mac showed up at the airport, bags in hand, and when I refused to let her come with me she tackled me in the middle of the airport and wouldn't let me go until I agreed to let her come with me. We were gone one year, but it wasn't a bucket list tour of the Seven Wonders. We went to the most remote and unappealing destinations, and witnessed some unimaginable living conditions.

We spent the last three months in Tibet, becoming learned in the practice of meditation. It wasn't a coincidence that we missed the anniversary of Malcolm's death; our time away was about healing and being there with Malcolm's parents would have ripped open old wounds that I'd spent too much time trying to sew shut.

MAC'S PARENTS MET us for an early lunch, which was a relief since I wanted to test the waters with them in a more casual environment before the black-tie affair Friday night. We arrived at the restaurant a few minutes late, but overall, we made pretty good time.

The maître d' escorted us to our table. Standing up, Gwen pulled Mac into a tight hug while Richard and Evan shook hands and exchanged manly pats on the back. When Gwen released Mac she gave me the most endearing smile and opened her inviting arms to me. I willingly accepted her warm embrace, knowing both of us were fighting back tears of emotion that had festered for years.

Gwen was a nurse until she married Richard. She too was tall and thin, with shoulder-length, strawberry blonde hair like Mac. Green eyes weren't that common, but their family had plenty to go around since both Mac and Malcolm had them too.

Their devoted mother spent the previous forty years raising their family, organizing church activities, volunteering at local non-profit organizations, and golfing at the country club. I was very close to Gwen until Malcolm's death, but since essentially dropping off the face of the earth, I was uncertain if I ranked very high on her list. Mac insisted she was never upset with me, just hurt that I had refused to stay and grieve with her and let her "comfort" me.

"Addy, you look wonderful. It's been too long. How are you doing, sweetie?"

"I'm good." I gave her a confident smile so she knew I was truly okay.

Richard pulled me into his big chest and almost squeezed the life out of me. "Adler, so good to see you, kid, we've missed you."

"Thanks, Richard, the feeling is mutual. You both look great." I exhaled, avoiding prolonged eye contact.

Richard Townsend was an attorney at a large firm. His sophisticated mix of ash blond and grayish white hair matched his authoritative personality. His skin had started to take on a mature, wrinkled appearance, but it was usually tan from hours on the golf course.

He made a lot of money over the years going after large companies who manufactured defective products. Firsthand experience solidified his already staunch belief that you couldn't put a price on a human life. He made it his life's mission to give those companies constant reminders that they were accountable for public safety and not above the law. The "constant reminders" were in the form of multi-million dollar injury and wrongful death lawsuits.

We ordered lunch and settled into comfortable conversation. Evan was an attorney too, so he and Richard talked shop while Gwen shared everything about her charities and golfing tournaments. Overall, lunch went quite well, and I felt like the weight of the world was lifted from my shoulders.

After lunch, Evan and Mac dropped me off at my hotel.

"I wish you'd stay with us at Mom and Dad's."

"I know, I'm just not ready to walk down the memory lane of pictures I know adorn every wall, table, and mantle."

"Okay … I guess I understand." Mac paused for a moment. "Do you want to meet for dinner later?"

"Thanks, but you two enjoy the evening with your parents. I'm going to get settled into my hotel room and maybe go for a run. I'll call you in the morning."

SO MUCH HAD changed since I'd left Chicago, but the comfort I felt with the familiar surroundings in Grant Park remained unadulterated: the beautiful gardens, the Art Institute, Buckingham Fountain, and my favorite, Lakefront Trail. It was a bit more humid than I normally liked for running, but a good sweat felt refreshing that evening.

The warm breeze caressed my skin as the rest of my senses came to life: the bobbing boats on the horizon; kids racing to catch every drip of their melting ice cream cones; the ambient white noise peppered with the call of the swooping gulls and rhythmic creaking of wooden docks; the mixed aroma of fish and food vendors.

As I stopped for a water break and made my way to the marina, an elegant, custom yacht caught my attention. I immediately recognized it.

"Hola, hermosa." I froze at the unmistakable, sexy, Latin-American accent behind me. "She's a beautiful vessel, sí?"

I nodded once. It was all I could do. His voice felt like a gun to my back. Despite the sweat still glistening on my skin, I shivered as I felt him move closer. I couldn't turn around. I refused to look into those deep brown eyes. My emotions were all over the place. I felt trapped and desperate to flee, but my body forbade all efforts.

He towered over me, so close that simply shifting my weight to my heels would have my back resting against his chest.

"I've missed you—" His finger traced down my arm.

"Don't!" I felt myself losing it ... but my control couldn't keep up with my words. Jerking away from his touch, I turned toward him. Anger poisoned my veins, and I knew the anger was with myself, that I let him elicit this reaction from me. A stupid note. Why couldn't I let it go? Fight or flight, I had to get out of there.

Finding my feet, I brushed past him. "Fuck you."

"You already did." His voice was smug.

Like the reflex to a mosquito biting me, I whipped back around and smacked Quinn across the face so hard I felt like my hand was on fire. Holding his cheek, I expected a look of shock or anger, but I was the one in shock and further angered when he gave me a smile of satisfaction.

"You're mad. That's good. I wanted you angry."

"You're a sadistic, egotistical, self-centered, son of a bitch! And just so you know, I'm not mad or angry at you because the truth is, I don't feel *anything* for you. You left me a note. You're either a coward or so full of yourself that you didn't think I'd let you go. Well, let me tell you something ... I was going to kick your ass to the curb."

I wasn't. I was going to have sex with him again, make him the best breakfast he'd ever had, and then part ways with a friendly handshake, maybe a chaste kiss on the cheek—but on my terms.

God, I'm a mess!

The energy coursing through me was like an electrical current and precisely what I needed to propel my body away from Quinn as fast as possible. I ran hard and fast, fueled by a toxic mix of emotions. By the time I reached my hotel room, my body was a bowl of Jello. I collapsed on the bed and prayed for a reprieve from the burning sensation in my lungs.

How dare he play me like that?

He acted like an animal batting around its prey, waiting for its final attempt to escape then going for the jugular.

I was drained and in need of a shower, but my body required food first. Dragging my tired ass off the bed, I ordered dinner from a nearby Korean restaurant.

Exhaustion won over while I waited for my food to arrive. A knock at the door startled me. Grabbing some cash on the way, I opened the door and my breath caught in my throat.

Quinn.

He held a paper bag in one hand, his other hand behind his back.

"Peace offering."

"You hijacked my dinner?"

"Not at all. I bought you dinner."

"Semantics." I grabbed the bag and started to shut the door on him.

"Wait, aren't you going to invite me in?"

"No, hijacking my dinner does not gain you access to my room." I attempted to shut the door again.

"Wait!"

I sighed. "What?"

Quinn brought his other hand out from behind his back, in it was another bag. "Vegan, dark chocolate ice cream ... with peanut butter."

The strong, sexy, godlike man gave me the look of an innocent young child and I hated myself for being so easily tempted. It was just a note—and my ego. Never underestimate the self-destructive capability of the ego.

"Fine." I opened the door wider and stretched out my arm

in a mock-welcoming gesture. "But I still don't like you."

Ego is a bitch. So is addiction to chocolate.

He chuckled and nodded. "I know, we'll see what I can do about that."

Refusing to make him feel truly welcome or comfortable, I sat at a small table by the window and dug into my dinner without saying a word or even looking in his direction.

He helped himself to the chair across from me, leaning back and resting one foot on the opposite knee while interlacing his fingers behind his head. His shirt tightened over his chest, and I could see the individual definition of every muscle.

Jeez, why did he have to be so damn sexy?

"It's good to see you, Addy."

"I wish the feeling was mutual," I mumbled with my mouth full, not deeming Quinn worthy of my table manners.

It was Quinn's turn to let out an exasperated sigh. "Where did you see us going, Addy?"

I paused, taking a moment to finish what was in my mouth before wiping it with the back of my hand like a true lady. "I don't know, maybe downstairs for breakfast at my café, maybe to a movie, maybe sailing on the lake, maybe no damn further than my front door for an amicable goodbye!"

Quinn was silent. He released his hands from behind his head and rubbed them over the top of his legs, his face lost in contemplation. The silence made me uncomfortable so I opened the ice cream and shoved a big spoonful into my mouth.

Oh, this is so good. Focus, Addy!

"What are you doing here, Quinn? You're a complete enigma to me. I don't know what you do for a living, or why you were in Milwaukee, since you don't live there. I know you don't drink, but I don't know why. I know you think of women as conquests and have never had a relationship last longer than six weeks. And who says that? Who says that on a first date unless your only intention is to have a mutually-consenting, one-night stand? Which is fine, because that's all you were going to get anyway, but you can have a one-night stand without being an asshole. 'Thanks for last night, it was *fun!*'"

My ego paraded around the room like a night at Mardi Gras. Not pretty.

Deep breath … I am peaceful, I am strong.

Quinn jumped to his feet, grabbed my arms and pulled me up to him. I clenched a big spoonful of ice cream in my hand.

"What did you want me to say? That everything about you drives me crazy? That I can't stop craving your smart mouth, sassy attitude, your mesmerizing blue eyes that make me feel like I'm lost in the ocean, your insanely sexy body, or that being with you makes me question everything I thought I wanted in life?"

Whoa! Clearly he doesn't understand the definition of a one-night stand.

Gloating ego. Even uglier.

Holding my arms between our chests, with chocolate ice cream dripping from the spoon down my arm, Quinn leaned in and eased his tongue over the trail of chocolate up my arm then put the rest of the spoon in his mouth, never once taking his eyes off mine. I pulled the spoon out of his mouth then crashed my lips to his. There was nothing more intoxicating than the taste of Quinn and dark chocolate.

He took the spoon from me while I grabbed his hair, pulling him in to deepen our kiss. As good as the ice cream was, all

I thought about was devouring Quinn. My body craved his touch, his smell, the moans he made as we kissed.

Our hands tore at each other's clothes, leaving them scattered on the floor. Clutching his large hands around my hips, he picked me up and I wrapped my legs around him. He grabbed the container of ice cream and lumbered over to the love seat.

He set me down. "Lie back."

"What are you doing?"

I sucked in a breath. His eyes widened. A wicked smile danced along his lips as a dollop of ice-cream melted down my breast, hardening my nipples.

"I'm going to cover you in ice cream then lick you clean."

"Oh ..."

Quinn's mouth descended to my chocolate-covered nipple. "OH!"

The Latin sex god knew more about my body than I did. His tongue did a whole tutorial entitled "How to Make Addy Scream, Beg, and Orgasm." I'm not sure what was sexier—his body taking mine to sensory overload or the look on his face after he devoured most of the ice cream along with two of my orgasms.

Once my body started to regain a sense of control, he nipped at my hip bone and looked up at me with a huge grin. "*Like* me now?"

Keeping a straight face, I dipped my finger into the remaining melted ice cream and sucked on it before pulling it out with a pop. "You're okay."

"Okay? Just okay?"

I nodded, biting my top lip to keep from smiling. With a dark look that made my body quiver, he reached for his pants and retrieved a condom from his wallet. I tried not to focus on the reason why men carried condoms in their wallets like women carried lipstick or tampons in their purse. The euphoria of knowing what was to come—literally and figuratively— helped me overlook his preparedness. He no doubt had been a Boy Scout and still lived by the motto, "Be Prepared."

Grabbing my hips, he scooted me to the edge of the love seat so we were face to face. He tugged at the elastic bands of my pigtails.

"Do you have any idea how much the 'fuck me' schoolgirl look turns me on?" Twisting my pigtails around his hands, he used them to pull my mouth to his.

When I was thoroughly kissed breathless, he released me for a gasp of air.

"Was that *okay?*" he whispered.

I nodded. "Wait …" I shook my head. "'Fuck me school-girl look?' They're braids."

"Baby, if you're going to wear your hair like this you might as well add the short, pleated skirt and a cardigan with nothing underneath it."

Shit! Mac was right. Dammit!

He hiked my legs up and wrapped them around his waist as he stood. He captured my eyes with his as he lowered me just enough to impale me. I moaned, tilting my head back.

"How about this? Would you say this is *okay?*"

"Oh God, yes …"

He walked us into the bathroom and straight into the shower.

Somewhere between meeting my orgasm quota for the year and collapsing to the floor of the shower, Quinn managed to meticulously soap and shampoo both of our bodies. He looked fresh and energized when he carried me like a corpse to the bed.

"Was that *okay* for you?" he asked, standing at the foot of the bed, drying himself with a towel.

Words escaped me. All I could do was lift my hand and put my thumb and forefinger together in a circle with my three fingers extended.

SITTING ON THE bed in a plush white hotel robe, I shamelessly watched Quinn drop the towel from his waist to get dressed again.

"Enjoying the view?"

I blushed. "Best in the city."

He shook his head and smirked while zipping his pants. His face turned serious, erasing his sexy smile. I sensed him carefully thinking about his next words.

"I'm an entrepreneur of sorts, meaning I have my hand in a wide variety of businesses, from investment firms and real estate to technology design and manufacturing. Some of the companies I own, others I'm just an investor. I was in Milwaukee as an *advisor* to Mr. Jamison, as well as taking a needs assessment of my hotel. I stopped drinking after someone I cared about was killed in a drunk driving accident. And only a gigantic prick, who's trying to warn a beautiful woman to stay away, shares his passion for other beautiful women and his inability to commit. What I did not anticipate was you taking me back to your loft and seducing me. The note in the morning was meant to make you mad and discourage you from looking for me."

So it was over for him after that night. He owned the Zen

Garden Hotel and I was casual entertainment while he was in town. I gave what he'd just shared some careful thought for a minute. A million questions ran through my brain, but just one mattered at that moment.

"And today?"

Quinn looked out the window with his brow furrowed.

"Today? Well, today was an unexpected surprise, a gift you could say. I've never been hit, by a woman, as hard as you hit me at the marina."

"Then why the stupid smirk when I did it?"

He chuckled to himself. "It showed me you've been holding in a lot of emotions and frustration…sexual frustration…" another smirk "…and it assured me we have unfinished business and well, that pleases me." I saw the devil return to his dark eyes.

"Why are you in Chicago?" I asked.

"Why are you?"

"Nice diversion. Mac's parents' fortieth wedding anniversary. And *you*?"

"Paintball tournament."

"Paintball tournament? Are you joking?" I questioned in disbelief.

"Joking? No. Are you?" He narrowed his eyes at me. "I'm not talking about some juvenile game of laser tag or Nerf guns in the backyard. Paintball is a real sport. Have you heard of the PSP?"

"Play Station Portable? Progressive Supranuclear Palsy? Payment Service Provider? Preschool Playgroup? Pyloric Sphincter Problems? Personal Solicitation Program? Personal Sausage Poker? Pretty Shoddy Product? Pretty Steep Price?"

Widening his stance, he crossed his arms over his chest.

"Are you done?"

"Police Service of Pakistan?" I bit my upper lip to prevent my impending grin as I nodded my head. "I'm done, sorry."

"Paintball Sports Promotions. It's a professional paintball league. They even have a World Series Championship. There's also the NPPL—"

"National Private Pilot Li—"

"Addy!" Quinn cut me off as he rolled his eyes and pursed his lips with a sigh through his nose.

"Sorry." I wrinkled my face and sucked in both lips to contain my goofy amusement.

"National Professional Paintball League. My point is, it's a real sport, and in a few years you'll likely see it televised more on national sports networks."

"So you're part of a professional paintball team, yet you didn't mention it the night I shared my hula hoop club membership?"

"I'm not on a team. I used to be though, but not at a professional level. I do have a day job, you know? My sister lives here in Chicago and her husband is on an amateur team and they needed someone to fill in for their tournament this week. We won today and play in the finals tomorrow morning."

"You play paintball?" I still had trouble wrapping my head around Quinn, corporate CEO, donning full gear and running around a paintball obstacle course. It seemed even more crazy that he would fly to Chicago mid-work week for a paintball tournament.

He sauntered over to stand in front of me then pulled my chin up with his thumb and index finger. He bent down and laid a soft, agonizingly slow kiss on my lips. "*Play* is an understatement. I dominated today. Why do you think we're in the finals tomorrow?" Resting his forehead on mine, he feathered the back of his hand over my cheek. "I have to go."

My mind reeled. Just when I thought I had him pegged, he surprised me. The more I was around him, the more he intrigued me. Suddenly, the idea of not seeing him again saddened me. "Is this goodbye?" I choked out. My insides tightened, and fear threatened to take over my emotions.

"Never goodbye."

CHAPTER FIVE

"One good thing about music, when it hits you, you feel no pain."

~Bob Marley

THE ANNIVERSARY PARTY was at a world-renowned independent research library which housed rare books, music, maps, and manuscripts spanning six centuries. I wore an Edun strapless dress with a bandeau neckline and horizontal cut out detail. It had a black bust and layered crosshatch-patterned skirt ending several inches above my knees. My black, open-toed, four inch heels were all style and no comfort, but I was resigned to endure a little pain for the greater good of looking and feeling amazingly sexy that night. I didn't get out much, so I welcomed the opportunity to forgo short denim cut-offs and racerback yoga tops for something more elegant.

Entering the gala hall, with its large windows and massive columns, I was stopped by the sight of a Steinway grand piano in the corner of the room. My fingers twitched just at the sight of it.

"I'd love it if you'd play for us tonight," Gwen spoke, standing beside me wearing a full-length, gold lace and sequined evening gown.

"Gwen, you look lovely."

"Thank you, dear, so do you. But don't think for a moment I'm going to let you leave before dazzling us with your musical genius."

"It's been a while since I've played."

She gave me a knowing look of shared sympathy then wrapped one arm around me for a tight squeeze while holding a stemmed glass of champagne in the other. "Tonight then. It's time, you're ready."

I nodded, more so in acknowledgment than in agreement.

"Addy!" Mackenzie squealed, shuffling over to me in her tight dress and high heels. "You look amazing! I have no doubt some insanely hot guy is going to snag you by the end of the night and make you forget all about 'he who shall not be named.'"

I didn't plan on keeping my recent developments with Quinn a secret from Mac, but it wasn't the time or place to share details. The mere thought of him had my body resonating with the tantalizing memories of the night before.

"I don't think so. You must be confusing me with your pre-Evan self."

"Yeah, well, sometimes I think you could learn a few things from her."

THE NEXT COUPLE of hours I spent mingling with Richard and Gwen's friends. Most were strangers, but a few I recognized from my past life with Malcolm. They were the ones I went out of my way to avoid.

"Addy, there's someone you should meet." Mac pulled me over to the bar and I noticed a tall guy with a bleach-blond buzz cut. He was thin, with a long distance runner's build, beautiful, straight, white teeth and dimples. Not my type and I was pretty sure that was because Quinn had ruined me for every other guy.

"Addy this is Raef. Raef, this is my best friend Adler Brecken."

I smiled and shook his offered hand. "Nice to meet you, Raef."

"It's a pleasure. Mac tells me you two are in business together?"

"Yes, we own a vegan café in Milwaukee."

"Addy is a brilliant chef. You should try one of her creations sometime," Mac gushed, like I was a piece of property she was trying to sell.

"I'd love that. Maybe I could make the drive up some weekend and check out your café."

A few other people crowded up to the bar pushing us closer together, he placed his hand on the small of my back.

"Raef is an instructor at the Art Institute. I told him you could give him a run for his money with art history trivia."

I had trouble registering what Mac was going on about because looking past her, I saw a dark figure in the corner near the door.

Quinn.

"Um, that's interesting. Will you two excuse me? I have to go to the ladies' room."

"Do you want me to come with you?"

"No, Mac, I'll just be a few minutes."

Quinn had a dark look on his face as he studied the entire length of my body. Despite the lust it fueled inside me, I was a bit miffed at the idea that he was stalking me. Again. His black suit and white shirt with the top buttons open exposing his flawless olive skin almost distracted me from my anger—

almost. His jet-black hair was a fashionable chaos. I fisted my hands, forbidding them to clench his hair, tug it, jerk it, and use it to direct those lips to my—.

"I don't think you were invited, sir, I'm going to have to ask you to leave."

He struggled to pull his eyes up my body to meet mine. I sensed he liked what he saw. His easy nod and tongue darting out to wet his lips confirmed it. "You're right, let's go." He put his hand on my lower back, guiding us out of the room.

"Stop, Quinn, I can't leave yet."

"Why not?"

"First, my purse is still in there, and second, I haven't said goodbye to Mac's parents or Mac. You'll have to wait and see me later."

"Not happening."

He grabbed my hand and pulled me down the hall to a single-stall bathroom that I think might have been for employees only. His long strides left me struggling to keep up in my heels. Closing and locking the door, he pushed me up against it. His look was intense and his breathing labored.

"Who's the guy at the bar with his hands all over you?"

"Nobody."

Lacing our fingers together, he raised my arms above my head, keeping me pinned to the door. His mouth aggressively worked its way down my neck. "Didn't look like *nobody,*" he mumbled over my skin.

Blood surged to my sex leaving my brain a jumbled mess of confusion as to why he was acting so possessive. "Jesus, Quinn, Mac had just introduced us, it's nothing. Let it go," I implored through my already gasping breath.

He thrust his hips into me, letting me know how hard he

was. "So you're telling me what I saw was nothing with nobody?"

"Yes."

I froze with a knock at the door. Quinn spun me around so my face was to the door, hands splayed against it above my head.

"Addy, are you in there?" Mac questioned.

The pressure of Quinn's hard cock straining against his pants as he worked his hips along my ass rendered me speechless. His hands cupped my breasts while he slipped his thumbs in the cutouts and circled my taut nipples.

"Uh, yes, I-I'm in here." I hoped she didn't sense the tension in my voice.

"Why are you using *this* restroom?"

Quinn pushed my hair away from my neck and skimmed his wet tongue along it while his hands traced the curve of my waist to my hips. One hand pulled the skirt of my dress up and the other slipped down the front of my black lace panties.

"It uh … um it was … closer." My voice was a shaky flustered mess.

He opened my cleft with two fingers and circled them to spread my ample wetness around before he slid them all the way into me. I threw my head back, mouth agape, and fought to hold on to the moan that was so desperate to escape. His palm rubbed over my clit, mirroring the grinding movements of his hips behind me.

"Addy, are you okay? You don't sound so good."

The all-consuming sensation made it nearly impossible to think. My body was a clash between opposing forces: to arch back and rub against his arousal or to thrust forward into his hand that worked its wicked magic on me.

"Yes! Uh, I'm ... I'm good." I leaned my head forward against the door and bit my lip, praying Mac didn't hear me panting.

"Fine, but hurry up. Raef's wondering where you are. I think he might be into you." Mac's giggle faded into the distance.

Quinn stopped, his body went rigid and utterly still. I was at the precipice, waiting for his next move, my body begging for more.

"Mr. *Nobody* might be into you?" he growled, clearly not too pleased.

"Ugh, it's nothing," I whined, while trying to move my hips against his hand. My attempts were futile. He had me braced so tight against his hard body it was like fighting a concrete wall. His fingers pulled out, and with the same hand he clenched my panties in his fist. With one swift yank, they were ripped off.

"What the hell, Quinn!" I tried to turn to see him but his hand was at my back keeping me bent over toward the door. I heard him take a deep inhale through his nose.

"God, you smell so fucking good."

Holy shit, did he just smell my panties?

My first thought was embarrassment at the thought of any man smelling my underwear and being so turned on by my scent, but Quinn doing it made me feel wanton. The next thing I heard was the sound of Quinn's zipper followed by the rip of a condom packet. He pulled my dress up exposing my bare backside while he reached around and rubbed his fingers between my thighs.

"Jesus, Addy, you're so wet."

My hypersensitive body teetered on insanity. I nearly orgasmed the moment he touched me. Then he leaned over me with his head next to mine and removed his drenched fingers from me bringing them close to his face so I could see them. He put them in his mouth and sucked. "Mmm, you taste as good as you smell."

Oh. My. God.

His knee nudged against the inside of my leg pushing out on it.

"Spread those long, sexy legs a little more."

I felt his erection slide between my legs, my four inch heels putting me at the perfect height. When I pushed back toward him he moved with me, rubbing the head of his erection around my opening but denying me what I craved.

He teased me over and over again, occasionally pushing past my opening to graze my clit, causing my body to buck and spasm in anticipation. His game was so agonizingly frustrating.

"Just because I'm not an only child doesn't mean I like to share. You know what I think? I think Mr. Nobody is more than *into* you. I think he wants *in* you."

That's it!

I shook my head in denial and in an attempt to clear my mind of the drunk-on-Quinn sensation that clouded my judgment. Shoving him away, I pulled my dress back down into place,—sans panties. It was no longer seduction; he was attempting to rob me of my dignity.

"What the hell, Addy?" Quinn yelled while trying to pull his briefs over his sheathed erection.

"Listen up, you jealous idiot! I'm not one of your brainless beauties you can fuck around and control by going all alpha male psycho on me. I don't appreciate being followed or *stalked*. And if I told you Raef is *nobody* to me, then you damn sure better believe me. I haven't had anyone else in my bed since you walked out of my loft six weeks ago. Can you say the same? Can you look me in the eyes and tell me you haven't screwed some other woman since we were together?"

Initially he looked angry, readying his comeback, until my last question. Then his eyes fell to the floor, lips in a straight hard line.

"That's what I thought." I spun around and opened the door then paused. With my chin to my chest and eyes closed, I released a long, slow breath. "I don't care." I shook my head. "I don't care if you've been with other women since me. You're not my boyfriend and Raef isn't either, but he's also none of your damn business." I walked out the door, and never looked back.

CHATTER AND LAUGHTER seeped through the doors to the gala hall, taking a moment before opening them, I fixed my hair and regained my composure. Mac spied me as soon as I entered and excused herself from the table where she and Evan sat with Raef and another couple.

"Jeez, Addy, you look all flushed. Are you sure you're feeling okay?"

"I'm fine. I've just had too much alcohol. You know what a lightweight I am."

"Well, hopefully you're not too drunk to play for my mom. She said her one anniversary wish is for you to play something for her."

"I'm not drunk, but I don't know, Mac, I haven't played in over seven years."

"Whatever, I know the piano is your proverbial bike. You'll

forget your name before your fingers forget how to play."

I sighed. "One song, then I'm going back to my hotel."

"Deal. I'll tell Mom."

A Steinway grand piano was as good as it got. I feathered my fingers over the ivory keys without playing them. Mac was right. Sitting behind that beautiful instrument felt like home. There was no music to follow, but I never needed it; I could always just play.

Gwen and Mac must have made their way around the room directing everyone's attention to me sitting at the piano, because the room had fallen silent with just a few soft whispers. I rested my fingers on the keys and closed my eyes. A warm smile pulled at my lips as I thought of the last time I closed my eyes and just let my body *feel*. Quinn infiltrated my mind in a way that somehow brought every thought back to him.

From the first note, my body entered a different dimension. I felt one with the piano, as if I had never stopped playing. The music was "Clair de Lune", my favorite piano piece and one of the most beautiful pieces ever written. Each note transported me to my past, where I experienced what would always be my greatest pleasure and my greatest pain. The previous seven years with Mac, in search of something resembling a life, seeped into my mind. I thought of Quinn and the exhilaration I felt with him, and the inevitable pain that would come with it.

Emotions that couldn't find words danced on every note, coming to life, resurrected from the dead.

The best of my life.

The worst of my life.

Every moment of pleasure.

Every moment of pain.

When I finished there was a moment of silence until I opened my eyes. Then the room filled with applause. Gwen and Richard beamed with what looked like parental pride. My lips turned up into a shy smile as I graciously nodded in appreciation.

"Addy, that was amazing. Thank you so much. You've made my whole night, sweetie," Gwen gushed as she hugged me.

"Thank you. It felt good to play again."

"Must suck being 'Adler, child prodigy'," Mac teased.

"I was hardly a prodigy."

"Bullshit."

"Mackenzie! Watch your language," Gwen scolded.

"Sorry, but she was. Addy's had an easy life."

The instant the words fell from her lips, she had her hand over her mouth. "Oh, Addy, I'm so sorry. It was terrible of me to say that. You know that's not what I meant."

"It's fine, Mac, stop walking on eggshells around me. I'm better, stronger … I'm good, okay?"

She offered a sad smile and hugged me, as if she didn't know what else to say.

"Now if you party people don't mind, I think this maestro is tuckered out and ready to head back to the hotel room to crash." My carefree response must have lightened the mood, because everyone was all smiles again.

After saying my goodbyes, I made my way out of the building. The sticky air clung to my skin. I hoped I wouldn't have to wait too long for a cab. That was when I recognized the black Bentley parked by the curb with Mr. Suit standing next to it.

"Good evening, Miss Brecken, may I offer you a ride to your hotel?"

"No, thank you," I smiled, praying a cab would show up soon.

"Mr. Cohen insisted I give you a ride."

My feet ached from the murderous shoes that held them hostage, but not enough to accept a ride with the ass. Sex god, but still an ass. The heavily-tinted windows prevented me from seeing inside.

"Is he in there?"

"No, miss." He opened the back door to prove it.

"Fine, but only to my hotel, no other stops, agreed?"

"Yes, Miss Brecken."

"It's Addy, remember?"

"Yes, I remember."

I slid in the car and immediately ripped off my shoes and rubbed my feet as the car pulled away from the curb.

"You said you work for Mr. Cohen?"

"Yes, miss."

"But he doesn't live in Chicago?"

"No, miss."

"So you drive here from New York City?"

"No, miss, I live in Chicago."

"Do you have a name?"

"Yes, it's Eddie."

"Well, Eddie, can you tell me what you do when Mr. Cohen is not in Chicago?"

"I follow instructions he leaves for me."

I sighed in defeat as we pulled up to my hotel. "Thanks for leaving the water muddy, Eddie."

He laughed. "Have a good evening, Miss Brecken."

I didn't bother shoving my throbbing feet back into my shoes. Instead, I looped the straps over my hand and headed into the hotel.

WHEN I REACHED my room my key wouldn't work. After several failed attempts, I trudged back down to the front desk for a new key.

"May I help you this evening?" the concierge asked.

"I need a new room key. This one wouldn't open the door when I swiped it."

"What is your room number?"

"418"

He typed something into his computer. "Ah, well that's because you've been upgraded to the Presidential Suite for the remainder of your stay."

"Excuse me? There must be a mistake."

"No mistake. Here's your new key and the security code required for the elevators to reach the top floor. Your belongings have already been moved for your convenience. If you need anything else just call down."

I was so tired I couldn't even think to protest what was obviously a mistake, so I headed up to the top floor. There were two doors, mine was the one to the right. Sliding the key card through the lock the light flickered green. I stopped before I even stepped in far enough to shut the door. The suite was twice the size of my loft. Floor to ceiling windows draped with elaborate fabric coverings lined an entire wall. What stopped me in my tracks were the glowing candles all around the room. There must have been fifty or more candles and all other surfaces were covered in lavender rose petals. Iron & Wine's *Flightless Bird* played over the surround sound.

With hesitation I walked into the living area, surely I was

not supposed to be there, but when I didn't see anyone I proceeded into the master suite. It too was filled with lavender rose petals and lit solely by candles. The king size four-poster bed was adorned in a deep plum duvet cover and showered with lavender petals. A single long stemmed lavender rose and a note lay in the middle of the bed.

Forgive me?

Holding the note, I sensed someone watching me. I turned to the door where Quinn stood with at least two dozen lavender roses tied with a large white satin ribbon.

"I was an ass." He cautiously made his way to me.

"Yes, you were. How did you know where the anniversary party was? *Were* you stalking me?"

"Having someone look into your whereabouts because I wanted to see you is not the same as stalking."

"You're right. It makes me feel so much better to know you had me followed because that's not creepy at all."

"Forgive me?"

"Why should I?" I crossed my arms over my chest.

"You probably shouldn't, but will you anyway?" His pleading eyes held hope.

I didn't answer.

"You were wrong ... about me."

I continued to stare at him, waiting for further explanation.

"The six weeks we were apart, I wasn't with any other women. My dad died. That day, before our date, I received the call. I knew I would have to leave the next morning, but I meant it when I told you I didn't anticipate you taking me back to your loft and us ... well, you know."

As the words left his mouth, I remembered back to the look

he had that night when I told him my parents were dead. The hurt in his eyes wasn't sympathy, it was empathy.

Given my past, I was all too familiar with death. I'd suffered loss in the worst imaginable ways, and those experiences taught me that true emotions cannot be defined by words. With that in mind, I did not tell Quinn I was sorry for the passing of his father; words were inadequate, words hurt. They could cut through your heart, but they didn't have the ability to heal.

So I did the one thing I could. Reaching for the roses in his hands, I took them and laid them aside. Then I wrapped my arms around him. He hesitated to return the embrace at first, but eventually his arms reciprocated. The moment was not sexual or desperate; it was an unspoken gesture of compassion and understanding.

"Thank you," he breathed in my hair.

His simple response made me think of all the times family and friends had tried to comfort me but failed so miserably. Their words of sympathy were suffocating, inadequate, and downright repulsive to me after a while. I refused to think something so awful was "meant to be" or "God's plan." No God I could ever imagine would be so cruel. *Predestined* didn't coincide with free will. The truth for me was: shit happened, life was not a fairytale, and bad things happened to good people, end of story.

My eyes filled with watery emotions, the flood gates opened, and I cried.

Tears for Quinn.

Tears for me.

Tears just because the toxic pain had to be released.

It was as much a physical need as an emotional need. He

didn't ask why, he just held me. After what seemed like an eternity, I let go and looked into his eyes. He cradled my face in his large hands and wiped away my tears with his thumbs. I sucked in a few jagged breaths and smiled.

"You're forgiven."

Quinn flashed me his million dollar smile then pressed a light kiss to my forehead, nose, one cheek, then the other cheek, both corners of my mouth, and finally, almost reverently, on my lips.

"I'M SURPRISED THE fire marshal hasn't knocked on the door yet."

"Too over the top?"

I held my thumb and index finger up, a few centimeters apart. "A smidgen, and I'm not just talking about the candles."

"You like the roses?"

"Honestly, I'm more of a lilac and daisy girl, but I meant this suite. It's too much."

"After you ripped me a new one and left me with a serious case of blue balls, I knew it would take a grand gesture for you to ever speak to me again."

I laughed at the thought of Quinten Cohen, Latin sex god, standing alone in that little bathroom with a raging hard-on and bruised ego.

"It wasn't funny. I about had to hand job it to get my pants zipped back up."

"No sympathy here, buddy, I had to go back to the party and sit center stage at a piano in this short dress *without* any underwear." My eyes narrowed.

He sat on the edge of the bed, clenched my hips, and

pulled me to stand between his legs. Rubbing up and down my bare legs, he released a groan from the back of his throat. "Damn, I forgot you're not wearing any panties."

His hands inched higher until they gripped my butt, kneading my muscles and flesh. That skilled touch turned me on like a faucet—a very wet need for him pooled between my legs. Just as I started to pull away, maybe to find a wad of tissues to stop the leak, he shot me a naughty grin, pulling the front of my dress up to my waist, wholly exposing me.

The soft kisses he pressed to the neatly waxed skin covering my pubis sent jolts of anticipation radiating to every inch of my body. He pulled me closer with the hand that was still on my butt, allowing his tongue to dip between my folds.

"Quinn," I whispered as my breath hitched.

"Hold your dress up."

My knees trembled so I held my dress up with one hand and put my other on his shoulder to steady myself. He sat up and removed his cuff links then unbuttoned his shirt like he had all the time in the world before shrugging it off his muscular shoulders. When he stood to remove his pants, I let my dress fall back over me.

"Uh, uh, uh. Pull it back up," he demanded.

Without hesitation I complied, giving him a shy smile. After removing the rest of his clothes, he sat back down. My heart raced as he moved his middle finger between my legs and slid it inside me. My hand grabbed his shoulder again. I closed my eyes for a brief moment, allowing my body to absorb the dizzying sensation.

I opened them to Quinn stroking himself with his other hand. My whole body flushed. Quinn's uninhibited, confident sexuality pushed me out of my comfort zone. He encouraged my inner sex goddess to blossom. Each time we were together, he peeled away the layers of self-doubt I felt about myself. I no longer saw ordinary Addy through my eyes, I saw the extraordinary version of myself through his.

A few moments later he slid his finger out and rolled on a condom. "Take your dress off."

My knees locked into survival mode. I was ready to collapse. "I can't."

"Yes, you can. Take. It. Off."

Releasing his shoulder, I reached around to unzip my dress while Quinn steadied my hips. I pulled it over my head and dropped it on the floor.

"Touch yourself."

What?

"I-I didn't think you liked me touching myself?" I distinctly remembered his reaction the night at my loft when I was desperate and tried to touch myself. How old was I? What kind of woman waited for a man to tell her what to do and when to do it?

"It's not for you, it's for me." His eyes were dark and hooded.

Oooohh.

My ambivalent thoughts gave me pause for a moment, but then I started to massage my breasts with a slow, kneading motion.

Fuck it!

Nobody needed to know about my weakness—submitting to alpha Quinn. What happened in the bedroom, stayed in the bedroom.

"Your nipples too."

I pinched and rolled my nipples between my fingers, occasionally rubbing light circles on the very ends with my index fingers.

The dark look on Quinn's face was the same look I imagined men at strip clubs having when their pants were about ready to bust open watching the dancers. I felt dirty, sexy, ashamed, and empowered all at the same time. Sex was the ultimate drug.

His sheathed erection twitched. My eyes refused to look away from it as I placed silent bets with myself as to whether he would orgasm just watching me. Quinn squeezed my hips with his hands while keeping his lust-filled gaze glued to the show. Pulling me closer, he slipped his tongue between my slit again.

"Oh, God," I moaned.

That time he didn't stop. He literally fucked me with his tongue. Over and over, he thrust it into me. I let go of my breasts and grabbed his hair for support, pushing my hips to him. Thoughts of romance, love, and commitment weren't even on my radar. Just sex. All I wanted to give him was my body because he played it like I played the piano. And oh … my … God, could he make me sing.

I yanked on his hair until his mouth broke from my center. Shoving him back on the bed, I crawled up beside him and straddled him facing backwards. Gripping his length I rubbed it around my wet entrance then sank onto him until he filled me to the hilt.

"¡Dios Mío. Usted es tan sexy." The erotic timbre of his voice was my undoing.

I started riding him—hard. Quinn tried to slow the pace, but I selfishly insisted on setting it to my liking. My nails dug into his defined leg muscles for support. I leaned forward so the head of his erection hit my g-spot.

"Oh my God, right there, yes, right there," I whimpered, throwing all my dignity out the window.

My impending orgasm was so close and I sensed his was too. Then, on the verge of a tantric orgasm, it happened. We both exploded at the same time into the most mind-blowing sensation ever.

"Jesus, Addy!" he growled.

My body was so overcome with stimulation I couldn't even form words. Deep moans were all that escaped me. The sensations just didn't quit. A fireworks finale rained inside of me. Quinn sat up, his front to my back, not breaking our connection. He finished riding out his orgasm, his arms wrapped around me, massaging my breasts and kissing the back of my neck. I arched my back, reaching my arms behind my head to grab his hair. I fisted and tugged at it while my body slowed its figure eight motion, absorbing every last bit of my orgasm.

Completely drained, we both collapsed with rose petals sticking to our sweaty bodies. I rolled, more like slid off Quinn's chest then turned to my side to face him. My fingers peeled the petals off his chest, occasionally pausing to trace the outline of his muscles.

"What was that?" Quinn asked out of breath.

"I don't know." I exhaled a huge, happy, thank-you-so-damn-much-for that sigh. "You bring out a part of me I never knew existed. I don't know who that girl was or what she was doing."

He laughed. "Well, I like her ... a lot."

"I think I may like her too." I giggled like I did when I'd been drinking, but I hadn't had much alcohol. I was drunk on Quinn. He was more intoxicating than anything I'd ever experienced.

I continued to trace my fingers over his abs. "So here's what I'm thinking. I come with some serious emotional baggage that no one deserves to have dumped on them, and my instincts are that you do too."

He stared at the ceiling but nodded in agreement.

"You live in New York, I live in Milwaukee. I'm not looking for Mr. Right to sweep me off my feet, buy me a house, and give me 2.5 kids. You haven't had a relationship last longer than six weeks, presumably because you're not that good looking, and a bit of a bore in the sack."

Quinn flipped over, pinning me to the bed, then he bit my nipple.

"Ouch!"

"Not that good looking and a bit of a bore in the sack, huh?"

I giggled, feigning innocence and tried, in vain, to struggle out of his hold.

"So here's what *I'm* thinking. I should tie you to this bed for the rest of the night and torture you with my tongue for hours and not let you come until you declare me to be the Ultimate Sex God." He sucked in the same nipple he just bit and soothed it with gentle strokes of his tongue.

"Okay, okay, okay, I'm just joking. Now back off, you didn't let me finish."

"Well you'd better shed the wiseass act or this won't be the only thing I don't let you finish tonight." He playfully kissed the tip of my nose and rolled off me.

"Jeez ... Bossyyy."

"Last warning."

"Whatever. As I was saying, how would you feel about

getting together for mind-blowing sex when our schedules mutually allow, maybe a great *vegan* meal from Milwaukee's hottest chef, and small talk about current events?" I couldn't tell for sure, but I thought he was in shock.

"What, like friends with benefits?"

"Not even that. More like acquaintances with benefits. Friends implies we know personal things about each other, share feelings and secrets. Mac's my *friend*. I have her for that type of relationship."

"Would we be monogamous?"

"Not out of necessity, I mean …" I didn't know how to tell him occasional sex with him was all I wanted but that I understood his needs were possibly different. "I guess I'm saying what we do when we're not together is our own business and nothing we have to share with each other. We don't *belong* to each other. You can't worry about guys like Raef, and I can't ask you if you've been with anyone since me."

He scrunched his face in contemplation then lifted my leg to look between them.

"What are you doing?" I smacked his hand away.

"Looking for your penis, because women don't come up with ideas like this."

"Shut up, I'm serious! So are you in or out?"

He rolled on top of me so that his growing erection rubbed against my leg. "I'm undoubtedly *in*."

I turned my head when he went to kiss me. "You won't be *in* without a condom."

"I only had two and you made me waste one in the library bathroom," he pouted.

"No, your possessive, dominant ego wasted that one. That's the behavior I'm talking about. You've got to shut that shit down."

"Have you ever considered going on the pill?"

"Never. Those synthetic hormones are poison to women. Besides, if we're not pledging monogamy you will never enter my shower without a cap."

"Such a lady." Quinn sighed while pulling on his pants.

"Where are you going?"

"Concierge. For six grand a night they should throw in a box of condoms."

"Six grand a night!" I was certain my jaw hit the ground.

"Pennies, sweetheart. It's just pennies to me."

Pennies, schmennies. There was no way I would stay in that room the next night.

"You don't have to get a whole box."

"You just said I don't have to spend half the night wooing you, so you can be damn sure I'm going to spend the whole night screwing you."

"Ah, you're such a poetic gentleman."

CHAPTER SIX

"There are people in the world so hungry, that God cannot appear to them except in the form of bread."

~Mahatma Gandhi

WHILE QUINN MADE his condom run, I explored the massive suite. The marble bathroom was fit for royalty. I put a dip in the swimming-pool sized tub on my to-do list. Making my way into the main room again, I stopped in my tracks and held my breath.

How'd I miss that earlier?

A baby grand piano claimed the far corner by the windows. It called to me. They always called to me.

I should've been concerned about walking around naked with the drapes open, but between the soft candlelight and knowing I was on the forty-seventh floor, I shed all modesty. Sitting at the piano, I closed my eyes and let my body take me to another place. God, I loved that place. My fingers chose Rachmaninoff's Prelude in G Major. After I played the last note, I opened my eyes to Quinn leaning against the doorway with candlelight shadows dancing across his smooth, olive skin.

"Amazing."

I smiled. "The composition is amazing. I just play it."

"A ten-year-old at a piano recital just plays it. I watched you … You feel it, you live it."

Those words were too intimate ... too personal, so I quickly diverted. "I see you're stocked up for the night."

Quinn pulled a long strip of condoms out of the box. "It'll get us started."

I stayed at the piano while Quinn began separating the condoms. My friskiness surfaced so I played a tune to get us in the mood. The moment he recognized it, he started laughing.

"Marvin Gaye, good choice since we will be *getting it on* very soon."

Distracted by Quinn placing condoms around the suite like he was hiding Easter eggs, I stopped playing.

"What are you doing?"

"Putting a condom on every surface where I plan to fuck you."

Sweet Jesus!

After making his way around the entire suite, Quinn moseyed up to me with one condom left and tossed it on the piano. He flashed me a devilish grin as he unbuttoned his pants.

Hmm, will we do Harvey Keitel and Holly Hunter in The Piano *or Richard Gere and Julia Roberts in* Pretty Woman?

AS IT TURNED out, we reenacted both. Also what I assumed was a six-pack of condoms turned out to be a twelve-pack and we used every one. By the time we made it to the gigantic bathtub around 5:00 a.m., we were out of condoms. At least I thought we were out. Somewhere between his mouth on my body in places that both terrified me and exhilarated me and a string of orgasms that he pulled out of me like a damn rabbit in a hat, I sort of lost count. I may have even lost consciousness.

We both conceded that just washing the sex off each other and crashing might be best anyway.

Quinn was good.

Sex was good.

Life was simple—life was good.

I woke to the faint sound of my cell phone ringing. Tossing the covers aside, I eased out of bed with a slight ache between my legs. Quinn succeeded at leaving his mark on me. By the time I found my handbag in the other room, I'd already missed the call. It was Mac. I wasn't ready to explain everything to her yet, so I headed back into the bedroom. The clock by the bed read 11:30 a.m.

Holy crap! I can't believe I slept until almost noon.

Quinn was still passed out on his back, one arm stretched out in my empty space and the other folded on his chest. I took a moment to admire his beautiful body. Every part of it was flawlessly sculpted. He obviously worked hard to maintain that godlike body. I questioned if it was fair for one man to possess so much physical perfection.

The duvet rested low on his hips, giving me a naughty idea. Being careful not to make any noise, I tiptoed over to the bed and inched the covers down, exposing his glorious morning erection. I eased between his legs, keeping a watchful eye on his face. Then with a slow stroke I ran my tongue up his erection from base to tip where I circled along the head. It twitched and his whole body jerked awake. Before he had time to respond, I took him in my mouth, sucking, licking, and teasing, while looking up into his sleepy morning gaze. With a pop, I released him from my mouth and gave him a huge grin.

"Good morning."

"Fucking best morning ever! But don't stop." He pushed

my head back down.

I sucked him deep and hard while he moaned in appreciation. His hands tangled in my hair, mixed with the deep sounds that reverberated from his throat, fed my desire to please him as unselfishly as he did to me so many times the night before. When I sensed him getting closer I pulled off and licked my way up his stomach to his chest. I flicked my tongue over his dark nipple while stroking him the rest of the way. He jerked his hips one more time into my hand.

"Oh, Jesus!" Breathless, he looked down at me and the mess pooled on his belly. "Guess you're not a swallower."

I shrugged my shoulders. "I'm a vegan." I laughed, and eventually he did too.

Then I slapped the side of his sexy ass. "Go get cleaned up. I'm starving."

"Then you should have swallowed."

"Smart-ass."

I ordered room service since a full breakfast was complimentary with the six-thousand-dollar suite. While Quinn was still in the shower, I gave Mac a call.

"Why haven't you answered your phone?" she scolded.

"Long story. What's up?"

"Just seeing if you want to take Chicago by storm like old times? Evan is going golfing with Mom and Dad so it's just us. We can start with lunch at the Chicago Diner, Art Institute, Magnificent Mile shopping, and maybe see if anyone in the city is protesting something worthwhile."

"Um, sure but it will have to be a late lunch, maybe around two? That way it will tide us over in case we end up tear-gassed and thrown in the slammer." We both broke into a giggle fit.

"Sounds good. Be prepared to share the 'long story.'"

"Bye, Mac."

"I'm serious, Addy, don't you think you're going to dodge me on this one."

"Two o'clock."

I pressed *End* right as two hands snaked around my waist from behind.

"Mmm, hope you're hungry. A massive buffet of food is on its way up."

He untied my robe and slid his hands up to cup my breasts. "I'm hungry, baby, but not for food." One hand slipped down over my belly, but I grabbed it before it went any lower.

"Food first. Besides, you're out of condoms."

"We don't need condoms for what I have in mind." He turned me around and backed me into one of the dining chairs. "Sit."

"Quinn, they're going to be at the door any minute." I tried to object but failed to sound convincing.

"Then you'd better cooperate. Sit."

I sat leaning against the back and gripping the wood arms with my hands. He knelt in front of me and pushed the sides of my robe open. Grabbing my ankles, he put my feet on his shoulders.

"Dr. Cohen, are you doing a pelvic exam on me?"

"Yes, and I plan on being very thorough." He slid a finger in me and I tilted my head back.

"Ooohh."

He buried his face between my legs and made haste with his "oral exam."

"God, Quinn, that ... uh ... that feels ... so ... good."

The pressure built and he started to slow down. "Don't stop, please!" He was an expert at bringing me to my knees—

begging, pleading, promising world peace, in exchange for a Quinten Cohen-induced orgasm. It. Was. That. Good!

There was a knock at the door and he started to pull away, but I grabbed his head and shamelessly pushed him back between my legs until he resumed.

"Don't ... just finish." I tilted my chin down, pinning him with a narrowed-eyed look.

Quinn's expert tongue and dexterous fingers worked their magic in record time.

There was another knock at the door.

"Oh, God! I'm coming!"

I'm sure room service must have thought I was starving, given my enthusiasm.

Quinn eased my legs down and pulled my robe closed, leaving me limp in the chair. That arrogant bastard had the nerve to wink as he wiped his mouth with the back of his hand, then answered the door, shoulders back, chin up, and beaming with male pride.

I never asked or wanted to know about Mac and Evan's sex life, but I had to wonder if oral sex in a dining room chair while waiting for room service was normal.

Was anything about Quinn normal?

"WHAT'S ON THE agenda today?" Quinn asked between bites.

I stared at his lips, those beautifully talented lips, then shook my head a bit. "Well, *my* agenda includes a day on the town with Mac."

"I see. Well, I have a meeting this afternoon, then I'm heading back to New York, but I'm glad you'll have plenty of reminders of me when you walk around this big suite tonight all alone."

I raised an eyebrow at him. "If you think I'm staying in this room another night, then you have completely fallen off your rocker, Mr. Cohen."

"Addy, I told you the money doesn't matter."

I hated when people who had money said that. It was a slap in the face to the vast majority of people, who lived paycheck to paycheck or without a job at all.

"If the money doesn't matter, then you shouldn't have a problem with me staying someplace cheaper and writing me a check for the six grand instead."

His eyebrows furrowed in worry. "Jesus, Addy, if you need money, all you have to do is ask."

I shook my head but didn't go into my financial status. "I'm not staying in this room another night, but I would like to show you something if you have your checkbook."

"Nobody uses checks anymore. Will cash work?"

"Yes."

"Fine," he grumbled "go get ready to go. I'll be back in an hour. Is six grand enough?"

"Yes, that's good for today," I said over my shoulder on my way to the bathroom.

By the time I showered, dressed, and packed up, Quinn was already waiting for me. He stood by the window in his tailor-made suit, with his hands casually shoved in his pockets. Once again he caught me ogling him.

He pulled one hand from his pocket and scratched his stubbled chin. "See something you like?"

My eyes flicked to his. "We'd better get going so you don't miss your meeting." I smiled and headed to the door.

He grabbed my bags and smirked. "God, I love how insatiable you are."

When we reached the front of the hotel, as I expected, Eddie was waiting at the curb.

"Mr. Cohen, Miss Brecken."

"Eddie," Quinn acknowledged as I smiled and gave a polite nod while sliding into the back seat.

When Eddie got in the front I gave the address to him.

"So are you going to tell me where we're going?" Quinn asked with a touch of agitation to his voice.

"A local food co-op." I smiled.

"Grocery shopping?"

"Wait for the enlightenment, Mr. Cohen."

Quinn's hand landed on my leg, working its way up my skirt. "I don't like waiting, in case you haven't noticed by now." His voice was raw, teetering between anger and desire.

I grabbed his hand and pushed it back down then interlaced our fingers. "Nice try, but I know it's not the wait, it's the control. Or right now, it's the lack of it."

Quinn cleared his throat, but it sounded like a growl then he squeezed my hand a bit harder than necessary glancing at his watch. "Enjoy your *control* while it lasts because in about fifteen minutes this vehicle will head to my meeting whether your show and tell is over or not."

"Show and tell, Mr. Cohen? Sounds kind of kinky," I mused. As we pulled to the co-op entrance, Quinn's brows pulled tight while I bit my lip to prevent the grin tugging at the corners of my mouth. "Keep your wig on. This won't take but a few minutes."

Quinn followed me into the co-op and up to the service counter.

"How may I ... um uh help you?" the twenty-something

girl behind the counter stuttered, obviously flustered by the Latin god standing in front of her.

Quinn, being a *friendly* guy, replaced his grumpy frown with the "I'm sexy and I know it" smile that rendered women speechless and possibly, on a good day for him, panty-less.

"Yes, do you still have a donation fund to feed the homeless through your co-op?"

It took a minute for the flustered mess of a girl to register my question, but she eventually peeled her eyes from Quinn to answer me.

"Uh, yes, three nights a week we fill the parking lot with tables and chairs to feed those in need. Most of the funding comes from our co-op members, but all donations are appreciated. Three dollars feeds one person, all the food is organic and most is locally-grown. Are you interested in making a donation?"

Quinn's phone was the lucky recipient of his attention. A million bucks said he didn't hear a word the girl spoke.

"We would love to make a donation and please let your management know how appreciative we are that this co-op gives back in such a social and environmentally-responsible way." Nudging Quinn in the arm to get his attention, I motioned with my head toward the girl. "Give her the money."

"What?" He narrowed his eyes.

Clueless. Just as I predicted.

"The money, Quinn, hand it over." I smiled and motioned with my head again.

"You want to just randomly give six thousand dollars to this place to feed some homeless people?"

Silently, I stood corrected. He *did* hear the girl. I suppressed the long speech that danced on the tip of my tongue and decided to keep it simple. "Yes."

Lifting his wrist to take another look at the time, he let out a heavy sigh and removed the cash from the inside pocket of his suit jacket. After tossing it on the counter, he turned and headed back to the car. "Let's go, Addy, you're wasting my time."

I smiled at the girl, who stared at the pile of hundreds on the counter, and pivoted on my foot to leave. The shock must have subsided just enough for her to yell out, "Hey, was that Enrique Iglesias?"

Not even glancing back I shook my head and raised my hand in a polite wave of goodbye. Laughing to myself, I hadn't thought of the comparison, Enrique and Quinn shared similar facial features, hair, eyes, and skin tone, but Quinn's body made Enrique look like a little teenager.

Eddie waited with the back door to the Bentley already open, an amused smile on his face. There was little doubt in my mind that Mr. Huffy Pants stomped out of the store a few minutes earlier having a time-wasting tantrum.

Quinn didn't look at me or say anything the entire way. Instead, he kept his nose buried in his phone. When we arrived at his meeting location he looked at me but still didn't say anything.

"You said you were good with numbers, so I shouldn't have to tell you that you just fed two thousand people."

He still didn't say anything, however, I could tell his brain was in overdrive, but not about the numbers. Eddie opened Quinn's door and as he started to scoot out, I placed my hand over his and he stopped. I shifted my body over and leaned in so my mouth was at his ear.

"You could have fucked me in the back of a station wagon

and it would have been just as memorable as in that outrageously expensive suite," I whispered.

He pulled his hand out from under mine and grabbed my neck, pulling me into him, pressing my lips to his. Our tongues slid together and I let out a soft moan. He took everything he could in that moment and left me breathless. Then in one fluid motion, he stood from the car, straightened his jacket and tie, and walked away.

EDDIE DROVE ME back to meet Mac for lunch. When I climbed out he handed me a black business card with Quinn's name and a phone number but nothing else, such as a business name or title on it. I stuck it in my handbag.

"Thanks for the ride, Eddie."

"My pleasure, Miss Brecken. Would you like me to wait and take you back to your hotel?"

"That won't be necessary."

Mac had already found a table and busied herself with studying the menu when I walked into the restaurant.

"Pretty fancy taxi that just dropped you off," she mumbled, not taking her eyes off the menu.

"I know, I think the driver thought I was some celebrity, and who am I to pass up a free ride. I guess they'll be pretty pissed when he's not waiting by the curb for them, huh?"

"Cut the crap, Addy, you can't lie for shit." She tried to keep a serious face but her mouth deceived her. "Spill. You've been riding that Arabian horse again, haven't you?"

I laughed. "Not the Black Stallion?"

After I shared the events of the last two days, Mac was speechless, which was a first for her—ever.

"Mac?" She nodded slowly, still at a loss for words.

"Come on, say something!"

"Wow!"

"Quinn and I have been screwing like bunnies for the past twenty-four hours, and we've agreed to have a non-monogamous, sex-only relationship, and all you can say is 'wow?'"

"Addy, I don't know what to say. I mean, it takes a special person to stay emotionally detached to someone they're having regular sex with and ..."

"And what? You don't think I'm special?" I batted my eyes and plastered on my beauty queen smile.

"That's not what I'm saying. It's not a character flaw that you're not a slut who uses men for your own satisfaction, or worse ... for money, then just drops them."

I grimaced a bit. "But, Mac, that's sort of what I am doing, minus the money part. I'm using him for my own selfish pleasure. I mean it's mutual, but you know what I'm suggesting, right?"

"Addy, I love you and you know my past leaves no room for judgment. I'm just worried that you think you're incapable of having those feelings again ... but I'm not so sure. Can you honestly say the thought of him in bed with someone else right now doesn't bother you at all?"

I answered her without delay, because if I would have hesitated for even a second, she would have seen right through me. I didn't want a relationship, just sex. However, the human side, my female gene that includes a heavy dose of natural jealousy, couldn't deny that the thought of him touching someone else would be hard to swallow, but I'd do it for the greater good of sex with no strings. "No, it's just sex. It's like ... golf ... just an activity."

"Golf?" she spit out in laughter right as our waitress brought the check. "You're equating sex to golf?"

"Clubs and balls." I giggled, falling into my own fit of laughter.

She shook her head, trying to hide her own amusement. "Time to change the subject. I was thinking about checking out the peaceful PETA protest at a nearby research lab. Turns out some pretty horrific things are being done to animals in the name of research."

"I think our peaceful demonstration days are over. Besides, we aren't PETA members."

"Who cares? The experiments are government-funded, *our* tax dollars." She gave me a pleading look.

"Ugh, I don't have a good feeling about this. Your parents are going to have a fit if they get called to bail us out of jail. Richard's firm doesn't like that type of publicity."

"We're not going to end up in jail. It's not like we're rebel teenagers anymore. Did you hear me say it's a peaceful protest?"

"Mmmhmm, I heard you, but I've heard 'we're not going to end up in jail' before."

"We don't have to go. We could always go ... shopping."

I rolled my eyes. "Jail versus shopping, great choices. Fine ... where's the demonstration?"

"That's my girl!" She winked.

IF MY PARENTS would have been alive to bail us out of jail after the police broke up our "peaceful protest," I would have been given the speech about Mac being a negative influence. I heard it countless times during college.

"Forgot how much I enjoyed being in the slammer." I rolled my eyes as we sat with some other protestors in a holding cell.

"Addy, you know the arrest was bogus. We were in the process of leaving when they arrived. We should have never been arrested."

"Is that what you're going to tell Richard when he comes to get us?"

"No way, I'm not calling him. Evan will come get us and he will not, I repeat, *will not* tell my dad."

We waited almost an hour before we were able to make a call. Mac tried Evan but he didn't answer.

"Did you leave a message?" I asked.

"No! Jeez, what would I say?"

I laughed. "Uh, we're in jail? Come get us the hell out of here, pretty please?"

"Well, I didn't say that or anything, so what's plan B?"

"Plan B? Who said we had a plan B?"

"You still have your one call, so call Quinn. He probably has influence here in Chicago."

"I am not calling Quinn. Our sex-only relationship doesn't include a get-out-of-jail-free card."

"Addy, we don't have a choice. Besides, after what you said happened last night I'm pretty sure he'll come get us."

"Yeah, well, that was before I shamed him into making a charitable contribution this morning. My guess is, his patience and contributions are tapped out for today."

Moments later, we both wrinkled our noses at a nasty smell that filled the air around us. My claustrophobia dug its claws into me with each passing second and with the odor, my lunch would appear soon too.

"Addy!" Mac pleaded.

"Fine! I'll call him. But he may have already left for New York."

I requested my phone call, but part of me hoped he didn't answer. There was a good chance he wouldn't recognize the number and therefore choose not to answer.

"Quinten Cohen," he formally answered.

"Hey," was all I got out.

"Addy? Where are you calling from?" His voice was neutral.

Thankfully he didn't sound angry, but I didn't detect any pleasure in his voice either.

"Um, well, actually ... funny thing happened this afternoon. Mac and I sort of got ... arrested."

There was silence on the other end.

"Hello?" I thought maybe we'd been disconnected.

"I'm still here. I'll be there as soon as I can."

"Where are—" I started to ask him where he was. I didn't want him flying back to Chicago if he was already back in New York, but he ended our call before I had a chance to finish. Then I was escorted back to my cell.

"So, what'd he say?"

"He's on his way."

"When will he be here?"

I shrugged. "Twenty minutes, an hour, two days ... He didn't say before he hung up on me."

An hour later we were released and told all charges had been dropped. Quinn stood in front of the police station, hands shoved into his pant pockets.

I gave him a sheepish smile. "Hi."

"Hi." He shook his head in disbelief.

Mac reached Evan on his phone and walked in the opposite direction while pleading her case.

"So how was your afternoon?" I went with small talk because I honestly didn't know what to say.

He narrowed his eyes at me. "Busy, yours?"

"Oh, same old, same old: fed some homeless people, had lunch with my friend, attended a peaceful demonstration, got thrown in jail. Nothing too exciting."

He nodded, brows drawn in thought. "So this is pretty much a normal day for you?"

I hitched my purse back over my shoulder then shoved my hands down into my front pockets while I stared at my feet. "We don't always go out to lunch."

With my head still down, I peeked up at him and smiled a goofy grin and he reluctantly returned a pursed-lip smile.

"Let's go. I'll drop you off at your hotel before I head back toward the airport." He grabbed my hand and led me to the car. I glanced back at Mac. She waved me off, phone still glued to her ear.

Eddie waited with the back door open.

"Miss Brecken." He smiled.

"Eddie." I grinned.

We were silent for most of the short ride. "Did you miss your flight because of me?"

"I own my own plane so I never miss my flight." He looked out the window but slid his hand over to grab mine.

My whole body relaxed with his touch.

"Do you want to know why we were arrested?"

He still didn't look at me. "I got you both out of jail and all charges against you dropped. I know why you were arrested."

"But don't you want my side of the story?"

Before I had a chance to elaborate, we arrived at my hotel.

Quinn turned toward me as Eddie waited outside my door. "No, I don't want your side of the story. I'm sure it's all about some poor animals being tortured and you thought trespassing on private property with a bunch of radical PETA demonstrators was just an expression of your constitutional right to freedom of speech. I won't lecture you any further on the matter if you don't try to convince me you didn't do anything wrong, okay?"

No, not okay!

Deep breath ... I am peaceful, I am strong.

I leaned in and gave him a quick kiss on the cheek. "Sorry to have inconvenienced you. Thanks for the bailout."

"Addy—"

I jumped out of the car and hustled into the hotel without looking back.

CHAPTER SEVEN

"Sex is emotion in motion."

~Mae West

THE CALENDAR FLIPPED two months and no word from Quinn. I wondered if he was waiting on me to call since he had Eddie give me his number. Maybe he didn't have mine, but he was too resourceful to let that be his excuse. After all, he knew where I lived and worked.

Our last day together replayed in my head more times than I cared to admit. As ridiculous as it seemed, he must have been quite upset about the donation. He himself said that kind of money was just "pennies," so why the grumpy reaction? Then there was the whole jail mishap, but come on, was I honestly the first girl he'd bailed out of jail?

Okay, probably.

It wasn't like I'd been arrested for robbery or prostitution. What about that kiss before he got out of the car to go to his meeting? It didn't feel like a goodbye. It felt like a tide-me-over kiss, like a squirrel saving acorns for the long winter. How long could Quinn's winter last?

Maybe I needed to be his groundhog and give him a sign of spring. Since it was just sex, I decided there was no reason to be so apprehensive about texting him and requesting a booty call. So that was what I did.

Me: *Hey stranger, I have a coupon for a value pack of Trojans.*

Any plans for Labor Day weekend?

Quinn: *Sorry, don't recognize the number, who is this?*

Oh my God, what was I thinking?

I should have called instead. Of course I wasn't the only woman texting him for sex. Before I had a chance to respond my phone chimed with another text.

Quinn: *Kidding ;)*

Might be able to squeeze you in.

Most likely though, it will be the other way around.

I grinned.

Me: *Don't flatter yourself.*

Quinn: *Too late.*

Holiday on Mon w fam

Can give U Sat. PM

Me: *Coming to me?*

Quinn: *Not without the damn Trojans!*

Me: *Dumb ass! Not in me.*

Quinn: *Lol, yes I'll come to Milwaukee.*

I THOROUGHLY CLEANED my loft, not because I was a neat freak, just because I had to burn off some nervous energy. After all, we were going to rub our naked bodies all over it. As his

ETA approached, anxiety had me fidgeting like a chain smoker. It was ridiculous, given the fact that he had seen every inch of my body in every possible position—more than once.

After changing my outfit five times like some stupid schoolgirl, I settled with the most appropriate choice for the occasion—nothing. The door connecting my loft to the café buzzed. Quinn must have thought I was there. It was nice of Jake to send him up.

Having second thoughts about greeting him in the nude, I grabbed an apron from the kitchen, slipped it over my head, and quickly tied it in back. It wasn't as sexy, at least until I turned around. I inwardly giggled with anticipation as I buzzed open the door and leaned against my kitchen island like a naughty chef.

"Hey, Addy, we're out of—"

Holy Crap, Jake!

He paused at the top of the stairs, eyes narrowed at first then wide with realization. I wasn't revealing anything, but my body was frozen in place.

"Um ..." He swallowed hard. "Rosemary, Mac said you had some on your deck."

"Yes, uh ..." My outside entrance door buzzed. Jake stared at me, his wide eyes roamed my body making me turn red with embarrassment. He waited for me to move.

"Are you going to answer that?"

"Yes, uh ... you get the rosemary, I'll get the door."

He nodded.

It was the most awkward standoff. He waited for me to answer the door before he made his way to my deck. Without taking my eyes off him, I inched sideways toward the door. As soon as I started to move, he walked over to the deck. I crept backwards to the door keeping my eyes on him the whole time.

The door buzzed again.

Jake took his sweet time getting the rosemary.

"Addy?" Quinn called.

In desperation I tried to find the perfect forty-five degree angle to hide my bare ass from Jake and Quinn. I didn't want Quinn seeing my bare ass with Jake still there.

"Got it. You've got a ridiculous green thumb, Addy. This plant looks like it's on steroids." Jake stopped and gave me a questioning look as I stood by the door. "Are you okay?"

Typical cocky male. He knew I was not okay.

"Yes. Fine." I narrowed my eyes and returned a tight-lipped smile.

"Addy! I can hear you, open up."

It was a mystery as to why or how I managed to fall into the most embarrassing circumstances with Quinn.

Deep breath ... I am peaceful, I am strong.

I opened the door, standing off to the side angled away from Jake.

"It's about time, what took you—" Quinn fell silent when he saw Jake and then eyed me up and down. He squinted at me then looked at Jake. "Hey, Jake, right?"

"Yeah, good to see you, just getting some herbs." Jake held up the rosemary.

Quinn focused in on me again, and while I knew he couldn't see my backside, he drew his brows together, pinning me with a don't-you-dare-move look.

Before I could find the right words, Quinn took it upon himself to dismiss Jake. "Well, good seeing you again, take care."

Jake took the hint and smiled. "You too."

We both stood motionless until we heard the bottom door close behind Jake. With no time for me to react, Quinn dropped his bag on the floor and turned me around to view my very bare backside. My whole body flushed again because this wasn't how I imagined things going.

I had planned on playing the sexy, seductive, naughty chef wearing nothing but an apron, sprawling my body out on the kitchen counter. Instead, it was more like the naughty twelve-year-old girl getting caught by her dad, sneaking out of the house wearing a mini skirt.

"What the hell is going on here?" Quinn's voice was ten percent curiosity and ninety percent anger.

The fact was I couldn't control how he acted, but I could control the way I reacted. He might have expected me to hang my head in embarrassment and regret, but I was not submissive. My chin was up, shoulders back, smile big.

"Why, whatever do you mean?" I strutted into the living room, shaking my bare ass with the confidence of a model on the catwalk. Quinn kept his distance, straight face, heavy breathing, maybe even steam seeping from his nostrils.

"You think parading around naked in front of your staff is funny or professional for that matter?"

I paused for a moment then, almost in slow motion, walked back to Quinn while untying the apron.

"I wasn't parading, it was an unfortunate situation, yet a bit funny if you think about it." I dropped the apron to the ground and went to work on removing his shirt. "However, I see you're having trouble finding the humor in it, and that's possibly because you're tense from your trip and need a little help relaxing."

After unbuttoning the last button I pushed his shirt back

over his shoulders and showered his hard chiseled chest in wet kisses, working my way down to his pants.

"You're trying to distract me," he grumbled.

"Your caveman thoughts of jealousy are the only distraction. They distract you from the naked woman trying to seduce you. Let it go. Stop wasting time, and take me already."

His hands dove into my hair, grabbing my head and pulling it to his. Our mouths melded and our tongues danced in a passionate frenzy. His forcefulness felt possessive, but I didn't care; I just needed him. My hands fumbled with his pants until they were undone. Fighting to break from his lips, I licked my way along his chest with my arms stretched above my head, clawing my way down the front of him. I yanked his pants and briefs down, and before he could protest, I had his thick, hard cock in my mouth.

"Fuck! No, Addy!" Quinn grabbed my arms and pulled me up to him, his breath labored. "You're going to end this before it even gets started."

I gave him my version of a devilish smile, because it thrilled me to know I affected him so easily. We both stood breathless, eyes locked for a few still moments. I pushed myself up on my tiptoes and brushed my tongue over his bottom lip.

"Then what *do* you want me to do?"

Keeping my attention with just his eyes, he removed the rest of his clothes. I wanted to look at him, all of him. However, he held my gaze with such command it left me drowning in his eyes. I looked away, not at him or anything in particular, simply away.

"Why do you do that?" he asked with a tenderness to his voice.

"Do what?" I whispered, still not looking at him.

Using one finger, he tilted my chin up, demanding my eyes on him again. "That. You look away like you're more insecure about me looking in your eyes than at your naked body."

I put my palms flat on his chest, closed my eyes, and kissed his dark, taut skin.

"Sex, Quinn, just sex, okay?"

He nodded. After a few moments of standing still with me leaning against his chest, he pulled me back, capturing my mouth and igniting the fire that burned for his touch. He lowered his head, taking my breast in his mouth, tugging and rolling his tongue over my nipple while cupping my other breast. I let my head fall back, a million sensations surging through my body.

"Oh, God," I moaned.

Moving his hands to grip my hips, he fell to his knees. My lungs sucked in a sharp breath when he grabbed my ass with both hands and pulled my center to his face, inhaling my scent.

"Jesus, Addy, you're my aphrodisiac," Quinn breathed, grabbing my right leg and hooking it over his shoulder.

I wove my hands in his hair for support as his mouth covered me.

"Ah, Quinn!" I gasped. My standing leg bucked beneath me.

His strong hands on my hips easily held my weight. I rocked into him, a silent plea for more.

More of his hands gripping my ass.

More of his tongue lapping a path through my folds.

More of everything.

Just sex. I added it to my list of mantras. I loved my body in his expert hands. I loved the voice I hardly recognized as my own—the one that begged for his touch. I loved the way my mind shut out the world, leaving us locked in the present moment with no regret and no expectations.

He moved up my body and backed me against the door before squatting down to get a condom from the side pocket of his bag. After he rolled it on, he pushed himself back up while grabbing my legs and wrapping them around his waist.

"Ahh," I cried as he impaled me.

That! That was what I wanted. Hot. Spontaneous. Mindless. Sex.

"Your body is so fucking sexy," he grunted, slamming into me over and over.

Desiring every solid inch of him, I pushed my back into the door to grind my hips forward.

"Harder," I pleaded.

He dropped his head to my shoulder and fucked me. That's what it was. That's all it was.

The door at my back and his fingers clenched tight into my legs would leave me black and blue for weeks, but I didn't care. He raptured my body and calmed my mind. Numb. I just wanted to feel with my body and let my mind go numb.

"Ah, God!" I cried out as the pain heightened the pleasure to the point of explosion.

His hard glutes felt like stone beneath my calves as he pinned me to the door with one final thrust, finding his release.

BOTH OF US gasped for air and dripped with sweat. Quinn carried me, wrapped like a monkey around his body, to the bedroom where we collapsed on my bed—my body draped over his.

"Holy hell, woman, I swear I could fuck you to the moon

and it still wouldn't be hard enough for you."

I laughed. "That's pretty funny coming from Mr. Latin Sex God."

"Sex God?" He tipped his chin, looking down at me.

"Yes. Latin. Sexy. Zero percent body Fat. Basically, I hate you."

He grinned while tracing his fingers up and down my back. "Good genes, I guess."

"Bullshit. Your looks are good genes. You don't get a body like yours without serious work."

"I may do a few push-ups occasionally."

"Just a few, huh? I might have to check that out later."

I rolled off him. He removed his condom, tied it, and tossed it on the floor.

"You did not just throw that on my floor." I scowled.

"I did. What are you going to do about it? Spank me?" He flipped onto his stomach giving me access to his glorious ass, but I was stopped in my tracks by the marks on his back. They were red and deep and looked like he'd been clawed, but not by an animal. They were from fingernails and not mine.

"What's wrong?" He narrowed his eyes when I didn't respond, my smile fading.

I couldn't take my eyes off the marks. "Nothing."

He sighed, as if realization hit him. "You said we weren't monogamous."

Shit! Don't feel. Don't analyze. Don't show any emotion.

Monogamy was not part of our agreement. Deep down, I knew he would be with other women when he wasn't with me. Hell, I gave him permission. However, the thought of him having visual souvenirs hadn't crossed my mind. I was over my head with two choices: Drown in self-pity and jealousy or keep my head up and take our relationship for what was agreed upon—just sex.

"It's fine." I smiled and shrugged. "Hungry? I'll get us something to eat. We should replenish our energy after that hot fuck by my front door." I slapped his ass and jumped up, grabbing my robe.

"Hot fuck?" Quinn quirked a brow.

Choked by the lump in my throat, I didn't answer. I couldn't answer. Instead I shrugged and fled for safety. The girl that called what was nothing short of incredible sex a "hot fuck" was unrecognizable to me, but after the reality check on Quinn's back, I was reminded that was all it was between us—*fucking*. Like animals.

I did this to myself and my stupid pride would never admit that I couldn't handle it. My heart couldn't handle caring for someone again, but my body couldn't handle not having Quinn again. There were two things I did know for sure: one, I would not end our relationship in defeat because I couldn't live up to my own rules; two, I would not be the one to contact him again.

If he wanted to see me he would have to call. It was the coward's way of saving face or, in my case, saving my heart, but it was all I could do at that point.

I called downstairs and asked Mac to leave some food by the door: curried veggie burgers, cinnamon spiced sweet potato soup, and cucumber limeade. Quinn walked out with a blanket tied low on his waist and looked more appetizing than anything we would eat.

"Didn't make it past the door with my clothes." He smiled and grabbed his bag and pile of discarded clothes.

Incapable of looking away, I stared without any guilt. He

kept his sexy grin while he shook his head and walked back to the bedroom. "It's just a body, Addy."

The lower door buzzed startling me out of my daze. I hopped down the stairs and opened the door. Mac stood with our tray of food, eyeing me up and down in my robe and giving me a suspicious eyebrow raise. "How's lover boy?"

"Shut up. It's just sex, not even that, we're just … you know."

"Yeah I know, do you?" she asked, knowing very well I was in uncharted territory.

"Thank you and goodbye, Mac."

When I reached the top of the stairs I found Quinn in a Mets T-shirt and running shorts seated on a barstool at the counter. He caught me standing in place, ogling him yet again.

"Thought I should put some clothes on so you could concentrate on eating, but I see it doesn't matter."

I set the tray down pushing his food in front of him. "You act like I just stand around drooling over your body."

"Don't you?" He took a bite of his sandwich, looking at me.

I blushed, shook my head, and focused on eating without further comment.

"This is good. I mean, exceptionally good," he mumbled before swallowing.

"You act surprised."

"I am, but not that you created something so great, just that I think this tastes better than any hamburger I've ever eaten. And I've eaten at some of the finest restaurants in the world."

"Yeah, well, there's only so many things you can do to flavor up animal carcass."

He coughed over his mouthful of food. "Jeez, you make it sound like restaurants are serving roadkill."

My lips pursed into a tight smile. "If the shoe fits…"

After sipping a spoon full of soup, he shrugged his shoulders. "I don't even have a good rebuttal because this food tastes so amazing."

I flashed him a smile of genuine gratitude. "Thank you." His praise meant more than he could imagine. My culinary creations were my art. They were an expression of myself and how I felt about health, the environment, and patrons of my restaurant.

"You're welcome." He looked pleased, yet I sensed the neurotransmitters in his head working overtime.

"What?"

With a barely detectable shake of his head, he smiled. "You're just … not what I expected."

"Really? What did you expect?"

"A clingy, narcissistic diva."

"Wow! So pretty much I'm the antonym to what you expected?"

"So it would seem."

"I guess you needed something in your life to change."

"Such as?"

"If you have to ask, then it must be something on a subconscious level that has switched off your 'clingy, narcissistic diva' magnet. We often attract what we need in life, even if we don't consciously know we're doing it."

"Well, Dr. Brecken, what is it about you that I subconsciously need?"

Rolling my eyes to the ceiling, I tapped the pad of my index finger against my lips. "You need to feel grounded and I am grounded."

Like a 747 that fell from the sky ... but nonetheless, grounded.

"Grounded? You don't think I'm grounded?"

"Not so much. You don't just *have* money, you think you *need* it ... lots of it. I imagine you make charitable contributions, but mostly because it's good for your reputation and a nice tax write-off. My intuition is you've never literally given the shirt off your back to another human, unless *she* was in need of a makeshift robe after crawling out of your bed naked. You avoid committed relationships because it ensures you stay disconnected ... from what? I'm not sure, most likely a fear of either giving or receiving love."

"Don't you think you could have given me the sugar-coated version?"

"That was." I smiled, before sipping some water.

"Okay, so I'm a greedy, selfish, arrogant prick who's afraid of commitment. What does that say about you? What exactly do you *need* from me?"

"That's what I've been trying to figure out."

"And what have you come up with so far?"

Shrugging my shoulders, I told him the truth, or at least the part of it my conscious brain willingly recognized. "Sex."

AFTER DINNER WE decided to go for a walk along the lake path. There was an intimacy in the way our fingers laced together as our arms swayed with each step. Those simple yet tender moments made me more self-conscious and exposed than his tongue licking chocolate ice cream off the most intimate parts of my body.

The ugly face of insecurity mocked me. Did he hold the

hand of the woman who marked his back the way he held mine? Eventually I gave my monkey brain a rest and simply let myself be in the moment. We walked in silence for the most part. Agreeing to not talk about anything personal left us with very little to talk about. The silence wasn't awkward, it was soothing. With Quinn, words were not always necessary.

The sun set in the horizon. A slight breeze brought cooler evening temperatures. Quinn pulled me into his side and rubbed my goose bump covered arms.

"That night at the pier you said you loved to sail. Do you rent a boat and go out very often?"

"Once or twice a week when it works out."

He nodded. "The last time I was in town I saw this great sailboat, yacht actually. It was docked at the marina. Made me think of you. I tried to find out who owned it, but no one would give out a name."

It was an odd statement, as if he was fishing, but I wasn't ready to bite.

"You looking into buying a sailboat?" I gave him a quick, sideways glance.

"Maybe." He shrugged.

I should have just let it go, but I couldn't. The bait was too tempting. "What about it made you think of me?"

"Aside from the fact that it was a truly spectacular sailing vessel and you said you loved sailing?"

I nodded.

"The name. It's called *The Sage*. Have you seen it before? I can't imagine you could have missed it."

I tried not to tense, knowing Quinn would notice since his arm was still wrapped around me, but I couldn't help it.

"Yeah, I know which one you're talking about, she looks

yare."

"Do you know the owner?"

"What do you think, Addy?"
"It's amazing, Mom!"
"Your dad and I knew you'd love it. A beautiful yacht for a beautiful girl."
"Promise us you'll never sell her."
"I won't, Dad, I promise."

"Hello, Addy?"

"Uh, what?"

"Where'd you go?" Quinn's brow wrinkled.

Turning to face him, I slipped my hands up the back of his shirt and pulled him into me. "You're leaving tomorrow and I haven't had enough of my sex god fix, so what do you say we head back and you warm me up with your hot body?" I slid my fingers under the waist of his pants and squeezed his magnificent ass.

He reciprocated by grabbing my backside and pulling me against his growing arousal. "I'd say you're changing the subject, but I don't give a damn right now."

He stroked his tongue along the crease of my lips then bit the lower one and sucked it into his mouth. My tongue met his and we melted into each other. I could have kissed him all day and never tired of it. My arms encircled his neck and I jumped up, wrapping my legs around his waist. He held me with ease as our kiss deepened. My need to feel his skin against mine became overwhelming.

"Take me back," I whispered in his ear, sucking his lobe into my mouth then running my tongue down his neck.

He released a groan from the back of his throat. I tried to

block out the image of him desiring another woman the same way; it slowly ate at me, like a cancer that could destroy me.

When we reached my loft he carried me straight to the bedroom. His eyes never left mine; he was trying to steal a part of me I wasn't ready to give. I reached over to my nightstand and pressed a playlist on my iPod. *Insatiable* by Darren Hayes flowed from the speakers throughout my loft. The seductive song heightened the sexual tension that was always so electric between us.

Quinn took his time, lacing his fingers through my hair, kissing my neck and lips, cradling my face in his hands as he rested his forehead on mine.

"You. Are. So. Beautiful," his breath whispered over my face.

My patched-together heart crushed beneath his words, to the breaking point. I hoped he would shove me to the wall and fuck my brains out, make me feel wanted, but Quinn made me feel desired, beautiful, special ... needed. I had to step back as the moment overtook me.

"I think I already made it clear that you're getting laid. Flattery is unnecessary." I laughed, trying to lighten the mood.

"Stop." He tilted my head up, forcing me to look in his eyes. "Just ... don't. We may not bare our souls to each other, but when I'm with you, like this..." he ran his finger over my lips then reverently kissed them "...I'm taking all of you, if *only* for this moment."

I hated him for that, but my body, as always with Quinn, deceived me. My mouth took his as I pulled the hem of his shirt up his back, breaking our kiss to pull it over his head. He reached for my shirt and followed suit. Leaning down, he pressed gentle kisses to the swell of my breasts as he unhooked my bra. I watched him leisurely cup my breasts, brushing his thumbs over my nipples. When I looked up, his eyes captured mine. "Beautiful," he breathed.

I shook my head.

"Yes, you are and I'm going to show you just how much I think so."

His movements were painstakingly slow as he finished removing my clothes. He kissed my feet, ankles, shins, and thighs. Stopping at my lace panties, he brushed his stubbled face over them before continuing up my belly.

He took his time kissing my breasts, then ghosted his lips along my neck, eventually capturing my mouth. We shared a long, lazy kiss like we had all the time in the world. I snaked my hand down to undo his jeans. Placing my palm flat against his stomach, I slipped it under his boxer briefs and wrapped my hand around his hard length.

"Addy," he moaned into my mouth.

We took our time exploring every inch of each other's body. Nothing about that night felt rushed, nothing about that night felt like sex. Everything ... every touch, every kiss, every look, felt intimate.

WAKING SUNDAY MORNING alone in my bed, I slipped on my black lace boyshort panties and a fitted white tank top, then headed past the empty bathroom to find an empty great room. I turned toward my deck and spotted my Latin sex god surrounded by a forest of herb plants, talking on his phone. He wore nothing but a rugged two day shadow and black boxer briefs that hugged every inch of his sexy ass.

Turning, he caught me, once again, ogling him. His steely

face looked serious. The polite reaction would have been to give him a few minutes of privacy, but my Quinn-addicted body vetoed that decision. Admittedly, the new brave—more like brazen—and confident version of Adler Brecken felt good in my skin.

I edged my way closer to him, his face still serious, making a few "yes, no, okay" comments to whomever was on the other end. Walking my body into his chest, I kissed his pectoral muscles and ran my tongue and teeth along his nipple while moving my hands behind him.

I pushed down just the backside of his briefs, exposing his perfect ass. Squeezing and digging my nails into his hard muscles, I stepped back and pulled him with me so we were no longer on the deck. His dark eyes seared me. I chewed my lip for a split second in contemplation then decided to go for it.

Encouraged by his arousal for me pressing against my stomach, I moved my hands around his hips and pulled the front of his briefs down with the back. Sinking to my knees, I took his erection in my mouth and sucked it hard. He drew in a sharp breath through his teeth. I looked up at him, swirling my tongue around the head. Grabbing my hair with his free hand, he closed his eyes, and urged my mouth back on him.

"Brett, I'll call you back." He tossed his phone on the couch and pulled out of my mouth, dragging me up to him. "I think I have a naughty little temptress trying to distract me when I'm on the phone. Would I be right?"

He palmed my butt and walked us backwards until I bumped into the kitchen island. Reaching behind me he ran his hand over the smooth surface, scattered with multiple specks of browns and golds with some scattered cobalt blue chips. "Recycled glass?"

I nodded, not interested in discussing my countertops.

"Hmm, cool to the touch."

I nodded. He pulled my tank top over my head, then yanked down my panties. Gripping my waist he set my bare ass on the *cold* counter top. I took in a quick breath.

He smirked. "Lie back."

I eased my back onto the counter. The cool glass sent chills through my body.

"Feet up."

I put my feet on the counter, and he pushed them back so my heels touched my butt.

"Don't move." He disappeared to the bedroom then returned a few moments later grabbing two dish towels that were by the sink. I balled my hand as he bound my wrist to my ankle.

Holy shit, I've never been tied up!

After securing one side, he went to work on my other side. "Relax, Addy. Just remember, you started this."

Was I being punished? What did I start?

My head spun as my heart raced from the claustrophobic anxiety of being tied up.

Don't panic, don't panic.

"Close your eyes and breathe, baby." He parted my knees wider, wholly exposing me. I searched for deep calming breaths as I closed my eyes. He waited until my breathing evened out. "Are you going to distract me again when I'm on the phone?"

"No," I whispered.

His tongue ran up my center.

"Ahh." My body jerked, pulling at my ankles and wrists.

"What's that, baby, I didn't hear you?" He inserted a finger in me.

"No," I breathed out a little louder.

Sliding another finger in, he flicked his tongue over my clit causing my body to spasm again.

"Oh God, no!" I tried to bring my knees together, but he had his hands on them, keeping me spread wide.

"No what, baby?"

"No ... I won't do it ... again."

"Good girl." He began moving his fingers in and out causing all the blood in my body to converge between my legs. The pressure was unbearable.

"Oh God, Quinn!"

"Yes, baby?"

"I can't take it anymore." I was a panting mess.

I heard the soft rip of a foil condom wrapper and then his fingers slid out of me, instantly replaced with his mouth.

I moaned in appreciation, wanting to move my hips into him, but he still held me down. "Untie me, please," I begged.

He stroked my sex with greater pressure, using the tip of his tongue to relentlessly flick my clit. Then, just when I was so close, he moved both of his hands up and pinched my erect nipples. The most explosive orgasm ripped through my body in long waves. He untied me while keeping his mouth on my core, lapping up every last bit of my orgasm.

All too soon he brought me out of the blissful aftermath by picking me up and easing me onto his erection. The exquisite fullness ignited my body again. He walked us over to the plush rug in front of the couch and knelt. We had sex—I think. Quinn defined mind-blowing and my IQ dropped ten points or more when his cock took up residence inside me.

After he came with a violent grunt, I breathed in relief, wondering what that was really all about.

"Do you have a secretary?"

He turned his head and gave me a puzzled look. "I have a personal assistant."

"Female?"

"Yes, why?"

"Just wondering if that's how you react every time she disrupts a phone conversation of yours."

He laughed. "First, she knows better than to interrupt me unless it's an emergency, and second, if and when she does, she just says, 'excuse me Mr. Cohen,' she doesn't wrap her mouth around my dick."

I chuckled. "Might make the work day better if she did."

"Maybe." He looked up at the ceiling with his hands folded on his chest.

Whoa, what was that supposed to mean?

Something was deliriously wrong with me for ever guiding the conversation in that direction. "Breakfast?" I asked, trying to focus on something other than Quinn's assistant literally giving him lip service.

He nodded but still didn't look at me. A few minutes later he stood in silence and headed for the bathroom. I heard the shower running so I slipped my panties and tank back on then grabbed some clothes for the day.

DEF LEPPARD'S *HYSTERIA* played through the speakers while I flipped banana oat pancakes on the stove. When Quinn came out, he was clean shaven, had a wet head, and was dressed in faded jeans and a fitted white tee. He set his bag by the door.

I flashed him a quick smile before turning back around to finish the pancakes. He sat on a barstool with no words yet to share. When the pancakes were done, I arranged them on our plates fanned in a circle with sliced strawberries and chopped pecans garnishing the top. Then I drizzled warm maple syrup over them. I set Quinn's plate in front of him and poured us small glasses of fresh-squeezed orange juice.

"Thank you…" he stared at his decoratively-arranged breakfast "…always the chef, huh?"

"Food should please the eyes before the palate." I shrugged.

He took a bite. "Well, you've succeeded at both."

His comment was friendly, or maybe courteous. It felt like small talk he would make with a waitress at a restaurant. Something was wrong, or off, but I wasn't sure what. Maybe it was my comment about his personal assistant. It was a joke. Thoughts of whether to say something or not quarreled. With a mental flip of a coin, I decided to just keep to polite conversation.

"Thanks. I make pancakes every Sunday morning, overindulge, skip lunch, then eat a light dinner."

He nodded, keeping his eyes on his plate while he continued eating. After he finished his juice, he grabbed his phone from the couch and walked to the door. The moment was immensely uncomfortable. I could hardly believe an hour earlier I had been tied up and exposed on my counter. I followed him to the door, pursing my lips while I chewed the inside of my cheek.

He bent down and picked up his bag. Then, with his back to me, he let out an exasperated breath.

"Why did you make such a big deal about a six-thousand-dollar-a-night hotel room and drag me to some grocery store to make a huge production about feeding the less fortunate when you're the sole owner of a yacht that's worth well over a million dollars?"

That curve ball punched me in the gut. I couldn't answer or even look at him.

He turned to face me. "Jesus, Addy, you own one small café, but you're talented enough to own a successful chain of them. You live in this dinky loft filled with mismatched furnishings and drive a car that's ten years old. You refuse to indulge in anything luxurious but you have a fucking million dollar yacht docked at the marina. Most women I meet want me for a shopping spree on Fifth Avenue and have dreams of a big diamond from Tiffany's. But you..." he ran his fingers through his hair in frustration "...you go out of your way to feed the homeless and are willing to be arrested just to voice your objection about something that offends you. Don't you get it? I'd lay the fucking world at your feet if you just asked me! But not you, Addy, you just want sex, with no strings attached."

My heart and my brain were at war. I felt lost. I didn't want him to walk out that door because I knew I would never see him again, but I also knew I had offered all I had to give. Quinn wanted to piece me together like a puzzle, but too many of my pieces were gone. I was forever incomplete.

Silence filled the space between us as he waited for my response. I had nothing.

"Is that all you got? Christ, Addy, can you at least look at me?"

It took everything I had to lift my head. Just as my eyes met his angry, dark glare, they spilled over with tears. Like blood oozing from a lifeless body, I stood motionless, not one sob, not one sniffle—only tears.

Quinn's brows knitted together.

Pity?

Pain?

Confusion?

He leaned into me and kissed the stream of tears on both of my cheeks then rested his forehead on mine. It had become a common gesture between us, maybe symbolic of an unspoken understanding or maybe it was his way of trying to read my mind.

"Goodbye, Quinn." I closed my eyes to fortify my courage.

He rocked his forehead side to side against mine. "Never goodbye," he whispered.

A sharp click resounded in my ears. The door was shut. I opened my eyes to the void before me. Like waking from a beautiful dream, I smiled thinking about the memories. Then it slowly faded as the disappointing pang of reality reminded me that it was in fact, just a dream. He left and once again—I was alone.

CHAPTER EIGHT

"Birthdays are good for you. Statistics show that the
people who have the most live the longest."

~Larry Lorenzoni

*D*EEP BREATH ... *I am peaceful, I am strong.*

It had been one month since Quinn walked out my
door. It had been one month since my past came back to haunt
my present and robbed a piece of my future. I'd found balance
in my life; it was a grueling journey, but I'd made it. Equal
parts pain and pleasure, but for me the balance was a sacrifice
on both sides. To keep the pain at bay I had to limit my
pleasure. Quinn magnified a pleasure I hadn't felt in seven
years, and pain reared its ugly head to bring my life back into
an acceptable balance.

The buzz of my door interrupted my thoughts. I peeked
out the window and saw Conner, my favorite furniture guy,
opening the back door to the Architectural Salvage delivery
truck. It was my birthday and I was certain my best friend sent
me something great; she had much better style than I could
ever dream of having.

"Conner!" I yelled, heading down the stairs.

"Hey, gorgeous, happy birthday." He gave me a big hug. It
made my day that much better.

"Thanks, whatcha got in there?"

"Maybe I was just in the neighborhood and wanted to stop by and wish you a happy birthday."

"Maybe, or maybe my BFF paid you way too much money to deliver my present on a Sunday."

He flashed me his sweetest smile. "Maybe."

Peeking into the back of the truck I saw a four-tiered shelving unit made from reclaimed wood and cast iron. "Oh my gosh, it's amazing." I was taken aback because the piece undoubtedly cost between three and four thousand dollars.

"She has good taste," he commented while sliding it forward.

"Too good. I don't deserve her."

"Well, you might not say that once I inform you she said you'd use your freakishly strong little body to help me carry it up these stairs." He looked me over. His perked brow questioned my physical ability.

"Tip it forward. I'll take the top."

His gaze lingered on me for a few more seconds. "Okay, but if you drop it, remember, it's a one of a kind."

"Yeah, yeah, let's do this."

We made it up the stairs but it was a heavy son of a buck. However, I think Conner left with a new respect for his favorite "little" chef.

I grabbed my phone and instant-messaged Mac.

Me: *Love, love, love it! Way too expensive, but I'm keeping it anyway :) Thank you, dear friend of mine!*

Mac: *Happy birthday, sweetie, you are very welcome. Can't wait to see you for dinner tonight. Your cake looks so yummy, if I may say so myself.*

Me: *Mmm, Mac's awesome carrot cake. My favorite, see*

you soon!

Later that afternoon while getting ready for my birthday dinner with Mac and Evan, my door buzzed again. A quick peek out the window revealed a floral delivery van.

Who's sending me flowers?

I opened the door.

"Adler Brecken?"

"Yes."

"Hope you have some empty counter space."

"Excuse me?"

"I have thirty-two floral bouquets for you."

"What? Who are they from?"

"Not sure. I think one of the bouquets has a card. Where would you like them?"

"Uh, the kitchen island and that empty shelving unit, I guess."

I stood at the doorway stunned, watching him bring in thirty-one bouquets of pink daisies and lilacs. The thirty-second and final bouquet was a dozen lavender roses with a card. Without reading it I knew who had sent them.

Happy birthday, beautiful!

"HE SENT YOU thirty-two bouquets of flowers and all the card said was 'happy birthday, beautiful'? He didn't even sign his name?" Mac questioned in shock.

"He didn't have to. The lavender roses were his signature."

When I said the words aloud, I uncovered emotions that compromised my guarded heart. The man I used for sex sent me thirty-two bouquets of flowers. I referred to Quinn as a stalker, but even though I would never have admitted it, I was flattered that he knew it was my birthday.

It had been a month, but I was still on his mind. The truth was, there wasn't a day I didn't think about him, and not just the sex. I missed being with him. Sharing a meal with him felt like we'd done it a million times before. When I talked, he was so attentive, as if I was the most interesting person in the world. He captivated me with his hardcore persona that didn't match the look in his eyes.

I couldn't help but wonder if he was just as scared of me as I was of him. The vulnerability of being with someone who could see past all the illusions, that were meant to guard something so deep, was terrifying. I'd just barely scratched the surface of Quinten Cohen. Somewhere beneath my own emotional shield was a voice that silently confessed: just being near him made me feel necessary.

"You should call him, at least to say thank you."

"I thought about it, but it would be awkward. I don't know what else I would say."

"You'd say, 'my lady parts are in desperate need of your service.'"

"Oh jeez, Mac, TMI," Evan blurted. "I'm going to get the cake from the kitchen, wrap it up while I'm gone."

We both laughed. It didn't take much for Evan to turn red with embarrassment, and Mac's unfiltered mouth kept him flushed most of the time.

"Seriously, Addy, you know I understand you better than anyone, which is why I don't push you on this. Having said that, I also love you more than anyone, which is why it breaks my heart to know that happiness waits for you on the other side of the mountain. I don't want to watch the pain you'd have to go through to make the climb, but I would love to see you alive and happy at the other side."

I nodded and gave her a forced smile. "You've always been good at narrating my life in metaphors."

"I don't know, Addy, I think all these candles may melt the frosting," Evan interrupted, easing his way into the dining room with my carrot cake decorated to perfection but with way too many candles.

"Evan! You butchered an hour of decorating by sticking all those stupid candles in the cake," Mac screeched.

"No way, babe, as I recall, you two ladies just about burnt the house down with all the candles you crowded onto my birthday cake last month."

Mac glared at him, eyes throwing daggers; talk of burning buildings was considered taboo around me.

"Oh shit, Addy, I'm so sorry. I can't believe I said that." He set the cake on the table and wrapped me in his arms like a little child.

"Stop, both of you. How many times do I have to tell you to stop walking on eggshells around me. I *know* you would never say something to intentionally hurt me. And I refuse to be the elephant in the room every time a subject comes up that might relate to my past, okay?"

They both stared at me, as if trying to gauge my mood.

"So are you two just going to stand there or are you going to feed this birthday girl some cake?"

Mac picked up the knife as Evan started to remove the candles.

"Don't, Evan! Put the candles back on and light them. I'm not worried about the house *burning* down," I spoke slowly to emphasize the fact that I was better. Not great, but certainly better.

I ARRIVED HOME from Mac and Evan's a little after ten. My loft was filled with the fragrance of lilacs, reminding me of my first encounter with Quinn. My spiritual journey that started seven years ago had taught me to find purpose in everything, no matter how random it might seem. I struggled to see why Quinn came into my life and what I was supposed to learn from him and our time together. I decided to text him instead of calling since I was unaware of his whereabouts or of whom he might be with. If he was home in New York, it would be an hour later so he might be asleep.

Me: *Thank you for the flowers.*

Extravagant, over the top, signature you.

I pressed *send,* leaving my phone on my coffee table, but before I reached my bedroom it chimed.

Quinn: *You're welcome. Hope you had a great day. Goodnight, birthday girl.*

His message haunted me. I couldn't stop staring at it. The stupid part of me hoped he would have said more. Hell, the stupid part of me wished the flower delivery guy had Quinn in the back of his truck, wrapped in a bow.

I missed him. Not just the sex, but him. I missed who I was with him, because I had a small reminder of what it felt like to have my heart beat for a purpose beyond circulating my blood. It thrilled me and scared me. Mac was right, he might be on the other side of my proverbial mountain, but most of the time it felt like he was at the bottom of a steep cliff that I stood atop. *Would he catch me if I jumped?*

CHAPTER NINE

"He that is not jealous is not in love."

~St. Augustine

"*A*DDY, *MY MOM and dad just showed up. Addy, are you hearing me? Sweetie, you need to help them make funeral service arrangements.*"

Th-thump. Th-thump. Th-thump. Th-thump ...

"*Addy, oh God, Addy, I don't know what to do for you. I'll do anything, just don't leave me, I'm worried you're slipping further away everyday. I can't lose you too.*"

Th-thump, th-thump, th-thump ...

"*Okay, Addy, I'm going to take care of everything, but when it's over you are going to get out of bed and find something worth living for, do you understand me?*"

Th-thump, th-thump, th-thump ...

OCTOBER FLEW BY. I spent all my spare time sailing with Mac and Evan. Sweatshirts and parkas were dress code on most days, but the sun graced us quite often. Sage Leaf Café transitioned the menu to incorporate a wide variety of root vegetables and squashes as well as lots of pumpkin and apple creations.

Early November surprised us with mild weather, but

Mother Nature changed her mind real quick. By the Monday before Thanksgiving we were shoveling snow. I spent Thanksgiving with Mac and Evan in Chicago at Gwen and Richard's house. It took hours of meditation, repeated mantras, and Mackenzie pep talks, for me to agree to go back to their house. I think Mac talked to Gwen beforehand because there was only one picture from my past that I saw. It was a family photo taken a few months before Malcolm died. Seeing it still cut me open, but not as deep.

When we returned from Thanksgiving, I prepared for my next trip. Mac had so very kindly volunteered my expertise at a culinary institute in New York. An instructor from there visited the café in November and gave my menu rave reviews, then inquired as to where I'd received my training. Mac told her the University of Chicago, which elicited the normal lost look. Then she proceeded to tell her I was self-taught and rarely ever used recipes.

If I ever needed an agent to sing my praises, Mac would have been it. Ironically, my lack of formal training impressed the instructor just that much more, and she insisted I come to New York in December. Eventually, against my better judgment, I agreed.

The day before I left Mac came over to help me pack. "You're going to love New York in December. Rockefeller Center decorated for the holidays is worth the trip all by itself."

"So you've told me a hundred times already." I rolled my eyes as I sat on my suitcase, trying to zip it shut.

"Well if the lights don't do it for you, there's always the optional booty call."

"Dream on. We haven't had any sort of contact since my birthday, that was two months ago, three since I've seen him … in case you've lost track."

"So?"

"So, if he wanted to see me he would have called by now. Besides, I'm quite certain Quinten Cohen does not have to make a trip to Milwaukee to have his sexual needs met. I doubt he has to leave his house. They're probably lined up at his door."

Honestly, the thought made me sick to my stomach. However, a part of me—the pathetic part—was secretly excited about being closer to Quinn. Although it was ridiculous since I had no idea if he was even in New York and I highly doubted I would get up the nerve to call him.

"Addy, just promise me you'll enjoy yourself. Do some Christmas shopping, maybe even spoil yourself a little. Good food that you don't have to make, a spa day, maybe take in a Broadway show. Just make the most of your time there, okay?"

I pulled her in for a big hug. "I'll try."

NEW YORK DURING the holidays was picturesque. Mother Nature delivered a light blanket of snow, creating a winter wonderland. Exquisite holiday window displays adorned the stores along Fifth Avenue. Ice skaters glided along the skating rink at Rockefeller Center under the massive tree that glowed beneath the skyline. I decided to immerse myself in the city and take it all in.

After arriving Monday evening, I checked into my hotel and ordered in dinner while I planned out my week. I was scheduled to speak and do demonstrations at the culinary institute Tuesday and Thursday from one to four. Friday morning the students were to make their own plant-based creations, and I was asked to "judge" their work.

I purchased tickets to two Broadway shows that week, *The Book of Mormon* and *Houdini*. Broadway shows were not a cheap endeavor, but I had promised Mac that I'd "live it up" while in New York.

Tuesday morning I grabbed breakfast, which turned out to be easy since New York City is quite vegan-friendly. Shopping, my least favorite activity, was next on my list, since I had to find some dressier items for the shows because my wardrobe at home was inadequate for Broadway. Over three grand later, I had two new dresses and coordinating shoes but vowed to sell them on eBay when I arrived back home and donate the money to a worthy cause. The sales associates at the boutiques assured me I got a bargain compared to other Fifth Avenue stores. However, *bargain* would not have been my description. My wallet was kidnapped and beaten, but not raped—that was the more accurate description.

The culinary institute was more enjoyable than I had anticipated. The students were gracious and eager to learn, and the three hours there flew by.

When I arrived back at my hotel, I changed into a non-Broadway dress for dinner and headed out to a raw vegan restaurant the instructor at the culinary institute suggested. She said it was a bit pricey but the atmosphere was intimate and I might get a secluded table where I wouldn't feel self-conscious about eating alone. She also told me their wine list was incredible, but I had no intention of getting tipsy by myself in the middle of Manhattan.

Mac spent the previous two days texting me, demanding a play-by-play of everything I did. When I told her where I was headed for dinner she freaked out.

Mac: *OMG! That is a very exclusive restaurant. I'm so jealous.*

Do you have reservations?

Me: *No, didn't think it would be necessary on a Tuesday night.*

Mac: *Think again, sweetie. Just make sure you have a Ben Franklin on you.*

That might be your only ticket to getting a seat.

Me: *Mac, I am not paying more for my seat than I am for my dinner.*

Mac: *Live it up ... remember you promised, have fun!*

The phrase "Mac was right" came out of my mouth way too often, but once again, she was right. The maître d' had to hold back a smirk when I told her I didn't have a reservation. My ego flared up, but I reined it in and handed over the cash—*the bribe money.* Within minutes, I was seated at a small table in the corner.

The atmosphere was dark and intimate, with candles on every table. Soft jazz played in the background, warming my skin with a seductive allure. It was the kind of music that awakened nerve endings and fed passion. The menu didn't list prices and I had to repress the guilt as I ordered my five-course meal.

My waiter offered me a taste of their house wine, and I couldn't refuse having just one glass. After my soup was served, I made a trip to the ladies' room before the next course. On my way back to my table I walked past a row of half-circle, button-tufted booths and someone grabbed my wrist, halting my motion. The touch was electric, sending a jolting energy up my arm. I looked down at the hand wrapped around me—It stretched out from a white dress shirt and black suit coat. I moved my eyes up the arm to a sharp jawline covered in dark stubble, and then dark eyes met mine.

"Addy," his deep voice vibrated.

My eyes shifted to a long, straight-haired brunette with hazel eyes. Her silver, sleeveless dress with a square neck line and form-fitted bodice complemented her model-thin body that was tucked very close to Quinn. Her hand rested high on the inside of his leg.

"Quinn," my voice broke just above a whisper.

"What are you doing here?" he asked.

Dragging my eyes from her hand on his leg to meet his eyes, I offered a simple reply. "Eating." That time my voice held more confidence, maybe even a little chill.

His grip on my wrist tightened. "What are you doing *in New York?*" Each word was slow, controlled, and demanding.

I twisted my arm, forcing him to release me. Miss Hazel Eyes moved her hand to the top of Quinn's on the table, interlacing her fingers with his, as if it was important to let me know he belonged to her.

"I'm guest-lecturing at a culinary school for a few days."

"Did you come alone?"

I glanced again at their interlaced fingers on display, but Quinn made no attempt to move his. "Enjoy your dinner." I faked a smile and hurried back to my table, wishing the god of mercy would plant a handsome man in the seat opposite of mine so I wouldn't have to look like such a loner.

My waiter showed up with my main course as soon as I sat back down. When he left the table, I risked a glance up and to my horror, I had an unobstructed view of Quinn and his date.

His eyes locked on mine. I diverted my gaze to my plate as soon as his date leaned into him and slid her hand into his shirt where the top buttons were undone. Her pouty, red lips grazed his ear as she whispered something to him.

Fortunately for me, the portions were small, because I'd lost my appetite, except for the wine. One glass turned into three by the time dessert arrived: raw chocolate molten lava cake with chopped macadamia nuts. The wine relaxed me so I was able to enjoy my chocolate binge—until I glanced up again to see Quinn and his date eating the same dessert. He took a bite and she touched her finger to a drip of chocolate at the corner of his mouth. Then she slid her finger into her mouth while directing her gaze over to me.

Check please!

My tolerance level hit its limit. I threw a wad of cash on the table and wrapped my scarf around my neck before donning my long gray coat. Then I practically sprinted for the door.

The cool December air filled my lungs, but the wine kept my body warm and tingly. I eased my way to the curb; high heels and a dusting of snow on the sidewalk was not a good combination. Anxiety raced through my veins as I prayed a cabbie would have mercy on me soon. A black Bentley was parked a few yards farther down the street with a driver standing by it, but it wasn't Eddie.

Why would he be in New York anyway?

"Addy, wait," Quinn called.

Looking behind me I saw him signaling to the driver of the Bentley. He leaned down and whispered something in Miss Hazel Eye's ear. Then he lightly pecked her cheek with his lips before she was ushered in the back of the Bentley by the driver.

I turned back toward the street, stretching my arm out for a cab. Just as I contemplated unbuttoning my coat to entice one of the cabbies with my exposed legs, I felt Quinn's body right behind mine. The white condensation of his warm breath meeting the cold air seeped into my peripheral vision. Startling me, he snaked his hands under my arms at my waist pulling me back until I was pressed against his chest.

I shook my head. "Don't, please."

"I miss you."

"Looks like it." My words were sharp. I hated myself, not him. Me, it was all on me and I knew it.

Human emotions sucked.

Jealousy sucked.

The irrational female gene sucked.

He let out an exaggerated breath. "I don't know what you want me to do."

"Just go." I tried again to catch a passing cab.

"Let me take you. Where are you staying?"

What?!

I whipped around, breathing out of my nose like a bull.

"What a great idea! Precisely how will this work? Wait, let me guess. You'll sit in the middle with a beautiful woman on each side of you, which you *enjoy*. I'll occupy your mouth while she sucks you off, since I'm quite sure after her little display in the restaurant that's exactly what's on your mind!"

His look was pure rage, but I wasn't finished. Why couldn't I be finished? I wasn't a beautiful woman that night, but the ugly swallowed me whole from the inside out and I couldn't stop it. Why, why, why couldn't I just stop?

"But I'm guessing for you that scenario might be a complete waste of having two beautiful women at once. Maybe Hazel Eyes and I will undress each other and put on a little show for you, before you take your turn having each of us in whatever sick way you want."

"Enough!" Quinn growled so loudly my body jumped backward.

He grabbed my arm, pulling me toward him at the same moment a cab screeched to a halt, inches from hitting me.

"What the fuck, lady?" The cabbie yelled from his rolled-down window.

Jerking away from Quinn, I slid in the back of the cab, giving the driver a quick apology then spewing off the name of my hotel.

Quinn banged on my window. "Addy!"

The driver glanced at me through his rearview mirror.

"Just go," I insisted.

WHEN I REACHED my hotel room, I threw off my heels and unzipped my dress, letting it fall to the floor. I dug out an oversized, long-sleeved T-shirt and slipped it on. Numb was all I felt because Quinn and wine were a toxic mix. My body went into autopilot as I washed my face, then brushed and flossed my teeth before crawling into bed. It was only nine o'clock, but I needed the day to pass as quickly as possible. I allowed a single tear to roll down my cheek before my body gave in to sleep.

My head was very angry with me Wednesday morning. I showered, threw on a sweatshirt and yoga pants, then headed out in search of a juice bar for a good detoxing tonic. After flooding my body with coconut water and lots of fresh juice, I found a Bikram yoga class at a studio I'd spotted the day I arrived. By evening, the Addy who had spent three months in the land of the Dalai Lama was back. I had no intention of letting that out of control, completely irrational imposter personality emerge again.

Deep breath … I am peaceful, I am strong.

Houdini was a great show that night. I felt a little sexy in my new dress and heels, capturing the attention of more than a couple of men, some married and showing no shame with their wives on their arms. It helped boost my flagging confidence from not having a date to the show.

Thursday morning I checked out some museums before heading to the culinary institute. I was just as excited to see the students as they were to see me. Once again, the afternoon flew by and I decided to have a low-key evening. I grabbed some dinner at a nearby café before heading back to my hotel to get out of the cold. In the elevator on the way up to my room, my phone chimed with a text from Quinn.

Still in NYC?

I chose not to respond right away. Thinking was my new requirement before responding. What good could come from acknowledging him? None. I ignored his text. An hour later my phone rang. I didn't recognize the number; however, the area code was local to New York so I answered it, thinking it could be someone from the culinary institute.

"Hello?"

"Why are you ignoring my text?"

"I couldn't see the relevance in the question, so I didn't waste my time responding." There was silence on the line. I wasn't even sure he heard me or if we were even still connected.

"Where are you?" he asked.

"What does it matter?"

"Jesus, Addy, just answer me!" His voice strained with exasperation.

"I'm at my hotel. Yes, in New York City. Again, what's the relevance?"

"I have to see you." He sounded calmer, even hesitant, as if he didn't want those words to come out, but they did anyway.

"Look, I overreacted, it was my fault. I apologize and it won't happen again." Yes, I'd practiced that line over and over like a new mantra. "I'm busy tomorrow and I'm doing some Christmas shopping Saturday, then leaving Sunday. So if you have something to say, just say it."

"Have dinner with me tomorrow night."

"Can't, I have plans."

"Saturday, then."

I sighed, trying to stay calm since he simply wouldn't take no for an answer. "Brunch Saturday, nothing fancy. I'll call you that morning." I ended the call, not waiting for his response, or more likely, his rebuttal.

FRIDAY MORNING AT the culinary institute was the best part of the week. The students worked hard creating their own masterpieces. The instructors expected me to be more critical of the students, but in all honesty, they all did a great job. I made a few suggestions: some were a bit salty; others were overmixed in the food processor, not leaving enough texture; and a few lacked good visual presentation but still tasted amazing.

That afternoon I indulged in four hours at the spa. I even had one of the employees take a picture of me in the mud bath, and I sent it to Mac. She replied with a smiley face and a long line of exclamation points.

After the mud bath, hot stone massage, manicure, pedicure, and hair styling at the salon, I caught a cab back to my hotel and slipped into my second new dress and heels. It was a metallic holiday red with a trendy single long sleeve and asymmetrical neckline. The snug, layered, sheer fabric was covered with diamond shaped glitter patterns in a darker contrasting red. It hit above my knees as a form fitting mini dress. For some reason it felt shorter than I'd remembered at the store. I made a mental note to keep my legs closed tight while sitting.

My long hair was swept to the side with curls cascading down my sleeved shoulder, leaving my neck completely exposed on the sleeveless side. My black crisscross Stella McCartney platform shoes had five inch fabric covered heels, and when I stood in them even I had to admit they made my legs look amazing. They were what Mac called "fuck me heels," which made me wonder how many inappropriate "fuck me" looks I would get that night. At that point, I second-guessed my whole ensemble. In spite of my inadvisable relationship with Quinn, I wasn't a slut.

The Friday night show was sold out. The reason I got a ticket was because I required a single seat. To my surprise, the seat was in the front just to the right of the stage orchestra. To my right was an older gentleman and his wife and to my left were two college-age girls.

Assuming the ladies' room would be a nightmare during intermission, I planned ahead by tapering off all liquids at 2:00 p.m. Not the healthiest move, but a necessary evil if I didn't want to miss out on any of the performance. I did, however, take the opportunity to stretch my legs during intermission. The self-consciousness I had when I left the hotel quickly dissolved when I noticed a plethora of women in "fuck me heels" and dresses every bit as short as mine, if not shorter.

"Adler?" A familiar man's voice echoed behind me.

I turned to see the familiar face that matched the voice. "Brent! Oh my gosh, good to see you."

He wrapped his big arms around me, lifting me off the ground. I gasped as my dress started to ride up into indecent territory. As soon as he set me down I made a quick move to shove it back into place.

"You live in New York?" he asked, flashing me his perfect, straight white teeth.

"Nope, just visiting, how about you?"

"Yeah, I moved here two years ago after completing my PhD and receiving a job offer at Columbia."

"That's great. I always imagined you teaching."

Before we could say much more, the lights dimmed on and off signaling the end of intermission.

"How long are you in town?"

"She's leaving Sunday, but busy until then." At the same time I heard Quinn answering for me, I felt his hand rest on the small of my back in a very possessive gesture.

"Quinn?" I blurted out in shock. I looked up at him standing right next to me, but his eyes were rigidly fixed on Brent.

Oblivious to the tension between us, Brent offered his hand. "Hi, I'm Brent."

Quinn accepted his hand, giving him a *very* firm shake. "Quinten Cohen. How do you know Addy?"

"We went to college together," Brent responded, unaware that he was in the middle of an interrogation.

"I see and where was that?"

"University of Chicago." Brent looked confused. I'm sure

he wondered why some guy who seemed close to me didn't know something as basic as where I went to college. As I started to suggest we all take our seats, Brent decided to elaborate.

"Adler graduated top of the class, Summa Cum Laude. Which was no surprise, since she had her pick of colleges. She received acceptance letters from every college she applied, UCLA, Stanford, Dartmouth, Harvard—"

I jumped in to interrupt Brent before it got any worse. "I'm sure Quinn doesn't need to hear a complete list, not sure how you even knew—"

"Mackenzie, she told everyone." Brent winked at me.

Of course she did.

"Well, at any rate, I should get back to my seat. So nice to see you, Brent."

"You too, look me up when you're in New York next time."

"I'll do that." I smiled.

As I started to walk back to my seat, Quinn moved in front of me, forcing me to stop. "What?"

I looked up at him, but his dark, hooded eyes were all over my body, sending a heat rush straight to my sex. Before he could answer, Miss Hazel Eyes appeared. She took his arm and reached up to kiss the side of his mouth then looked at me with a catty smile. It was decidedly time to turn the table on Quinn, so I offered my hand to her.

"Hi, I'm Adler. I don't believe Quinn introduced us the other night."

She stared at my hand like I had cooties, then eventually gave it a weak shake with just her fingers. "Olivia."

Quinn's jaw worked over time, muscles twitching. It wasn't my fight. Quinn and Olivia were not my concern.

Smile and walk away.

Reason was my friend again—for about two seconds.

"So how do you know Quinn?" she asked with a fox's smile as she hugged him to her, hand splayed out over his chest.

Reason went out the window, splattered along the side of the road, leaving nothing but uncensored emotions. "I don't, per se. We just meet up when our schedules allow for a quick fuck. Enjoy the rest of the show."

I stepped to the side and walked past Quinn with a sway in my hips, fighting to hold back my huge grin. It was my own *Pretty Woman* moment. My ego gave me a high five but my conscience knew it was a childish move. However, at the time it felt like self-preservation.

Shortly after the second act started, my phone vibrated in my purse. I wasn't even supposed to have it turned on, but I risked a quick glance anyway.

Quinn: *Well played. FYI, I will be fucking you in nothing but those heels by end of the night.*

Ho-ly crap! I poked the bear.

Book smart. I was ridiculously book smart. My memory—flawless. Common sense? Zilch. It seemed to be a law of nature: Those gifted above-average intelligence had to give up common sense. I'd give up my perfect grades in exchange for the sense to not. Poke. The. Bear.

The show ended with the audience on their feet, in a standing ovation. I slipped into my coat and headed toward the door before the rest of the audience finished their applause. There was no time to look around for Quinn and Olivia. I had to vacate the premises before the predator caught up with its prey.

I hailed a cab and called out my hotel before I even had the door shut. The cabbie started to pull away from the curb then suddenly halted. A man walked to the driver's side. The cabbie rolled down his window and the man said something to him, but I didn't hear what it was. Then he handed the driver some money before the cabbie continued to pull out.

During the drive I checked messages on my phone, Mac of course wanted to hear everything about my spa day and the show. I sent her a quick, generic text.

Spa was fabulous, show was great!
Talk more Sunday ;)

I looked out the window and struggled to recognize any of my surroundings. "Where are we?"

The cabbie pulled to a stop in front of a multi-level Queen Anne-style townhouse. "Upper West Side."

"This isn't where I told you to take me."

"I have three hundred dollars cash that says it is."

And then there were the people who had no conscience—the ones who could be bought.

"Who lives here?"

"Beats me, but from the looks of things, someone pretty wealthy."

Logic would have told me Quinn, but the building I looked at said wealthy family, several kids, maybe a dog. It was definitely not a bachelor pad. My curiosity got the best of me, so I opened the door and eased out of the cab onto the curb. "Thank you."

"My pleasure, miss."

The cab disappeared into the exhaust-filled air of the cool winter night.

CREEPING UP THE stairs, I gripped the rail so my Stella McCartneys wouldn't send me to the ER with a sprained ankle or worse. My gloved finger pressed the doorbell. No answer. I proceeded to use the large metal knocker. No answer.

Crap!

Since someone went to so much work to ensure I got there, I decided to be bold and simply see if the door would open. *Bingo!* I peeked around the door. "Hello?"

Nothing.

I stepped inside gently shutting the door behind me. The lighting was dim, mostly incandescent picture lights and hanging track lights illuminating the various art pieces adorning the walls. Soft music played in the background. That was the lone sound I heard until I noticed a shadowy movement in the corner. At first all I saw was the outline of a dark figure, but I knew it was Quinn.

He stepped into the light. His white dress shirt was partially unbuttoned, and untucked from his black dress pants, tie loosened, and sleeves rolled up to his elbows, exposing the vein-laced muscles of his forearms.

Addy, ten years earlier in that situation, would have been shaking like a leaf and staring at the floor. It no longer took much effort to embrace the confident woman I'd become over the past few months. After setting my purse on the entry table, I untied my coat and eased it off my shoulders letting it fall to my feet.

Quinn's eyes were just as they were at the show, hooded and almost black. Keeping my eyes locked on his, I stepped a few feet closer, while inching the zipper of my dress down with one hand. His eyes followed my every move as I pulled my arm out of the sleeved side then used both hands to push my dress over my hips, letting it pool at my feet.

Quinn's mouth opened and he ran his tongue over his lower lip while his eyes perused my body. I tucked my thumbs under the waist band of my lace thong and pushed it down to meet my dress, before stepping out one foot at a time, and another step closer to Quinn. Finally, I removed my hairpins and combed my fingers through the messy waves.

My part was done. It might have been a threat or it might have been a promise, but it didn't matter. He had me just how he wanted me: standing before him in nothing but my fuck-me heels.

Common sense be dammed. I just wanted the man before me. I just wanted to *feel* because no man had ever made me feel so much. Olivia? Their relationship? Our sex-only relationship? I'd figure it all out later.

Bloodstream by Stateless flowed from the speakers. Quinn took one more step toward me as he unbuttoned his shirt, then tossed it on the floor. He removed a condom from his pocket and held the edge of the wrapper with his teeth as he removed his pants. After rolling on the condom, he went from slow and calculated to animalistic in a matter of moments.

He pushed me against the wall and smashed his lips to mine, as his tongue began its impetuous exploration. With his hands braced against the wall on either side of my head, he used only his torso and mouth to hold me in place. I gripped his firm biceps to steady myself, then fisted my hands in his hair when he grabbed my leg and hiked it up to his hip. His other hand aggressively kneaded my breast before navigating to my sex. Slipping two fingers between my slit, he barely grazed my clit before I felt his fingers glide into my wet channel. I moaned, closing my eyes.

Quinn pulled his fingers out and replaced them with his hard cock. He slammed into me, then stilled for a brief moment before he pulled back and repeated. His fingers dug into my leg, which he held firm to his hip. The calf of my standing leg burned as it supported my weight and absorbed the jarring impact every time he surged into me. His pace was fast and urgent; it felt like a race to the finish. Quinn took the checkered flag just seconds before I crossed the finish line.

Neither one of us had spoken a word since I arrived. All that came out of our mouths were labored pants and deep moans. Completely exhausted, I dropped my head and bit his shoulder as my body came down from its intense orgasm.

After a few moments of standing still, clenched to each other, he relaxed his hold on my leg and eased my foot to the ground. I ghosted my nails over his back while he brushed a soft kiss over my swollen lips. His forehead pressed to mine.

"Hi," he whispered, offering the first spoken word since I'd arrived.

"Hi," I breathed back.

I wanted to cry. I wanted to scream. He infiltrated my chest, gunning for my heart. How could I be so stupid to think it was just sex? I was the fool. He didn't play me. I played myself.

He lowered to his knees, sitting back on his heels, and unfastened my shoes one at a time, rubbing each foot after slipping them off.

"You're like my favorite dessert." I confessed.

He looked up at me, confused, while he worked his magic on my sore feet.

"I crave you constantly—borderline addiction—but I fear

the consequences of overindulging." I stuck with the food metaphor, it seemed safer than just handing him my heart.

Quinn stilled for a moment, still looking down at my feet. Nodding, he pushed his body off his heels, straight up on his knees. He wrapped his arms around me and rested the side of his face on my abdomen. I combed my fingers through his hair, momentarily caught up in the tender moment.

A few minutes later he stood and pulled his boxer briefs back on then slid his white dress shirt on me, buttoning just the bottom three buttons. He reached for my hand and guided me up the stairs to a bedroom. Tossing back the duvet, he lay on his back pulling me with him so I was sprawled across his torso. My ear was against his chest, and as I focused on his heartbeat, I let my mind drift back to a time where the sound of that rhythmic pulse haunted me. Quinn pressed his lips to the top of my head, bringing me back to the moment.

"Whose house is this?"

"Why do you ask?"

"Because I don't think it's yours."

He chuckled. "What makes you think it's not mine?"

"Everything. The location, the Queen Anne architectural design, the warm interior design, the wall art, I could go on forever. This is a family home. I expect a couple of kids to run and jump in bed with us at any moment."

He didn't respond.

"If you don't say something soon I'm getting the hell out of here before your *wife* shows up."

He wrapped his arms around me like I was his hostage. "It was built in the late eighteen hundreds, five floors, over 8,500 square feet of living space, six bedrooms, six baths, three half baths, elevator access, roof solarium and deck, natural hardwood floors with radiant heat, wine cellar, library, grand piano, chef's kitchen, exercise room, custom built-ins throughout, et cetera, et cetera."

I chuckled at his realtor spiel. "And your *wife?*"

He kissed the top of my head. "It's my parents' house … well, I guess my mother's now."

"You live with your mom?"

"No, I own a condo in Midtown." He traced random figure eights on my back.

"Where is your mom?"

"After my dad died she went back to Spain with my brother and the rest of her family for a while."

"Why are we *here?*"

The hand that traced my back paused for a moment then continued its doodling. "I have a friend staying at my place." His words were not spoken with confidence, but more like testing the water with them. I didn't push the subject anymore.

"I should not have said what I did to Olivia tonight. I was out of line."

"You were honest."

I laughed. "Yes, but that's not why I said it."

"Then why did you say it?"

Because it pissed me off to see her all over you and I wanted to put her in her place.

"I'm not sure."

"You're not sure or you don't want to tell me?"

Sighing, I whispered, "A messed-up mix of both." A big yawn escaped me while I waited for him to respond, but I wasn't sure if he did because I fell into a peaceful sleep.

CHAPTER TEN

"Fate controls who walks into your life, but you decide
who you let walk out, who you let stay, and who you
refuse to let go."

~Unknown

I WOKE THE next morning feeling as though I'd slept forever.
Quinn was no longer in bed, but I snuggled under the warm
covers that smelled of him. Rolling over, I hugged his pillow
and buried my nose in it.

"Lucky pillow."

I jumped. "Shit, you scared me!"

Quinn was showered and dressed in dark jeans and a black
button down shirt but it wasn't buttoned. My heart was still
racing from being startled and showed no signs of slowing
down with him dressed like that.

"I was thinking of stealing this pillow so I could wake up to
your intoxicating smell every morning."

He crawled up the bed like an animal on the prowl and
straddled me.

"Sounds fair, since I will not be washing this shirt anytime
soon." He tugged at his white shirt that I still wore.

Moving between my legs, he shrugged off his shirt and
unzipped his pants. I grinned. He smirked. It was just sex. I
needed to remember that because his rogue smile wasn't mine.

It was on loan. I was on loan. We were a moment. No regrets. No promises.

QUINN MADE BREAKFAST while I showered. When I got out there was some lingerie, jeans, a sweater, and a pair of boots set out on the bed. After drying my hair and dressing I made my way to the kitchen.

"Hey, beautiful." He smiled, sitting at the table reading the paper.

"Hey there, yourself." I took his paper and set it on the table, then straddled his lap. "Thanks for the clothes. They look brand new. You must have invisible elves working for you." I nuzzled his neck working my way to his earlobe.

"Mmm, something like that." He ran his hands up my back under my sweater. "Just for the record, the prAna jeans are organic cotton, as is the sweater, since I wasn't sure if you were a wool-wearing vegan. The boots are eco-friendly faux leather and some sort of non-wool."

Unexpected. That one word encompassed all of my emotions for Quinn. Leaning forward, I ran my tongue along his bottom lip before teasing it between my teeth.

"I stand corrected, Mr. Cohen. Your attention to detail may have just elevated your status from acquaintance to *friend*."

He moved his hands around to my stomach then slid them up to cup my breasts while slipping his thumbs inside my bra to rub my nipples. "Here's the thing, baby, you can talk the talk, but your body doesn't lie, and I can tell it has me elevated to a god status."

I shoved his hands out of my shirt. "Don't flatter yourself.

Which reminds me, do I want to know how you knew my bra size?"

He gripped the top of my legs and squeezed them. "Probably not. My elves also brought you breakfast in that bag."

"You said you were going to make breakfast."

"I didn't factor in the absence of my mother in the house also meant no food."

I pulled out a large lidded cup filled with green liquid and another smaller one with hot tea. I took a sip of the tea then put a straw in the lid of the green beverage and tasted it.

"Yum, resembles my Green Goddess smoothie. And Chai Tea?"

"Yes, made with coconut milk."

"Well done, Mr. Cohen. What did you have?"

He wrinkled his nose and brow. "You don't want to know."

"Out with it. What animals were sacrificed for your breakfast?" I narrowed my eyes.

"Two baby chickens. I had a veggie omelet, no cheese, but I'm thinking of going to confession later."

"You're Catholic?"

A slight laugh vibrated from his chest. "My mother's from Spain, so yes."

"When's the last time you went to church or confession for that matter?"

"Does this morning count? Because it felt like I was in heaven worshiping your beautiful body."

I shook my head. "Ah, you're smooth, real smooth."

I moved off his lap to grab my phone.

"Crap, it's almost noon. I have to get going. I have half the city to tackle today and I'm leaving tomorrow."

"Well, good luck. You should take a closer look outside."

I walked to the French doors that led out back and was shocked I hadn't noticed the massive amount of snow that had fallen overnight. "Well, your elves delivered my clothes and breakfast so they must be able to navigate the city well enough to get me back to my hotel. From there I can walk to the shops."

"True, however, more snow is expected tonight and flights out of all three major airports have been canceled for today, and I'm guessing tomorrow isn't going to be any better." He came up behind me, wrapped his arms around my waist, and bent down to kiss my neck. I leaned my head to the opposite side, giving him better access.

"You may be right. I'll just book my room for another night and settle in to wait out the snow storm."

He worked his way up my neck, sucking and nibbling on my earlobe.

"You think you're going to just hang out in your hotel room for the next two days by yourself?" One of his hands dropped to cup my crotch, rubbing the outside of my jeans while his other palmed my breast.

"Sure, I'll order up room service, get out my vibrator, and watch some good porn."

He flipped me around and pinned me to the glass doors with his body. "The hell you will. If you're into toys and porn I can help you with that." His voice was deep and rough.

The bulge in his pants strained against his jeans. I pushed him away and walked back to the table, leaving him to adjust himself. Sitting down to finish my smoothie and tea, I gave him a sideways glance.

My curiosity got the best of me. How would he go about

"helping" me with porn and toys? It was, once again, another reminder that I knew very little about Quinn. The only thing I knew about his past relationships was none of them lasted longer than six weeks. How could I not wonder just how many "relationships" he'd been in? Or, if he was simply a manwhore playboy bachelor.

He was rich, off the charts in the hot and sexy department, enjoyed traveling and extreme sports—all swoon worthy qualities—and that didn't include his god status in the bedroom. I fought to keep my brain from wandering, but I couldn't stop the questions from popping into my head.

Was he into kinky BDSM? How many women had he been with? What did Olivia mean to him? I'd seen them together twice in the same week. Were those her nail marks on his back months earlier? How old is he? Who's the friend staying at his place? How did he know The Sage *belonged to me?*

My head told me to keep a lid on it, but my mouth didn't cooperate. It never did. "How old are you?"

He sat down across from me. "Twenty-five."

My smoothie stopped midway down my throat and I started coughing.

"You're twenty-five?" I choked.

A lopsided grin formed on his lips. "No, I'm thirty-four, but your reaction was totally worth it."

I squinted my eyes at him, not amused by his sense of humor. "How did you know my age or my birth date for that matter?"

"Jake."

"When did you talk to Jake about me?"

"I stopped in one time when you were out."

When was that? "So you thought it was okay to question my

employee about me?"

"Yes."

"And you don't think that sounds a little stalkerish?"

"I call it research."

The response left me wondering if I should have felt flattered or violated. "Are you into BDSM?" I asked, keeping my eyes glued to my drink.

This time it was Quinn who choked on his coffee. "Jesus, Addy, where did that come from?"

"Your comment earlier implied you are knowledgeable about toys and porn so …" I bit my lips together, then opened with a pop.

He stared down into his coffee for a moment. "I don't know how to answer that, but I'm sure Miss Photographic Memory-Summa Cum Laude has her own intelligent opinion, so let's hear it."

I knew Brent's diarrhea of the mouth would get brought up again, and I sensed Quinn would go on his own fishing expedition in the Adler Sea of Secrets.

"BDSM is a catch-all phrase for many aspects of sexual orientation and role play. You've exhibited characteristics of it with me when you've carried your already-dominant personality over into the bedroom. You've used bondage with me and delayed sexual gratification to force me into submission, the *B & D*. It's the sadomasochism, *S & M*, I haven't seen … yet. I guess I need to know if what I've seen with you is everything, or are you just working me up to floggings, spanking and whipping, suspension, wax play, and golden showers? Do you get gratification from inflicting pain, degradation, or subjugation? Is it your *lifestyle?*"

He rubbed his face with his hands.

"You're the one who mentioned the toys and porn, and now I'm the one being interrogated about BDSM? Unbelievable." He tried to control his voice, but I sensed a hint of agitation.

"You asked me for my 'intelligent' opinion and I gave it to you, so unfortunately this can of worms has been opened and now I want an honest answer."

"Have I experimented with different facets of BDSM? Yes. Is it my lifestyle? No. Do I like the dominant role during sex? Yes. Do I need it? No. Do I get gratification from inflicting pain? No. Degradation? No. Subjugation? Sometimes. As for your list of means of inflicting pain, the answer is no. Now are we done talking about this?"

If this wasn't a lifestyle of his then why did he sound so annoyed by my questions? Why did I have to know?

"Yes." I was relieved when I looked at him and saw the corners of his mouth turned up. "What?"

"You're such a contradiction. You want to know everything, yet you share nothing."

I bit my thumbnail between my front teeth contemplating my next move, and I surprised myself with what came out of my mouth. "Fine, before you take me back to my hotel, you get to ask me one question, fair?"

He laughed. "Not hardly, but I'll take it."

He placed his elbows on the table and rested his chin on his steepled fingers. While he contemplated in silence, my nerves fired in anticipation to the point of fidgeting with my cup, the placemat, a loose string on my jeans—anything to hide my level of discomfort. Most likely, he would ask me about something in my past. I had mastered the art of vagueness, so I hoped I would easily come up with an honest answer that didn't expose too much.

"Will you stay the rest of the weekend with me?"

I looked at him, eyes wide, jaw slack. "Are you kidding me? I give you free rein to ask me anything and you choose to ask me to spend the rest of the weekend with you?"

"Yes."

"Why?"

"Why, what? Why do I want you to spend the rest of the weekend with me?"

"No, why did you choose that question?"

He stood and grabbed my hands, pulling me up to him. His arms were around my waist resting on my butt, my hands on his chest.

"Because it's the only question that matters to me right now."

There was that word in my head again. *Unexpected.* Lifting onto my toes, I pressed my lips to his, allowing myself to get lost in the moment.

Did he have any clue what he did to me?

The less he asked for, the more I wanted to give to him.

QUINN GOT HIS answer twice, once on the granite counter in the kitchen and once halfway up the stairs. We headed out in the snow in a black Range Rover. He looked like a kid on Christmas, four-wheeling his way around.

We went to my hotel first, to get my things and check out. He insisted on paying my bill so I indulged him. We still hadn't addressed my million-dollar sailboat, and I wondered if he thought I came into a bit of money at some point and blew it all on a yacht. For him, that would explain my "dinky loft and mismatched furniture" or my "ten-year-old car."

Maybe over the years women had come to expect him to foot the bill for everything and he assumed we were all alike. Regardless, I let him *take care* of me because it was a soothing stroke to his rich, dominant, male ego and money never mattered to me.

I promised Mac I'd do some holiday shopping, so after checking out of my hotel we made our way to the shopping districts. Quinn suggested Madison Avenue. I had no doubt that he was a regular at Barneys, but it wasn't where I wanted to shop. He assured me he would pay for everything. I let him foot the bill for my hotel, but he wasn't going to buy Christmas presents for my friends.

When he suggested Fifth Avenue & 57th Street, I assured him it was too early for us to browse Tiffany & Co. Luckily he caught my facetiousness, especially after my long speech on blood diamonds.

TMI? Probably.

Much to Quinn's displeasure, we ended up in Chinatown among what Quinn referred to as "junk." I promised him I'd find some "ethically-sourced" diamonds in the rough and I did. In an attempt to put a smile back on his face, I let him buy me a nice tea set and little Buddha statue. He did smile but it was accompanied with an exaggerated eye roll, so I don't think it was genuine.

"After I drink my tea I like to meditate. It opens all my senses and is a great segue to tantric sex."

His arm was around me while we walked, but he stopped to look at me. I stood on my tiptoes and brushed my lips against his, then nuzzled our cold noses together before giving him a suggestive raise of my eyebrows.

"In that case, best purchase we made all day." He grabbed my ass and squeezed it as he led us back to the vehicle.

"We should stop and get some groceries since the cupboards are bare," I suggested.

"We're not going back to my mom's. We're going to my place."

"Oh, did your friend leave?"

"Yes."

"When?"

"This morning."

I nodded and then bit my curious tongue, *hard.* The pit of my stomach knew who the *friend* had to be, even if my brain refused to acknowledge *her.*

THE SNOWSTORM WAS in full force on our way back to Quinn's. Travel was not recommended for the rest of the evening and into Sunday. We pulled into his secured underground parking garage and then took the elevator up. He set down my suitcase to fish his keys out of his pocket. Once we entered and the door closed, I stopped to take in the elaborate surroundings.

This place was Quinn. Double-height ceilings were supported on three sides by oversized floor-to-ceiling, glass-paneled windows which overlooked the city and were surrounded by a huge private terrace. The custom-designed staircase had marble treads and a glass railing. The kitchen was a mix of brushed and polished nickel cabinetry with white marble slab counters. A sea of wide, solid oak planks, custom-stained in ebony, sprawled out beneath our feet. The place screamed money and bachelor.

A noise came from upstairs. Quinn held his hand in front of me.

"Wait here." His voice depicted a sense of anger more than alarm.

"Is someone here?"

He didn't answer as he took the stairs two at a time. A few moments later I heard the shouting of a woman's voice, followed by the clicking of heels on a hard surface coming to a halt at the top of the stairs. *Olivia.*

Damn gut instinct!

As soon as she zeroed in on me she came down in a flash, Quinn hot on her heels. He carried what appeared to be an overnight bag and headed straight past her to the door, not chancing a glance at me. He opened the door and tossed the bag into the hall.

"Out, Olivia," he growled.

She glared at me. "I didn't know you were bringing your whores to your house, Quinn." Her eyes then fell to the shopping bags by my feet and she let out a spiteful laugh. "A bargain-basement whore at that, from the looks of it."

"Get the fuck out, now!" Quinn yelled.

She brushed past me smirking before she stopped and traced her finger down his chest.

"Call me when you're done with her."

He slammed the door on her. Standing frozen next to me and looking at the ground, his only movement was the twitching of his jaw muscles. I crossed my arms over my chest and walked to the window. The blizzard conditions made it impossible to see what I knew had to be a spectacular view of the city. Not that I cared, but I wondered how Olivia would get to wherever she needed to go since catching a cab was not an option.

Maybe she had a car in the parking garage. All I knew for sure was I wanted to be anywhere but there with Quinn. Even if I'd found a hotel, I had no way of getting there. It was just me and Quinn for the night, separated by an ocean of garbage between us. It was my fault. I chanted those words over and over. It didn't help. My feelings had their own thoughts that didn't ask for my brain's approval.

Quinn ascended the stairs. When I could no longer hear him I looked back at the door. All my bags were gone. A few minutes later the sound of his shoes hitting the marble stair treads signaled his return. The lighting allowed me to see his reflection in the window.

He walked straight to the kitchen and grabbed a glass-bottled water out of the refrigerator. After a long pull, he sat down in a gray leather chair with a nickel-plated steel frame.

"Olivia was your 'friend' staying here?"

There was a long pause.

"Yes."

I nodded. "Does she live here, in New York?"

"Yes."

"Does she stay here often?"

Fuck me. I was the masochist. We were supposed to be in the moment. No regrets. No expectations. Why couldn't my brain tell my feelings to mind their own business?

He set his water down on the end table then rested his elbows on his knees, running his hands through his hair. His shoulders sagged in defeat.

"Sometimes ... yes."

With every question I asked, it felt like I was running a blade deeper into my skin, or possibly my heart. Quinn may have been the knife, but I was the one holding it. I was the one asking the questions. He didn't want to hurt me. I was hurting myself. I self-destructed right in front of him and there was nothing he could do about it.

"Did she stay here the night I saw you at the restaurant?"

"Yes." It was a whisper, but I still heard him.

As I looked at his reflection in the window, I saw him look up and meet mine. I knew he saw the few errant tears that fought their way, streaking down my cheeks.

"What is she to you?" I asked, swallowing the lump in my throat.

He remained silent for a few long seconds. "A distraction."

"A distraction from what?"

"You."

His last word pushed the knife the rest of the way in, leaving me there to bleed out. I turned and walked to the stairs, pausing at the bottom when I heard his voice.

"Your bags are in the guest room, up the stairs to the right," He sounded as defeated as he looked.

Without acknowledging him, I continued up the stairs. As soon as I shut the door to the bedroom I heard a loud roar, "FUCK!" followed by the shattering of glass.

Leaning against the door, I slid myself down to the floor before shattering into pieces as well.

"ADDY, WHERE ARE you going? Jesus, this has got to stop! I told you I'd take care of everything and I did. You've got to get it together and move forward, not run away. This is bullshit. There's no way I'm letting you leave me. Addy!"

AT A TIME unbeknownst to me, the mercy of sleep wrapped its arms around me. I woke up in a fetal position on the floor next to the door around four in the morning. My eyes were swollen and my head throbbed. Every muscle in my body was achingly stiff from lying on the floor. I crawled to the bathroom.

After turning on the shower, I stripped out of my clothes as steam started to cloud the room. I eased into the shower and let the water cascade down my body. It felt so good. Despite the surreal memories of the past twenty-four hours bouncing around in my head, my thoughts drifted to Quinn and his whereabouts. It pained me to think that he'd left and was somewhere else *with* someone else. Maybe a woman who could give herself to him in a way I couldn't. Quinn probably blamed himself, but I didn't. I couldn't. I'd offered him my body and nothing more. It wasn't fair to ask for everything and give nothing in return.

Did he want more? Did I?

After a long shower, I put on a pair of yoga pants and an oversized sweatshirt that hung off one shoulder. I tiptoed downstairs. The clock in the kitchen read 5:15 a.m. It was still dark outside but I could see the snow blowing in the glow of the city lights. The large windows gave the illusion I was in a snow globe. I flipped a switch that turned on a floor lamp, illuminating a trail of shattered glass.

Opening doors around the kitchen, I searched for a broom and dust pan, eventually finding them hanging from the wall. I slipped on my boots that were by the door to protect my feet, and started sweeping up the shards of glass.

"Leave it." I flinched at Quinn's deep, raspy voice. A deep breath later, I continued to sweep.

"I. Said. Leave. It." What sounded and felt like anger

caused the few unshed tears I had left to surface.

I dropped the broom and dust pan, hugging my knees to my chest, I fought to keep from sobbing. I didn't want him to see how broken I was.

Please go back upstairs. Just turn around and leave me with the shattered glass. Please, I just don't want you to see me, not like this ...

A sob escaped at the same time two strong arms lifted me. He cradled me to his bare chest and kissed the top of my head, breathing me in. Then he carried me up the stairs to the guest room, set me down on the bed, pulled off my boots, and crawled in behind me. As he pulled the covers over us and held my shaking body to his, I sobbed without reprieve. At some point my body stilled and I surrendered to sleep, wrapped in Quinn.

Several hours later I opened my eyes. Neither one of us had moved. The warmth of Quinn's breath caressed my back, but I wasn't sure if he was awake.

"My parents gave me *The Sage* for my twenty-third birthday. I was advanced in school and I'd just started working toward my PhD in Ecology and Evolution. Their dreams for me were so big. It crushed them when I graduated from high school and declared I wasn't going to college. I had my own dreams and they didn't require a college degree.

After listening to everyone I knew give me the speech on wasted potential and my parents basically threatening to disown me if I didn't go to college, we came to a compromise. If I got my degree, I could do anything I wanted and they would support me. A stipulation being it had to be a PhD. So I filled out every college application they set in front of me. I had a 4.0 GPA, near perfect college entrance exam scores, a long list of community service activities, and glowing recommendations from my supervisors at various summer internships I had during high school.

The cherry on top was my affluent family. I received acceptance letters from every college to which I applied. Numerous scholarship offers added to my 'wasted potential' guilt trip. Anyway, when they gifted the sailboat ... or yacht to me, they made me promise to never sell it, so I haven't."

Quinn didn't move the whole time I talked and continued to remain motionless and silent. I thought maybe he was asleep and hadn't heard a word I said. I was fine with that too. Just saying it out loud helped lighten the emotional load I'd been carrying for so many years, but then he tightened his arms around me.

"Thank you," he breathed in my ear then kissed my shoulder.

I rolled toward him so we were face to face. The look in his eyes comforted me. Searching for "our" connection, I rested my forehead on his and closed my eyes. "I can't do this with you anymore. I thought I could, but I can't."

"I know." His voice was barely a whisper.

"Seeing you with Olivia ... it broke me. My fault. Not yours. I asked for nothing. I gave nothing. It wasn't fair to expect anything. But still ..."

He nodded against my head. "I wasn't with her to hurt you."

One rebel tear escaped. "I know." That was the hardest part. I *knew* he wasn't trying to hurt me.

He kissed away my tear. God, I loved that about him. It was such a tender, intimate gesture.

He released me enough to meet my eyes. "I want you. I

want to *be* with you in a way I've never wanted to be with anyone. But ... when I look into your beautiful blue eyes I see a sadness that is so vulnerable, so fragile. I don't know what haunts you, but I want you to know it doesn't change me wanting to be with you."

Desperate to lift the mood, I smiled. "See, I knew you were an *okay* guy."

When he laughed, my heart skipped a beat, seeing the carefree smile that I felt he reserved just for me.

"Baby, I don't know what I'm going to have to do to get upgraded from your stringent *okay* status, but I'm very willing to give it my all."

I kissed his neck and ran my hands over his firm chest and down each sculpted bump of his abs.

"It's going to take time." I moved up his neck to suck in his soft, smooth earlobe. "Maybe over time you'll grow out of this homely-looking phase you're obviously going through."

He bear-hugged me to his chest and kissed the top of my head. "Maybe, but don't count on it."

CHAPTER ELEVEN

"Sex is always about emotions. Good sex is about free
emotions; bad sex is about blocked emotions."

~Deepak Chopra

AFTER AN INTENSE morning of make-up sex, we both were
in desperate need of food. I made myself right at home in
Quinn's kitchen, finding everything necessary for banana oat
pancakes. It seemed unlikely that he did his own grocery
shopping and made a mental note to ask him about that.

He said he was going to run upstairs and stick in a load of
laundry, something else I doubted he did regularly. Opting not
to spoil the mood, I didn't question him; however, my
suspicions were that he wanted to change the sheets on his bed
since his "friend" had been staying there. That must have been
why he carried me back up to the guest room instead of his
own, early that morning. Refusing to dwell on that thought, I
focused on the fact that I was the one with him in that
moment.

But who will be with him when I leave?

"Hey, beautiful." Quinn grabbed some juice out of the
refrigerator.

"Nope, put it back, buddy. I already have juice for us." I
pointed to the table.

He sauntered over, lifted the glass, and examined it. "Did

you squeeze this?"

"Of course. Who would drink that pasteurized crap when you have a refrigerator drawer full of oranges?"

He shrugged his shoulders. "Didn't know I did."

"Yeah, about that, who does your grocery shopping?"

"Why? Are you missing something?"

I flipped the pancakes and gave them a gentle pat with the spatula. "No, quite the contrary. It's as if you knew I would be here and had your kitchen stocked just for me."

I gave him a sideways glance, trying to gauge his reaction. He didn't look my way, swirling the last little bit of juice in his glass. "Hmm, what a happy coincidence."

"Happy, my ass. Someday I'm going to catch your elves doing your laundry list of crap you refuse to do yourself."

He put his hand over his chest, jaw unhinged. "I'm hurt you'd think so little of me. I'll have you know, I am very resourceful and skilled at multitasking."

"More like, you're rich and have mastered the art of delegating." As I set his plate down in front of him, I placed a chaste kiss on his cheek.

"Touché, baby, touché."

"I checked my flight for today and it doesn't look like anything is departing or arriving until this evening at the earliest."

He finished a bite but left his fork in his mouth, biting just the end of it as he flashed his sexy eyes my way. I knew where his mind was.

"I'm sure we can find *something* to keep ourselves occupied while we're snowed in."

I crossed my legs under the table to ease the tension building from just his look. "Actually, I was thinking we should play in the snow today."

His sexy look morphed into a raised-brow curiosity. "You want to play in the snow?"

I licked a drip of syrup off my lower lip. "Yep, maybe ice-skating, cross country skiing, sledding ... something like that."

Quinn's whole face lit up. "Get dressed, baby. I'm taking you to play in the snow."

TRAVEL WASN'T RECOMMENDED so I suggested something within walking distance. There were people who took heed to such recommendations, such as myself, and then there were those who didn't, such as Quinn. He didn't think recommendations—suggestions—or any rules in general applied to him, so we spent half the day driving in the winter terrain before arriving at the ski resort.

He was in his element, and his enthusiasm was contagious. I knew how to ski but had never attempted snowboarding. In no time at all, I was decked out in the latest and most expensive snow gear the Pro Shop had to offer. Quinn changed into his gear and looked ready for the Olympics. He also looked smokin' hot. I started to question my decision to not stay in bed with him all day. He easily read my mind.

"Don't give me that look now that you have me all excited about hitting the slopes."

"What look?" I grabbed his hair and pulled his face to mine, brushing my lips over his before easing my tongue into his mouth.

He hummed a deep groan as I pulled away, then discretely tried to adjust himself while shooting me a dirty look. "You're going to pay for that later."

I batted my eyelashes at him, flashing a wry smile. "God, I

hope so."

He swatted my ass. "Get in the snow."

We spent what was left of the afternoon and the better part of the evening snowboarding. I surprised myself at just how easily I picked it up. Quinn was amazing, that being an understatement. After getting my fill of the slopes, I enjoyed planting my butt in the snow and watching him fly off the ramps, boxes, and rails. He gave me a taste of the extreme sports he enjoyed and I enjoyed every minute. His carefree, adventurous, no-limits personality was as sexy as the body in which it resided.

He finished his last run, stopping on a dime just inches from me.

"Hey, beautiful, you cold?"

I bit my lower lip and slowly shook my head. I wanted him so badly, he could have taken me right there in the snow.

"Are you hungry?"

My head continued to move side to side.

He grabbed my gloved hand and pulled me to my feet. Our faces were inches apart, separated by a small cloud of warm condensation. "Do you want me to get a room?"

I nodded.

He grinned.

Twenty minutes later, that felt like hours, we stumbled into our room. Our frantic bodies created a tornado of snow gear and clothes being ripped off, tossed aside, and thrown around the room. He pulled his thermal shirt off exposing his glistening, sweaty torso.

"I'm a sweaty mess. We should shower," he said breathing hard.

"Nuh-uh," I groaned, removing what was left of my own

clothes, then making haste with his pants.

I pushed him onto the bed, losing what little control I had left. Never in my life had I wanted anyone so much. He felt it too, but even his eagerness fell a step short of mine. I crawled up his sweaty body and ravaged his mouth with mine, pushing myself onto his waiting erection.

His whole body tensed. "Ah, fuck, that's so good, but…" he closed his eyes "…I'm not wearing a condom Add—"

"Shh …" I breathed out as I rode him. "I want you *so* much." My voice strained, almost painfully.

He leaned up on one elbow, flexing his washboard abs, and took one of my breasts in his mouth.

"Ah!" I arched into him, grinding my hips harder.

Our bodies were covered in sweat as they slid against each other. He released my breast and hissed as I slammed down onto him. He eased his hand between us and massaged my clit, releasing my orgasm. My movements slowed, milking every last sensation. Still breathless, he flipped me on my back and plunged into me several more times.

"Fuuuck!" he growled. As I clenched my muscles around him, I felt his warm release fill me.

He rolled to his back searching for his breath. "What the hell got into you?"

I laughed. "You."

"Jeez, that was … I mean, I thought *I* was the adrenaline junkie."

"I guess having my way with your *homely* body has become my extreme sport. You are very, very bad for me, Mr. Cohen," I gasped for breath, outlining the muscles on his chest with my fingernail.

"Speaking of … are we going to discuss the no condom

part of the evening?"

I traced my fingers lower, circling his belly button. "That's simple. I'll be starting my cycle in about two days so the chances of me getting pregnant are about nil. However, if you're carrying around some STD that I end up with, I promise you I will go batshit and cut your balls off, then feed them to you in your sleep."

He turned toward me, covering his man parts with the sheet as if attempting to protect them. "I'm clean."

"Good to know."

"Have you been tested?" he asked, raising an eyebrow at me.

"No."

"You've never been tested?" Shock filled his voice.

I shook my head.

"You know that condoms aren't one hundred percent. I can't believe you're so cavalier with your sex life."

"For the record, you're the only *cavalier* part of my sex life..." my voice turned to a mumble "...or sex history for that matter."

"What did you say?"

I raised my voice a notch. "I said you're the only cavalier part of my sex life."

"No, not that, the last part that you mumbled under your breath." He raised his body up on his elbow, looking down at me.

Dodging anymore questions, I sat up and headed to the bathroom. "Never mind. It doesn't matter. You don't have to worry about me passing anything to you, that's all."

After hurrying into the shower, I took a moment to gather my composure and thoughts. What *had* gotten into me? I wasn't worried about getting pregnant and the naive part of me *did* trust that Quinn was clean, but it still was not an excuse to be so reckless. My hunger for him was insatiable; my greed clouded my judgment, which made it easy to find an excuse not to use protection. *Stupid. Stupid. Stupid.*

The door opened to the bathroom and Quinn stepped into the shower with me. Not saying a word, he grabbed the soap and went to work lathering my body, caressing and massaging every inch of me. He took the handheld shower head and rinsed me off, pausing briefly as he aimed it between my legs. The sensation made my body jerk. He moved it away, flashing me his wicked smile. Shaking my head at his mischievousness, I reached for the soap and worked the suds over his body.

No matter how many times I saw him naked, I remained in awe of his body and its flawless beauty. "You're perfect." It was just a thought, but it slipped out of my mouth as I stood behind him washing his back.

He turned around, capturing my gaze. "I'm not." Cupping my face, he inched lower, ever so slowly, until his mouth covered mine. I wrapped my arms around his neck as he lifted me up. His naked erection filled me again as our bodies melded. He released my mouth and moved his lips to my ear.

"This, my beautiful, this … is perfect."

MOTHER NATURE LEFT a thick layer of snow over New York City, but I was able to get a flight booked for Monday afternoon. We left the ski resort Monday morning making it back to Quinn's by noon. He had a business meeting scheduled for that afternoon, but considered rescheduling it until I insisted he go; it would have only given us an extra hour together before I had to leave for the airport.

I agreed to come back to New York between Christmas and New Year's. He and his sister were leaving for Spain the week before Christmas to be with his brother and mother then they planned on returning the day after.

On the way to the airport, in the back of Quinn's Bentley, I received a text from him.

Quinn: *Can't concentrate, thinking of you in some naughty Santa lingerie.*
It's going to be a long two weeks.

In any other life I would have thought meeting Quinn was the equivalent of winning the dating lottery. In this life, it felt like a cruel joke. It seemed like the chances of us working through all our baggage and finding some semblance of happiness were virtually impossible. Cutting my losses early and just getting out would have been the smart thing to do, but I couldn't. He had become my addiction.

Me: *Not sure I own anything to that effect.*

Quinn: *Elves, babe, my wish is their command.*

Me: *Kinky, spoiled, little rich boy. ;)*

Quinn: *Little boy? Was that a little boy who fucked you at the front door before going to work this afternoon?*

Our "never goodbye" kiss earlier took a small detour. Quinn wore a gray three-piece suit, white shirt, and dark purple striped tie. He had a day's worth of dark stubble on his beautiful face. My outfit was less formal: a fitted, charcoal, recycled wool dress that fell above my knees with three quarter length sleeves. What sent Quinn over the edge were my soft pink, lace cable-knit boot socks peeking out above my black knee-high boots. I had expected the tease to be my hair, divided into my signature pigtails.

When I walked down the stairs he was donning his wool overcoat but slipped it back off the moment he caught sight of me. Spewing a string of dirty expletives about my "naughty little schoolgirl look," he had his pants dropped to his feet, my panties ripped off, and me pinned against the front door in no time flat. He took me quick and hard, with my dress pulled up to my waist, my legs wrapped around his, and boot heels digging into his butt. I was quite certain he would have a reminder of me on his ass for a few days.

> **Me:** *Ah, I stand corrected.*
> *It was definitely all man who violated that innocent little schoolgirl.*
>
> **Quinn:** *She deserved it, fucking tease.*
>
> **Me:** *Have your mom clean up that potty mouth of yours while you're gone. ;)*
> *Gotta go, I'm at the airport. Bye!*
>
> **Quinn:** *Safe trip, beautiful ... but never goodbye.*

CHAPTER TWELVE

"The worst kind of pain is when you're smiling just to
stop the tears from falling."

~Unknown

M AC PICKED ME up from the airport and grilled me for
every detail before I even retrieved my luggage. I put
her off, not wanting to start with all the details until I was
home.

As soon as I walked in the door, my phone chimed with a
text from Quinn.

Quinn: *Home safe?*

Me: *Yes, thanks!*

Quinn: *You should send me a picture of yourself.*

It hit me at that moment that we never had taken photos of
each other together or separate. It warmed me to think that
maybe he wanted a picture of me to show his family when he
went to visit. I decided the best picture I had of myself was the
one from my website, so I copied it to a text and sent it.

"Are you sexting Hot Pants already?" Mac asked while she
threw off her boots and coat, getting comfy for all the details of
my trip.

"No, he just wanted me to send him a picture of myself, so

I sent him the one from the café's website."

She laughed.

"What? You don't think that's a good one?"

"No, Addy, it's great. I just doubt that's the kind of picture he was thinking about." She suggestively raised her eyebrows.

"Shut up! That's not what he meant, leave it to your filthy mind to go there."

Before I finished, my phone chimed again.

Quinn: *Cute, babe, but that's not quite what I had in mind.*

My jaw dropped.

"What'd he say?"

"Uh, nothing really."

"Bullshit, let me see." She lunged toward me as I tried to hide my phone in my pocket.

"It's nothing, stop!" I squealed as she pinned me against my kitchen counter.

"If it's nothing then let me see." She peeled my fingers off it and yanked it out of my pocket, quickly turning her back to me so she could read it before I took it back. "Ha! Told you! He wants a nudie, Addy. God, I love how innocent you are." She cackled.

Mac tossed my phone at me. I caught it and sent back a quick text. "Yeah, well it's not happening."

Me: *You first!*

After pressing send, I shut off my phone before he could respond, fearing he might in fact do it and that would *not* be shared with Mac.

"I could take the picture for you before I leave. Wouldn't

want the poor guy jerking off to an empty pillow."

"Nice, Mac. Forgot to put in your filter today, I see."

"I have a hard time believing any woman who's been with *that* man could possibly be offended by my mouth. Tell me about your trip, skipping all the yada yada about the culinary institute. Get straight to the good stuff."

"Fair point." I blushed just thinking of my intimate and erotic moments with Quinn.

I spent the next hour filling Mac in on most of the details, skipping the R—or maybe X—rated specifics. It was almost midnight before she left, and I was exhausted from my day of travel, not to mention the hour time difference. I threw on an old T-shirt, washed my face, and brushed and flossed my teeth before collapsing into bed.

MY ALARM BROUGHT the morning too quickly. I was surprised how much I missed waking with the comfort that came from being wrapped in Quinn. It would be two weeks before I would see him again, so I made the most of my time at home and jumped right back into my routine.

I put in a full hour of yoga, but skipped the run, since Milwaukee was also covered in snow and the icy paths could be pretty treacherous. After my shower I went down to the café for the world's best smoothie and wheatgrass shot. As I cleaned up, Jake arrived for work.

"Morning, Addy!" He gave me a big hug.

"Hey, Jake, how'd everything go while I was gone?"

"If I say great you'll think you're not needed, if I say terrible you'll feel guilty and never leave again, so what do you want to hear?"

I smiled and kissed him on the cheek before heading back to the kitchen. "Hmm, maybe you should tell me things went okay, but you sure are glad to have me back because it eases the pressure of you having to take the credit for all my fabulous culinary creations."

He started washing kale and lettuce. "I wish. Unfortunately the popular response was 'tell Addy everything is amazing as usual.'"

"You could have changed up the menu and added some of your own recipes. I wouldn't mind; I trust you."

"Really?" His eyes widened.

My time at the culinary institute reminded me just how great aspiring chefs can be if given the right guidance and opportunity. I wanted the same for Jake. He was very talented and no longer required much guidance. It was the opportunity he was waiting for and it was time I gave it to him.

"Absolutely. In fact, I'll be gone again around Christmas and you can have free rein over the menu.

He narrowed his eyes for a brief moment, as if it was a joke. Then he grinned as he turned back around and continued prepping.

I needed to text Mac and have her stop to pick up some more limes and that's when I remembered I'd left my phone upstairs. Finding it on my kitchen counter, I turned it on. An alert buzzed for two missed calls and three texts. One call was from Mac with a message saying she would stop and pick up limes on her way in. *Great minds think alike.* The other call was from Quinn and his message was a hostile one, demanding I respond to his texts or calls. *Bossy much?.* I immediately checked my texts.

Quinn: *For your ogling pleasure.*

Attached was a photo of Quinn, but something was off about it. He looked younger, not that he showed any signs of aging. It was more about his build. He stood in a pair of white briefs with a black waist band, his back to the camera, his head was turned looking over his left shoulder with a "sexy and I know it" look. His left hand was pushing the back of his briefs down just halfway over his left buttock, exposing part of his tight, tan ass. He was fit and trim in the photo, but having recently inspected every inch of his beautiful body, I knew his muscles were a bit larger and even more defined than they were in the picture. The photo also looked professionally taken. I moved on to his next text.

> **Quinn:** *Waiting? I'm wearing my shirt that smells like you and sex. Where's my photo?*

> **Quinn:** *A little pissed you haven't responded. Guess I'll have to resort to other means.*

All three texts were sent within a two hour time frame from the previous night. What the hell was *other means* supposed to mean? *Olivia?*

> **Me:** *Shut my phone off to talk to Mac and forgot to turn it back on. What other means?*

I waited a few minutes but no response, so I went back downstairs and started filling lunch orders with Jake and the girls. About ten minutes later my phone chimed.

> **Quinn:** *No time. In a meeting.*

I immersed myself in work to keep my mind off the short, cold-sounding message from Quinn. It was hard not to read into it, but I tried to avoid overthinking it. By the end of the day I was in better spirits, not because I'd heard back from Quinn, but simply because I loved being back at my café, working with fun, like-minded people, and serving such grateful customers.

Later that evening around seven, I returned to my loft, ready to chill out on my couch with a good book. Around eight o'clock, my phone rang.

"Hello?"

"Hey, baby, good to hear your voice." Quinn sounded tired.

"Yours too. Bad day?"

"Just long. I spent most of the day dealing with unfinished business my father left behind."

"Wanna talk about it?"

"Not so much. I'm wishing you were here to take my mind off everything."

"Two weeks."

"Two weeks too long."

"Well one week before you leave for Spain and there's nothing like family to provide a good distraction."

"Not in my case. It will simply be more talk about everything that went on today."

I sensed it was time to lighten the mood and change the subject. "Nice picture by the way, but it's not recent. When, where, and why was it taken?"

The tone of his vice immediately lightened. "Ah, very observant of you. It was taken about ten years ago. I did some part-time modeling in college."

Of course he did.

"And what precisely were you modeling in that picture?"

"Cologne."

"Cologne? Are you joking? Where exactly was the bottle?"

He chuckled. "The picture I sent you was from the photo shoot, not the actual ad."

"The message being what? If your man wears this brand of cologne, he will turn into a Latin sex god with a perfect ass?"

"Worked for you."

"How do you know? You've never seen my man."

"Watch it or I'm going to violate your smart mouth in more ways than one." His voice carried an edge to it.

What the...? Hello, dominant Quinn.

"Well, I'd love to chat all night but I have a pulsating shower head and a new romance novel calling my name."

He sucked in a sharp breath. "If that's how we're playing it, then you'd better be ready for a four poster bed and handcuffs in two weeks."

"We'll just see about that. Goodnight, sex god."

"Goodnight, beautiful."

I filled my soaker tub with hot water; it was one of my less than eco-friendly indulgences. I lit several candles and shut off the lights. While adding some lavender soap to create bubbles, an idea came to me. Throwing my robe on, I grabbed my camera. After several minutes of adjusting its placement on my vanity and testing the timer, I pulled my hair up into a loose pile on my head, leaving some wispy strands hanging down, giving me a sexy look. Then I dug out my make-up, that hardly ever got used, and smoked out my eyes, adding a little mascara and lip gloss.

Setting the camera remote on the table by the tub, I eased into the bubbly water. I bent one leg so part of it was exposed and draped the other over the side of the tub. I arched my back which brought just the top swell of my breasts out of the water, the small bubbles exposing a hint of my nipples below the surface.

Fifteen or more shots later, I prayed there was at least one good shot with a sexy look on my face instead of the giddy little grin I had trouble hiding. After forty-five minutes of soaking and reading, I removed my make-up and climbed out of the tub. I slipped on my lace boyshorts and pulled an old T-shirt over my head. Sitting down at my desk, I looked through the pictures and found the perfect one. As soon as I download-ed it to my phone, I sent it off to Quinn in a text.

Me: *Wishing you were here to scrub my back.*

I expected an instant response but it was a good ten or so minutes before my phone chimed.

Quinn: *Fuck. Me.*

Me: *You like?*

Quinn: *No words, baby ... no words.*

Me: *What took you so long to respond?*

Quinn: *Too difficult to text one-handed.*

Me: *Huh? ... Ooo, you didn't?*

Quinn: *Sure as hell did, twice, hence the ten minutes.*

Me: *Now I have no words. Goodnight.*

Quinn: *Very, very good!*

THE REST OF my week fell into the comfortable routine category. The café was slower on the colder days when snow was in the air. We took advantage of our down time and messed around in the kitchen creating new menu items. We had an informal staff meeting to discuss work scheduling during the time I was to be in New York between Christmas and New Year's.

It was bittersweet to realize my café ran just fine without me. Mac was still involved with the business part, but I suspected that would change whenever she and Evan decided to start a family. Jake, on the other hand, made the bulk of his living underground fighting, but his passion was my café. He had become my apprentice of sorts, but whether or not he chose to believe it, my guidance was no longer necessary.

Mac and Evan talked about moving back to Chicago someday if a spot at Richard's firm ever became available to Evan. They wanted me to move back too, when or if that day ever came. Closing the café wasn't an option for me. First, we had too many loyal customers, and second, the café stood for a change in the way we needed to think about our health and the environment. However, over the past year, Jake's interest in everything about the business gave me hope that if I moved, the café would survive in very capable hands.

Quinn texted me every day, mostly in the evenings when we both were done with work. It usually started out with small talk that evolved into some very inappropriate sexting. I was desperate to see him. It was one week away, but when Quinn left for Spain the week before Christmas I missed him even more. It was silly. It shouldn't have mattered if I was not seeing him in New York or not seeing him in Spain, but for some reason it did.

At the café we spent the week before Christmas filling special holiday orders: pies, pastries, and appetizers. I planned on spending Christmas with Mac, Evan, Richard, and Gwen, but in a sudden, last-minute change of plans, Mac and Evan went to see his parents on Christmas instead. They insisted I go with them, while Richard and Gwen insisted I keep my plans with them. It wasn't going to be an easy decision, so I decided to decline both offers.

Quinn had given me a key to his condo and the security information to get in, in case I arrived before him on the 26th, so I decided to leave a day early for New York and spend Christmas at his place. I knew I would be alone, but a quiet, uninterrupted day to myself was a good thing. Mac and her parents weren't too pleased about me skipping out on Christmas in Chicago, but they didn't have a choice. I had already purchased my plane ticket before I told them so it was presented as a done deal.

It was frigid when I arrived in New York City on Christmas, and there was still a thick layer of glistening snow on the ground. The sun beamed in the clear sky, making sunglasses mandatory to see anything against the piercing reflection off the snow. Traffic was light, so it didn't take much time at all to get to Quinn's. I didn't mention my early arrival since he wasn't going to be home anyway, and I knew it would make for a better surprise when he did show up the next day. My plan was to have his whole condo filled with the smell of sweet holiday treats that I would bake early in the morning.

When I arrived I didn't have any trouble with the code to the elevator, but I had to dig through my bag to find the key he gave me. As I started to push the door open, I expected to hear the beeping sound of his security alarm, but I didn't. Everything from that moment on played out in horrific slow motion.

NUMEROUS PAIRS OF shoes on the floor lined the entry, and the coat tree was covered in winter wear. I heard voices.

Leaving my suitcase in the hall, I stepped in and the door shut behind me. The room became silent. A group of people were seated at Quinn's dining room table, having Christmas dinner. I recognized Quinn's sister and her two kids from the yacht. There was a man who shared Quinn's features that I assumed was his brother, and another man with medium-length blond hair that hung close to his blue eyes, maybe his brother-in-law. Quinn sat at the end of the table opposite his brother. An older woman with chin-length black hair sat to his right and *Olivia* sat in the chair to his left.

"Addy," Quinn spoke, shoving back in his chair to stand. I could never have imagined Quinn looking pale, with his dark complexion, but the face that stared at me was drained of all color.

Olivia's face morphed into an ugly bitch smirk, but the rest of his family, with the exception of the two young children, pinballed their eyes back and forth between me and Quinn in complete confusion.

Quinn wasted no time making his way to me. He tried to grab my arm, but I jerked away.

"Don't. You. Dare. Touch. Me!" My jaw was rigid as my heart attempted to burst out of my chest.

He took a step back like distancing himself from a rabid animal. "What are you doing here?" His voice was low, just above a whisper.

"I could ask you the same thing." My fists clenched, nails

digging into my hands.

"It's not what—"

"Stop! So help me, if you use some stupid 'it's not what it looks like' bullshit cliché, I will unleash on your intimate little dinner party with such fury that you'll pray for the earth to open up and swallow your pathetic, lying ass! Do. I. Make. Myself. Clear?"

Quinn mirrored my tense frustrated stance. With his hands fisted, attempting to hold it together, he nodded carefully, tracking my every move. What move? I wasn't sure.

Turn and run? Make a scene? Test the waters? Yes, test the waters, because I have nothing to lose at this point, and it's time to make Quinn squirm.

Taking my sweet time, I removed my shoes and hung up my coat.

"What are you doing?" he whispered.

Deep breath ... I am peaceful, I am strong ... hmm, might need to work on the peaceful.

I leaned up to Quinn's ear, putting my hands on his chest to steady myself. "I'm going to ruin your Christmas like you have mine, and then I'm going to walk out that door and you will *never* see me again." I stepped back, giving him a tight smile before brushing past him and making my way to the table.

"Merry Christmas, everyone! I've *so* been looking forward to meeting all of you." My voice was syrupy-sweet.

Quinn caught up with me, clearly in uncharted territory for such a control freak. There was a moment of silence before the woman with chin-length black hair spoke.

"Quinten, are you going to introduce us to your guest?" Her voice was soft, friendly, genuine. I liked her already.

"Yes, Quinny, don't be rude," I remarked with my voice a pitch higher than usual.

His family exchanged amused glances at each other, his brother mouthing "Quinny?" with a grin.

Quinn cleared his throat. "Uh, yes, forgive me. This is Addy … or um, Adler Brecken. We met in Milwaukee last spring when I was visiting one of my new hotels. Addy—Adler, this is my brother Chase, my sister Alexis, her husband Mitch, their two kids Ethan and Ellen, my mother Elena, and … you've met Olivia."

All eyes landed on Olivia, she played her part, although I didn't know what that was, and smiled politely. "Pleasure to see you again." *Lying bitch.*

Everyone, including myself, waited in eager anticipation for Quinn to explain who I was, other than Adler from Milwaukee, and what I was doing there on Christmas, unannounced, with a key to his condo.

"I forgot I had told Adler I would be out of town over the holidays and I offered to let her stay here while I was gone. Then when we had a last minute change of plans I completely forgot to call her."

I nodded my head but it wasn't in agreement, it was in acknowledgment. We were all waiting for more of the story.

"What brings you to New York City on Christmas?" Elena asked, brow tense. She had to be confused by the whole unlikely scenario. I sure as hell was. I looked to Quinn since he was clearly the one directing the show.

"Uh, she's looking to move here so she has to find a place to rent."

"Over Christmas? Don't you have family that you should be with?" Chase jumped into the conversation.

"They're dead," Quinn immediately responded.

Everyone except Olivia and his sister gave him a look of shock and horror. I had always been blunt too when I told people my parents were dead, but Quinn managed to make it sound even more cold and insensitive than I ever had.

"Quinten Lucas Cohen!" his mother snapped.

"It's fine, my parents *are* dead, and I'm an only child." *He was right about that but dead wrong about me moving to New York.*

"I'm sorry, I didn't mean to sound so cold." Quinn looked at me and I knew he was genuinely sorry, but it didn't matter.

"Well, you're here and it's Christmas, so you might as well stay. Quinn, grab another chair and I'll get another place setting," Elena suggested graciously.

Touched by her kindness, a small lump formed in my throat. I couldn't speak, so I just smiled and nodded. Quinn brought in a chair as his mom arranged another place setting between her seat and Quinn's. Olivia sat idle, seething. The moment could not have been any more awkward.

"Turkey?" Elena offered, after I was seated.

"No thank you, I'm a vegan," I smiled politely.

"Oh." She looked surprised at first. "Well, good for you. It's such a healthy lifestyle and you look radiant, maybe I should give it a try."

She wasn't the first person to say something like that to me, but she was the first to say it with such sincerity.

"Thank you, Elena."

Olivia hid her boiling temper well by moving her hand to Quinn's leg in a casual but intimate gesture. His body stiffened, but he didn't push her away. He caught me staring at her hand and when I looked at him his eyes were pleading. I wanted to shove her hand away and claim him as my own, but he wasn't and never would be mine.

His family took turns passing me the dishes on the table that were vegan. I had a colorful mix of veggies on my plate, but no appetite. I picked around and forced a few bites.

"So, Adler, what has you looking to move to New York?" Chase asked.

"I'm not sure, maybe a change in profession."

"What do you do now?" Chase continued to probe.

"I'm a chef, but since I met Quinn he's helped me recognize some hidden talents I didn't even know I had."

Everyone looked at Quinn to elaborate, while he looked at me with uncertainty. I smiled and continued to rearrange my food around my plate.

"Hidden talents, huh? Sounds interesting," Mitch added.

I stuck a green bean in my mouth and nodded while slowly chewing. "Yes, turns out I have … what did you call it, Quinny? Oh, yes, a naughty school-girl charm, so I was thinking of taking Quinny up on his offer to be part of his new business venture."

The room fell silent and there wasn't a closed mouth at the table including Quinn's.

Chase cleared his throat. "And what business might that be?"

"Well, an escort service, of course." I smiled and batted my eyelashes at everyone.

Elena gasped while all three men choked on their food. Olivia and Alexis glared at Quinn in contempt.

I stayed with my ditzy blonde talk because it elicited the desired reaction. "Oh, it's not what you think. Quinny assured me it would be entirely upscale, ya know, high society type service, nothing under fifteen hundred an hour. It's not like he would be my pimp or anything." Another round of gasping and choking ensued.

"Dude, you're starting an escort service?" Chase asked flabbergasted yet a little intrigued.

"Enough," Elena insisted. "I think whatever business your brother and his *friend* have together is none of our business."

I shifted my gaze to a fuming Quinn. Every muscle in his neck twitched and his veins looked like they were going to rupture. My work was done.

"I'm expecting a delivery tomorrow so I think I'd better go inform the front desk that I'm staying here. I'd hate for them to turn away my package." My bravado had begun to falter and I needed to get out of there before the shit hit the fan.

Quinn grabbed my arm. "Where are you going?" he whispered between clenched teeth.

"I told you, I'm going down to let the front desk know I'm expecting a package tomorrow," I whispered back with a plastered-on smile since all eyes were on me.

I lied and he knew it. He wasn't going to call me on it and I knew that too. We were at an impasse. He kept hold of my arm, desperation in his eyes, but that was all I saw and it wasn't enough to make me stay.

I tugged my arm away and walked to the door. After pushing my feet down into my boots, I grabbed my jacket hoping no one would question why I needed it. As soon as my hand grabbed the door knob, Quinn's voice stopped me.

"Addy ... her friends call her Addy."

Stopped in my tracks, I felt paralyzed. Unable to turn around, I closed my eyes and just listened with my heart lodged in my throat.

"She's an amazing vegan chef. She has her own restaurant, the Sage Leaf Café. She's caring and nurturing. She's smarter than everyone in this room combined. I love that some days she smells like rosemary and basil and other days she's a sweet mix of mango and coconut. The purr of pleasure that escapes her when she's eating chocolate brings me to my knees. When she smiles, it stretches to her eyes and lights up the room. Her eyes are the most mesmerizing depths of blue and I could spend eternity lost in them. She's beautiful, delightful, elegant, exquisite, charming, divine, captivating, gorgeous, stunning, bewitching, admirable, and a million other inadequate words. Her heart is pure and honest and I know lying to everyone today is killing her. She's in New York to see me, to be with me, and I don't know why because I don't deserve her. There's an injured soul inside that beautiful body, and it rips my fucking heart out to see that I have caused her further pain. And if she walks out that door … I won't be able to breathe."

The silence was deafening. Even Ethan and Ellen were captivated by Quinn. Tears flooded my eyes and I fought the urge to blink. It was painfully overwhelming. My body's awareness of him had become my sixth sense. I knew he was close even without warning or confirmation from any of my other senses. His hand ghosted along my waist until he stood in front of me. I stared at his feet, keeping my eyes wide while rapidly trying to blink back the tears. Then his forehead found mine and just like that … I was his.

"I hate you," I sobbed.

"I know, baby, I hate me right now too," he whispered.

It was as though everyone else in the room disappeared. Quinn swept me up in his arms, and I hugged him and cried into his chest. He carried me upstairs and into his room. It was the first time I had been in his room. He set me down on the end of his bed, kneeling on the floor at my feet.

"I epically fucked up. Just don't leave, please. I have to go see my family out. Then I'll be back up and I'll do whatever it takes for as long as it takes to make this … to make *us* right."

He kissed away my fallen tears before leaving.

I WAS SURPRISED when Quinn came back upstairs only about fifteen minutes later. He was carrying my suitcase and handbag that I had left outside of the door. I hadn't moved from the end of his bed, but he chose to give me space by taking a seat in the chair near the windows.

"Is your family gone already?" I asked in a gentle voice.

"Everyone except my mother. She's putting the food away then she'll let herself out." He sounded tired.

There was an extended period of silence with neither one of us searching for eye contact.

Quinn's willingness in the past to answer my questions even if it hurt me was commendable, but I wasn't in the mood to drag information out of him.

"I'm not going to ask you anything. I don't have it left in me. So if you think you can *make it right* then now's the time, otherwise, I'm leaving."

As much as it hurt, I forced myself to look at him even though he still didn't look at me. He rubbed his hands over his face.

"I didn't lie to you. I was scheduled to go to Spain for the week, but then I got a call from my attorney at the last minute and had to cancel my trip."

He paused for a moment, maybe trying to piece together

his thoughts.

"My father left behind a shit storm of a mess for his family to clean up. He had some business issues that got him into trouble over the last ten years and when he died they fell into our laps or more accurately mine, since I took over most of his business dealings. My attorney needed to question my mother, brother, and sister too, so we changed our plans and they came here for Christmas instead."

He briefly met my eyes before he looked back down at his feet. The elephant in the room had yet to be addressed and for me, it was the deal breaker. I heard the sound of his front door closing and I assumed it was his mom leaving. He must have been waiting for that moment before diving into the subject that could have ultimately sent me running for the hills.

"When plans changed to stay in New York, my sister insisted I invite Olivia to dinner since she wasn't going back home for Christmas. I met Olivia at a fashion show two years ago and she and Alexis became good friends. It was just dinner, so with all the other drama my family has been going through, I didn't want to deal with the Olivia situation too."

I waited to see if he would elaborate, but he didn't. *Not good enough!* I grabbed my suitcase and handbag and headed to the stairs.

"Stop! I'm not finished."

I dropped my bags but didn't turn around.

"Olivia and I have never been together for longer than six weeks ... at a time. I omitted that detail on our first date because it's become a defense mechanism for me. Women want to know they will be more than a one night stand and I want them to know it will be a short relationship. Olivia isn't a gold digger. She has her own money. She likes to be showered with gifts just because she thinks she deserves it, not because she can't afford them herself."

I thought he was done, but as I started to move he continued.

"She's convenient for the random date and unattached sex. Her modeling career comes first so there is never any pressure to give her a long-term commitment, which has made it easy for her to overlook my ... indiscretions. My sister's relationship with her has kept our on-again, off-again relationship going longer than it would have, had they not been friends. But you must know, I don't have to be with her."

What?!

I wanted to storm out of there so fast it would singe his eyebrows, but I knew he would try to stop me. Exhausted, I didn't have the energy to put up a fight. "I'm going to lie down for a while ... alone."

I left my luggage at the top of the stairs and went into the guest bedroom. Quinn didn't follow me. He gave me the space I needed. A few minutes later, I heard the front door shut again. I hopped up and took my bags downstairs. Finding some paper and a pen, I left Quinn with the words I couldn't say, words he didn't want to hear.

Quinn,

I need time to think and you do, too. I believe we may have been the perfect couple, in another life. I can't keep asking you to give me more than I can give you. I don't know if I will ever—

The door opened and I jumped, dropping the pen on the ground. Quinn looked down at my bags by the door and then at the piece of paper in front of me.

"What are you doing?" he asked with his eyes fixed on mine.

"Nothing." I folded the paper and clenched it in my hand.

"What's that?" His eyes fell to my hand.

I didn't answer. He walked over to me and grabbed my hand, but I tried to pull it away.

"Stop!" I yelled, but he ignored me and pried the paper out of my hand then unfolded it.

"You're leaving?"

Silence.

"What was the rest going to say? You don't know if you'll ever what?"

Silence.

He slammed his hand holding the paper down on the counter. "Tell me!"

I flinched. He looked monstrous and it scared me. It was a side to Quinn I had never seen, and I wondered how far his anger would take him. I eased past him, praying he wouldn't reach for me. Quickly grabbing my boots, I nervously fumbled to get them on.

"Fine, Addy, leave. That's just great. Good riddance … Merry fucking Christmas to you, too." He wadded up the paper and threw it aside, then went upstairs, not once looking back.

IT WAS TOO late to get a flight out so I got a room for the night and flew back to Milwaukee the next morning. I hadn't shed a single tear since I'd left Quinn's. I cleaned my loft, scrubbed the café from top to bottom, walked dogs at the local shelter, and volunteered at the soup kitchen to pass time until Mac and

Evan came back two days before New Year's.

Having texted Mac with the "highlights" of my one day trip to New York, she was very worried about me and thought about returning early, but I had insisted she stay. When they returned home from Chicago we had dinner at their house. As soon as we were done eating, Mac kicked Evan downstairs to watch TV while we discussed my pathetic life.

"He hates me, Mac."

"I think just the opposite. I think he loves you." Her face wrinkled as if she was afraid of my reaction.

"You're crazy," I laughed.

"Hmm, I wonder if he's ever told Olivia that hurting her 'rips his fucking heart out,' or that if she left him he 'wouldn't be able to breathe,' or my personal favorite that he would 'lay the fucking world at her feet if she just asked'. He's a finance guy, Addy, not a Hollywood actor. You can't just make that shit up on a whim unless it's coming from your heart."

"Where was his heart when he refused to tell his family about us? Where was his heart when he allowed Olivia to grope him right in front of me? Where was his heart when he said he didn't *have* to be with her? I don't *have* to eat chocolate, but I sure do want it."

"Did you ask him?"

"No."

"Addy?"

"What?"

Mac moved to sit with me on the sofa, and she wrapped one arm around me, pulling me closer. "Do you want to be with him?" Her voice was tender and compassionate. Mac loved me and had endured so much to be my friend. I felt guilty for not finding happiness in my life because she needed it for me almost as much as I did.

"Yes," my voice broke, "bu-but ... I don-don't know h-h-how," I sobbed. Everything that had built inside me since leaving Quinn's came out.

"Oh, sweetie, one day at a time. Be with him one day at a time." She rocked me in her arms.

When I shed my last tear, she handed me a tissue and I blotted my red, swollen eyes.

"I'm not who he thinks I am."

"You're exactly who he thinks you are. Your past is horrific, unimaginable, and I wouldn't wish it on anyone, but don't let it define you. It was part of your journey, but it's not your future."

"I can't tell him. He deserves to know, but I just can't."

"Then don't. It only affects him if you let it affect you."

"What if he finds out, like what happened with Brent?"

"Brent doesn't know everything."

"He knew Malcolm."

"Addy, don't buy trouble. If it comes out, then it comes out. If Quinn cares about you the way I think he does, then it won't matter."

"God, I hope you're right. You're the best you know?" I gave her one last big hug before leaving.

"I know," she teased.

CHAPTER THIRTEEN

"We are not rich by what we possess but by what we
can do without."

~Immanuel Kant

I T WAS AN insane idea, but Mac talked me into flying back to
New York for New Year's Eve and surprising Quinn. It was
a bold move on my part. The last time I tried to surprise
Quinn it didn't end so well. I mentally prepared myself for the
possibility that he wouldn't be alone when I arrived. Ready to
fight for him, I wasn't opposed to kicking Olivia or any other
hussy to the curb. There was also the possibility that he would
kick me to the curb.

My flight arrived mid-afternoon with light snow but luckily no delays. I was eager to catch Quinn before he left for any
possible New Year's Eve parties. I couldn't imagine him staying
home alone on such a night. As luck would have it, the
doorman recognized me and let me in the elevator without
announcing my arrival. Butterflies fluttered in my stomach as I
neared his door. Pausing for a moment, I took a deep breath.

Deep breath ... I am peaceful, I am strong.

I knocked on the door. No answer. Then I tried the key
that I hadn't given back before I left. The door unlocked and
his security system beeped. Hurrying to type in the code, my
hands shook. After my second attempt and sweat beading along

my brow, the light switched to green. The silence haunted me. He wasn't home. The breath of hope deflated from my lungs. I wanted to surprise him, but plan B was to text or call if he wasn't home.

Not ready for plan B, I freshened up in the bathroom and lounged on his couch, staring out the window. I messed with my phone, checking Facebook, emails, and a missed call from Mac. I even read some of a book I downloaded onto my phone. Before I knew it, it was after five o'clock. Doubt crept in, stealing any certainty that I would see Quinn. Swirling emotions threatened to flood my eyes but I fought them back. It wasn't how I'd planned it. I didn't want to do this over the phone. I had to look in his eyes. My courage was compromised and my confidence faded. Could I handle seeing him come through the door in the early morning hours draped in another woman? Having nothing to lose by that point, I texted him.

Me: *Where are you?*

I waited, ten minutes, twenty minutes, a half hour. My heart sank. I knew he would've had his phone with him, but the realization hit me that he just didn't want to talk to me. I'd flown to New York and gotten my answer. He was done with me. A silent goodbye.

My next step was the daunting task of finding a hotel room on the most crowded night of the year in New York City. I pulled on my boots and just as I was buttoning my jacket my phone chimed.

Quinn: *I'm sitting outside my door.*

What?

I opened the door and sure enough, there he was, sitting on

the ground against the wall in faded blue jeans and a white thermal shirt, with a white ball cap. I hardly recognized him, he looked so young. It felt like someone just breathed life into me again.

"What are you doing?" I hesitantly asked.

"Waiting."

"Waiting for what?"

"Waiting to see if the beautiful angel I saw walk into the lobby earlier was really here or just my imagination. I was afraid to open the door and have her not be there."

I squatted in front of him, placing my hands on his, over his bent knees.

"Well, I don't know if that beautiful angel is here ... but I am."

He spread his knees and I knelt between his legs, this time cradling his face in my hands and leaning my forehead against his. "I have another proposition for you."

"Anything." He lifted my hips and extended his legs out flat then set me back down so I was straddling him. His arms wrapped around my waist and mine around his neck.

"You don't even know what I'm going to say yet."

"Doesn't matter. If you're here, then my answer is yes."

My emotions overflowed. Quinn made me feel wanted, needed, desired, and even if he hadn't said the words yet, maybe even loved. "Maybe we could discuss this inside?" I suggested.

"First things first." He turned his hat around with the bill to his back and closed the small gap between us. He kissed my top lip, then my bottom lip, before I pulled his head into me, deepening our kiss, our tongues reuniting and exploring familiar territory again.

"God, I missed you," he mumbled against my lips.

"Mmm," was my response, not wanting to leave his lips.

After several minutes of making out like teenagers in the hallway, he lumbered to his feet, holding me in my signature monkey position, and walked us into his condo, his mouth never leaving mine. He collapsed on the couch as his free hands worked the buttons of my coat until he could shrug it off me. I felt his hardness beneath me as his mouth became more urgent, moving down my neck.

"Quinn, we should ... talk ... first." My voice lacked conviction, but he stopped anyway.

"Make it quick," He said in a ragged breath, a smirk plastered to his face as he wiggled under me, adjusting himself.

I had rehearsed my speech a thousand times over the previous twenty-four hours, and it was uncharacteristic—virtually impossible—for me to forget something, but being there with Quinn, my mind went blank. I had to search for new words, and hoped I would piece them together well enough to make sense.

"Do you think we can be together without our pasts?"

"You mean Olivia?" He narrowed his eyes.

"Yes, no ... I mean ... jeez, I thought this would be easier. It sounded so good in my head."

"I'm not with Olivia, and I told you that nothing you tell me about your past will change the way I feel about you." He held me closely in a comforting embrace. I rested my head on his shoulder, my nose to his neck, and I breathed him in.

"I know ... I do ... it's not that. I'm not trying to hide anything from you. My past is tragic and sharing it with you would be like reliving it. I can't do it. Not now, maybe never."

He kissed the top of my head and stroked my hair. "Baby,

if you can let go of your past, then I don't need to know about it. But I hope someday I can look into your beautiful eyes and see past all your pain."

Pressing my lips to his strong jaw, I combed my fingers through the hair at the nape of his neck. "Me too."

"Baby?"

"Hmm?" I mumbled as my lips and tongue tasted every inch of his neck.

"You should move to New York."

Whoa!

I bolted up straight, eyes wide. "I can't move to New York."

"Why not? You told my family you were thinking of moving here." He smirked.

"I'm glad you can find the humor in that. What's in New York that I can't have in Milwaukee or even Chicago?" I threw back without thinking.

"Me." He grinned and so did I, because his beautiful smile was unavoidably contagious. "You could open another Sage Leaf Café here in Manhattan. Hell, you could open a chain of them."

"I didn't open my café to make money. I opened it because I wanted to share what I love with others. One café is personal, a chain of them is not. It's not that I'm opposed to having more cafés like mine open up. It would be a good thing to have healthy food options more readily available. But Mac handles the 'business' part of our business, and I don't see her rushing to expand anytime soon."

"Then let me help you expand. I don't know if you've noticed, but inside this ruggedly handsome head of mine is a brilliant mind for business. You wouldn't have to deal with banks or worry about start-up capital because I would give you all the financial backing you would need."

"I don't need your money—"

"*Need?* Or do you just not *want* my help or my money. Your feminist attitude is admirable, I get it, but—"

"Wait! I don't have a feminist attitude. This may be hard for you to wrap your money-driven brain around, but I don't want or need your money. If I wanted to start a chain of cafés I would, and maybe someday I will. If or when that day comes, I have plenty of financial backing. However, right now I'm just trying to live in the moment and squeeze every bit of happiness I can out of it. I lost my purpose a long time ago, or at least I thought I did. But maybe it's not about the right time or moment to find a new purpose. Maybe it's about finding purpose in every moment."

He squeezed my legs as I sat astride him. The look on his face was complete adoration. "You fucking amaze me, you know that, right?"

"That's why you lov—"

Quinn raised his eyebrows as I fumbled for a recovery. He'd poured his heart out to me on more than one occasion, but in all his words of admiration, passion, and desperation, never once did he use the word love.

"Um ... that's not what, or what I meant—"

My gallant knight rescued me by putting us back on the road we were on before I detoured into no man's land.

"So then come to New York and get a teaching job at the culinary institute, or use your degree, or get a janitor's job at Juilliard and do the 'Goodwill Hunting' thing by leaving anonymous masterpiece compositions on the chalk boards."

I punched him in the gut, laughing at his ridiculous ideas.

"You're a dork, you know that right?"

He didn't even flinch when I hit him. "Your IQ is probably 180 or higher and 'dork' is the best you've got?"

I gave him a slow kiss. "What can I say, I'm an idiot—stupid, dumb, thick, deficient, simple-minded, dopey, witless, stolid, moronic, brainless, and cretinous—when I'm around you."

"Okay, Merriam-Webster." He dipped his tongue in my mouth and cupped my breasts, and I knew we were done talking.

His erection came back to full attention. I reached between us and rubbed him over his jeans. Pulling away, he removed his shirt in one easy motion. I reciprocated then he paused, taking in my new, black lace, demi-cup bra. His wet his bottom lip then sucked it into his mouth.

One look. The guy gave me one look and I was gone.

I reached both arms around to unhook my bra but he grabbed my arms and shook his head.

"Leave it on." He traced his fingers over the swells of my breasts then his eyes lifted to mine with a naughty boyish grin. Sitting there with his hat on backwards, shirt off, and faded jeans, he looked young and playful.

"You're right, we should leave it on. I'm not sure you deserve to get past second base tonight."

He flipped me on my back and pushed his hips into mine. The hardness straining at his zipper rubbed between my legs. My hips reached to meet his. He'd taken me in almost every way possible, but being with him on the couch, half-dressed and grinding into each other like two teenagers dry humping, was raw and sensual. We hadn't been intimate for a while, so taking it slow and letting our desire build was intensely gratifying.

He kissed his way up my neck then paused, looking deep into my eyes. "Sin ti no puedo respirar. Te necesito enmi vida." *Without you I cannot breathe. I need you in my life.* He smoothed back a few errant hairs from my face and kissed both of my cheeks. "Tu eres mi luz en oscuridad. Tú eres la mujer más bella que he visto." *You are my light in the dark. You are the most beautiful woman I have ever seen.* "Te amo." *I love you.*

My emotions caught in my throat. He seduced me with his words. When they melted off his tongue, it felt like he was serenading me with a song. They were a whisper, a confession, a promise. He eased off of the couch and lifted me up, cradling me in his arms. I fought back the tears as he carried me upstairs and laid me on his bed. He pulled off my pants then stood at the end of his bed looking at me. His eyes shone with adoration, appreciation, and yes, love. He slowly removed his pants and briefs then looked at his bedside table.

"Don't," I whispered, "you don't need it."

He nodded in trust before crawling over me and removing my bra.

"I thought you wanted it left on?"

"Quiero hacerte el amor." He breathed into my bare chest, reverently kissing both of my breasts before sliding off my panties.

The moment was beautiful and seductive. He opened up to me, yet hid behind a language he assumed I didn't speak. Fear held our emotions hostage; we both wanted to say the words we'd already physically expressed. They were just words, but saying them somehow nurtured small insecurities in our souls. It was my turn to rescue him. I wanted him to know the feelings were mutual. I needed him to know before our physical connection blurred our emotions.

He kissed his way back up my legs, pausing at my sex. When his tongue parted my folds, my body melted into his mouth.

"Ah, Quinn…"

I grabbed his hair and pulled his head, aching for him to be inside me, but I wanted this to be slow and more emotional than physical. He followed my lead and continued to move up my body. He kissed my neck and my earlobe. It was time to let him know.

"Quiero hacer el amor contigo también," I whispered.

He went still—his face resting at my neck—and it was in that moment my instincts were validated. He thought his confessions were hidden in a woven tapestry of language. He lifted his head, searching my eyes, and translated my words as if his mind hadn't yet absorbed their implications. "I want to make love to you too?"

I nodded before the tears escaped. Baring all, I was completely exposed to him, body, mind, and soul. He kissed away my tears while one hand slid under my knee, pulling my leg up, as he eased into me.

A soft moan escaped my mouth as he filled me. He kissed me deeply and passionately as his hips found a slow rhythm. We took our time, letting our hands explore each other's body, like we hadn't done it so many times before. It felt familiar and new at the same time; our bodies iterating our verbal confessions.

We made love, and in that moment I was exclusively Quinn's. Not one part of me was held hostage by my past. I wasn't the pretty girl feeling inferior to the god-like man. Together we were one, and we were beautiful.

"God, I love you so much, Addy." His voice was urgent as his release approached. He reached between us and massaged my clit. "Let go with me, my beautiful."

"God, I love what you do to me," I breathed, orgasming around him as his warm release filled me.

Our movements gradually faded, like the ending of a song. He rolled to his side, hugging me in close and kissing my forehead. "Well, well, my beautiful girl speaks Spanish. I suppose it was an insult to your extreme intelligence to think you didn't speak another language."

I laughed in between kisses to his chest. "Five, my Latin lover ... I speak five other languages fluently."

He pushed me back so he could look into my eyes. "Are you shitting me?"

I shook my head, biting my lips together as I shrugged.

"What other languages?" He looked at me wide-eyed with his mouth agape.

"Spanish, French, Arabic, Mandarin, and Hindi."

"Hindi?" He furrowed his brows.

"Yes, I spent several months in India."

He pulled me back into him. "Huh."

"Surprised?" I smiled, inhaling his intoxicating scent with my nose nuzzled into his chest.

"I guess I assumed someone who could have gone to any college she wanted and yet chose to stay close to home, probably didn't even have a passport."

"Oh, I'm full of surprises, Mr. Cohen."

He scooted down until he was even with my breasts. Then he cupped and kneaded them before flicking his tongue over my nipples. "That you are, and it's so fucking sexy." He wrapped his arms around me and continued his oral assault on my breasts. "Now that we've established that you are mine, I'm going to claim every inch of your body. There's not going to be any part of you where I haven't left my mark."

We spent the next two hours claiming each other in every possible way. We spooned, and Quinn continued to whisper words of love in my ear. I opened my eyes and looked at the clock. It read 12:01 a.m.

"Happy New Year." I spoke with a trace of excitement in my voice.

He lifted his head to see over mine. "Happy New Year to you too, my beautiful."

I turned my head back toward his and we kissed, bringing in our new year together.

I WOKE ON New Year's Day in my favorite place—in bed, wrapped in Quinn. The night before replayed in my mind so many times; I wondered if in the light of day everything would change. His grip around my waist tightened, letting me know he was awake. I rolled to face him.

"Morning, beautiful." He nuzzled into my neck.

"Good morning. I love waking up wrapped in you." I ran my hands down his chest.

"How long are you staying?" he asked as he unabashedly lifted the sheet to gaze at my naked body.

I rolled my eyes, trying to ignore his horny teenager antics. "Good question. I hadn't thought that far ahead. How long will you have me?"

He smiled bigger than I had ever seen him smile before. "Not a day past ... hmm ... forever. I can have all your belongings here tomorrow."

"What if I have all *your* belongings in Milwaukee by tomorrow?" I chided back.

"Not possible."

"And why not?" I gave him a single raised eyebrow.

"Well, for one, your resources are not as good as mine, and for two, my stuff would not fit in your loft, and for three, I can't leave New York."

I chewed on the inside of my cheek, thinking my response through. "I see. Well, for one, I guarantee my resources are just as good as yours, if not better, and two, the reason all your stuff would not fit into my loft is because your overindulgent life has allowed you to acquire way too many unnecessary possessions, and three, you could leave New York, you just don't want to."

Quinn pulled me in for a long kiss before resting his forehead on mine. "I'm tempted to say yes just to check out your 'resources,' but I'm not going to because negotiating with your feisty little ass gets me hard." He palmed my butt and pulled me into his waiting erection. Then his tone went from playful to sober as he met my eyes. "But, Addy, at the end of this day and every day forward, you need to know there is nothing I wouldn't give up for you."

I'm free falling off the cliff and all I can do is trust Quinn to catch me … please catch me.

"Oh, I bet you say that to all the girls." I wanted to fall, I really did, but every word felt like my stomach lodging further in my throat. I couldn't breathe. Quinn literally took my breath away.

"Don't … I hate that you don't see how incredibly amazing you are. I've never said that to anyone else. The truth is, there is very little I would even consider giving up for any other woman. You're only the fourth woman I've ever loved."

And just like that … he popped my balloon. It ranked up there with "I enjoy beautiful women." I looked away, trying to hide the pain in my eyes, but he pulled my chin forward, forcing our eyes to meet again. Then he smiled.

"The first is my mother, the second is my sister, and the third is my niece."

I blinked away the impending tears and shoved him in the chest. "You shit!"

He laughed. "Sorry, baby, I know that was mean. God, I love you."

I bit his lower lip, hard.

"Ouch! What was that for?"

"Just a reminder to watch your smart mouth, if you know what's good for you."

He flipped the sheet up over his head and wiggled his body down mine, nestling between my legs with his head positioned at my sex. Then he grabbed my thighs and spread my legs out wide. His tongue swept through my slit and my hips jerked off the bed.

"Baby, I'm pretty sure I know what's good for me."

I ONCE HAD a conversation with Mac about the male characters in romance novels that had endless stamina. They required virtually no recovery time and defined the images of endurance and vitality. That was Quinn. If I was a "musical prodigy" as Mac referred to me, then Quinn was the ultimate sex prodigy. He spent the morning showing me all of his talents.

"Since you mentioned insanity, I'm curious about this unprotected sex we've been having … It's been great but I'm wondering if you're going to be showing me a stick you've peed on?"

"Uh … no. I have a copper IUD now. I don't want to leave it in for years, but right now I like the spontaneity it provides."

"Agreed…" he interlaced our fingers "…I'd ask more questions about the copper IUD but I know I'd be lost in the first few words, so I'll just trust you on the matter."

"Yeah, well, as I said, don't get used to it. You're the only 'foreign body' I like in mine, so the IUD won't be staying long."

After a quick kiss, he sat up and walked his delicious nakedness to the bathroom. "Listen, beautiful, I'm going to see my mother and brother today before they go back to Spain. Make yourself at home while I'm gone and we'll go out later and make up for missing the excitement of New Year's Eve in New York City."

I stayed in bed, half-covered in tousled sheets as he showered. Dumbfounded. It wasn't the most eloquent word but if one word described me in that moment, that was it. Oh how I fell so quickly from cloud nine. Quinn confessed his feelings for me at Christmas in front of his family, and then just twelve hours earlier he declared his love to me, so why did I feel like the dirty little secret he was leaving behind?

Before Quinn finished his shower, I slipped on one of his T-shirts and went downstairs for some hot tea. I didn't want to overreact after such an amazing night. Unquestionably, the logistics of being together had to be ironed out, but keeping me from his family hurt.

A few minutes later, he came downstairs wearing dark jeans and a grey V-neck sweater with his hair a perfect mess but dry. Did he use a hair dryer? The thought made me smile.

"What are you smiling about?" he asked as he pulled me

away from the counter into a hug. I held my arm out so my tea didn't spill on him.

"You. I was picturing you with a hair dryer styling that sexy mop of yours."

"Mop?"

"*Sexy* mop." I stretched up on my toes to give him a quick kiss. "Can I make you some breakfast?"

"Mmm, as great as that sounds, I can't. I'm meeting my family for an early lunch at Masa. Do you want me to bring you something?"

Deep breath … I am peaceful, I am strong.

"No, the thought of eating one meal that costs as much as it does to feed a family of four for two weeks spoils my appetite."

"Jesus, Addy, not this again." He released me and grabbed a water from the refrigerator. "If you had a fraction of the money I do, you wouldn't suffer from such guilt-ridden sentiment indulging once in a while. It's not like I don't make plenty of charitable contributions."

He had no fucking clue, but I wasn't ready to enlighten him on the matter … yet. After taking a long swig, he set his water on the counter and cradled my face in his hands.

"I don't want to argue with you. If it will make you feel better, we'll feed some homeless people or make some donations later. Whatever you want, okay?"

"Whatever I want?" I asked for clarification.

"Yes, whatever you want. Now I have to run, babe, okay?" He pressed his lips to my forehead and headed to the door, grabbing his coat on the way out.

My teeth dug into my tongue but my ego won anyway. "Tell your lovely family 'hi' for me and maybe next time they're in town we can visit more."

Quinn's back was to me but I could see his whole body flinch. I headed to the stairs contemplating the gamble that would be my next statement. "Oh, and make sure Olivia knows if she so much as breathes in your direction, I will break her skinny-ass twig of a body, okay?"

Halfway up the stairs, I paused when he spoke. "Why would you think Olivia will be there?" His question was slow and cautious.

But my answer was quick and forthright. "Because you didn't invite me."

He sighed. "It's complicated, Addy."

I turned and glared at him so he would know my next words were serious and nonnegotiable. "Well, you have approximately three hours to un-complicate things." Not waiting for a response, I continued to his bedroom.

Rarely do people want to be wrong, but I did. I wanted Quinn to tell me Olivia wasn't going to be at lunch. I wanted him to feel like an ass for not inviting me and extend me a last minute invitation, which I would have declined. But that wasn't the point. I needed him to show me love beyond the bedroom.

Alexis was family and I admired Quinn's loyalty. However, Olivia was quite simply a complete bitch who didn't deserve one minute of his time. He told me there wasn't anything he wouldn't give up to be with me. Whether he liked it or not, the time had come for him to ante up.

I SPENT THE next three hours going through Quinn's stuff, to carry out my plan. I didn't pick out the most expensive things,

I saved those for later, but I chose the items that were most repulsive to me.

Quinn was later than I expected. Sprawled on the couch and armed with my favorite distraction, a good book, I waited for the inevitable. Quinn didn't disappoint.

He stormed through the door. "What the hell is going on?"

Man, I loved to poke the bear. Why? Just for fun.

My eyes glued to my book, my words soft and steady. "I'm not sure yet. I'm just on the second chapter."

"I'm not talking about your fucking book! I'm talking about the silent auction in the lobby … Of. My. Stuff!"

"Oh, that? I know, PETA would have a field day with that horrific junk."

"Junk? My thirty-eight thousand dollar Testoni alligator skin shoes are not junk, neither is my forty-seven thousand dollar Montblanc alligator skin briefcase … and the trophy zebra skin rug. Do you have any idea how much of my money is sitting down in the lobby being ogled by the other residents?" He looked just seconds from self-combustion: clenched fists, narrowed eyes, and fire flaring from his nostrils. Almost.

I set my book down and strolled into the kitchen to grab a banana. "Well, we'll know by ten o'clock tonight how much your stuff is worth. That's when the silent auction ends. I can't wait to see the warm fuzzy feeling you're going to have in the morning when we donate all the money to the African Wildlife Foundation."

He paced back and forth like a caged animal, but I didn't let it faze me. "Why are you doing this?" His voice was still strained, but he managed to take the volume down a few notches.

"Because you said I could," I mumbled through a mouth

full of banana.

"And when exactly did I say that?" Both of his hands were on his hips, chest puffed out.

"Before you left for lunch. You said, 'we'll feed some homeless people or make some donations, *whatever* you want.' I said, '*whatever* I want?' and you said, 'yes, what—"

"I know what I said. I don't need it repeated back verbatim. But that's not what I meant. God! You're so fucking frustrating." He raked both hands through his hair.

"Did you get everything straightened out at lunch?" It was my turn to glare at him with my hands on my hips.

"What? We're not..." he sighed an exasperated breath "...that's not what we're talking about right now."

"It is now. I'm done watching your tantrum over a bunch of overpriced shit that was made from killing innocent animals."

"If I didn't buy it, someone else was going to. I don't understand what the big deal is."

"The big deal is the simple concept of supply and demand, if there is not a demand for something then there wouldn't be a need to kill these animals to supply a non-existent demand. It's about being part of the solution, not part of the problem. Be the change, Quinn ... be the change you wish to see in the world. Are you familiar with Gandhi? Now. What. Happened. At. Lunch?"

He walked away, stopping at his massive windows. His silence answered my question. He didn't have the balls to say to his family what had to be said, and that was the only answer I needed. I marched upstairs and threw my stuff back into my suitcase. My back was to the door but my "Quinn-sense" detected him looking at me.

"What are you doing?" His voice was softer.

"I'm going home until you're ready to do more than *say* you love me."

"You didn't even let me tell you about lunch."

I turned around but didn't make any advance toward him. "Then tell me."

"I texted Olivia and told her not to come to Masa. I had to practically tie my sister to her chair to keep her from storming out when she found out what I did."

I was stupefied and way beyond speechless. He moved closer to me until he was so close I had to strain my neck to look up at his face. He brushed his knuckles over my cheek.

"That's all I'm going to tell you, and I know it's a huge leap of faith I'm asking you to take … but please trust me. I made things right with my family where you are concerned. Okay?"

I nodded.

He bent down and kissed me, slow at first but it became more intense and urgent. I dropped the clothes I had clenched in my hands as he pushed me back onto his bed. His hands moved up my shirt, cupping my breasts as his thumbs slipped under my bra, brushing over my nipples. A deep groan escaped his throat. When his length rubbed against my thigh, I broke our kiss. He moved to my neck as I tried unsuccessfully to push him back.

"Quinn?"

"Hmm?" he hummed into my neck.

"I've had a cup of tea and a banana today. You're going to have to feed me before this goes any further."

He grabbed my wrist and placed my hand over his erection. "I think I can be accommodating to your hunger cravings."

My hands grabbed his hair and yanked it hard.

"Ouch, okay, okay!"

"I'm serious. My stomach isn't filled with a parasitic breeding ground of raw fish and caviar like yours. I'm starving and you're going to take me to dinner and feed me a sensibly priced meal."

"Parasitic breeding ground? You'd make one hell of a food critic, Addy."

I laughed, thinking about how proud Mac would have been of me. Her unfiltered mouth had rubbed off on me over the years. "Don't act all offended. You know you love my honesty."

"I love *you,* my beautiful, as for your *honesty,* that's yet to be determined." He kissed the tip of my nose before crawling off me. He grabbed my hand and pulled me off the bed. "Let's feed you ... I think the golden arches might have something in your socially responsible budget."

WE WENT TO a quaint little café that reminded me of my own. Sitting at a table in the corner, we enjoyed casual conversation over exceptionally good food.

"Favorite food?" Quinn asked.

"Not a fair question."

"Okay, favorite fruit?"

"Still too hard, but I'd say a tie between figs and avocados."

"You?"

"Abacaxi."

"Yum, pineapple, I love it too."

"Now you're just being mean." He shook his head.

"What?"

"When I say Abacaxi most normal people would say,

'what?' but not you. You act like people use pineapple and abacaxi as interchangeably as sweet potato and yam."

"Well, actuall—"

"Don't." He tried to be serious but a chuckle escaped him. "Don't give me the speech on the botanical differences between sweet potatoes and yams. Do you have a weak subject?"

I wrinkled my nose and rolled my eyes to the side.

"Hmm ... sports, well at least traditional ones. I don't follow baseball, football, basketball, etcetera."

Quinn smiled as if finding my weakness was a small victory for him. "What's your favorite sport? We should play it together sometime. I love *physical* activity."

"Oh, don't you worry, we will." I gave him a cheeky grin. "Okay, my turn. Favorite book?"

"*The Science of Getting Rich* by Wallace Wattle." He smirked.

"Seriously?"

"Yeah, seriously."

"Oh, jeez, *The Original Guide To Manifesting Wealth Through The Secret Law Of Attraction.* 'No man can rise to his greatest possible height in talent of soul development unless he has plenty of money.'"

"Words to live by, don't you think?"

I couldn't control my laughter. "My 'words to live by' are not even close to those. I'd love to know the version of Quinten Cohen, blue collar worker, living paycheck to paycheck."

"Is my money a turnoff for you?" His question was almost one of shock.

"No, not your money—your attitude towards it." I stopped short to carefully piece together my next question. "Would you give it up?"

He looked a little nervous. "You mean hypothetically, right? Sure, I made it once, I could make it all again."

"That's not what I meant. Would you live on say … fifty grand or less a year, in exchange for being with the one you love? Would you live with little or no health insurance? Would you clip coupons to make ends meet? Would you take public transportation because you couldn't afford a car and the upkeep on it? Would you shop garage sales and discount stores for clothing? Would you plant a garden to save money on food?"

"This is ridiculous. I don't even know why you're asking me all of this. It's not realistic, not in this life."

I paused a moment, picking at my food with my fork. "I would … I would give it up for you. I would choose you with nothing, than everything without you." My demeanor was cutthroat serious. I meant what I said. I wasn't sure why Quinn had come into my life, but something in some undefinable place within me knew we needed each other.

He reached for my hand on the table and squeezed it. "I don't deserve you."

Smiling, I looked up at him. "You're probably right."

I STAYED TWO more weeks in New York with Quinn. We saw more Broadway shows, settling for the cheaper seats. Quinn called it slumming, but his willingness to appease me was endearing. We tried all the vegan-friendly restaurants and shopped Whole Foods for the meals I made at his place.

I shared my opinion on grocery prices, and the financial geek in Quinn considered the possibilities both from a business standpoint and an ethical one, which was great progress from our night at the café. We ice-skated, visited museums, art galleries, and served food at the local homeless shelter. Quinn was like a little kid with money burning a hole in his pocket. He wanted to lavish me with gifts, but I only allowed him to pay for a spa day that we both enjoyed together and a few Bikram yoga classes. Quinn in workout clothes showcasing his muscles in various yoga poses had me drooling on my mat.

After the first class, we only made it as far as the bathroom, where we locked the door and he took me from behind at the sink while we watched each other in the mirror. The sex was always incredible. It didn't matter if we slowly made love first thing in the morning or fucked like bunnies in a public restroom. Our mutually-insatiable desires just grew stronger.

He spent time working out of his home office for several hours each afternoon while I read, caught up on emails, and checked in on Jake. I knew Quinn hadn't achieved his level of success by working a few hours a day. He made time for me, and it meant a lot, but I knew it couldn't last forever.

We fell into a comfortable routine, but our time had come to an end. He had meetings and a few business trips that could no longer be delayed, and I needed to get back to my café and relieve my hardworking employees and business partner.

The drive to the airport was quiet. We hadn't had any further discussion on the future of our relationship, and neither one of us was ready to pack up and move to make it work.

"I'm going to be in Chicago on business in a few weeks. Maybe I'll drive up to see you and check in on my hotel."

I gave a forced smile. "I'd love that. If I'm lucky you might get snowed in while you're visiting and I can keep you a little longer."

He leaned over and kissed me while we pulled up to the terminal. "I love my greedy girl."

"I love you." My eyes started to tear up, so I quickly opened the door. He grabbed my hand.

"Look at me," he demanded.

I shook my head, looking down as I tried to will away my tears.

He tilted my chin up with his index finger and the flood gates broke. "Oh, baby, no ... don't cry." He kissed my trails of tears and wiped my cheeks with his thumbs.

"I hate goodbyes," I sobbed.

"Never goodbye, my beautiful, you know that. I'll do whatever it takes to be with you, okay?"

I sniffled and nodded as he handed me a handkerchief from the inside pocket of his suit.

"See ya soon." He gave me one last deep kiss.

"You'd better." I smiled back at him as I exited the car.

CHAPTER FOURTEEN

"I want to be your favorite hello and hardest goodbye."

~Unknown

MAC WAS ECSTATIC when she picked me up at the airport. It was a déjà vu moment when she nearly tackled me in the middle of the airport. As much as I loved being with Quinn, I missed Mac so much it often felt like a piece of me was in Milwaukee waiting to be reunited and made whole again. The ride home was nonstop questions.

"So you've declared your love for each other, but no plans have been made to be together?"

"Correct."

"And you're okay with this?"

"I don't have a choice right now."

"Adler Sage, you know that's not true. You could pack up and move tomorrow, so what's the real reason?"

"So could he, but he's not throwing his stuff in boxes yet either."

"What is this, some western movie standoff between you two? You just said you told him you would give up everything to be with him. What are you waiting for?"

"I would, but I have to be certain that I'm not giving up everything to move in with some guy who doesn't share my commitment. If he called me tonight and said he was moving to Milwaukee, I would have my stuff in New York before I hung up the phone. I just want confirmation that what we have is real, no matter where we live or what we have."

"This sounds like the makings of a tragic love story, except for the sex. Holy cow, I can't see you screwing in a public restroom. I didn't think you had it in you."

"You and me both. Quinn brings out a part of me I never knew existed. It's thrilling and intoxicating, yet frightening and reckless too. We don't have that much in common. We are the cliché of opposites attract. I know he's helped me heal parts of my soul that I thought were permanently damaged, and I love the Quinn that I see when he isn't trying to impress me with all of his money."

Mac giggled. "I take it that's a part of you he doesn't know about yet?"

"I've alluded to it several times, but he hasn't taken the bait and you know it's not something I flaunt."

"That's an understatement." She remarked rolling her eyes.

"He's coming for a visit in a few weeks since he has some business in Chicago. Maybe by then I'll have a better idea of where we stand or where we're going."

"I hope so, sweetie, because limbo is miserable."

"I know. It's where I've been for close to eight years, though, so what's a few more weeks?"

"I suppose so."

I UNPACKED AS soon as I got home and started some laundry. My loft wore a nice glove of dust, so I cranked up the music and dove into cleaning. When I wiped off my counter where my phone was, I noticed two missed calls and a text, all from

Quinn.

> **Quinn:** *Missing you, lucky for me my bed smells like you.*
>
> *If my housekeeper washes my sheets I'm going to fire her.*
>
> *I'm going to get a blown up print of that picture you sent me.*
>
> *It will get hung on the ceiling above my bed.*

> **Me:** *Missing you too but my bed doesn't smell like you.*
>
> *Not fair. Lucky for me I have a good memory.*
>
> *I plan on replaying them in my head each night while touching myself.*

> **Quinn:** *Holy Fuck, Addy, I am so hard! Keep talking.*
>
> *The thought of you touching yourself has me halfway there.*

> **Me:** *Goodnight, babe!*

> **Quinn:** *Not yet, seriously, you're killing me!*

THE WEEKS IN New York with Quinn spoiled me. I thought being home would remind me of how much I enjoyed time to myself, but all I felt was alone. Everything was better with Quinn. All my senses were heightened, the world was a brighter place, even my creativity was inspired.

I came up with five new menu ideas during my time in New York. I was alive, not just living. He brought me to life, yet he had no idea. It had been weeks since I'd had any flashbacks, which was a record for me.

The weather was cold and the piles of snow were so high the DOT ran out of places to put it. Jake was glad to have me back, but it wasn't because he needed me. He just liked to bounce ideas off me. At the end of my first week back, we had a late dinner together after the café closed.

"So, I want to discuss the future of the café with you."

"What do you mean?" It was as if he'd been oblivious to my recent time away and what it might mean.

"Would you be interested in taking over ownership with Mac?"

His brow furrowed. "I don't understand. Are you wanting to sell out?"

"No, that's not what I mean ... I'm offering you the business, and Mac will help out until she and Evan move back to Chicago, which will happen when they decide to start a family or if Evan gets offered a position at Richard's law firm."

"Addy, I'm flattered, but I don't have that kind of money, and I don't know if I can get a loan from the bank right now."

I grabbed his hand from across the table. "Jake, I don't want to sell you the café. I want to *give you* the café."

Shaking his head, he narrowed his eyes. Was it just the lighting or did he truly have tears in his eyes? Seeing this tattooed, muscular man crying would have caused me to lose it too.

"Why ... why on earth would you just give me the café?"

"We have such a great following of loyal customers and it's been a great addition to the city." I shrugged. "I can't imagine closing it. I'm not going to go into all the reasons why I don't need to *sell* it to you, I just want you to say yes and promise to treat my little café with all the love and dignity she deserves."

"Are you moving?"

My lips twisted as I focused on a small scratch in the table, not knowing the answer to his question. "I'm not sure yet, but maybe. I just want to have all my loose ends taken care of if I decide to leave Milwaukee."

"Would this have anything to do with a Latin businessman from New York?"

Unable to hold back the happiness I felt when I thought of Quinn, I smiled. "It may."

Jake stood and took my hand pulling me to my feet. Then he embraced me. "You deserve the very best, Addy. I hope Quinn knows what a lucky guy he is and if he hurts you I will break him."

I laughed. "You're a lot younger than me, but you sure sound like a big brother."

He pulled back and slowly wet his lips. The firm look in his eyes made me a little uncomfortable. "Addy, my feelings about you are anything but brotherly."

Not good, not good at all.

Flirting was nothing new with Jake, but he had a girlfriend. I assumed it was just playful and innocent, however, the way he held me and looked at me felt intimate. He was much younger than I was and quite good-looking in his own right, which made our flirtations that much more flattering.

I looked away as I pulled back. "Thank you. Jake, you're a great friend and everything you've done for me means so very much."

"Anything for you, Addy."

We ironed out the details over the next couple of days while my attorney got the paperwork together to officially sign ownership over to Jake. I made plenty of excuses to spend limited time at the café, because the uncomfortable moment I shared with him left me a bit apprehensive.

Mac was happy for me and I think she felt an equal sense of

relief knowing the café was in good hands. I suspected it might expedite her and Evan's decision to start a family.

Quinn and I texted several times a day and talked on the phone at night. I hadn't yet told him about the café transition. Since I was not yet one hundred percent sure I was moving to New York, I didn't want him to think it was a foregone conclusion.

QUINN TOLD ME he would arrive around eight in the evening on Sunday, so that morning I slept in, knowing we would be up late reacquainting. To my surprise, I woke to the warmth of a large naked body at my back. I screamed bloody murder until a strong hand covered my mouth. My heart hammered against my chest as I kicked and flailed around trying to escape.

"Shh, baby, it's just me," Quinn whispered in my ear as he removed his hand from my mouth.

I whipped around, out of breath. "Oh my God! What the hell, Quinn? You about scared the crap out of me. What are you doing here?"

He pulled me into his body and stroked the back of my head. "I wanted to surprise you."

"Well, mission accomplished. How did you get in?"

"The door."

"You need my security code to open the door." I pulled away from him, waiting for his explanation.

"I watched you enter it while saying the numbers out loud the night we ate at the pier. You'd had a little too much to drink. You really should come up with something a little more secure than five, five, five, five."

"It's easy to remember." I shrugged.

"Do you know how ridiculous that sounds coming from you?"

"Not for me, it's more for Mac, Evan, and Jake."

"Jake? Why does Jake have access to your loft?"

"He and Mac keep an eye on things while I'm gone and I grow most of the herbs and edible flowers for the café up here."

He nodded, keeping a stern look. "I'm not sure how I feel about Jake."

Me neither.

"Well if you're not planning on taking him to bed anytime soon, then what does it matter?"

"Addy! What's that supposed to mean? You think I'm gay?" He pinned me to the bed, his face a breath away from mine.

"All the sexy guys are, don't you know?"

"Looks like I may need to remind you how *not gay* I am."

Lifting my hips, I tried to rub against his naked erection. "I think you may."

He flipped me on my stomach, pinning both of my hands above my head with one of his. He knelt between my legs, spreading them with his knees. "Lift up that sexy ass of yours, baby."

I pulled my knees under me. His free hand kneaded my breasts, pulling my nipples into hard peaks, then moved down and stroked my sex until it dripped with desire and need for him. He sucked on his wet fingers, which still made me blush from head to toe, but turned me on at the same time.

"Mmm, I missed the taste of you."

He then slipped his fingers into my mouth and I sucked them, tasting both of us at once. As I sucked his fingers, he lined his cock up at my entrance then slammed into me.

"Ah, Christ, Addy, I wanted to take it slow but it's been

too long, baby."

He pulled partway out and repeated.

"Ah! Oh my God!" I yelled.

Relentlessly, he pulled out then slammed back into me, so hard my body inched up the bed. Every thrust hit deep, eliciting a dizzy sensation. His pace picked up and he kissed my back, leaving a wet trail with his tongue. He let go of my hands, allowing me to brace myself better so I didn't ram into the headboard. With one hand on my breast and the other at my clit, he brought us both to orgasm within seconds of each other, each of us moaning the other's name.

Afterward, he laid me on my back and feathered kisses along every inch of my body. Words were not necessary. I felt his love with each touch.

We spent the rest of the day in bed, only getting up for food and bathroom breaks. After that first intense time in the morning, everything else was patient, slow, sensual lovemaking. My body belonged to Quinn and I loved how he worshiped it. He made me feel sexy, beautiful, wanted, needed, and very loved.

After showering for the third time that day, we decided to curl up on my couch with a big bowl of popcorn and a movie of my choice: *Pitch Perfect*. Quinn rolled his eyes at my choice, but he hadn't seen it, so I felt confident he would change his attitude by the end. I was right. He laughed throughout the movie, but in stubborn Quinn fashion, he still just called it "okay." I think it was his attempt at payback but I didn't give him the satisfaction of arguing with him.

We stayed spooned on the couch, under a blanket, for a while after the movie ended.

"What type of business did you have in Chicago?"

"More loose ends with my dad's stuff."

"Such as?"

He sighed. "Legal stuff. My dad got into an unfortunate situation with one of his companies many years ago and the legal ramifications from it have been ongoing."

"How did he die?" His body tensed around mine, but I couldn't see his face, so I waited for a response even if it was not an answer.

"Suicide."

Shit, me and my big mouth.

Another sigh. "It wasn't ruled a suicide but that's what it was. When the legal issues started, my dad took to drinking, a lot. He was never abusive toward anyone else, but he became reckless. He had a driver, but he insisted on driving himself to burn off some steam."

I waited, but Quinn didn't continue.

"That's the call you received that day in Milwaukee, that he had been in an accident?"

"No, the accident happened three months earlier. He was on life support and that was the day my mother signed the papers to have him taken off it. I couldn't be there to watch. I hated him. He was such a coward."

I rolled over to face him. His eyes were glazed as he absently stroked his fingers down my arm. I wrapped myself around him, and we held each other until sleep took us both.

"MORNING, BEAUTIFUL." QUINN kissed the top of my head. We were still cuddled naked under the blanket on the couch.

"Mmm, don't move. I could stay here forever," I mumbled into his chest.

"I leave tomorrow morning, so our forever on your couch is about a day."

"You're such a downer." I pouted.

He hitched my leg over his hip and eased his hard length into me. "I wouldn't really say I'm a downer, would you?"

"Ah, good morning, Mr. Cohen, welcome back." I grinned before kissing the smirk on his face and tilting my hips further into his, encouraging him to start moving against me. We took our time, slowly making love. He knew all the places I liked being touched and I knew all the ways to make his breath hitch. I loved driving him crazy. He was my drug and I could have happily died on a Quinn high.

By the time we both found our own release, we were sweaty and tangled in the blanket.

"Mac and Evan invited us over to their house for dinner tonight. We don't have to go but—"

"I'd love to go." Quinn pulled me on top of him and ran his fingers through my hair, which flowed down my back.

"You would?"

"Of course. You consider them your only family, so I'd like to get to know them … maybe make nice before I sweep you away from here to live with me."

"Mr. Presumptuous today, huh?"

"Mr. Hopeful is more like it. Every morning I wake up that I'm not buried inside you is another wasted day of my life."

"Ah, how romantic … in your own twisted, sex-crazed way."

"Twisted, not really, but yes, completely sex crazed. If I weren't my own boss, I'd be without a job. I can't focus on work, and I have to cut out of meetings early to whack off in my office because my mind is always on you, which leaves me with a perpetual hard-on."

I busted out in a fit of laughter. "Whatever."

"I'm serious. If you move to New York you can come to work with me every day and help relieve my tension so I can be more productive."

"Oh, okay, so you think I'm going to go all Monica on you and just camp out under your desk waiting to service you?"

"No, you'd be too cramped under there all day. I have a nice leather couch in my office. I was thinking about tying you to it naked … Shit! I'm getting hard just thinking about it." He tried to push into me again but I rolled off him.

"Where are you going?" he pleaded in a strained voice.

"Food. I love it almost as much as my Latin sex god."

"I'll give you ten minutes to throw something in the microwave for us then get your sexy ass back here."

"Whoa! First of all, I don't even own a cancerwave, and second, you distracted me from having my banana oat pancakes yesterday morning so I'm having them today."

"Oooh, you might talk me off the couch after all. I like your pancakes, maybe not as much as I like distracting you, but they are great."

"You know I could teach you how to make them, then you could serve me breakfast in bed."

"Baby, if you move in with me, I'll make you anything you want, anytime you want."

"That's a big promise … don't forget the last 'anything you want' promise you made."

He narrowed his eyes. "Trust me, losing over one hundred thousand dollars of my personal property to a silent auction that raised half that amount of money is not something I will be forgetting very soon. It may take even longer for me to forgive you."

I snickered. "Fine by me since I'm not sorry anyway."

"How would you feel if I sold off your favorite belongings for a charity of my choice?"

I shrugged. "Proud."

"Proud?" He sat his naked ass down on my barstool and watched me mix the batter.

"Absolutely. You can never give too much and in time, it all comes back to you in the most unexpected ways."

"You mean to tell me there's nothing you're overly attached to?"

I looked back over my shoulder and winked while blowing him a kiss. "You."

He rolled his eyes, losing the battle to hide his grin.

"I'm not saying I don't like *things*, I just don't *need* most of them and they don't make me happy."

"What planet are you from?" He shook his head.

"Planet *Awesome*." I turned toward him, fists on my hips, chest puffed out in superhero fashion.

His sexy chuckle reverberated from his chest as he gave me my favorite grin. "That you are, baby, that you are."

WE SPENT THE rest of the day laughing, talking, snacking, and of course, having lots of sex. Quinn spotted my chess set and challenged me to a friendly game. I agreed and gave him a run for his money, but he eventually won. I was a fan of his overinflated ego if I was the one voluntarily feeding it.

We got ready to go to Mac and Evan's by five, even though dinner wasn't until seven. We had to allow plenty of time for shower sex, closet sex, and door sex. We were still piecing our clothes back together as we walked out the back door.

"Car sex?" Quinn asked, wiggling his brows.

I smiled. "You obviously forgot what type of car Karma is."

Just as we rounded the corner of the building Quinn got his first look at Karma. He was speechless and I couldn't blame him. She was a real beaut. Aside from her flashy, cherry red paint, she was tastefully adorned with meaningful bumper stickers such as the religious-symbolled "COEXIST" representing religious freedom, tolerance, and understanding; *The Earth has music for those who listen; Prius Pride; My car sips gas, Yours sucks!; Water-More Precious than Gold; Save the Planet, Kill your Ego; Save the Bees; Mother Nature Has Been Good To You, Return the Favor; Practice Random Acts of Greenness; Hug me I'm a Vegan; Eat Leaf not Beef; Visualize World Peas; and I Think Therefore I'm Vegan.*

"She's amazing isn't she?" I beamed with pride.

Quinn's eyes were the size of saucers. "She's uh ... wow, I mean ... there are no words."

"I know, right? I've had her for over ten years and I still get excited about driving her. She's the only possession I have that might tug at my heartstrings to let go."

Quinn nodded while biting his top lip. He traced his fingers over her rough spots.

"Poor thing, huh? She's not exactly a young girl anymore. She's had her share of unfortunate incidents." I shook my head.

"Yeah, um, *dents* definitely being the operative word," he said quietly, almost to himself.

"I call them bruises and wrinkles. Anyway, we'd better get going."

He walked around to the driver's side and I followed him. "Sorry, babe, I don't let anyone else drive her, not even Mac. I just don't want to see anything happen to her and someone else feel guilty about it."

He laughed but when I didn't join in he stopped. "Oh, you're serious?"

"As a heart attack. Just go get in and enjoy the ride. Besides, you don't know where to go."

After a moment's pause, Quinn got in on the passenger side and we buzzed off to Mac and Evan's.

He didn't say much on the way, but as we walked up to their door, Quinn grabbed me and pulled me in for a knock-me-off-my-feet kiss.

"Whoa, what was that for?" I asked out of breath.

"You. Just when I think you can't be any more amazing, you are. I've fallen so hard for you, my beautiful girl, you completely take my breath away."

"It's Karma. She makes me look better than I am."

He swatted me on the butt and guided me up the front steps. "Karma is … something else, but trust me, you make the car, the car doesn't make you."

"Addy!" Mac yelled, opening the door before we even reached it. She pulled me in for a big hug.

"Quinn, good to see you again." She hugged him too, but I suspected it was to size up the feel of his muscular physique.

"Mackenzie, nice to see you again too. Thank you for the dinner invitation." He could charm the socks off of a rattlesnake, and Mac was no exception to his powerful spell.

"Come on in, it's freezing outside." She closed the door behind us and took our coats.

"Did you have to dig Karma out of a snow drift?" she teased.

I rolled my eyes. "No, she's protected by the carport, you

know that."

"So, Quinn, what do you think of old Karma?" Mac asked, giving him a sly wink.

"If you know what's good for you man, you won't answer that," Evan's voice sounded from the living room as we entered. He walked up to Quinn, shoulders back with big-brother confidence, and gave an easy nod while offering his hand. "Hi, I'm Evan. It's nice to meet you."

Quinn accepted his hand. "Quinn, and the feeling's mutual."

"Have a seat. Dinner's almost done. Can I get you something to drink?"

"Water's fine, thank you," Quinn replied.

Evan looked at me. "Water's fine for me too, Evan, thanks"

"Oh come on, Addy, just one glass of red wine with me. Evan's on his second beer and I shouldn't drink a whole bottle by myself," Mac called from the kitchen.

I glanced at Quinn, knowing how much he hated his alcoholic father. I didn't want to make him uncomfortable.

He smiled and it was carefree, not at all disapproving.

"Just one glass, Evan," I conceded.

"Great, I'll be right back with the drinks after I see if Mac needs anything in the kitchen."

"You can drink without my permission," Quinn whispered when Evan left the room.

I don't know why it surprised me that he'd read my body language so accurately. "I know, I just don't want to make you uncomfortable."

"Addy, I'm not an alcoholic. It's just a choice I've made, okay?" He kissed my temple, pulling me into him.

I hugged him back. "I love you, *Quinny.*"

He grabbed my sides and tickled me until I couldn't hold it in any longer. Mac and Evan walked in just as I was doubled over laughing and squealing.

"Do you two need a minute?" Mac asked, raising her eyebrows.

Quinn sat back with one arm on the couch behind me and one ankle resting on the opposite knee looking all "Cool Joe." I, on the other hand, felt the heat of my blush burning my cheeks with disheveled hair sticking to my face. As I straightened out my sweater, I looked at Mac and Evan. "We're fine. Quinn's just trying to deal out some payback."

"Good luck with that, Quinn. Don't let Addy fool you. She's very competitive," Mac shared as she sat down next to Evan.

"Well, then she might have a bruised ego from the chess game I beat her at earlier," Quinn quipped with a smirk.

The room fell silent as Evan and Mac gave each other confused looks and then shared the same expression with me and then Quinn.

"What?" Quinn questioned.

I avoided eye contact with him and tried to give Mac and Evan my best warning glare without Quinn seeing me. My warning went unnoticed, or most likely unheeded, by both Mac and Evan.

Mac cleared her throat. "I hate to be the one to burst your bubble, Quinn, but you didn't beat Addy at chess. She let you win."

"What? No way, we played for almost two hours and it was close but I simply was the better player in the end. I've played for years and I would know if someone was *letting* me win."

His ego was on the defensive and I wished they would just

let it go, but I knew better.

Evan tried to help Quinn understand. "Have you heard of Bobby Fisher?"

"Sure, why?"

Quinn studied Mac and Evan's tight-smiled expressions, then looked at me. I glanced up at him with a wrinkle-faced, contrite expression.

"What are you? Some sort of chess grandmaster or world champion?" Quinn's brow knitted together as he tilted his head to the side and scratched his stubbly jaw.

"No, nothing like that. It's more like I see the board differently than most people do, that's all."

"She's so downplaying this, Quinn, but I know Addy hates being the center of attention so we'll just drop it. Besides, dinner is ready," Mac declared, standing and walking to the kitchen with Evan in tow.

As I started to stand, Quinn pulled me back down, his lips next to my ear. "The only thing I despise worse than being duped is being embarrassed in front of your friends. Don't be surprised if when we get back to your place I tie you to the bed and don't let you orgasm for hours." He sounded angry.

I looked at him with a questioning grin. "Really? That's the card you want to play? Unless an ex-boyfriend shows up for dinner and fondles me in front of everyone while you have to sit there feeling humiliated, then I'm pretty sure I'm not the one who will be bound and tortured later. Okay, pumpkin?" I plastered on a fake smile and strutted my way to the dining room.

Quinn soon followed after he scooped his jaw off the floor and sent out a search party to look for his castrated man parts.

Dinner went well. Neither Quinn nor I appeared to hold a

grudge and conversation was relaxed and easy. It saddened me to think about living away from Mac and Evan. I wondered if Quinn would ever have considered moving to Chicago, since his sister lived there and he frequented it on business.

"Addy tells me you two would like to move back to Chicago someday," Quinn said while taking a bite of cake.

"Yes, we would. I'm hoping to take a position at Mac's father's law firm and Mac would like to be closer to her family when we decide to start one of our own," Evan responded, giving Mac a sexy smile and wink.

"Do you have any siblings?" Quinn questioned, wiping his mouth with the corner of his napkin while he looked at Mac.

Their eyes shot in my direction but I kept a stoic face.

"Uh, I did, a brother, but he died years ago," Mac said.

"Sorry to hear that. Were you close in age?"

"He was three years older."

The breath in my lungs remained idle as I fought to keep my face indiscernible, but then Quinn placed his hand on my leg and I knew he felt my tension.

"You okay, baby?" he mouthed.

Letting out a deep sigh, I nodded and laced my fingers with his on my leg.

"Well, enough about us. How long are you staying in Milwaukee, Quinn?" Mac diverted.

"Actually, I leave early in the morning. I have to be back in Chicago by ten."

"Are you going too, Addy?" Evan asked, because honestly the guy was in the dark when it came to my relationship with Quinn.

Quinn looked at me with sanguine eyes as if I had some good news to share.

"No, Evan, I'm not. But maybe we'll create our own Hollywood love story and meet up at the top of the Empire State Building on Valentine's Day."

Everyone laughed, except Quinn. The rest of the evening was a little more somber. Quinn did his best to seem engaged in our conversation, but his smile failed to meet his eyes.

"Mac, Evan, dinner was wonderful and we've had a great time but I think Quinn could use some sleep before his early morning flight."

"Yes, you're right, and it was lovely. Thank you for your wonderful hospitality, and I hope you both make it out to New York soon so I can return the favor," Quinn offered.

"We're going to hold you to that," Mac insisted.

After hugs all around and bundling up, we walked arm-in-arm through the snow to Karma. Quinn used my ice scraper and brush to clean her off.

"Be careful with her, babe, she already has one crack in the windshield."

"Her windshield is the least of my worries. Have you looked at the street?"

Their driveway was protected from the blowing snow by trees and shrubs on both sides, but the street looked like a whole other beast. I noticed Quinn was on his phone but only briefly.

"Who'd you call?"

He finished brushing off the back window. "Elves."

"Why?" I knew why but I was still offended he didn't have faith in Karma.

He tossed the scraper on the floor in the backseat and then jumped in and shut the door. We were in a cloud of breath vapor as she worked hard to warm up.

Quinn rubbed his ungloved hands together and blew into them. "Just in case Karma proves to be the warm weather diva I suspect her to be."

"Buckle up, she's fine." The confidence in my words waivered, but the truth was I rarely took her out in the snow.

I put her in reverse and backed down the driveway, but by the time I reached the street, the plowed snow at the end of their drive was a couple feet deep. I stopped before I got stuck.

"Listen here, Cohen, not one word, do you understand me? I don't want to get her stuck so I'll get her tomorrow. Evan will drive us home in his Sequoia."

Quinn bit his lips together and covered his mouth with one hand, no doubt hiding his stupid grin. "Not necessary, our ride is here."

I looked in the rear view mirror and spotted a familiar white Range Rover parked along the street. With a defeated sigh, I pulled up the driveway closer to their garage. His smug smirk taunted me as we walked to the snow-worthy vehicle so I tried to push him down in the snow. He didn't so much as budge. Instead he threw me over his shoulder and carried me to the Range Rover. Opening the back door, he tossed me inside before sliding in next to me.

"Jeez, Tarzan, must you manhandle me all the time?"

He grinned while reaching around to buckle me in like a child.

"Evening, Mr. Cohen and Miss Brecken."

"Eddie," Quinn replied.

"Hey, Eddie, nice to see you again."

"You as well."

As Eddie drove toward my loft, Quinn nuzzled my neck. The closer we got the more intense he became. I wasn't up for putting on a show for Eddie, but Quinn didn't seem to care as he moved my hand between his legs and rubbed it over his erection. He let out a soft groan.

"Quinn, stop," I whispered, pulling my hand away.

"I can't, baby." He tried to unbutton my coat but I batted his hand away.

Luckily the drive was short and before Quinn made it to second base, Eddie stopped.

"Have a pleasant evening," Eddie called out.

Quinn, in his horny rudeness, just hopped out, pulling me behind him. I barely got the words "Thanks" and "Goodbye" out before the door shut and I was thrown over his shoulder and hauled up the stairs. He had my complex security code entered in record time, and without even stopping to turn on the lights, he proceeded to my bedroom and tossed me on my bed.

"How chivalrous of you," I laughed.

He already had his coat, shoes, socks, and shirt ripped off, and his jerky hands fought to unfasten his pants. "Shut up and take everything off, now!" His voice was commanding but his hooded eyes and stone face told me his control teetered on empty. It wasn't going to be gentle.

I managed to get my coat and boots off before he was on top of me, unbuttoning my jeans, then pulling them down and tossing them aside while I pulled my sweater over my head. His hands were all over me, rubbing and squeezing, his wet mouth sucking my skin so hard I feared what I'd look like in the morning. He unfastened my bra and just about ripped the strap off pulling it from my arms. His mouth attacked my breasts and it was ridiculously intense. He took me to the fine line between pleasure and pain.

"Ah, God!" I moaned. He teethed my nipple so hard I grimaced, then he soothed his tongue around it.

He moved down between my legs and slipped his fingers under the waist of my panties and yanked them down, leaving them in shreds. His hands gripped the inside of my knees and opened me up. His mouth covered my sex and his greedy tongue stroked me. He didn't stay there long; I knew he wouldn't. His need to be buried in me was too great. Every move he made with his mouth was followed by a hungry moan. I couldn't deny him anything.

We had sex, but it was no longer just sex. With every need there was an emotion and every emotion expressed a need. I was sexy for him. I was sexy because of him. And the love? It became exhilarating, all-consuming, just … everything.

Collapsed on his chest, we continued to kiss until I slid off him. He spooned me to his strong body.

"Why were you so quiet after dinner?" I asked.

He brushed a kiss on my shoulder then rested his chin on it. "I knew you weren't coming back to New York with me tomorrow, but hearing you say it and then joking about meeting on Valentine's Day, which is a month away, well … it bothered me. It took me thirty four years to find something—someone—I can't live without, and seeing you a couple of times a month or less isn't going to work for me."

"I know," I whispered. "We'll figure this out, I promise."

CHAPTER FIFTEEN

"Wealth consists not in having possessions, but in
having few wants."

~Epictetus

QUINN FLEW OUT early the next morning, leaving the memory of his goodbye on my lips. To keep from missing him, I followed my morning routine: exercise, meditation, shower, breakfast, and finally the café. I let Jake decide the menus and order supplies. Mac and I went to the market but Jake insisted he could take over that responsibility too. He seemed fine around me, but I was still a little uncomfortable after our awkward exchange. A year earlier, I might have jumped at the chance to have a casual relationship with Jake.

I liked his bad boy persona that he put on for his fighting. I loved his tattoos too. He'd caught me starting at them on more than one occasion. Quinn changed everything; all I wanted from Jake was his friendship and his promise to take care of the business I had built.

Within days, "Quinn brain" started to consume me. Every day without him felt empty. I sifted through my belongings, organizing and reorganizing.

On Sundays, Mac and I saw almost every movie that came out in the theaters while Evan watched football. I texted, phoned, or FaceTimed Quinn everyday. Long work hours consumed his days, which I assumed was to make up for the time he'd devoted to me when I was in New York. He traveled on a weekly basis and always offering to pick me up in his private jet to go with him. I wanted to say yes, but I knew it would be short-lived and we'd be back to our long distance relationship.

After a full month without him, I cracked. My ego was the only thing keeping me in Milwaukee.

Lonely sucked.

Misery suffocated.

I called Mac. She squealed, we both cried, and my decision was confirmed. The moving company was scheduled to come on Thursday morning. I spent all day Tuesday and Wednesday packing. Mac let the movers in because I had Karma packed and ready to go by 4:00 a.m. and they weren't expected until ten o'clock that morning. With minimal stops, I anticipated arriving at Quinn's by eight or so that night. He texted me numerous times that day so I used my short pit stops to text him back. It was so hard not telling him my plans, but I was over-the-top excited about surprising him.

When I arrived at Quinn's it was almost 8:30 p.m. We usually talked around nine. I parked Karma a block from his building. As I got out of my car I dialed him up.

"Hey, beautiful, how was your day?" His voice soothed me.

"Long. I missed you."

"Mmm, I can relate."

"Are you home or out and about tonight?" I often asked him that so I knew it wouldn't make him suspicious.

"Home. I just got back from dinner with Zach."

"Ah, yes, I can't wait to meet him. I'm sure your college roomy has some pretty good dirt on you."

"Guy code. He'll never talk."

I stopped at his door. Adrenaline pumped through my veins. "So ... what are you wearing?" I asked in my sexiest voice.

"Oh, baby, I like where you're going with this. What do you want me to be wearing?" His voice deepened.

"Pants, bare feet, no shirt, messy hair."

"Already have bare feet ... Now I've lost my shirt and you know my hair is always messy."

"Did you shave this morning?"

"Not since yesterday. Does my baby like her man rugged?"

"Mmm, makes me want to slide my hand between my legs and touch myself," I breathed out.

"Fuck, baby, I'm so hard." His deep voice vibrated from his chest.

I had him just where I wanted him so I knocked at the door, but put my hand over the peep hole.

"What the—" Quinn threw out a long line of expletives. "Just a minute, baby, somebody's at my door and whoever it is will get their ass beaten."

A few seconds later he swung open the door almost sending it through the wall.

My eyes grew with appreciation. Quinn was indeed only wearing a pair of pants, I wanted to take in the surprise I knew was all over his face, but I had trouble peeling my eyes from his firm, sculpted chest.

"Hey, honey, I'm home. Miss me?"

In a sudden shocking move, Quinn shut the door on me.

What. The. Hell?

My phone chimed; it was a text from him.

Sorry, baby, this long distance phone sex thing isn't

working out for me. I'm leaving you for the most beautiful woman in the world, who just showed up at my door.

He opened the door again and swept me into his arms, taking me into his condo and shutting the door behind us. He kissed me with such fervor and passion I saw stars.

"You said home. Please tell me there's a moving truck outside."

I shook my head. His smile faded.

"Not until tomorrow." I chuckled.

"Why didn't you tell me? I would have arranged everything," he murmured into my neck as his tongue traced a path to my ear.

"And miss your reaction? Not a chance. Besides, I'm more resourceful than you give me credit for."

"You should have at least let me pick you up from the airport."

"Once again, not a surprise and I didn't fly. I drove Karma."

He halted his sensual quest over my body. "You drove that car here?"

"Not *that car,* Karma, and I wasn't going to leave her behind. If I'm going to be living here you should make sure she has a space in the underground parking garage. I can't leave her parked on the street. Someone might take her."

"Take Karma, are you serious?" He raised an eyebrow.

"Yes, I'm serious!"

"What, like a hippy from the hood?" He laughed as he set me on my feet.

"You did *not* just say that!" I warned. "Here..." I handed him my keys "...she's just a block north. Park her between your Range Rover and Lamborghini. Bring up the rest of my stuff and don't ding her doors getting in and out. I'll be upstairs making myself comfortable in the *guest* room until you're ready to apologize to me for your brash attitude towards Karma."

After three steps up I turned around to witness Quinn looking at me like I'd just grown another head. "Get going, she's not going to park herself. This may be your one chance to drive her so don't blow it."

By the time Quinn got done unloading my stuff, I was in the shower. I felt his hands snake around me cupping my breasts, his erection pressed to my back. He pulled my hair away from my neck and pressed his lips to my wet skin.

"Did you make nice with Karma?"

"Mmm hmm," he mumbled.

I reached behind us and dug my fingers into his glutes. His breath caught as he rubbed his hard length against my back while moving one of his hands down to cup my sex.

"Now I'm ready to make nice with you."

I AWOKE FRIDAY morning alone in the middle of Quinn's bed. I peeked over at the clock on the nightstand: 8:15 a.m. Next to the clock was a note.

Killed me to leave you naked in "our" bed this morning.

Should be home by 4:00. Call me if you decide to venture out.

Dinner reservations at 7:00. Qx

The moving company was scheduled to arrive around noon. I had a fair amount of my stuff sent to storage. Quinn's condo was huge, but it was also fully furnished. It wasn't my intention to think of us as temporary, but I honestly didn't see myself living in New York forever. However, this wasn't a conversation I was going to jump into right away. I wanted every moment with Quinn to be like the first but lived like the last.

I paused at the bathroom threshold. Everything from my toiletry bag was unpacked and given its own spot. One slow step at a time I shuffled across the tile to Quinn's gigantic walk-in closet. The last time I saw it, every shelf and every hanger was occupied.

Elves. The guy really did have elves.

The entire right side of the closet was empty with the exception of the few clothes I'd brought with me, hanging all by their lonesome. I eased open the white drawers below the hanging area. They were empty, too, with the exception of a few yoga outfits and my undergarments sorted out in a divided drawer.

After getting dressed in my comfy yoga clothes and separating my hair into pigtails, I headed downstairs for breakfast. Two missed calls from Mac flashed on the screen when I turned on my phone, followed by texts from Quinn.

Quinn: *Making yourself at home?*

If you get bored I have a break from 1:30 to 2:15.

My office sofa would love to meet you ... naked.

Me: *Looks like the elves already made me at home B4 I woke.*

Sofa will have to wait. I'll be busy unpacking after the moving truck arrives.

Missed you this morning, how early do you start work?

Quinn: *Not until 8, but I have to devote a little time to keeping up my Latin god appearance.*

Me: *How much is a 'little' time?*

Quinn: *Two hours, five days a week.*
However, the naked goddess next to me every morning could change that.

Me: *Hmm, I bet I could think of a good morning workout for both of us.*

Quinn: *Meeting with wealthy business men from China in ten, thanks for the boner.*

Me: *Hope it's to discuss fair trade practices.*

Quinn: *Pleading the fifth.*

The movers showed up on time and had everything unloaded in less than thirty minutes. I spent the rest of the afternoon unpacking and becoming more familiar with "our" place. True to his word, Quinn arrived home by four o'clock while I reorganized some things in the kitchen to my liking. He walked through the door wearing a charcoal grey pin striped three piece suit. All I could do was stare.

"Hey, beautiful, cat got your tongue?" He hung up his wool coat and slowly shrugged off his suit jacket, revealing his broad, firm shoulder muscles, barely contained by his crisp, white shirt.

I gawked.

He smirked.

My lungs drew in a desperate breath as he strolled into the kitchen with a cocksure confidence that I constantly fed. He grabbed my waist and lifted me onto the counter.

"How was your day?" I tried to sound interested as I worked his tie loose.

"Boring." He ran his hands up my thighs gripping my butt and pulling me to the edge of the counter. I wrapped my legs around his waist just as my phone rang. He kissed my neck. "Ignore it."

"It might be Mac. Give me just a minute."

Quinn grumbled but lifted me off the counter. "Fine, I'll be in my office."

I grabbed my phone. "Hey, Mac."

"Hey yourself. It's been one day and you've already forgotten about me?" she whined.

"Not hardly. I've been trying to get my stuff unpacked quickly so Quinn doesn't think he's been invaded upon. He's a bit of a neat freak, and I think piles of boxes could send him over the edge."

"Well, at least I know Karma got you there okay."

"I never doubted her. She's nestled in the secure, temperature-controlled parking garage between Quinn's Lamborghini and Range Rover."

She exploded into a fit of laughter. "I'd love a picture of that! The caption would say, 'completely pussy whipped.'"

"Don't be so dramatic. He loves me, that's all."

"I'm sure he does, but I guarantee you're going to have to put out like you've never done before if Karma so much as brushes his Lamborghini. I'm talking some serious dick sucking and even … *swallowing.*"

"Eew, Mac, nice mouth. I'm not going to touch his precious car, and even if a small mishap takes place, I will not suck his cock as an apology."

Before I could say anymore, I received a text from Quinn.

Get in here, NOW!

"Mac, I'll call you tomorrow. I'm being beckoned by my sex god."

"Okay, glad you're in New York safe, even if I miss you like crazy already."

"Me too. We'll talk soon. Bye."

"Bye, sweetie."

Quinn must have worked himself into a blue-balled emergency. I casually padded down the hall to his office. The first thing I noticed was one of my boxes that I had set on his desk earlier and forgotten to unpack. He held some papers in his hand and the look on his face was an odd mix of shock and anger.

"What the hell is this, Addy?"

"What is what? Is that mine? Are you going through my stuff?" I moved closer to him.

"I was going to put your stuff in some of my empty drawers and file cabinets, but then this caught my eye."

I took the papers from him. They were financial statements from my bank and various investment firms. "So?" I shrugged, shoving them back in the box and pushing the lid on it.

"So? Are you fucking kidding me? Addy, according to those papers and some quick figuring in my head, you're worth over a *billion* dollars."

I shrugged again. "It's possible. I don't really keep track because it doesn't matter."

"Well it sure as hell matters to me!" he yelled.

My eyes narrowed. Why would my financial portfolio would matter to someone like Quinn?

"Quinn I … I don't understand?"

"Well, that makes two of us, because I don't understand

why you would lie to me about this." His anger had its own relentless stamina.

"I didn't lie, we just never talked about it."

"So if I was married, but we just never talked about it, you wouldn't be upset, right?" His voice dripped with sarcasm.

"Uh, not really the same thing but … are you upset because you think I lied to you or because I have my own money?"

He released an exasperated sigh as he ran his hands through his hair. "Why didn't you just tell me? It's not like I tried to keep my wealth a secret from you."

"Oh my God! Are you kidding me? Everything about you reeks of wealth. I don't know if you could hide it if you tried. I've never cared about your money and it's not because I don't need your money, it's because … It. Really. Doesn't. Matter. To. Me. You've seen the way I live. The only part of my life that is extravagant is my sailboat, and it sure didn't take you long to sniff out that part of my life. Speaking of that, would you like to tell me why you played twenty questions about it with me when you knew it was mine anyway?"

He spun his chair around to look out the window so his back was to me. "It wasn't exactly a well-kept secret, and everybody talks for the right price. I just wanted you to open up to me about your past a little more. I wasn't trying to push you, but I thought if I brought it up you'd trust me enough to share at least that much with me."

Rubbing my hands over my face, I tried to rationally cope with my insecurities. My past would always haunt my future.

"You know my past is not an open book. I don't know if it ever will be. When I told you about my yacht, I also told you I came from an affluent family. All that money has come into my life from tragic events. The people I've loved most in my life have all died and now I have more money than any one person should ever have—all because they died."

The burning pain seared through my body. I hated thinking about it. I hated talking about it. But I genuinely hated the fucking sympathy that came with my story. Emotions tore through me. Anger, rage, heartache, guilt—the toxic mix boiled over as I yelled out in broken sobs.

"All you see is the fucking money, the bottom dollar, the yacht, the house, the car, the private jet, the fucking alligator skin crap, the social status. I don't give a shit about any of that! Don't you think I would give it all up and live in a box to have even just one of them back in my life? Just..." my voice dropped to a whisper "...one."

He didn't look at me.

How could he not look at me?

How could he not feel my pain?

How could I be so wrong about him?

I turned and walked out of his office with a heavy heart and tears streaming down my face. Before my next breath, Quinn's arms wrapped around my waist. A sob ripped from my chest. The memories. They hurt so bad.

"Shh, I'm sorry, baby," he whispered behind my ear. "I didn't mean to open old wounds. I hate hurting you ... I'm just stupid. The money doesn't matter. I wanted it to matter to you so I wouldn't feel like such a materialistic fuck-up. I don't deserve you. You are a better person than I could ever be in a thousand lifetimes. The more I love you, the more I think you deserve better." He turned me around and kissed away my tears.

This man had taken a piece of me that I couldn't live without. Our love felt beautiful, vital, and sometimes toxic.

I looked up at Quinn through my tear drenched lashes. "There is no one better. I know you don't see it, but you are the *one*. If given a thousand lifetimes, I would choose you every time."

"MRS. TOWNSEND, YOU *are our most important client and if there is anything you need or changes you'd like to make with your financial portfolio please let us know."*

"Miss Brecken."

"Excuse me, ma'am?"

"Miss Brecken. My name is Miss Adler Sage Brecken."

"Uh … okay, yes, of course. As I was saying, let us know if you need anything. I'm sure you're aware you will never want for anything, and you have my personal guarantee that everything that belonged to your parents will be taken care of according to their wishes."

"I don't want it, any of it."

"Mrs. Towns—Ms. Brecken, I understand all of this is a lot to take in, and you are probably still grieving, just know that I'll be here if or when you need anything."

"ADDY? HELLO, CALLING Adler Brecken," Quinn called from the other side of the table.

I had been in New York living with Quinn for two weeks. The cold weather discouraged me from doing much exploring, so I spent most of my time cooking, reading, and looking for my "New York" calling. Just because I didn't have to work for money didn't mean I could hang around all day by myself waiting for Quinn to come home, even if he was completely worth the wait.

I was finally getting to meet Quinn's best friend Zach and his girlfriend. Quinn's schedule had been crazy, but we managed to find a night that we were all available to meet for dinner.

"Sorry, babe, what were you saying?"

"I said Zach and his girlfriend should be here soon. I think you're going to like them a lot."

I laughed. "I'm sure I will, but I'm curious as to why you think so?"

"Zach's like me, a venture capitalist and adrenaline junkie, just not as ruggedly handsome, but Eden is a lawyer and she works under the clinical professor of environmental law at Columbia University. Another smart tree hugger." Quinn grinned as he sipped his water.

"It would be advantageous of you to recognize the words smart and tree hugger as synonymous." I gave him a wink and cheeky smile.

"Here they come." Quinn stood as his friends approached, then pulled my chair out to help me up as well.

Zach was tall, with short, ash blond hair that was spiked in the front. His build resembled Quinn's. The tail of a serpent tattoo met the nape of his neck. Ice blue eyes accompanied a bright smile. If I hadn't already been sitting there with the sexiest man alive, Zach would have easily caught my eye.

Eden looked like a model, Quinn's type—tall, extremely thin, long, straight black hair with blunt cut bangs, full glossy lips, and dark brown eyes framed in even darker eyeliner and thick mascara. Her skin was flawless and sun kissed.

Quinn greeted Zach with a quick man-hug ritual, consisting of a complicated handshake with a one-handed pat on the back, and a shoulder-chest bump. "Hey, man, good to see you."

"You too. It's been a couple of weeks. I assume this lovely lady is the reason?"

Quinn's smile overtook his face when he looked at me. He then placed his hand in the middle of Eden's back and gave her a chaste kiss on the cheek. "Eden, looking lovely as always."

"Thank you." She blushed.

Hmm, this beautiful woman is very shy, or is it just in the presence of my Latin sex god?

Quinn wrapped his arm around me, placing his hand almost indecently low on my back. It was a very possessive gesture, but given the non-threatening company whose presence we were in, I felt flattered. "This is Adler Brecken, love of my life."

I glanced up at him in shock. Friend, girlfriend, significant other, sex partner ... but love of his life? He beamed with something more than pride.

Happiness?

In that moment I gave him yet another piece of myself I couldn't live without.

"Addy, this is my crazy but awesome best friend, Zach, who had better remember all the rules of guy code tonight if he doesn't want his ass kicked later." They exchanged playful but challenging looks.

"And this is his girlfriend, Eden."

Zach gave me a friendly but awkward hug since Quinn refused to release me. "Addy, nice to meet you. Quinn has been singing your praises like a sappy, lovesick schmuck for months."

I laughed, the thought so endearing. I offered my hand to

Eden. "Nice to meet you, Eden."

She nodded and smiled, averting her gaze to the ground. The girl was stunning, and yet I don't know if she knew it. I guessed her age to be mid-twenties.

We ordered hors d'oeuvres and I indulged in a glass of wine when Zach and Eden ordered a beer and a martini.

"So, Addy, Quinn tells me you have, and I quote, 'the brains of Einstein and the wealth of Oprah.'" Zach grinned, ignoring Quinn's dagger-shooting glare.

"Did he?" Glancing at Quinn, I laughed. So much for guy code. "Well, I wouldn't say Einstein; I'd prefer someone more intelligent but not as recognizable, such as Nikola Tesla." Zach caught my humor and raised his glass at me.

"You're good, Addy. Quinn needs a quick wit like you. That is if he can get over the fact that you're worth more than he is."

Quinn cleared his throat, shifting in his chair. I don't know why it hadn't occurred to me that Quinn could feel intimidated or maybe inferior at the thought of me having more money than him. I wasn't sure how much money Quinn had and I didn't care. He knew that.

"Eden, Quinn tells me you have a degree in environmental law. What's your focus going to be?" I refused to go down the "make Quinn uncomfortable road" with Zach any longer.

Eden sipped her martini. "Um, well, I'm not sure yet, but I'm leaning toward renewable energy practice."

"Great area. The renewable energy policy development is constantly changing with regard to the expanding field of clean technologies," I offered back.

"Well, my current boss thinks I'd be well suited for that type of work and the job opportunities are vast." She smiled like her whole personality ignited. All she needed was the opportunity to shine.

"Smart girls are fucking hot." Zach raised his fist and Quinn gave him knuckles; they wore shit-eating grins.

I excused myself to use the ladies' room. It wasn't an original idea because there was a line backed up to the edge of the bar. I tried to look casual as I stood with my back to two guys sitting at the bar. The more casual restaurant was my suggestion. My growing need to relieve my bladder made me regret it. There was never a line for the restrooms at the fancy places Quinn liked to go. A lady coming out bumped me, causing me to step back into one of the guys at the bar.

"Oh, excuse me, I'm very sorry." I blushed, embarrassed to have almost landed in his lap.

He grabbed my waist to steady me but then didn't let go. "Well, well, what do we have here? If you wanted my attention all you had to do was ask."

A putrid mix of beer and cigarettes wafted from the man's mouth, turning my stomach. Everything about him was repulsive: a large protruding gut, dirty brown hair pulled back into a pony tail, and a greasy face riddled with acne scars. He moved one of his hands lower and grabbed my ass as his friend laughed.

I jumped struggling to get away. "Let go of me, asshole!" I said with a raised voice just short of a yell. It was enough to get the bartender's attention.

"Hands off or you're out of here," the bartender warned with a deep voice. His large tattooed body, shaved head, and pierced lip were enough to intimidate anyone.

He removed his hands and held them in the air. "Hey, sorry, she was the one coming on to me."

I stepped away as he dragged his eyes up and down my body. A creepy shiver raced through me. I opted to hold my bladder and just head back to the table.

When I arrived Quinn gave me a questioning look. "What's wrong? What happened?"

I forced a smile just as Zach and Eden turned in shared concern. "Nothing, just a couple of drunks at the bar trying to razz the ladies waiting in the bathroom line. The bartender took care of them. No need to worry."

Quinn's jaw clenched and I could see his muscles twitching. "Are you sure?"

"I'm sure." I stared at my veggie penne that the waiter placed in front of me.

"Is there anything else I can get anyone?" the waiter asked.

Quinn looked around then answered, "We're fine, thank you."

We all fell into a more relaxed mood over the next hour. Quinn and Zach talked business for a while but then started in on stories of snowboarding, climbing, skydiving, race cars, and other extreme sports. Eden asked me about my past, college, jobs, and my vegan lifestyle. I had developed a routine response over the years to those questions and nobody had ever thought much of my vague answers. Deception had started to feel like reality some days as I made my past sound as normal as most people my age.

I went to college, worked, enjoyed various hobbies, and had certain things I was very passionate about. I never freely offered information about my family, but if asked I went right for the immediate silencer, which was, "I'm an only child and my parents are dead." It was the guaranteed end to any conversation.

"Are we ready to go?" I was ready to get the hell out of there the moment the check was paid.

Quinn held my coat as I slipped my arms into it. Eden and I waited on the sidewalk while our men retrieved the cars. Zach arrived first and I said my goodbyes to them. As they drove off I hugged my arms around myself to keep warm. Stealing my breath, a set of arms pulled me backward.

"Hey, you little tease, want a ride." It was the drunk from the bar.

I twisted, struggling to get free of him. "Let. Me. GO!" I yelled, this time attracting attention, but oddly enough no one jumped to my rescue.

What was wrong with people?

Panic set in, my stomach in my throat. I yelled again. Before I could make sense of what happened, his hold on me vanished. The drunk asshole was lying flat on the ground with a bloody face and his body curled into a ball. Quinn stood over him, hands fisted, chest heaving.

He spoke with an unrecognizable menacing voice. "You're lucky we have an audience because if we didn't, I'd beat you within a breath of your miserable fucking life."

Quinn pulled me to him and ushered me into the Range Rover. He cupped my face in his hands. "Are you okay?" His voice was still strained with anger.

Still shaking, I nodded. "I'm f-f-f-fine."

He shut my door. I couldn't tear my eyes from the group of people gawking between me and the drunk on the ground. We didn't say much on the way home. Quinn's white knuckles clenched around the steering wheel and stone-set jaw said it all.

What frightened me the most was my reaction to the situation. After fate stepped in years ago and shattered my heart, soul, and whole existence, I stopped fearing death. Hell, I all but begged it to come get me.

But when that asshole grabbed me outside the restaurant I was frightened because for the first time in a long time, I wanted to live. I wanted to live for Quinn.

The quiet ride home lulled me to sleep. The next thing I knew, I was enveloped in Quinn's arms. He carried me to the bedroom, laid me down on the bed, and eased his body next to mine. I turned to face him and ran my palms over his beautiful, stubbled chin and cheeks.

"My hero."

He closed his eyes and took in a deep breath. "It hurts to love you so fucking much. If I would have shown up a few seconds later—"

"Shh ..." I pressed my lips to his.

He didn't kiss me back at first. Then I bit his lower lip and sucked it into my mouth. He moaned and opened up to me. Our tongues explored each other until I pulled back. Taking my time, I unbuttoned his white shirt. After the last button was released, I nudged him and he rolled to his back. His eyes followed me, dark and hungry. I brushed my lips all over his chest, tracing every detailed muscle with my tongue. His shallow breath hitched as I dipped my tongue under the waistband of his jeans.

I grinned as his abs quivered from my fingers unbuttoning his jeans. Many unspoken emotions passed between us: desire, need, gratitude, and love. Always love.

Quinn loved me with a look. I felt everything that words couldn't say as I removed his clothes and then mine.

"I love you," I whispered.

He sat up and pulled me to him, straddling his legs. My

hands pressed to his cheeks. "I do, I love you. I now understand why my heart is still beating."

His brows tensed I didn't want his sympathy. That's not why I said it. They were just thoughts. The truth. Until I heard my own voice, I didn't realize I'd said them aloud. His love was all I wanted.

Rising to my knees again, I kissed him like my salvation. As he entered me, I thanked God for him. It had been many years since I'd consciously acknowledged a higher power with an actual name.

I wanted to live. I wanted to live for Quinn.

Our hips started to move as we looked deep into each other's eyes, closing them only for slow, heavy blinks. We made love and it was intimate and emotional.

It was personal.

It was everything.

Our mouths connected and moved in perfect harmony with our hips. I loved the sensuality of his body melding to mine. He found his release first but continued to move inside of me while he moved his hand to massage my swollen clit, pulling me over the edge to meet him. Our foreheads connected. We shared matching smiles.

"You were made ... just for me," he declared between ragged breaths.

My response was immediate, simple, and certain. "Yes."

CHAPTER SIXTEEN

"One should always be drunk. That's all that
matters ... But with what? With wine, with poetry, or
with virtue, as you choose. But get drunk."

~Charles Baudelaire

THE NEXT FEW months defined bliss. I volunteered at several animal shelters, the culinary school, local soup kitchens, and my favorite: Quinn's office. His personal assistant requested a short leave of absence to deal with some family matters so he asked me to *assist* him.

I assisted him on that leather sofa in his office in more ways than seemed possible. I assisted him on his desk, his chair, the door to his office, his private bathroom counter, the large windows overlooking the city, and the elevator in his building. In my free time I did take some calls and schedule a few appointments. I even accompanied him on several business trips, which added the mile high club to my resumé.

We made three weekend getaways with Zach and Eden snowboarding and skiing. Quinn and Zach were content staying on the slopes from sunrise to sunset. However, by early afternoon, Eden and I found drinking wine by the roaring fire in the lodge was the best way to warm our chilled bodies. Massages, manicures, and pedicures also helped pass time while the "boys" played.

In mid-March we went to Chicago for a meeting. Quinn suggested we stay with his sister, but I wasn't thrilled about that idea. Alexis was still close friends with Olivia, and although she swore to Quinn that she was fine with our relationship, I always sensed otherwise when we were with her.

A position for Evan opened up at Richard's law firm in late February. My best friend and her husband wasted no time packing up and moving back to Chicago. They bought a beautiful house about a mile from the marina where my parents had surprised me with The Sage. When Mac and Evan decided to move back to Chicago I had The Sage transported back as well.

"Maybe we could stay with Mac and Evan," I suggested on the short flight to Chicago.

"Alexis thinks we're staying with her, and it's just for one night, so what's the big deal?"

I pinched my lips together and lifted my shoulders. "I don't think Alexis likes me and I am a little uncomfortable around her."

"Nonsense. You know she's fine with us being together."

I nodded slowly. "Maybe I could stay with Mac and you could stay with your sister."

"What? That's ridiculous. Why would we not stay together? It would look like we're fighting or something, and besides, I've been spoiled having you with me."

"You said it yourself, it's just one night. I haven't seen Mac's place since I helped them move."

"Well, you can go see them during the day then you can get your ass back to my sister's for dinner and ..." Sitting opposite of me, he leaned forward and moved his hand up my leg, eyes hooded.

"We're not screwing around at your sister's house." I pushed him away.

"Why not?" He jerked his head back.

"Because her guest room is right next to the kids' rooms and neither one of us is very quiet. However, Mac and Evan don't have kids yet and their guest room is on the other side of the house from the master bedroom." I raised my eyebrows hoping he would be persuaded.

"You drive a hard bargain, Miss Brecken."

"If we stay at Mac's, I'll be driving your hard bargain." I slipped my shoe off and moved my foot between his legs curling my toes around his bulge.

He glanced at his watch. "Call her and tell her we'll be there within the hour."

"Thank you, babe." I went to remove my foot but he grabbed it and held it next to his firm erection.

"We don't start our descent for about twenty minutes, and I think you know actions speak louder than words, baby. So just how much do you really thank me?"

Quinn got a thorough thanking before we landed; so much that he was in need of a shower but he opted for a quick wash up in the bathroom and a change of clothes before Eddie took us to Mac and Evan's.

"I love the way you negotiate." He smiled while texting his sister about our change of plans.

"I learned from the master." I leaned in and kissed his neck. "What time is your meeting this afternoon?"

"Three. I should be done by five, so check with Mac and Evan and decide where you want to go for dinner."

"Actually, Mac and Evan already made plans to go to Richard and Gwen's for dinner. I told them not to cancel on our behalf, so it will just be the two of us. Besides, there's something I want to discuss with you."

He narrowed his eyes. "Is something wrong?"

"Nope, I just have an idea I want to run by you."

"What is it?"

"Not here. We'll be there soon and I don't want to be interrupted."

He still held his concerned look but finally nodded and went back to messing with his phone.

When we arrived at Mac and Evan's, Mac gave us a quick tour before Quinn had to head off to his meeting.

Evan was still at work so we had some girl time on her three season porch with hot tea.

"Have you talked to Quinn about moving yet?" Mac sipped her tea.

"Not yet, that's what my plan is tonight. I thought being in the city might make it more imaginable and hopefully realistic."

"What are you going to do if he flat out says no?"

I shrugged. "He won't, even if he doesn't want to he won't close the door on the subject. He's told me too many times he'd do anything for me." I set my tea on the coffee table and curled my legs under my butt.

"I hope you're right. Have you decided what you're going to do with your—"

I cut her off. "No, not yet. I won't sell it until I see it one more time, but I'm not ready to see it. Maybe if Quinn agrees to my suggestion it will prompt me to deal with it sooner versus later."

QUINN ARRIVED BACK at the house a few minutes before Evan returned home. We all talked for about an hour before Mac and Evan left for dinner at Richard and Gwen's.

"I'm surprised Richard and Gwen didn't invite us to dinner too. If they're like family to you, I assumed they'd want to meet your guy," he questioned while we changed clothes for dinner.

"I'm sure they want to meet you, but I think they invited other people from the firm. You'll meet them eventually," I answered casually while brushing my hair and putting on my makeup.

What I didn't share was the fact that they didn't know we were in town and Mac and Evan were not supposed to share that information either. I postponed the inevitable with several important matters, and that little introduction was one of them.

"I have another meeting here next month, so maybe we can plan ahead and have dinner with them."

"Maybe," I answered from the bedroom as I slipped on my dress.

Quinn picked the restaurant. It was quiet and intimate but not too over the top expensive. I even ordered a glass of wine, which I hadn't had in months, but I thought a little liquid courage was necessary.

"Well, what is it you wanted talk to me about?" he asked between bites of his salad.

I tapped the rim of my wine glass with my fingernails. "About Chicago."

"You're going to have to be more specific than that." Quinn laughed.

"I'd like to move back to Chicago sometime in the near

future."

His eyes shot to mine as he swallowed hard. "Are you leaving me?"

"What? No, I'm not leaving you. I want *us* to move to Chicago." I tried to keep my voice at an acceptable level.

"Addy, you know I can't just pick up and leave my business behind."

"You could move your offices to Chicago. Other than some business meetings, your offices just serve to house your employees during the work day while everyone attends to business not only in New York but throughout the world. Does the location really matter?"

He leaned forward to stress his point without drawing attention. "It does to my employees who live in New York with their families. They have lives there and kids in school. Money aside, they might not be too anxious to uproot and move to Chicago because the boss's ... whatever you are ... doesn't want to live in New York."

"Whatever I am?" I gritted my teeth.

"You know what I mean, Addy. We're more than friends but you're not my wife and girlfriend sounds too juvenile. That's not the point anyway."

He sighed as he sat back, his voice calmer as he grabbed my hand on the table. "Addy, I'm not saying never, I'm just saying not now. If this happens, things will have to be planned out, okay?"

I nodded.

"Are you that miserable in New York?"

"No, of course not. I love being with you, but you work a lot of hours and travel regularly, which I understand. I grew up in Chicago and while it holds a lot of sad memories it will always be home to me."

I laughed a little. "I spent most of my childhood dreaming or counting down the days until I would leave the Midwest. I wanted mountains and oceans. I wanted to be where the action was; I wanted to be part of the trendsetters. New York would not have been my first choice, but at the time it undoubtedly made the top five. My mom downplayed the excitement of living near the coast. It felt like she was trying to squash my dreams. She told me to bloom where I was planted. That's why, after she died, this flower didn't move out of her 'hardiness zone.' I miss Mac, and I know she and Evan are going to start a family soon and their kids will feel like my family. It's comforting knowing my friend is a short drive away."

His forehead wrinkled as he squinted his eyes. "I thought you and Eden had become friends. You do yoga together, go out to lunch, shopping—"

"We are friends, and you introducing us was a lifesaver for me. I love having a girlfriend to hang out with. I'm going to miss seeing her as often if or when we move. But this is my home and Mac is my family."

Every word was true. Eden was young and full of contagious energy. We could talk for hours about anything. She didn't make me feel unworthy of Quinn, like Olivia and Alexis, and I didn't have to picture her in bed with him or playing the spoiled little sister card. However, she didn't know me like Mac and she never would.

A sad smile pulled at his mouth. "I understand, Addy, I do. Now is just not the right time, okay?"

I felt dismissed and even a little angry. At the same time I also felt ashamed that I hadn't given much thought to Quinn's employees and the logistics that went along with him moving to Chicago. Maybe I sounded selfish, but the truth was I felt like I deserved to be a little selfish. Giving was better than receiving. I had been a giver for so long, doing what other people expected of me, but it felt like my time to receive, even if just a little.

By the time we returned to Mac and Evan's, they were already there. They must have made up an excuse to leave early.

"So ... how was dinner?" Mac asked, but that wasn't her real question. I could tell by the way she phrased it and by the look on her face, she was waiting for some big announcement about us moving to Chicago.

I gave her an indiscreet shake of my head. "Dinner was fine. How about yours?"

The disappointment in her eyes was evident, but she didn't let on any further. "It was good, you know, blah, blah, blah, about Mom's social schedule and the same with Dad and Evan's shop talk."

Quinn hung up our coats then pressed his hand to the small of my back. "I have about an hour or so worth of work on my laptop that I need to get done. So if you all will excuse me, I'm going to head to the guest room and get started." He leaned in and kissed my cheek before making his way down the hallway.

"Tea? Wine? Both?" Mac offered.

My brain said tea and then off to bed, but after my evening with Quinn, the one word that came out of my mouth was, "wine."

It wasn't long before Evan headed off to bed too. Mac and I once again found ourselves on the porch wrapped in throw blankets with a bottle of wine and two glasses. I confessed my frustrations to her, and she did her best to play the impartial party, but she couldn't hide the fact that she wanted me in Chicago as much as I wanted to be there.

The first bottle of wine went down easy. Too easy. I couldn't say no when Mac offered to open another bottle. We talked about everything, often falling into fits of laughter that were exacerbated by the alcohol. Before we knew it the clock read a quarter after midnight. I felt warm, numb, and tingly. Another side effect was a bad case of the giggles. Mac turned off the lights and stumbled in the opposite direction to her bedroom.

The guest bedroom door creaked a bit as I eased it open, peeking inside. Quinn was asleep and the room was pitch dark. I needed to brush my teeth, remove my make-up, and put on my pajamas. But the only thing I could think of was stripping down naked and having my way with Quinn. I fumbled with the zipper to my dress and bumped into the armoire.

"Shit!" I whispered then followed it with a giggle.

He stirred during my clumsy attempt to quietly undress. After finally winning the battle, I managed to remove my dress and bra but forgot about my panties as I crawled over the covers on top of Quinn.

"What are you doing?" he whispered, voice groggy.

"I'm se … duuu … cing you." I giggled as I fought to pull the covers off him. "Remember, this is why we're here." I ran my nails down his chest.

"What?" He shook his head like his brain was foggy.

I giggled again. "Youuu … know … if we would have stayed at your sister's, no fun for my Quinny, but since we're here we can fuck like bunnies." My hand slipped under his boxer briefs and his partial erection hardened to one hundred percent. He must have thought it was a traitor because the rest of his body said no.

"Addy, stop!" He pulled my hand out of his briefs.

I giggled again. "Oh come on …" I scooted up so I straddled him then I rubbed and circled my pelvis over his erection beneath the sheet.

He grabbed my hips to stop me. "I said stop it!" His voice was still a whisper but it had a very serious edge to it.

I leaned forward and smashed my mouth to his trying to force my tongue inside his mouth, but he grabbed my arms and pulled me off him, tossing me to my side of the bed.

"Dammit, Addy! You're fucking drunk and I'm not doing this with you. Just go to sleep." He pulled the covers over himself and shifted so his back was to me.

"Fine then." I pouted. "I'll just have to please myself." I slipped my hand inside the front of my panties and let out a soft moan.

He sat up, grabbed his pillow and his phone off the dresser, and left the room.

It was hard to remember much after that. The next thing I did remember was Quinn's stern voice. "Get up. We're leaving in an hour."

I squinted my eyes. My head thumped in time with my heart.

Brilliant, Addy. Nice hangover.

Through my blurred morning vision I looked at the clock—6:30 a.m.—then I looked down at myself sprawled on top of the covers in nothing but my underwear. Quinn was in the ensuite bathroom brushing his teeth. When he finished he grabbed his suit coat and packed suitcase.

"I'll be in the kitchen." He didn't even look at me before

he walked out shutting the door behind him.

I showered and packed my stuff before making my own personal walk of shame down the hall to the kitchen. Quinn was seated at the table sipping his coffee and looking at the newspaper. Evan had already left for work but Mac was blending something. She looked better than me. I chalked it up to her having wine daily and me having it, as of lately, rarely.

"Detox smoothie," she announced, setting a tall glass in front of me.

"Thanks, Mac," I whispered, rubbing my temples.

Quinn ignored us and refused to even sneak a peek in my direction.

"Quinn can I get you some toast?" Mac asked in her cheerful and most hospitable voice. "We don't have any eggs or bacon, sorry. Although I'm sure Evan has packets of beef jerky hidden somewhere."

He didn't look up from the paper when he answered, "That'd be wonderful."

"Anything on it?"

"Peanut butter if you have it. Thanks."

"You got it. Addy, toast?"

Tipping my chin to slurp my drink, I shook my head. It hurt. That's what I deserved.

After a silent breakfast I hugged Mac goodbye as Quinn and Eddie waited in the car for me.

"What was this morning all about?" Mac asked.

"Last night … my thinking was impaired and I somehow pissed him off."

"I'd say so. I came out to the kitchen around three this morning to get a drink of water and he was curled up on the couch in nothing but his underwear." Mac flashed me an appreciative smile.

"Oh God!" I groaned as memories of the night before resurfaced.

"What?"

I scrunched my face in embarrassment. "When he turned me down for sex I think I may have attempted to pleasure myself."

She screeched in laughter. "Oh my gosh, that's hilarious, Addy!"

"Ugh, it's not. I'm so humiliated and he's so pissed. This is not going to be a fun flight home."

"Good luck, sweetie." She waved to me as I headed to the car.

Eddie waited with the door open to the back. "Miss Brecken."

"Eddie," was all I said.

I scooted in beside Quinn. He was, as always, checking emails and messages on his phone.

"I'm sorry," I whispered.

He didn't pause what he was doing for even a moment. He just nodded his head in acknowledgment. I chose to leave it at that, knowing eventually we would have a more in-depth discussion when he was ready.

THE FLIGHT BACK to New York was excruciating for me. Quinn stayed busy with his computer and business calls while I read every magazine on the plane from cover to cover.

When we arrived at the condo he put our luggage upstairs then headed straight for his office without a word. I followed him because I wasn't about to let the silence go on between us any longer.

"Out with it," I demanded as he sat at his desk flipping through some papers.

"Out with what?" I still wasn't worthy of so much as a glance.

"Out with the crap, Quinn. You're pissed, I understand that. I said I'm sorry, but you still insist on giving me the silent treatment. I'm sorry I asked you to move to Chicago. I'm sorry I drank too much. I'm sorry I propositioned you for sex. I'm sorry I ..." I couldn't finish. The words, "I'm sorry I tried to masturbate in front of you" stayed lodged in my throat.

He finally made eye contact with me and relinquished the first smile I'd seen on his face in almost twenty-four hours. "Go on, finish."

The longer he looked at me the more his smile looked like a cocky smirk.

"I'm finished." Crossing my arms over my chest, I stood my ground, refusing to let him drag any more out of me just to watch me squirm with embarrassment.

He pushed away from his desk and leaned back in his chair. "I don't think you are. I think you stopped just short of apologizing for touching yourself when I refused to fuck your drunk ass."

"Whatever, you smug bastard." I turned, grabbed my purse, and stomped out the door. By the time the elevator reached the parking garage, Quinn was a step behind me coming down from the stairs.

"Addy, wait!"

I turned and pushed my finger into his chest. "No, I apologized but you weren't going to be satisfied until you brought me to my knees. That's not what people who love each other do."

I got into Karma and fastened my seat belt before jerking the gearshift into reverse and stomping on the gas. In my anger and frustrated state, I turned the wheel a fraction of a second too early and caught the rear fender of Quinn's Lamborghini.

My heart and stomach fought for space in my throat as I slammed on the brakes. Jumping out of Karma, I looked at Quinn. He was frozen and utterly speechless. He looked like someone just punched him in the stomach and he was going to double over at any moment.

"Oh shit! Quinn I'm ... I'm ..."

He didn't move and the wise words of Mac took over my body. I dropped to my knees in front of him and made haste with his pants, jerking them down to his knees. He looked down at me in complete confusion, but his body and mouth were paralyzed. His length was soft, but I wasn't surprised to find out that crashing the back side of his precious car wasn't arousing to him.

I wrapped my mouth around him anyway and sucked him like I'd imagined he'd never been sucked before. It took a few moments but his smaller brain kicked in and he expanded in my mouth. I stroked, licked, and sucked him relentlessly, grabbing his ass and pulling him into me.

Don't gag. Don't gag ...

By the time he found his voice it was strained and raspy; he had to lean to the side just enough to rest his hand on his car to balance himself. He first let out an agonizing moan as his other hand grabbed my hair and started to pull me back, but as I sucked him deeper, he let go and squeezed his butt, gently thrusting into me.

"Addy ... ah ... Jesus!" His breathing was labored and I

knew he was close. The recent fight or flight reaction continued to dominate my instincts, which allowed me to take him all the way.

"Fuuuck!" he yelled, grabbing my hair again as he flooded my mouth with his warm salty release. All I could hear in my head was Mac's words of warning as I dug down deep and ... swallowed.

WITHOUT FURTHER ADO I left him standing in the parking garage with his pants at his ankles while I jumped in Karma and sped away.

My heart raced.

My hands trembled.

I parked in front of a local coffee shop just down the street. Bursting through the door, as if someone was chasing me, I ordered a soy Chai Tea Latte and a bottled water. I chugged down the water before the barista had a chance to give me my change. Then I found a table in the corner and texted Mac.

Me: *I hit Quinn's car.*

A few minutes later she responded.

Mac: *On purpose?*

Me: *No, it was an accident. I was upset and in my rush of trying to leave I caught the back of it.*

Mac: *And?*

Me: *He was speechless.*

Mac: *And?*

Me: *I took your advice.*

Mac: *NFW!!!*

Me: *Yes fucking way. It was like some other force took over my body.*

Mac: *And?*

Me: *And ... it will never happen again!!!*

Mac: *LOL! Not a fan of the spunk?*

Me: *No, but now I'm afraid to go back.*

Mac: *Where are you?*

Me: *Coffee shop down the street. I didn't even wait for him to pull his pants up B4 I bolted.*

Mac: *OMG! That's hilarious. You have to go back. I have to know how this ends. Text me later.*

Me: *We'll see.*

Hiding out at the coffee shop for over an hour, I finally received a text from Quinn.

Quinn: *Where R U?*
Me: *Coffee shop down the street.*
Quinn: *Come home.*
Me: *Come here, neutral ground.*

He didn't respond, but ten minutes later he walked through the door and made his way to my table in the corner.

"This seat taken?" He smiled.

I returned half a grin and shook my head.

"Interesting afternoon, wouldn't you say?" He was calm—eerily calm.

"That's one word for it," I mumbled, looking out the window to my side.

"I have to know, is that your usual MO for dealing with fender benders?"

I couldn't believe he asked me that. I wanted to be pissed at him, but I couldn't because it was quite funny.

"It's actually a sliding scale based on the value of the car. Most of my other mishaps only required a hand job but Lamborghini owners require ... more." I laughed as I met his eyes.

He tried to hold in his amusement to my comment but failed. We both laughed until the tension completely faded between us.

"I'm sorry, Quinn."

"Hell, I'm not, in fact, I plan on parking much closer to Karma next time." He smirked and reached for my hand.

"Not funny." I smacked his hand away.

"It's a little funny." He reached for my hand again and interlaced our fingers. "I can't believe you weren't concerned that someone would drive by us or come down the elevator."

"That's just it. I wasn't thinking. I would have been horrified if someone would have seen us."

He grinned like the devil.

"What?" I questioned.

He shook his head. "Nothing."

"Don't try and feed me that. What are you grinning about?" I demanded.

"Let's just say you'll likely be getting an extra-enthusiastic greeting from Tom the next time you see him."

"Tom? Tom at the front desk?"

He nodded.

"Why would that be?"

"Tom is the one who reviews the security tapes ... from the parking garage." He bit his lip and waited for my reaction.

"Oh my God! Are you serious?" I shrieked. "There are security cameras in the parking garage?"

He laughed. "Uh, yes. Hence the title: secured parking garage."

"I am such a ditz sometimes. I can't believe that never even occurred to me. God, I'm mortified. There's no way I'll enter or exit through the lobby ever again."

"Oh, it's not that bad. You don't have to avoid Tom. I'm sure he's seen a lot of interesting stuff on the security tapes. It's his job to be professional and discreet."

"Easy for you to say! I surely just fulfilled a fantasy off your bucket list."

"You think being given head was on my bucket list?"

"No, I think being sucked off in public while being taped is on your bucket list."

Quinn rolled his eyes to the side and puckered his lips. "Hmm, it wasn't on my list, but it probably should have been. I have never, and I mean ever, had a blow job as good as you gave me."

"Enough, let's go home." I stood and he followed.

I made us an early dinner. Then we hung out on the couch together and watched a movie. When the movie was over Quinn grabbed my foot and started massaging it. It had become a regular ritual with us.

"I can't say for sure when, but I'm going to do my best to get us moved to Chicago."

My heart skipped a beat at his words. The unavoidable smile on my face felt amazing.

I looked into the eyes of the man I loved. "I know you will, and I'm truly sorry for not considering everything that will entail. One of the many things I love about you is your concern for your employees."

"Coming from such a philanthropist, I will take that as a compliment." He winked at me.

My smile faded. "I'm sincerely sorry for getting drunk and coming at you in bed. I know drinking is a sensitive issue."

He laughed. "Coming at me in bed?"

I pushed the foot that he was rubbing into his gut. "You know what I mean."

"I know, I'm sorry. I was just frustrated after dinner, and then I waited up for you, but you didn't come to bed. I acted like an immature adolescent pouting when he didn't get what he wanted when he wanted it. Then when you came in drunk it just pissed me off even more."

"I can't believe I acted that way with you. I didn't even remember you leaving to sleep on the couch until Mac told me in the morning that she saw you when she went out to get some water."

He grinned. "Well, there was no way I was going to just lie next to you in bed while you touched yourself."

I grimaced. "Not one of my finer moments."

"Not one of my finer moments when I detoured to the bathroom and jacked off before hitting the couch. You had me so fucking worked up there was no way I was going to get to sleep, thinking about you down the hall touching yourself."

"You didn't!" I gasped.

"Did." He nodded.

"We're quite the stubborn pair aren't we?"

He adjusted himself. "Yes we are, now all this talk has me thinking we should go upstairs and make up properly."

"Mmm, I think you may be right."

CHAPTER SEVENTEEN

"When your mother asks, 'Do you want a piece of advice?' it's a mere formality. It doesn't matter if you answer yes or no. You're going to get it anyway."

~Erma Bombeck

QUINN'S BIRTHDAY WAS in April. We had unofficially been together for almost a year. By some miracle, we successfully managed to live in the present and grow new roots together, without digging up the past and all its dirty mess.

I wanted to do something grand for Quinn's birthday. I was very content living a simple life, but Quinn loved grand gestures, so grand he got. We left the day before his birthday for three weeks in Spain. I paid for everything and to my surprise he didn't argue … much.

Our first stop was Valencia, to visit his family. After the awkward first encounter with them at Christmas, we made an effort to video chat with them every couple of weeks, so by April they felt like my own family.

Since this trip was all about Quinn, we took his private jet—the one exception to my footing the bill for the trip. We planned to fly out early in the morning, so with the time difference we would be at his mom's in time for a late dinner.

I nestled into my large captain's chair and unfastened my seat belt after we were safely in the air. Quinn messed with his phone—his life.

"I hope your mom doesn't go to too much trouble for dinner. In fact, we should pick something up on the way."

He grinned but didn't take his eyes off his phone. "My mother will no doubt be knocking herself out; I'm certain she's spent the last week researching and planning vegan meals to impress you."

I was flattered. The thought of Quinn's mom trying to impress me was crazy, but it warmed my heart. It made me think of my own mother; I wondered what she would think of the path my life had taken. Would she be proud of me? What would she think of Quinn?

Undoubtedly, she and my dad would be proud of Quinn's financial accomplishments, but he was Malcolm's polar opposite in so many other ways and they had adored Malcolm. He'd kept me focused, which my parents loved. He'd pushed me through college and was such a cheerleader for my accomplishments, just like Mac.

I hated comparing Malcolm to Quinn. Not only were they two completely different men, it felt like two completely different lifetimes. Still, I couldn't look at Quinn and not have flashes of Malcolm in my head. Like the slow tick of a film projector, my past ran on an endless reel in my head.

Malcolm had short, wavy, copper-blond hair and green eyes, opposite of my Latin sex god. He had a nice smile with cute dimples. His body was lean, but not overly muscular, and his stomach was flat, but not toned, not even close to Quinn's.

Malcolm was my first love and everyone thought of him as a "cute, nice guy." He had all the sexual temptations of a young man in his early twenties, but his strict religious upbringing was a halo of guilt over his head whenever we were together. In the early stages of our relationship, our sex life was quick, like if we hurried, God might have his head turned and not see us sinning.

I longed for sensual, erotic intimacy, the kind I read about in my romance novels ... the kind of passion I had with Quinn. I loved Malcolm, but I didn't crave him. At the time, I had no idea that sort of desire existed. He gave me the greatest love ever, and for that I would always love him. He also took it from me the day our house burned down, and for that, there would always be a sharp pain of resentment.

"Penny for your thoughts?" Quinn's voice brought me back from memory lane.

"Hmm, rich guy owns his own private jet. I think my thoughts should be worth more than a penny to him."

He sat opposite me so I slipped off my wedges and moved my foot in between his legs, biting the corner of my bottom lip and looking up at him from beneath my long eyelashes.

He tossed his phone aside and scooted forward in his chair, pushing my foot harder into his bulge. My toes, with French pedicured nails, curled over the top of his erection, and he hissed as he sucked in a breath through his teeth. The cabin door clicked open behind me and I tried to pull my foot back, but Quinn held it soundly in place as he looked at the flight attendant and shook his head. The door closed again. He was used to getting what he wanted and having his way with me, anytime and anywhere.

HE HAD HIS way with me three times over our more than seven hour long flight. By the time we landed in Valencia, his brother, Chase, was waiting for us. The twenty-eight year old, shorter and slightly stockier version of Quinn with a bad boy smile embraced my man. It wasn't a man-hug, but a genuine embrace. It was my turn next, and Chase lifted me off my feet and twirled me around. I gasped, with a huge grin plastered to my face.

"Easy there, killer, she's mine." Quinn cleared his throat.

Chase set me down and grabbed my left hand zeroing in on my ring finger. "Not yet, big bro. She'll be mine within a week, once she realizes it's the younger Cohen who has the stamina to keep a sexy goddess like herself thoroughly satisfied."

Quinn collared Chase's neck from behind and led him to the car. "Get in and drive before I bust your cocky young ass."

Chase laughed and winked at me. Quinn opened the back door to the white Audi A6 and we both got in.

"Mom's car, huh?" Quinn asked.

"Yep. Addy would have had to ride on your lap if I'd have brought mine."

Quinn squeezed my upper thigh. "Probably would not have been safe." Then he leaned in and whispered in my ear, "However, I'd love nothing more than you riding on me."

Chase faked a cough. "Uh, I heard that."

Quinn grinned. "Good, then you'll know by Addy's shade of red that she's a *very* satisfied lady."

I went from pink to bright red. "Enough! Jeez, what is this, embarrass Addy day? You two are acting like a couple of horny, competitive teenagers."

Chase winked at me through the rearview mirror. He was such a flirt. "How long are you two staying in Valencia?"

Quinn shifted his eyes to me. Our itinerary was on a need-to-know basis and he didn't need to know.

"Just a few days," I answered.

"Oh, really? Where are you off to next?"

Quinn narrowed his eyes a bit like he could break me with a look. "Addy won't tell me. This trip is all her planning. She wants to surprise me."

"Let me get this straight—Addy's in control?" Chase glanced in the rearview mirror; his expression said Quinn just told him the Earth wasn't round. "I never thought I'd see the day."

Quinn leaned in and kissed my neck. "Me neither," he mumbled into me.

The heat of his touch elicited a whole-body response. I crossed my legs to ease the pressure, but I couldn't do anything to hide my hardened nipples straining against the thin cotton fabric of my white and hot pink floral sundress. The low-cut back and halter tie didn't allow for a bra, which was regrettable and embarrassing at that moment.

As if he sensed my thoughts, Quinn's focus dropped to my perky peaks, and his eyes widened as his smile met his eyes. I hated how responsive my body was to his every touch; it made for some very uncomfortable situations.

CHASE PULLED INTO a gated community. The shadows of the night hid the detail of the houses, but they looked modest and well kept. We pulled into the drive which belonged to Elena's sister. She, too, was widowed, and Elena had been staying with her since Quinn's dad died. Chase stopped next to a silver Mercedes Benz SLR McLaren. I assumed the two-seated sports car was his. Quinn offered his hand to help me out as Chase retrieved our luggage.

"You wearing that damn piece of material you call a dress is not the distraction I need when we're about to see my mother," he whispered in my ear as he adjusted himself.

"Well, as long as you keep your hands to yourself, it shouldn't be a problem."

Chase headed to the door with his arms loaded as Quinn grabbed the rest. "We'll give my mother a quick hello then take our luggage to our room and *correrse.*"

I gave Quinn a funny look.

"Ah, got you on that one. Think more vulgar definition. 'To get off, or orgasm.'"

"You really should write for Hallmark, babe. The words that flow from those sexy lips are so romantic," I quipped.

"Addy!" Elena smiled as we approached the door.

She wrapped me in her arms and squeezed me so tight my lungs begged for air.

"Elena, so lovely to see you in person again." I dropped my purse and hugged her back.

"Nice to see you too, *Mother.*" Quinn feigned hurt that she acknowledged me first.

"Si, si, mi hijo mayor." Elena released me and Quinn pulled her in under his arm for a hug while he still held a suitcase in his other.

"¿Cuándo vas a casar con ella?" Elena asked Quinn with abundant enthusiasm.

When are you going to marry her? I pretended not to hear her comment and instead looked around the foyer attempting to appear fascinated with the decor.

"What the hell, Mother? You know she speaks Spanish," Quinn shook his head.

I risked a glance at Quinn with a meek smile on my face.

"We're going to take our luggage to our rooms and, uh,

freshen up before dinner, okay, Mother?"

Elena kissed Quinn on the cheek. "Fine, but don't be too long. I don't want the first meal I make for Addy to be cold."

As I followed Quinn toward the stairs I grabbed Elena's hand and gave it a warm squeeze. "I'm sure it will be wonderful. We'll be back down in a few minutes."

"Need help with anything up there, bro?" Chase called with a devilish smile.

"Nope, nothing I need *your* help with," Quinn threw over his shoulder without looking back.

OUR ROOM WAS the last one down the long ceramic tiled hallway. I leisurely made my way down the hall, stopping occasionally to take in the beautiful framed art that so elegantly adorned both walls.

"Addy!" Quinn called from the bedroom door, his look impatient.

I knitted my brows. "*What?*" I mouthed.

He jerked his head toward the bedroom. I sighed and picked up my pace, making a mental note to ask Elena about the black and white sketch of Don Quixote.

As soon as I reached the threshold to the bedroom, Quinn grabbed me and closed the door behind us. His mouth eagerly captured mine as his hands tangled through my hair momentarily before untying my halter straps.

I moved my face just enough to throw out a few quick words. "Quinn, what are you doing? Your mother and Chase are waiting on us."

His mouth moved to my then naked breasts as he lifted me up and moved us to the bed. "I know, that's why we have to be quick."

He glided my dress up over my legs and hooked his thumb under my panties just under my hip bone. I tilted my pelvis to allow him to slide them down. I wanted to put up more of a fight on the matter, but Quinn was my drug and in that moment I couldn't think past him being inside me.

I worked the buttons on his jeans as he sucked and nibbled my hard nipples. He used one hand to push his pants down just far enough to free his erection. Then he hooked the same arm under my knee, hiking my leg up as he slid into me. His other hand massaged my breast and his mouth overtook mine. We kissed hard and deep, swallowing each other's moans, and we rocked our hips together in a frantic rhythm.

Quinn found his release first and started to pull out while I was still teetering on the edge. I grabbed his ass and dug my nails into his firm flesh. "Not yet," I whimpered.

He gave me his damn cocky grin but obliged me by thrusting his hips into me a couple more times as he thumbed my swollen clit, sending me to the island of euphoria. I bit his shoulder to suppress the scream that wanted to escape my throat.

He pulled out and stood to pull up his pants and straighten out his shirt. "Damn, baby, you're insatiable."

I glared at him as I slipped my panties back on. "Wouldn't be a problem if you weren't so incorrigible." The sass in my words failed to trump the satisfied grin on my face.

He stretched his V-neck T-shirt to the side exposing deep bite marks on his shoulder. "You marked me, baby; you'll pay for that later."

My jaw dropped, eyes wide. I couldn't believe I did that to him and I also couldn't imagine what he meant by "paying for it later." Was he going to bite me? He tied my dress around my neck as I lifted my hair. When he finished he kissed my exposed shoulder then nipped at it with his teeth, releasing an iniquitous growl.

Elena was setting the food on the table just as we entered the kitchen.

"This looks amazing, Elena." My words were genuine.

"Oh my, I hope you like it. There are three different kinds of homemade vegan cheese with flax crackers and sliced apples. Then the large bowl is creamy cashew kale with chickpeas, olives, and julienned bell peppers and carrots."

Quinn pulled out a chair for me then sat at the end of the table to my right. Chase sat across from Quinn and Elena was opposite me.

"Well, did you two get all *freshened* up?" Chase asked giving a quick wink.

"Yes, we did, but Addy was quite hungry…" Quinn rubbed his shoulder smirking at me "…so we didn't take too long."

Smart-ass.

"What are your plans while you're here in Valencia?" Elena asked.

Quinn shrugged his shoulders while chewing a big bite of food.

"It's a surprise. I have some travel plans for us over the next three weeks and apparently, much to everyone's amazement, Quinn is being a good sport and patiently waiting for the next reveal."

"Amazing indeed." Elena grinned. "I've never known Quinten to patiently wait for anything. He always found his hidden birthday and Christmas presents within a day of my purchasing them."

Quinn wiped his mouth then squeezed my leg. "Everything about Addy is worth waiting for."

Elena's eyes shifted to mine. She was a blink away from tears. I looked at Quinn before she pulled me into a big bawl fest. He winked at me as I squeezed the hand he had placed on my leg.

We finished dinner with casual, easy conversation. "Dinner was amazing, Elena. You have a gift."

"It was nothing. My gift is being able to follow directions. I'm not at your caliber of effortlessly and confidently creating my own recipes, but I'm glad you enjoyed it, dear."

The bond I had with Quinn's mother was true and special. I fell for her with the same effortless ease I fell for her son.

"It was wonderful, Mother, but it's been a long day, so if you don't mind I think we're going to head off to bed." Quinn stood then pulled out my chair for me.

"Are you sure I can't offer you some tea, Addy?" Elena added.

As anxious as I was to have Quinn all to myself again, I wanted to spend more time with his mom, and it was the perfect setup to my first birthday surprise for Quinn.

I didn't get up. "That would be lovely, Elena."

Quinn narrowed his eyes a bit.

"Go on up to bed, babe, I'll be up in a little while." I smiled and batted my eyelashes at him.

His shoulders sagged inward. Had we not been in the presence of his family, Quinn would have thrown me over his shoulder and hauled me off to bed because *no* was not an answer Quinn accepted without an argument.

"Fine, but don't be too long." He pinned me with a look that demanded a yes sir response.

I returned a tightlipped smile.

"It's time for me to head home too." Chase kissed Elena, then me, before leaving us alone.

I didn't want to keep Quinn waiting too long. The memory of that night at Mac and Evan's was still fresh in my mind. I did, however, want a little alone time with Elena.

"BLUEBERRY POMEGRANATE TEA sound good?" Elena called from behind the counter.

"Perfect."

She brought back a beautiful glass teapot with a bamboo handle and two double-layered glass tea cups.

"I'm glad we have a few moments alone," she said while pouring the tea into our cups. "How much has Quinn told you about Lucas, his father?"

I wasn't expecting our conversation to go in that direction. "Just that he died from injuries sustained in a car accident and uh—"

"Did he tell you about his drinking?"

"Yes, and that's the reason why he doesn't drink?"

Elena nodded, tension drawing her brow tight as she focused on the cup of tea in her hand. "Lucas was the love of my life. He worked hard to provide for our family, and once we moved to the United States he had a lot of opportunities to make money. Years back he had some legal issues with one of his businesses, and after years of litigation he lost ... well ... let's just say a lot. It was hard on our marriage because he wouldn't open up to me and then he started drinking. The drinking led to infidelity. Our children suffered too much, but Quinn had the most to deal with. He never wanted to be in business with Lucas, but when his father wasn't sober enough to run his companies, Quinn had to step in and help. After Lucas died it was Quinn who dealt with the lawyers. He's still dealing with the mess his father left behind."

She wiped a stray tear away. "He did it for me, Chase, and Alexis. He takes care of all of us and ..." Several more tears fell to her cheeks. "Quinn thought his father walked on water for so many years. He wanted to be a brilliant businessman just like him, but the women and the alcohol severed their relationship. Quinn doesn't drink, and for that I am grateful, but the women..." she reached over the table and took my hand "...he swore he would never settle down, never marry, and never have a family because he feared he was too much like his father. But, Addy, he loves you and I hope he doesn't get scared and run, but I want you to know that Quinn is a good man. He is not his father and I hope if he tries to push you away you will fight for him."

I blinked away the tears that pooled in my eyes. "My past is rocky too, but I love your son. I can't promise more than one day at a time, but I won't go down without a fight, okay?"

She gave me a beautiful smile; it was the same as Quinn's. I honestly couldn't promise her forever with Quinn, but he was waiting for me upstairs and in that moment he was my whole world.

The clock read five minutes past midnight. It was officially Quinn's birthday and I was ready to give him his first of many presents. I hugged Elena and told her goodnight.

QUINN WAS PASSED out on the bed by the time I made it upstairs. Part of me regretted staying downstairs with Elena for so long, but it was a conversation we needed to have. It was Quinn's birthday, but it seemed more like mine when I took in his naked body covered by the sheet at his midsection. He was the most delicious eye candy. I still had to pinch myself. It was ridiculous that such a perfect body was for my pleasure and mine alone. Even in a relaxed, sleeping state, his muscles looked flexed and sculpted. I itched to run my hands over his day's worth of stubble, or to feel it between my legs. His full, cherry red lips were slightly parted, and his high cheek bones and thick, dark eyebrows framed his sleepy eyes and long, full lashes.

Quinn didn't mention his mother's faux pas about getting married and I was glad, but there was a part of me that wondered where Quinn imagined us in the future. I, like Quinn, had sworn off marriage years ago. But was he a game changer for me? Was I for him?

I removed my shoes and tiptoed into the bathroom. I fixed my hair, added a little lip gloss, and rubbed jasmine oil over my body before I slipped into black satin and lace thong panties and a fitted nighty that had see-through lace over the breasts and just below my navel, with hot pink satin flower embellishments bordering the lace.

The elegant four-poster bed was perfect for my plan. I had two long pieces of black satin that I used to tie Quinn's arms to the posts. Quinn was a heavy sleeper, which played in my favor. I crawled up between his legs and pulled the sheet off of his midsection, exposing all of him. I dug my fingernails into his firm inner thighs, and as soon as he started to stir I wrapped my lips over the head of his length. I didn't want to get his hopes up; this wasn't going to end like it did in the parking garage.

His groggy eyes opened in confusion as he tugged, to no avail, to free his hands. "What the hell?" Even his voice was heavy with sleep.

I sucked hard on his cock, stroking it at the base with one hand as he hardened in my mouth. I popped off, licking my lips.

"Happy Birthday, babe." I sat up and straddled him, allowing his eyes to take in my scantily-clad body. "Does my Quinny like?" I ran my hands up his chest then brought them back down, raking my nails over his skin just enough to elicit a heavy moan but not hard enough to leave marks.

He nodded then tugged at his bound wrists. "Fuck, baby, what are you doing to me?"

"Any. Thing. I. Want." I crawled up his body. "I'd better make sure these ties are secure." I straddled his head, leaning forward to check the knots. His lips reached for me, but my sex was just out of reach. He took a slow inhale. I played it cool, like the slow breath of air he drew in didn't melt my panties, but it did.

For his torture, or maybe mine, I lowered just enough to let his nose graze the thin patch of silk and lace at the front of my thong. He sucked in another breath and flicked out his tongue, swiping my sensitive flesh on one side of my string.

"Mmm, again," he hummed.

The shots were mine to call, but he was the master of my body and it followed his command on instinct. I dipped my hips back down, lowering my center to his face again, lingering a little longer, allowing his tongue to dip under the material enough to brush past my clit.

Under heavy lids, my eyes rolled back in my head. He robbed my ability to focus. I scooted down his body again to straddle his legs just below his erection.

"Aw, baby, come back up here…" he licked his lips "…you know you want to, and I fucking love the taste of you."

I smiled as I reached for a container I set on the bedside table. Removing the lid, I dipped my finger in it then sucked it off, drawing my finger out an inch at a time.

His breath caught then another moan escaped from deep in his throat. "What is that?" he asked as his butt flexed, lifting his hips a little.

"Edible body chocolate, organic and vegan, of course."

I dipped my finger in it again and brought it to Quinn's lips. He opened his mouth, but I smeared it on his lips instead. I leaned into him and licked his top lip as his tongue traced his bottom. I continued to suck and lick his lips before I dipped my tongue into his mouth to taste him. The chocolate was good, but it was Quinn that I craved.

I smeared more chocolate around his nipples and over his abs. My tongue seduced and savored every inch of his chest. Quinn squirmed and jerked at his restraints as I hummed with each stroke of my tongue.

His erection twitched.

"Looks like someone's feeling a little left out," I cooed.

His eyes were dark and heated. His arms, tense with veins, pulled against the restraints, his hands fisted. I covered his hard cock with chocolate. My two favorite aphrodisiacs together was a heady combination. I wanted to play this out, slow and sensual, but my body screamed *fuck the birthday boy!* Literally.

I'm not sure who was more turned on at that moment.

I wrapped my mouth around him and sucked him like a Popsicle, over and over again, lapping up the warm chocolate.

"Fuuuck, Addy stop!" Quinn's breathing was labored—his

voice ragged. "Take these goddamn things off my wrists or I'm going to rip this fucking bed frame to pieces."

Flashing him a wicked smile, I slipped the straps off my nighty, exposing my breasts, then rubbed chocolate on my nipples. "Mmm, not yet, babe, but soon."

I scooted up just enough to graze my sex over his erection. His hips jerked up to me. Hooking my finger under the thin strip of material, I pulled my thong to the side and eased down onto him.

The bed creaked as Quinn tensed, pulling down on his arms. "God, untie me, baby!"

I moved up and down his length while circling my chocolate smeared nipple with my finger. Then I sucked it off my finger with an appreciative moan.

"For the love of Christ, Addy, I swear to God if you don't untie me now my mother will be knocking on the door because I'm going to fucking lose it."

I eased off him. "As you wish, birthday boy." Leaning forward I stopped with my nipple over his mouth. He licked it several times then sucked it into his mouth. I untied one arm then the other expecting him to attack me or even tie me up, but he didn't. He didn't move his arms at all as I sat up. I took one of his hands and kissed his wrist before resting it on my hip. I did the same to the other arm.

"I don't like tying you up."

His narrowed his eyes. "Why?"

"I need your touch almost as much as my next breath."

His hands tightened around my waist. "I love that you need me." Then he clasped his hands around my wrists and kissed my palms.

"I know." I smiled.

I slid my straps back over my shoulders.

"I don't think so." He pulled them back down. "My birthday, my wishes." His grin was playful, and I loved playful Quinn.

"So let me just get this straight, you don't like tying me up and I've confessed I'm a dominant not a submissive, yet you tied me up anyway?"

I nodded.

"Why?" he questioned.

"I wanted to use the chocolate on you but the last time we mixed food with sex you ate it all."

He laughed and pinched my sides causing me to squeal and wiggle off him. He pinned me to the mattress, hovering just inches from my face. "As I recall, you begged for more of me, not more ice cream."

"Mmm, you might be right." I lifted my head just enough to bite his bottom lip, and I sucked it into my mouth.

He melted into me and took his time caressing and kissing every inch of my body as we made love until the sun started to peek over the horizon. Then we held each other in silence, surrendering to sleep.

CHAPTER EIGHTEEN

"As usual, there is a great woman behind every idiot."

~John Lennon

"GOOD MORNING, MY handsome son and his beautiful ..."

"Love of my life, Mother, she's the love of my life," Quinn stood at the counter in nothing but his running shorts, pouring himself a cup of coffee.

Elena's grin spread all the way across her face as she looked at me. My whole body heated from his words. Would I ever get used to Quinn calling me the love of his life? My parents had been married for over thirty years before they died and I couldn't remember my dad ever referring to my mother as the love of his life. The realization that Malcolm had never used that endearment for me was bittersweet as well.

Elena hugged me and whispered in my ear, "No one has ever called *me* the love of their life."

I returned her embrace, wishing I could share his sentiment, but I couldn't. Quinn wasn't the love of my life, at least not this life.

"So what's on the agenda for my birthday boy today?"

Quinn sat at the table and peeled a banana, handing it to me before getting one for himself. "Addy wants me to take her to my favorite places in Valencia, minus bull-fighting.

Something about systematic torture and eventual killing of innocent animals, blah, blah, blah—"

"Ouch!" he yelped after I smacked the back of his head.

"The *love of your life* just so happens to love all life, but at this moment I might not hesitate to throw your ass into the ring and I'd root for the bull."

Elena choked on her tea, stifling a laugh.

"That's a little harsh, baby. Spanish bull-fighting is an art form."

"So is castration in Wisconsin."

Quinn moved a hand to cover his man parts.

"Feisty little thing you've got there," Chase smiled as he walked in the door.

Quinn thumbed through the local paper. "You have no idea."

"I'm going to shower." I stood and kissed Quinn on the head.

He tossed the newspaper aside and scooted his chair back. "I'm right behind you."

"Quinten, give the girl a few minutes alone. Sit and finish your coffee," Elena demanded.

"I would, but trust me, she doesn't want to be alone." He made his way to the stairs.

"Guilty as charged," I hollered from the top of the stairs.

We took an extra-long shower, and I had to work hard to clear my mind of the fact that Elena and Chase were downstairs, fully aware of what Quinn and I were doing. Quinn, however, wasn't fazed by it in the least.

After the dirtiest attempt to get clean on record, I finished messing with my hair as Quinn put on his shoes.

"My mother loves you."

"Why do you say that?" I knew, but I was curious why Quinn thought so.

"She told me if I weren't her son she'd think you were too good for me."

I shrugged. "She doesn't know that much about me and I'm sure she's thought the same thing about other women you've been with."

"Not even close. She's tolerated them, and some just barely. You … you she loves."

I slipped on my sandals then moved in front of him. "Well, I love your mother. In fact, if we don't work out I think I'll ask her to adopt me."

He laughed. "If we don't work out I'll be looking for someone to adopt me because my mother will disown me." He wrapped me in his arms and kissed the top of my head.

WE SPENT MOST of the day in the City of Arts and Sciences, a cultural and architectural marvel that housed, among other things, a planetarium, science museum, aquarium and botanical gardens. The stunning futuristic buildings and landscape were nothing short of awe-inspiring. However, we enjoyed the moments that would seem mundane to others, such as walking hand-in-hand, occasionally taking snapshots of the great architecture, and grabbing lunch to eat in the sunken park that had been created in a former riverbed that Mother Nature drained during a catastrophic flood.

"Good birthday so far?" I asked between bites of salad.

"Mmm, I'm not going to lie, you set the bar pretty high early this morning, but I'm having a wonderful day. Every day with you is perfect."

"Every day?" I questioned.

"Every day. Yes, even the days when you ram into my car." He smiled as he took a bite of his sandwich.

"Can you believe it's almost been a year since you nearly ran me over with your careless driving?"

Quinn choked a bit. "Excuse me? I hate to insult your memory of all things, but I remember very clearly you were twirling around in the middle of the street with no regard for your own safety, or anyone else's, for that matter."

"The speed limit was thirty-five through there and you're supposed to yield to pedestrians."

"I'm quite certain the fact that you're sitting here alive, with me, is proof that I did yield to the pedestrian."

"Do you jump out of your vehicle and throw a tantrum for all the pedestrians to whom you yield?"

He laughed then leaned in and kissed me. "Just the sexy ones. Had I ran you over, you wouldn't be here to serve your purpose, and that would be a real tragedy."

I raised my eyebrows in curiosity. "What are you calling my purpose?"

"Well, to please me of course."

I shoved him back on the grass and lay on top of him. "That reminds me of another thing I love about you."

He rubbed his nose against mine. "What's that?"

"Your vivid imagination."

WE MET ELENA and Chase for a late dinner at Quinn's favorite restaurant. After we finished eating, close to midnight, I excused myself to use the ladies' room. On the way I stopped by the hostess station to pick up the garment bag Elena dropped off when they arrived before us. I changed into a strapless, purple and black sequined cocktail dress with black, open-toed, chunky high heels.

Smoky eye shadow, black mascara, and a thick layer of tinted lip gloss completed my sex-kitten look. The question of whether Quinn would like my dress was a no-brainer. The real question was if he would like other people admiring it on me. He would either love it or hate it.

I turned the corner. Quinn's back was to me, but Chase and Elena caught sight of me and smiled. Quinn turned, his eyes dropping to my feet and slowly making their ascent up my body. The desire in his eyes made my knees a little unsteady.

He didn't smile.

He didn't speak.

He didn't move.

I steadied my shaky legs and walked to him stopping just shy of his chest, tilting my head to meet his gaze. It was dark with an intensity that sent a fiery heat straight to my core.

"Addy, you look beautiful," Elena broke the awkward silence.

Chase came up beside me and kissed my cheek, placing his hand on my lower back. "You're sexy as hell is what you are."

Quinn grunted or maybe it was a growl. Chase stepped back with his hands up. "Hey man, she is. Are you blind?"

"I'm. Not. Blind. More like blindsided. Why are you dressed like this?" His attempt to control his tone was weak at best.

"It's for your surprise," I murmured, ending with a timid smile.

"Come on, bro, wait until you see where we're going." Chase patted Quinn on the shoulder as he and Elena headed out the door.

I entwined my fingers with Quinn's and led him out as well. His grip tightened, expressing his unspoken displeasure. My skimpy attire had him wound tighter than a monkey's nuts. I could relate. My Latin sex god looked utterly consumable in his dark, frayed-at-the-bottom jeans and fitted black T-shirt that accentuated his sculpted chest. I was excited for him to see his surprise, but his caveman attitude left me buzzing with sexual electricity.

WE ARRIVED AT our destination in silence. It was an exclusive night club which I had rented out for the night. The starving children in the world crossed my mind more than once when I let go of the large sum of cash required for our private party.

Quinn pulled me into him as the security guy opened the door for us. As soon as we entered, a crowd of people yelled out "Happy birthday!" His extended family—aunts, uncles, and cousins—from Spain, as well as his sister, Alexis, and her husband Mitch, flew in from Chicago. Standing next to Chase were Zach and Eden. I'd invited them not only to the surprise party, but also to stay an extra week with us for some more surprise adventures I had planned. Toward the back of the crowd we saw Mackenzie and Evan with huge grins plastered on their faces.

After Quinn scanned the familiar crowd with wide eyes, lips parted, he looked down at me. "I'm speechless, baby. No one has *ever* surprised me like this."

His lips found mine just seconds before friends and family surrounded us pulling us in opposite directions. The money didn't matter at that moment. Quinn was surprised and very,

very happy. Even my dress had managed to fall off his radar for a while.

"Addy!" Mac screamed as she pulled me in for a big hug. "You're the best girlfriend ever for doing this for Quinn, but you're an even better BFF for flying me and Evan here for the party. And would you look at you! I'm talking grade-A hottie. He must have flipped when he saw you in this." Mac held me at arm's length as she checked out my dress.

"He was speechless." I left it at that.

Evan hugged me. "Hey, gorgeous, we've missed seeing you."

"Thanks. I've missed you guys too. It's so easy to get caught up in Quinnland, I sometimes forget the rest of the world exists."

"He's exactly what you need, sweetie," Mac added.

"I hope so." I scanned the room looking for my hot guy in the crowd, but before I found him, Zach and Eden grabbed my attention.

"This is the bomb, Addy," Zach yelled over the music that had been kicked up to dangerous decibels.

"Thanks. I'm so glad everything worked out."

Eden moved closer to my ear so she didn't have to shout so loud. "Does he know about the rest?"

"Not yet. He's been uncharacteristically easygoing about letting me take charge of everything."

"Even that dress?" Eden added.

I smiled, fidgeting with it, struggling to find the perfect balance between pulling it up to keep my nipples contained versus tugging the hem down to keep my ass covered. "The dress ... not so much." I rolled my eyes.

Hanging out with Zach and Eden had become a regular

part of our routine since our first dinner together. Eden and I texted on a daily basis, usually just to vent about our men who acted like horny boys most of the time. She knew all about Quinn's list of quirks, which at the top of the list was his obsession with my body being properly covered in public.

I jumped as large hands suddenly snaked around me from behind. "You've outdone yourself with this lavish party, baby, but don't think I've forgotten about this." One of Quinn's hands traced the swell of my cleavage while the other skimmed my bare thighs just below the hem of my dress.

I turned in his arms and grasped his hair in my hands, pulling his lips to mine. He slipped his tongue past my teeth and explored every inch of my mouth. We were boldly crossing the acceptable PDA line, but when I felt his erection rub against me the rest of the world faded away.

The deep clearing of a man's throat startled me. "I hear the restroom lounge areas are quite posh and dimly lit if you two have something you need to do ... or uh ... work out. Otherwise, I'd keep in mind that you have a very intimate audience, including our mother, watching your every move, birthday boy." Chase wore a cocksure grin on his face.

I wiped the smeared lip gloss from my lips as Quinn used the back of his hand to do the same.

"Now it's time I take this beautiful lady out on the dance floor while our guest of honor mingles some more." Chase offered his arm to me and I took it smiling at Quinn.

"Watch your hands or you'll be leaving without them," Quinn warned with a daring smile. Chase just winked at him and led the way to the disco-lit dance floor.

After two dances with Chase and a handful of fast-paced dances with Mac, Eden, and several of Quinn's cousins, I beelined to the bar for a cold drink. I leaned back against the bar, letting the cool liquid extinguish some of the heat I'd built up from all of the dancing. As my breath started to even out again, I searched the crowd for Quinn, but he was nowhere to be found.

"Great party, Addy."

"Hey, Mitch, thanks." I gave him a big hug.

Alexis was not a huge fan of mine, but Mitch and their kids had always accepted me with open arms. He never said so, but from reading between the lines, I had the impression Mitch was not a big Olivia fan. Quinn had casually alluded to the fact that Mitch questioned Olivia's influence on Alexis. Mitch wanted Alexis to be a homemaker and hands-on mother with their two kids. However, when Olivia was around, Alexis wanted to pretend she was carefree, without anything else to do other than go to fashion shows and exclusive clubs.

"I was just wondering where the birthday boy was. Have you seen him?"

"Not for a while. Maybe he's using the restroom," Mitch offered.

"You're probably right. I think I'd better do the same. Talk with you later, okay?"

"You bet."

I swayed down the dark hall to the lounge area with my shoes scuffing against the floor and my hands held out for balance. I hadn't been drinking, but all the dancing mixed with my toe-crushing shoes made my legs wobbly.

When I rounded the corner outside of the lounge area, my feet came to an abrupt halt. My eyes tried to make sense of what I saw. Quinn was sitting on the bench with his back to me, and his head was hunched over *Olivia's* bare shoulder. His hand was resting comfortably on her knee. One of hers was on his thigh, while her other hand was on the back of his head, pulling him close while she whispered in his ear. Her eyes met mine and a smug smile graced her face as she pulled away, leaving her hand planted on his leg. Quinn must have seen her gaze fall behind him because he slowly turned, his eyes trailing up to meet mine.

He quickly stood and closed the distance between us. "Hey, baby, I was just getting ready to come find you."

Olivia slithered into the ladies' lounge like the evil serpent she was, leaving us alone in the hallway.

Livid.

What was she doing there? Who the hell invited her to travel halfway around the globe to a party I was giving Quinn?

Moreover, what were they doing hidden back in the corner, huddled together with their hands on each other in such a cozy and familiar fashion?

"I'd better get back to our guests." I turned on my heel, not wanting to get into an argument at a party filled with our family and friends. He grabbed my arm.

"Get. Your. Fucking. Hands. Off. Me." The words came before a second of thought.

He jerked his head back like my words physically smacked him in the face. "Addy—" His eyes moved past me and then I was the one following his gaze. Elena stood a few feet behind me, all the blood drained from her face. My heart skipped a beat. The last thing I wanted was to embarrass or hurt her. In that moment, I was more concerned for her feelings than either mine or Quinn's.

"Addy, what's wrong?" she whispered.

"Nothing ... um, I just was, or I saw ..." Was I supposed to tell her the truth? I didn't want to lie to her, but it wasn't the time nor the place to get into it. "I'm sorry, Elena, I can't talk about this now. Please, let's just get back to the party. We can talk about it later, okay?" I pleaded as much with my eyes as I did with my words.

She looked past me to Quinn, and if looks could kill, then I should have heard the sound of his body hitting the ground. Instead, I kept my gaze on her as she grabbed my hand and pulled me back down the hall to the party. Neither one of us looked back at Quinn.

I spent the rest of the party planted at Elena's side. She was like a mama bird watching out for me. Quinn kept his distance, as if he feared the wrath of his mother. I put on my best face so nobody would think much of us navigating the party separately. Mac knew something was up, but I shook off her attempts to approach me about it.

Elena told Chase to bring Quinn home because she was taking me back first and wanted some time alone with me. I knew Quinn was not privy to that bit of information because he never would have allowed it, even if it meant being at odds with his mother.

WE ARRIVED BACK at Elena's around four in the morning. I was exhausted, physically and emotionally, but she insisted we have a quick chat before Chase arrived with Quinn.

"I don't want all the details, Addy. I saw Olivia there and I know something must have happened to set you off. You have to know I'm on your side. I love my son, but as we discussed before, Quinn is oblivious to his actions around women."

She held my hands, squeezing them and bringing her head closer to mine, eliciting my gaze. I brought my teary eyes to meet hers.

"But, my dear Addy, I *know* with every cell in my body that he loves you. You *are* the love of his life. I'm not asking you to turn a blind eye to his stupid actions. You should talk to him. He will listen. He's not like his father. He loves you and he wants to please you. Okay?"

I pulled my hands from hers to wipe my tears. The lump in my throat thickened. All I could do was nod. She hugged me tight and kissed my head. I released a tight sob.

"Now get some sleep, my dear. Things will look better after you give your body and mind a chance to rest. My stupid, stupid boy won't be bothering you until I've had a long heart-to-heart with him."

IT FELT LIKE I'd slept forever. Squinting open one eye, I glanced at the clock on the nightstand: it read a quarter to noon. The room was dimly lit from the light that filtered through the long, sheer curtains. I rolled toward the middle of the bed and froze. Quinn was facing me, on his side, with his head propped up on several pillows.

"Hey, beautiful."

I blinked. My swollen eyes hurt. It was the nasty side effect of crying myself to sleep.

"Addy, I think there a huge misunderstanding last night and I feel really bad about it. I want to make it up to you, but I don't know how. All I know is my mother reamed me out for over an hour for being an insensitive jerk, along with a whole list of other names I never imagined my mother would call me. But in the end, I guess the insensitive jerk part of me still didn't understand what exactly I did that was so awful. So … I'm sure the only thing worse than doing whatever it was I did is not knowing what that is." He scrunched his nose, like I could go ballistic on him.

He was right to think I might lose it. Quinn literally had big balls, but I was shocked to find out that figuratively, his balls were just as big. Most men would throw out random apologies until something stuck, not Quinn. He didn't understand what he did that was so wrong and he had no qualms admitting it.

Deep breath … I am peaceful, I am strong.

I sat up and turned my back to him, with my legs dangling off the side of the bed. "I didn't invite Olivia to your party."

"I didn't figure you did."

He wasn't helping the situation. "Then who invited her?"

"She said she was in Madrid for a photo shoot and my sister insisted she come to the party."

I nodded my head but it quickly changed direction into a side-to-side shake. "Why would Alexis invite her?"

"I've told you they're friends, and I've known Olivia for quite a while, too." He sounded so casual, as if I was the one who was crazy to even be surprised that she was there.

My pulse thundered in my ears as I fisted the sheets. "Quinn, she's your ex-girlfriend, lover, fuck buddy … whatever!"

"Yeah, *ex*, but I'm with you, Addy. I love *you."*

"Jesus, Quinn!" I jolted up and turned with my hands still balled at my sides. "She basically called me a whore the same day you broke my heart for the what … I don't know, second, third, fourth time? She's the spark that ignites most of our fights. You still have faint white scars on your back from what I've always assumed were her fingernails from when you were touching, kissing … *fucking* her the same way you fuck me. AND the first I saw of her at the club was with you—" My voice caught as heartbreak and agony tackled my anger and took over. Tears flooded my already swollen eyes, and I hated myself for breaking down in front of him. He scooted to the edge of the bed and started to stand. "Don't!" I held out my hand. "Just don't." He stopped, sitting where I had been a few moments earlier.

I regained my composure and talked slower to make it through what I needed to say before my weaker emotions took over again. "The first I saw of her at the club was with you … alone … in the hall by the lounge. She was … whispering something in your ear, her hand was on yo-your leg and—" I swallowed through the lump in my throat and wiped more tears away as my bottom lip quivered. "Your hand wa-was on her-hers." I released a sob and Quinn tried to move toward me again, but I shook my head and retreated a few more steps until he stopped. "I know you d-don-don't understand, bu-but the gesture was … int-intimate and … and … familiar … and comfortable."

His shoulders curled inward, eyes cast downward. I had to fight for courage to stand my ground and not be made to feel like a jealous fool for making a big deal out of "nothing."

We both were silent as my breathing evened back out again.

"I mean … you gave your brother a verbal and non-verbal warning, more than once, about keeping his hands to himself and I've never fucked him. So it's okay for you to go all caveman with your own brother, but I'm supposed to just sit back and watch you and Olivia have a private moment with your hands on each other? Really, Quinn, is that how it's going to be?"

He eased toward me, the predator testing its prey. I no longer had the energy to stop him or even back away another step. He folded me in his arms. I was too tired to sob anymore, but a few residual tears made their way down my face and onto his shirt.

One of the qualities I both loved and hated about Quinn was his brutal honesty when directly confronted. He didn't sugarcoat things to ease the pain. In fact his honesty about Olivia usually cut my heart like a knife.

"You're right, my history with Olivia makes being in close proximity to her familiar and comfortable, but it wasn't … it's not intimate, not for me. I was an asshole. I am an asshole. She should not have been at the party, and I should not have been with her, the way we were. Although it really didn't mean anything to me at the time, I know that it looked bad to you and possibly anyone else who saw us together. It was embarrassing and hurtful to you and I will never be able to take back what happened, but I will make sure it *never, ever* happens again."

He sat on the bed and pulled me onto his lap so I was straddling him. He leaned his forehead against mine. "I feel you … when you see the scars on my back. I feel you tense up a little and it breaks me inside. I hate that they're there. But, Addy, you're the only woman I've ever made love to. I have never kissed anyone the way I kiss you, the way I touch you, the way my body connects to yours, the way my soul longs for yours. My heart beats with yours, for you, because of you." I watched tears drip between us ... but they weren't mine.

That man.

His love for me was so real it had its own breath ... its very own heartbeat.

CHAPTER NINETEEN

"Love is composed of a single soul inhabiting
two bodies."

~Aristotle

OUR LAST DAY with Elena was not what I had planned.
Quinn spent most of the day either arguing with Alexis
about the Olivia catastrophe or settling fights between his mom
and Alexis, also about Olivia. I disappeared with Chase for part
of the day to have lunch with Mac and Evan before they
headed home. Quinn was disappointed he couldn't join us, but
I understood he had some things to settle with his sister.

Later that afternoon, we said our goodbyes to his family
and boarded his private jet with Zach and Eden, off to the next
surprise destination.

Scuba diving in the Canary Islands had Quinn all smiles
again. He had lots of scuba diving experience and so did his
sidekick, Zach. Eden and I were both certified to dive, but
neither one of us had very much actual experience. What made
our foursome work so well was the combination of two cocky
guys, who had done just about everything, coupled with two
adventurous girls, who were willing to try just about anything.

The Canary Islands were nothing short of breathtaking.
Being volcanic in nature, they were beautiful both above and
below the water. Picturesque views of the crystal-clear waters of

the Atlantic, mixed with the turquoise sea and rich marine life, gave the islands a dreamy paradise atmosphere. It was a diver's dream, with arches, tunnels, caves, caverns, coral fish, game fish, pelagic species, a rainbow of flora, and scattered shipwrecks.

We stayed for five days in three different locations, each on a private beach, surrounded by warm, salty, ocean air and an infinity of blue waves. Our last night, we enjoyed dinner outside on the patio, illuminated by a combination of the full moon and the flickering flames of golden garden torches.

Quinn raised his glass. "A toast to the most amazing time in paradise with my best friend, his lovely and adventurous girl, and to the love of my life, for making this all possible, but mostly for making us possible. You dropped everything and took a blind leap of faith to be with me ... I will never be worthy of you, but I will live every day in abundant gratitude that you haven't figured out yet what a monumental ass I really am."

Everyone laughed and raised their glasses in unison. "Cheers!"

Quinn took a sip then leaned over and pressed his lips to mine. "I love you, baby."

I ran my palm over his cheek and smiled. "I love you too."

"Any progress on mission 'destination Chicago'?" Zach raised his brow at Quinn.

I looked at Quinn too.

"I haven't had that much time to figure it all out, but when we get back I'm going to investigate some possible solutions," he answered very matter-of-factly.

"We're going to miss you both, ya know?" Eden said with a sad smile.

"We're going to miss you too, but with Quinn traveling so much I'm sure we'll still be in New York quite often." I smiled back. When I glanced at Quinn he had a tense look of contemplation on his face and I wondered what had him distracted.

After another hour of talking, laughing, and drinking, Zach and Eden decided to call it a night. Quinn suggested we take a farewell walk along the beach before heading out in the morning for our next surprise destination.

I WAS STILL in my bikini, with a long, sheer wrap around my waist. Quinn wore nothing but board shorts that hung low on his waist. His perfect olive skin had taken on a deeper shade, which intensified his sex appeal. We walked hand-in-hand in silence for a while, as the waves rocked back and forth over our feet. When we were a ways out from the house he stopped and turned to face me.

The ocean breeze whipped my hair in my face. He grinned, pushing the unruly strands behind my ears before feathering the tips of his fingers down my neck and over the swell of my breasts. Despite the warm breeze, my skin erupted in goose bumps under his touch. Wetting my lips with my tongue, I looked up into his dark, seductive eyes.

He bent down and kissed my bottom lip, then my top, and finally his tongue slid past my lips, flicking just the tip of mine. Our mouths eased together as our tongues slow danced. His hands skimmed down my arms and then to my back, gradually untying my bikini top until the strings fell to my sides. With an equally patient ascent, his hands cupped my face ever-so-slightly, deepening our kiss, before sliding them under my hair to the back of my neck, undoing the final tie to my top. The two triangles and their connecting strings fell to the sand.

Quinn continued his leisurely journey to my breasts, where he cupped his fingers under them while he delicately rubbed the pads of his thumbs over my erect nipples, sending a flood of heat to my sex.

"Oh God, Quinn," I breathed out, arching into his touch.

His tongue trailed along my jaw to my ear. "Beautiful ...You're just ... So. Damn. Beautiful."

He drew my earlobe into his mouth. My hands rested on his firm chest to steady my weak knees. He sucked and nibbled along my neck as his hands pressed down the concave part of my figure stopping at the top of my wrap. One hand loosened the knot until it opened and glided down to my feet.

My hands feathered around his torso to his back, then dipped under the waist of his board shorts until both of my hands reached his strong glutes with my fingers splayed across them.

His fingers dug into my hips as he bit his lower lip and released a moan, briefly closing his eyes. "Oh, Addy ..."

Then his fingers simultaneously tugged at the hip ties to my bottoms, releasing them to the growing pile at my feet.

He pulled back and looked down at my feet. I stood naked, exposed, and vulnerable to him. He thoughtfully moved his eyes up my body, as if he was committing every inch to memory, until his eyes met mine. He stripped me to the essence of my soul with just his eyes.

I felt his words before he spoke them, but then he did ... he said them. Two words. They weren't a question, or a demand. They weren't planned or rehearsed. They were just the natural unfolding of time, the perfect moment, the now.

They were as essential and instinctive as our our next breath.

"Marry me."

I paused for a moment before I slid his shorts down, keeping my eyes locked to his. He fell to his knees as the waves crashed along the shoreline, enveloping us in their warmth and pull. His hands supported my body as I lowered to him, stopping to capture his mouth with mine. I closed my eyes and let the white noise of the sea, the smell of the ocean air, and the warmth of Quinn take over my senses.

He wrapped one arm around my back and guided my legs around his waist with the other. He gradually lowered me onto him, filling every inch. In that moment, I gave myself to him completely. He held me tight as our bodies melted into the sand and water. Every move was in perfect harmony and rhythm with the ebb and flow of the sea, with our hearts, with our souls. Every cell in my body yearned for Quinn. He couldn't get close enough to me. I wanted every part of him, so badly it was all consuming.

"Harder, Quinn, please I need … more."

My legs wrapped around his and my arms hooked under his while my hands gripped his shoulders for dear life. I arched my whole body into his.

"I know, baby…" he held me just as tightly with each deep thrust "…it'll never be enough … God, I'll always need more of you," he whispered through strained breaths.

And in that perfect moment, our bodies let go. Quinn pushed our hands over my head and intertwined our fingers, both of us squeezing so hard our knuckles turned white. His mouth crashed to mine. Our bodies moved together, grasping for every last sensation. The slow fading of ecstasy was almost physically painful.

I WOKE ON my stomach in a tangle of white sheets and sand. My hand fanned along the sheets in search of Quinn. I craved the reassurance that last night wasn't just a dream.

No Quinn.

With a sigh of disappointment, I peeled my eyes open, squinting against the morning sun's rays that filtered through the window. A kaleidoscope of purples and blues reflected on the sheets, ceiling, and walls. I stretched out my left arm and spread my fingers. Planted on my ring finger was a stunning tanzanite ring. Two halos of smaller gems surrounded a larger, cushion-cut tanzanite gemstone that must have weighed at least six or more carats.

"Good morning, my beautiful." Quinn stood in the doorway with a white towel wrapped around his waist and rivulets of water dripping from his hair to his chest.

Saliva pooled in my mouth as my vision hazed, fixed on my Latin sex god. He messed with his towel and I drew in a quick breath, anticipating its fall to the ground, but he just readjusted and tightened it.

He chuckled. "I'm glad you like it."

My eyes shifted to his. I nodded and sucked in my bottom lip, then worked it with my teeth. I liked him. I liked him a lot.

"The ring ... I'm glad you like the ring. It's all ethically sourced for my socially-responsible bride-to-be."

"What?" I shook my head. "Oh, um, yeah ... it's stunning, too much really." I looked back down at it and twisted the band back and forth.

"Too much was what I wanted to buy you, but strangely enough, my billionaire beauty has frugal taste." He sat down on the edge of the bed.

I ran my finger down his chest chasing a drop of water. "Not with you. I have to stay grounded in every other part of my life because you, Mr. Cohen, are as elaborate as they come. In that department, I picked the top of the line. I undoubtedly splurged with you … you are my guilty pleasure." I traced his tight abs at the edge of his towel dipping a finger under to tug it loose.

He grabbed my hand. "Sorry, baby, my *fiancée* has us on a strict schedule and we leave in less than an hour to a destination unbeknown to me."

I stuck my bottom lip out. "She sounds like a real spoilsport."

"She's actually quite the little ogling minx." He leaned down and sucked my nipple into his mouth then bit it with a tug before releasing it. "Now get going, baby. I can't wait to see where you're taking us next."

After a quick shower, I threw on a sundress and wedges then braided my hair into Quinn's favorite pigtails. My suitcases were in need of some reorganization, but that would wait until our next stop. Anal retentive Quinn wanted to keep our stuff segregated when we packed for our trip. He said it would be easier, but I'm pretty sure the idea of mixing his pressed shirts and pants with my wash and wear wadded sundresses and capris sent his OCD into overdrive. When I moved to New York, I insisted his housekeeper/cook go part-time since I wasn't working full-time. After a month of wrinkles, miss-matched socks, and thousands of dollars worth of shrunken clothes, I relinquished all of Quinn's laundry to Helen, his housekeeper. I stayed in the kitchen, which was perfect for Quinn.

Before Zach and Eden saw the rock on my finger, I wanted

to share the news with two other people. I grabbed my phone off the dresser and snapped a picture of my left hand held up by my face with a big grin. I texted it without subject, caption, or comment, to Mac and Elena. Then I silenced my phone, knowing I would get an instant call from Mac, and possibly Elena too. They would have to wait for details, but I felt better knowing they knew before the rest of the world.

Zach and Eden piled their suitcases by the door as Quinn checked his phone while popping grapes into his mouth. His face lit up when I walked in the room, as did mine. He grabbed a banana and peeled it back before handing it to me.

"I'm starting to think I'm your pet monkey."

He hugged my waist and lifted me off the ground. I wrapped my legs around him and took a bite of my banana. "You kind of are." He kissed my neck then stole a bite of my banana before setting me back on my feet.

"Holy crap!" Eden yelled, grabbing my hand. "Quinn proposed?"

I grinned, looking at him. "Sort of."

He gave me a sexy wink. Eden embraced me while squealing and bouncing us both up and down.

Zach shared a man-hug with Quinn. "Dude, that's awesome. I take it she said yes?"

Quinn laughed. "Sort of, I think."

"You two don't make any sense. Sort of? I think? What's that supposed to mean?" Eden planted her fists on her hips.

Quinn looked at me but I didn't say anything. "Addy and I have … a unique way of communicating."

"Words are overrated," I added.

"Niiice … body language … I totally get you two. That's fucking hot." Zach spoke without thought, just like Mac.

Eden's eyes doubled in size. "Ooohhh, I see, well congratulations anyway … sort of."

Everyone laughed just as the driver pulled up.

CHAPTER TWENTY

"Speak when you are angry and you will make the best
speech you will ever regret."

~Ambrose Bierce

OUR NEXT STOP via Air Cohen was Seville. Quinn, being
the world traveler, knew where we were before either I or
the pilot had a chance to announce it.

"Seville, right?" Quinn asked with a confident smile.

I nodded.

"How long are we staying here?"

"Just two days."

"Two days to do what?" He looked at Zach and Eden.

Zach had a good poker face, but Eden struggled. She didn't
look at Quinn. Instead, she focused on fidgety hands in her lap.

Quinn stayed focused on her because she was the weak link
at the moment. "Eden?"

"Hmm?" she answered, still not making eye contact with
him.

"Are you nervous? I know you too well. You can't hide
your nerves."

She tried to steady her hands as she shook her head.

"Are you pregnant?" Quinn smirked.

"What? No you idiot, I'm not pregnant. I'm scared shitless
about jumping out of a plane!"

"Eden!" Zach hollered.

"Oh shit, I'm sorry, Addy, he just … he's just so—" She blew out a breath of air.

"He's a nosy little bastard, I know." I squeezed his leg then he laid his hand over mine and laced our fingers together. His finger absentmindedly traced the contours of my ring.

"Seville, Spain, baby, one of the top ten best places in the world to skydive," Quinn declared as he gave Zach a high five.

"I know you two wild hares have already taken the fifteen thousand foot plunge here, but this time—"

"We'll have hot chicks attached to us," Zach finished.

"You'll be tandem jumping with two beautiful novice divers," I corrected Zach.

"That's what I said." He feigned innocence as Eden gave him a stiff elbow to the ribs.

Quinn's knee, that our hands rested on, started to rapidly bounce. I looked at him and then his knee.

He stopped. "Sorry, the adrenaline is already taking over."

"We're not jumping until tomorrow."

He raised his eyebrows. "Who said it was about skydiving?" He shifted our hands just enough to let me feel his growing erection. I wasn't as flattered. Extreme sports turned him on almost as much as sex.

"Maybe we should just skip the jump and stay in bed all day tomorrow." I flashed him a challenging smile.

He knitted his brows. "We could, but that wouldn't be fair to you and Eden, and since we've come all this way—"

"Oh, just admit it, you're like a kid on Christmas Eve. You won't be able to get to sleep tonight."

"Not if my fiancée is lucky."

WE WERE TRANSPORTED to the Gran Melia Colón, a five-star luxury hotel in the historic old quarter of the city. After lunch we explored the city, including a tour on a double-decker bus. Quinn and Zach turned up their noses to the idea.

"This isn't how people with means tour the city," Quinn protested.

"I'm sure you're right, so good thing we're not a bunch of snobby, pretentious, rich people." I leaned in and kissed his cheek.

I took a slew of pictures just like every other tourist on the bus, in complete awe of the Islamic monuments and gardens. Our bus stopped at the Tower of Gold, Bridge of San Telmo, and Casino Exhibition Hall. We made it back to our hotel in time for dinner, but we agreed to call it a night and order room service instead of going out. I was anxious for a little alone time with Quinn.

As soon as we got to our room, I plopped down on the plush bed and glanced through the menu. Quinn sat beside me with his back against the headboard. He grabbed one of my feet and took off my sandal to massage my foot.

"Ah, that feels so amazing," I moaned in pleasure.

His strong hands moved slowly over my arch, applying firm pressure with his thumbs to all the right spots. He could have sent me to the spa for a massage, which I always enjoyed, but I loved his hands massaging me more than anyone's. It was such a tender, nurturing, and loving gesture, not just quick foreplay before sex. However, it was just our nature that after enough physical contact we both craved more and weren't satisfied until we had sweat beading down our bodies and our lungs begging for air.

"Did you enjoy slumming on the layman's tour? I'm guessing that was your first time on a bus like that?"

He smirked. "It was basically a party bus, and I'm not going to lie, I've been on a few, mostly during college. As for the tour itself, the best view in the city is sitting next to me. I watched you, not the tour. Other foot." He clapped his hands and I lifted my other foot to his lap.

"You've ruined me for every other guy, you know?"

"I hope so."

"Caveman."

He fisted his hands and pounded his chest.

I giggled. "You goof. So how about veggie enchiladas? I'll call down and see if they can veganize something for me."

"Ask how long it will be too. We need a shower."

"Oh do *we?*"

He pulled off his T-shirt then stood and removed his shorts, leaving him in nothing but his sexy, white, boxer briefs that contrasted his tan skin in the most mouthwatering way. "Well I do." He strutted off toward the bathroom.

"Two can play this game, buddy," I yelled in his direction.

He didn't answer but I heard the shower turn on. Wasting no time I ordered dinner and slipped into the bathroom to play my hand at the strip tease he started. I retrieved my lavender shaving gel and razor from my toiletries bag, then untied my sundress letting it drop to the floor. My sudsed-up man wiped a small area of the glass shower door so he could see me. I was in a red lace demi bra with matching panties. I lifted my foot and rested it on the edge of the sink. The toilet seat would have been a more practical choice, but I was going for a more dramatic effect. Slowly, I massaged the gel over my leg, but not like I normally would, more like I was auditioning for a commercial. Out of the corner of my eye I saw Quinn watching me. I glided the razor up my leg, over and over, removing all the gel before switching to the other leg. When I was almost done I stole a quick glance at Quinn again.

Holy Shit!

He pinned me with a dark look, but that's not what stole my breath. It was his hands—one rested against the glass wall, but the other was fisted around his enormous erection— stroking it. The erotic show sent my body into nuclear meltdown. I bit my bottom lip for a moment while I watched him stroke himself.

Could I play his game?

My inner sex goddess declared, Game. On. I reached behind and unclasped my bra, letting it slip from my breasts. With the same steady ease, I followed with my panties, keeping my eyes on his as he picked up the pace at which he stroked himself.

Cupping my breasts and taking my sweet time, I massaged them. Even over the noise of the water, I heard a deep moan escape him. I closed my eyes for a brief second then opened them again to his dark, heated stare. Inching my right hand down over my abdomen, I slid my finger over my clit. His eyes followed my hand. Then his hand against the glass wall fisted. He pulled open the door to the shower and grabbed my waist, jerking me inside. He positioned me so I stood next to the shower seat before he lowered to his knees. He lifted my leg and set my foot on the seat. Then he buried his face between my legs.

"OH! My god," I cried.

I wasn't expecting him to attack my sex with such intensity. His lips and eager tongue ripped through my frayed nerves. There wasn't a gradual work up; he quickly brought me to an intense orgasm as I screamed out his name. My knees buckled under me, and he held me in place with one hand under my leg while he stroked himself with the other. His lapping tongue between my legs matched the intensity and rhythm with which he gave himself. The same thought that usually crossed my mind during such intense moments with Quinn danced through my mind again. *Would we ever get enough of each other?*

Hungry.

It was just a theory that I could live off Quinn and sex. Wrong. I needed food. A knock at the door sounded just as Quinn slipped on his shorts and I tied the sash to my robe. We took our food and beached out at opposite ends of the couch with our legs tangled in the middle and our plates on our laps.

"Whatcha thinking about, beautiful?"

That's not the question I wanted him to ask me. I could feel my skin turning red. No answer was necessary, Quinn knew.

He smiled a sexy, all-knowing grin. "It was hot, baby. You're such a naughty temptress. You had me so fucking hard."

It wasn't fair for anyone to be so comfortable in their skin and with their sexuality. I always tried to hide my inexperience, but there was no way for Quinn to hide just how *much* experience he had. It wasn't a thought I relished, but it often crossed my mind. I knew he had women falling at his feet, willing to fulfill every sexual fantasy he'd ever imagined and probably some he hadn't yet thought about.

"It's easy for you—" I paused, to rethink how I wanted to approach the subject.

"Getting turned on by you? Hell yes, it's easy for me." He casually took another bite as if we were discussing the weather.

"No, I mean the sex or the things like what we just did.

You're so comfortable and confident about it." I stared at my food.

"You mean masturbating? You can't honestly tell me you've never masturbated before." He laughed with hesitation.

"No, I'm not ... I mean yes of course I've done *that* before ... I've just never done it in front of anyone else before you."

"Well, beautiful, you should know that I would never have guessed that. You're sexy as hell when you touch yourself. I'm flattered and a little aroused at the thought of being your first audience."

I glanced up at him as he continued to eat without skipping a beat. Was the topic of sex considered normal conversation with Quinn and other women? Lucky him. I was speechless.

"Anything else?" he asked between bites.

"What do you mean?"

"Well, I'm the first person you've masturbated with. Am I your 'first' anything else?"

"Jeez, is your ego hungry or what?" I rolled my eyes.

"I'm serious, and I'm not asking to 'feed my ego.' By the time most people reach their thirties the lists of 'firsts' starts to dwindle. I promise if you tell me I'll make sure your ego goes to bed more inflated than mine tonight." He licked some sauce off his thumb while giving me the "so what do you say" look. "Deal?"

I let out an exaggerated exhale. "Fine, but then we never speak of this again. Deal?"

He turn-key gestured his lips.

Sucking in a deep breath I let it all go at once. "You were my first ... sex someplace other than in a bed, position other than missionary, oral sex, multiple orgasms, nipple stimulation orgasm, bondage, food with sex, and you're the first person to rip an undergarment off me."

There was a deafening silence while Quinn looked certifiably shocked. I gave him a sheepish smile and shrugged. "You wanted to know, so say something. Don't simply look at me like I just told you I'm only sixteen or something."

He set his plate to the side. "Addy, how many guys have you been with?"

Shit, shit, double shit!

"Two," I whispered.

"What?" He sat up and leaned closer to me.

"I said two." My voice was still soft but no longer a whisper.

"Two? Are you serious? You've only been with two other guys before me?"

My face contorted in anguish. "Not exactly."

"What do you mean 'not exactly?'"

I nervously worked the corner of my bottom lip between my teeth. "Well, you're, uh …"

"I'm what?"

"You're number two." I grimaced, then covered my face with my hands.

He dropped to his knees in front of me, laughing with equal parts humor and sympathy, as he pulled my hands away from my face. "Baby, don't. Look at me. I'm not trying to judge you, I'm just amazed that you're thirty-two years old, with the body of a twenty-year-old and you've only been with one other guy. How is that possible?"

My eyes met his. The moment felt right and safe, so I let another piece of myself go. "Number one died, and it took me awhile—years—to give myself to someone again, physically or emotionally."

"Oh, Addy," he whispered as he cradled my face in his hands. "I love you, and I want to be your only."

"You are." I smiled and leaned into his lips.

I needed his touch to ground me again. He didn't ask me any other questions, and I loved him for trusting me to share my past in my own time. He had no idea what an emotional milestone I reached by sharing that with him and not shedding tears. I was healing. With Quinn, I was healing.

"All right, buddy, your turn ... You promised to boost my ego, so let's hear it."

He looked at me for a moment, eyes narrowed a bit, then he wrapped his arms around me and whispered in my ear, "You're the first person who has made me want—*need*—something money can't buy. You're the first person I've made love to, you're the first person I've held in my arms until morning, and you're the first person I knew I couldn't live without ... and I want you to be my only, my very last."

We tightened our embrace and kissed. It was long, passionate, tender, and loving. We did this for what seemed like an eternity. Most people think of sex or making love as the ultimate form of intimacy, but for me it was the kiss. It was my infinity of love. Relationships often started and ended with a kiss, but when Quinn kissed me, I couldn't remember when we started, and I never wanted it to end. Quinn was my infinity.

ANOTHER GREAT MORNING wrapped in Quinn. I felt extra-special that morning, knowing I was the one privileged person who had experienced waking in his strong arms. Actually, it was his legs and half of his body too. Quinn hugged me like a body pillow. Sometimes the weight of his body felt suffocating, but I breathed through it because once I made it past the crushing sensation, it was pure bliss.

Butterflies fluttered through my stomach as I thought about jumping out of a plane fifteen thousand feet up in the air. Quinn and Zach spent two summers during college as instructors, plus they both had extensive experience in all areas of skydiving. Unequivocally, we were in good hands, but that didn't completely calm my nerves. I was certain Eden was much worse off that morning, while on the flip side it was just another day in the life of Quinn and Zach.

I wiggled my butt against Quinn's morning wood as a wake-up call.

"Mmm, does my wanton fiancée request servicing this morning?" he mumbled into my neck as he tilted his pelvis into me.

"Tempting, but we'd better get up—"

"Done." He rubbed into me again.

"We'd better get *out* of bed and check on Eden. I'm guessing she's already wrapped around the toilet, dry heaving."

"Then we'd better give her some time. Zach will figure out a way to calm her nerves." He splayed his palm over my stomach then slid it down until two of his fingers grazed over my clit. "How's *my* baby? Can I help relieve some tension?"

"Quinn, we don't have time," I insisted.

He lifted my leg and slid into me. "Ah ... but I can be quick." His hips started a slow rhythm and his fingers circled my swollen bud.

"Well..." I panted, eyes rolling back into my head "...I suppose, if you're quick."

He kissed my back and shoulders then moved his free hand to my breast. My nipples hardened beneath his touch.

"Better hurry, babe. I'm going to beat you to the finish," I said between strained breaths.

His thrusts became unyielding as he tugged harder at my nipple. "Ahhh!" I cried out.

"That's what I want to hear. Let go, my beautiful," he demanded while his fingers worked the most sensitive part of my clit even faster. I gave it up to him while I reached around and dug my fingers into his hard ass bringing him to his release.

He fell back against the bed. "I'm sooo glad you waited for me before you let go of your sexual inhibitions. Your body is so responsive and it fucking drives me crazy."

I rolled toward him. "It's responsive to you, and I'm sure you're *real* unfamiliar with women being responsive to you." I rolled my eyes.

"Not like you, not like us. I never understood the concept of chemistry between two people until you. I've never felt addicted to a person—sex maybe, but not a specific person. You bring out an insatiable desire in me—addiction, like an actual chemical reaction. Everything about you is an aphrodisiac to me and it doesn't matter how many times we have sex or how much time we spend together, it never seems like enough."

I propped my head up on my arm. "I'm going to geek-out on you, but just for about thirty seconds. They're called pheromones—naturally-occurring odorless substances excreted by the fertile body, triggering a response from the opposite sex. Dr. Winnifred Cutler, of the Athena Institute for Women's Wellness, conducted the first controlled study documenting pheromones' existence in humans. Basically, we have very compatible pheromones; we crave each other. It's the same concept in animals, but scientists have known about that for years. Studies in humans are a relatively newer discovery. You can experience sexual pleasure or gratification without the chemical or pheromone attraction, but it's the craving of that specific person that you're experiencing with ... me. Very, very, very lucky me." I leaned into him and kissed his nipple before rolling my tongue around it. "Glad to know you experience the same attraction. Here I thought it was just me ogling you all the time like a bitch in heat."

A sound of amusement escaped him. "A bitch in heat, huh? God, I love the way you talk a mile over my head one minute, then explain it to me like you would a five-year-old the next."

I laughed. "I probably wouldn't talk to a five-year-old about a bitch in heat, but I'm glad you understand."

An instant later he hopped out of bed, then pulled me up behind him. "Let's go jump out of a plane. Then we'll come back here and I'll fuck you to the wall until my euphoria starts to wear off."

I smacked him on his bare ass as I cut him off on the way to the bathroom. "Wow, so relieved to know you're already working on your wedding vows. Nothing says forever quite like 'I'll fuck you to the wall.'"

IT TOOK ABOUT fifteen minutes for Quinn and Zach to give us our instructions on the ground before we geared up and took off in our little plane. I was nervous-excited, but Eden was a complete basket case. As we approached our drop zone Quinn and Zach made all of the final preparations.

"We won't be able to verbally communicate during the free fall, only hand gestures. Just enjoy the ride. I know you're going to love it. And remember," Quinn added while looking at Eden, "it doesn't feel like falling, it feels like flying."

She returned a forced, nervous smile as we made our way to the door. Zach and Eden went first and we followed them. I held my breath for a few seconds then screamed. The guys told us to scream to force us to breathe.

Incredible.

The second we left the plane, I knew I would do it again. It wasn't a roller coaster sensation. We were like Lois Lane and Superman. I felt weightless, flying through the beautifully unobstructed sky over Seville.

My one complaint was it was over too soon. We were in free fall for only about a minute before Quinn deployed the parachute, which floated us back to the earth in a little over five minutes. We all landed without a hitch.

"Holy shit!" I yelled. "That was the most extraordinary rush ever!" My heart slammed against my chest.

Quinn released our equipment and I jumped into his arms, wrapping my legs around him as we kissed with crazy intensity. I was euphoric, sharing his adrenaline rush.

"I knew you'd love it." He pulled back with a huge grin on his face.

Eden was a little shaky still but her smile masked any residual nervousness.

"I would totally do that again!" she declared.

We headed back to the hotel for showers and brunch. I didn't eat before we left that morning and neither had Eden, but inevitably once my body settled back down I felt famished. Quinn held true on his promise, but it was technically the shower wall he fucked me against. It was quick and hard, and I wanted it just as much as he needed it.

He made a few business calls while I dried my hair in just my bra and panties. I ran my fingers through my long, wet tangles as he sauntered up behind me. His faded jeans were made to hang from his sculpted hips. They were also made to be worn without a shirt. My man wore the hell out of that look.

I turned toward him and flipped my hair out of my face before I aimed the dryer at his hair, reaching up to run my fingers through it. Quinn smirked as I fisted and tugged at it while the warm air blew in every direction. After shutting it off and pulling the plug, I dropped it to the floor. Quinn stepped closer until the backs of my legs hit the edge of the vanity.

I rested my hands on his chest as he pushed my hair back off my shoulders. Leaning down, he kissed my neck, letting his tongue wet a trail to my jaw. He wrapped his hands under my legs and lifted me onto the vanity.

"Quinn, they're waiting on us." My weak protest was followed by a moan as his hands squeezed my legs and his thumbs grazed my inner thighs just below my panties.

"So?" he murmured, as his lips found mine.

His tongue casually explored my mouth as the minty flavor from our toothpaste mixed between us. Keeping his mouth soundly pressed to mine, he worked the buttons of his jeans. The word "no" wasn't in his mentality of understanding at the moment, which was fine, because I wanted him—I always wanted him.

WE WERE FORTY minutes late for brunch. Zach and Eden were

nearly finished eating by the time we walked up to the table.

"Sorry we couldn't wait," Zach said as he took his last bite.

"Neither could we." Quinn winked at me as he pulled out my chair.

I blushed when Zach gave me a knowing eye.

Eden cleared her throat. "I was thinking we could use some shopping therapy, or at least I could, and I know Addy will be better company than someone else." She glared at Zach.

"What? I'll go shopping with you."

"No, you'll go pick up necessary items, you won't let me shop. You expect me to find what I'm looking for, but I like to let it find me."

We laughed and I patted Eden on the hand. "I'm your girl." She smiled in appreciation, knowing I wasn't much of a shopper. We had a lot in common, but designer clothing, shoes, and hand bags were her weaknesses, not mine.

"That settles it. You lovely ladies enjoy your afternoon and we guys will do ... guy things," Zach declared with a mischievous grin.

Quinn shrugged his shoulders, feigning innocence.

We ate our fill while Zach helped Eden enter all the best shopping locations into her phone.

She noticed my empty plate then jumped out of her chair. "Let's do this, Addy!"

Zach retrieved a credit card out of his wallet and handed it to her. "Go wild, sexy." She leaned in for a kiss.

Quinn stood and pulled my chair out while I got up. He wrapped me in his arms moving his hand down over my butt. "I'd rather drag you back upstairs," he grumbled in my ear.

"Mmm, later." I pulled away and grabbed my purse. "Aren't you going to offer me *your* credit card?" The humor wasn't lost on Quinn alone, as I heard Zach and Eden trying to stifle their snickering.

"Funny, baby, we'll see who has the last laugh later when you're tied naked to the bed."

Eden's gaze met mine, eyes wide, cheeks flushed. I didn't dare a glance at Zach, although I imagined him giving Quinn knuckles, a high five, or some other sort of childish frat boy approval.

EDEN AND I spent the next four hours shopping. I purchased T-shirts, shorts, shoes, socks, toiletries, food, and water. Then I handed it all out to various homeless people we encountered.

In the car on our way back to the hotel, Eden was unusually quiet, even for her.

"It's been a great day, don't you think?" I asked, trying to gauge her mood.

"Yeah," she said with a small voice.

"Are you okay?"

"Yes ... well, no. I mean, I feel like such a pathetic loser around you."

"What?" My head jerked backward.

"It's just that I'm heading back to the hotel with all of this stuff and everything you purchased you gave away. You make me feel so materialistic sometimes."

"Oh, Eden, that's not my intention at all. Everybody has their own unique journey and mine has led me to this point in my life. I haven't always been so willing to just give everything away. There's so much about me and my past that you don't understand, but I don't ever want you to think that I'm judging you for your choices. You're a very caring and giving person, okay?"

She gave me a half-smile. "Okay."

"Okay then, put on your happy face before we get back to our guys."

"You're the best, Addy. Quinn was right to choose you."

Uh, what?

My eyes narrowed a fraction. "What do you mean 'choose' me?"

"Just that we all wanted to be the one that captured Quinten Cohen's heart. Nobody ever thought it would happen. You know, with him having been such a player for so many years."

I shook my head, uncertain if I heard her correctly. "'We?' Are you implying you—"

"Oh shit, Addy, I thought you knew." She covered her mouth, as her face contorted in a horrified grimace.

"You've been ... intimate with Quinn?"

She stared at me, holding her breath, then slowly nodded.

"And ... Zach knows this?" My words were louder than I intended them to be.

"Of course, Quinn introduced us."

The car pulled up outside our hotel, but I couldn't wait for the driver to open the door before I jumped out, leaving Eden behind, buried in her bags of designer crap.

"Addy, wait!" she yelled, as her impractical heels clicked the ground behind me.

I breezed through the door into the hotel lobby and the party kicked up another notch. Quinn and Zach were standing off to my right talking to some older couple I didn't recognize. Quinn caught sight of me and smiled briefly before both he and Zach were distracted by Eden's voice echoing through the door.

Quinn looked back at Eden with a confused look.

"Quinn, I'm so sorry, I thought she knew."

He didn't require further explanation before he immediately chased me to the elevator. "Addy, wait!"

He lunged for the doors a moment too late. I closed my eyes, releasing a sigh. I needed the thirty seconds alone in the elevator to gather my thoughts before facing Quinn, who I knew was sprinting up the stairs to greet me when I reached our floor. The anger and hurt inside of me was boiling over. I felt like such a fool.

Eden was my friend too, and I knew the way I looked at her would never be the same. It wasn't her fault, but the image of Quinn with her was too much.

The doors opened.

"Addy, don't be upset," Quinn pleaded through labored breaths as he tried to pin me in the elevator.

I brushed past him to our room. He was right on my heels. As soon as the door shut behind him I turned, took off both of my shoes, and hurled them at him one right after the other. The first missed his head only by a few inches, but the other bull's-eyed to the middle of his face, the right side of his upper lip taking the brunt of it.

"What the hell are you doing?" he yelled as he touched his hand to his lip, smearing the blood with his fingers.

He lifted the hem of his shirt and pressed it against his lip.

"What does it look like? I'm lashing out because I received yet another reminder that I'm engaged to a manwhore. Tell me, Quinn, would it just be easier to make a list of the women who you *haven't* screwed?"

He removed his bloodied shirt and walked into the bathroom, returning a few minutes later with a wet washcloth pressed to his lip. His next words dripped with contempt in a slow, angry voice. "You know I've been with a lot of women. Just because I'm the only man still alive that's been inside you doesn't give you the right to act all fucking noble."

My hand contacted with his face so hard I thought my whole arm was going to fall off. "Go to hell, you fucking asshole!" I growled between clenched teeth.

He had blood smeared all the way across his face because my hand reopened the cut on his lip that had just started to clot. I looked down at my left hand and my ring covered in blood. It must have been turned slightly when I hit him. There was too much blood on his face to assess how much damage my ring did to his already injured lip. Unlucky for Quinn, I was ambidextrous, so using my left hand to smack him was as likely as using my right.

I glared at him, blood dripping down his face, his whole mouth bloodied like a boxer's after a fight. He didn't move. He still had the washcloth in his hand, but both of his arms hung limp to his sides in defeat.

An apology dangled on the tip of my tongue, but I couldn't. I had trusted Quinn with a painful piece of my past, and he threw it back in my face in the ugliest fashion. Without question I provoked him, but I had to know that I could trust him with the broken pieces of my heart without fear of him crushing them further. He needed to know it, too.

Silence. There weren't any more words to be shared. I took the washcloth from his hand and pressed it to his lip. He didn't jump, but the corners of his eyes creased a little. After a few minutes I folded the washcloth over and gingerly wiped the blood off his face. He never took his eyes off me. It angered me and broke my heart at the same time.

I reached for his hand and pulled him to the bathroom, and he willingly followed and sat on the toilet seat. After rinsing the blood from the wash cloth, I finished wiping his face off. His lip was swollen but the bleeding had stopped again. I soaped up my hands and scrubbed them clean, working my finger over the gemstones set in my ring.

Closing my eyes for a moment after drying my hands, I took a deep breath and swallowed my emotions. Stepping between his legs, I peered into his sorrowful eyes then focused on the mangled corner of his lip. Cupping his face in my hands, I leaned in and whispered a kiss over his lip before I rested my forehead to his. A few moments later he wrapped his arms around me and rested his head against my chest while I ran my hands through his hair and held him tight.

CHAPTER TWENTY-ONE

"Life is either a daring adventure or nothing at all."

~Helen Keller

W E NEVER SPOKE of that incident again. I apologized to Eden for how I treated her and she tried to apologize for mentioning it, but I assured her it wasn't her fault and no apology was necessary. Zach insisted they had to bail on the rest of the trip because he had something with work come up. I didn't press him on it, but I suspected he and Eden wanted to step back from the hurricane that was Quinn and Addy. Things felt a little uneasy after that day, and time was what we all needed to heal our wounds.

I considered suggesting to Quinn that we head home early too, but that would have meant admitting there was still something between us that wasn't quite right. We felt the need to forget and forgive in the silence of each other's arms, so that's what we did. When we made love, there was a desperate intensity that hadn't been there before. It was our unspoken apologies to each other and our way of soothing the emotional scars.

Our last stop was Rodellar, in Northern Spain, for sport climbing. Quinn loved to rock climb and I did, too. He and Zach had been climbing for years all over the world. I wasn't nearly as experienced, but it didn't matter. We had to finish making amends before we headed back to New York, and burning off energy on an amazing crag was our remedy.

Fall was the best time to climb in Rodellar, but we were fortunate enough to find plenty of crisp, dry routes. We beat the summer crowd so it felt as though we were alone with just the vast wildlife and breathtaking views. Rodellar, a little town atop a limestone gorge with a lovely green river running below, was a climber's haven.

I was surprised and equally excited to find out that Quinn had never climbed there. We were sharing a first for both of us and it felt even more perfect that we ended up there alone, like a pre-wedding honeymoon.

We flew into Zaragoza, rented a black Mercedes-Benz SUV, and stocked up on food before we headed to the little village of Rodellar. Our mansion was not a five-star hotel but a small, two-bedroom cottage with one bath and a small kitchen. I was in my element: simple, cheap, and über casual. Everything I packed for our stay either had a rip or hole in it. To my complete shock and awe, Quinn's attire was much the same. I hardly recognized him when we changed clothes after arriving our first day.

"Well for the love of all things scruffy, where did my permanent-pressed, anal retentive, GQ fiancé go?" I mused when Quinn came out of the bedroom in cargos and a T-shirt that must have dated back to his college days or before. It was paper thin and wrinkled, like it had been wadded in the corner of his suitcase, or more likely mine. He was already scruffy in the face before we arrived. I loved that look on him.

Glancing down at his clothes he smiled. "I know, I look like … you." Then he poked me in the side, making me jump before he bear-hugged me and threw us both onto the couch as

I squealed in delight.

"You've never looked better."

He rubbed his scratchy face over my neck and cheeks.

"Stop!" I yelled. "Seriously, where did you get these clothes? I cannot believe they came from our condo."

"I keep them in a special spot, for occasions such as this."

I laughed. "Occasions such as what? When you want to fit in with the town folk? Do you have a secret chest labeled *incognito* that you keep these clothes in?"

"Something like that." His hands went to work on my khaki capris that had a pink and green checkered patch on the back pocket, covering a rip I had in them.

"I thought we were going to check things out?" I managed to say between kisses.

He grabbed the hem of my shirt and pulled it over my head before tossing it behind the sofa. He nuzzled his face into the exposed part of my breasts. "What do you think I'm doing?"

I grabbed his hair and pulled until he was forced to look up at me.

"Checking me out?" I raised my eyebrows.

He wiggled his.

My eyes fell to his lip. It was no longer swollen but the cut hadn't completely healed and the skin around it was still tinged with hues of purple and yellow. I brushed the pad of my thumb over it. He moved his head enough to suck my thumb into his mouth and playfully bit at it with his sexy grin enticing me. One look was all it took.

Each time we made love, the line between Addy and Quinn blurred into an *us* that had no beginning and no end. My need for him was unmistakable, but his need for me was just … unimaginable and beautiful, but in a part of my heart that didn't know why, it was also heartbreaking.

WE LAY SATED wrapped in each other's arms, drifting in and out of sleep.

"Why are you marrying me?" he asked in a soft voice.

"Because you asked me."

"So you'll do anything I want, all I have to do is ask?"

"Sure, in your dreams." I smiled. "The real question is, why do you want to marry me?"

"You're it for me. You're my forever. I want us to belong to only each other."

"Well, I hate to shatter your fairytale dreams, but marriage doesn't mean forever." I chuckled.

"Would you stay with me forever if we never married?"

I thought for a moment about his question, and I knew the answer but it wasn't so simple. "I'm going to be with you for however long I'm going to be with you, regardless of whether or not we're married. I don't want to belong *to* you, I want to belong *with* you. I don't need a paper certificate that makes it hard to leave; I need a love that makes it easy to stay."

He laughed but it sounded more like choking. "Wow, what planet are you from again?"

"Planet Awesome, babe, Planet Awesome."

"You don't have dreams of a big wedding, the dress, bridal showers, flower girls, a first dance, a honeymoon, babies, birthday parties, teaching a child to ride a bike or watching them score their first goal?"

Deep breath … I am peaceful, I am strong.

"Is that your dream?" I deflected.

"I'm not sure. I never took time to dream about anything

other than money and success, until I met you."

I rolled over to face him. "And now?"

"And now … I want you." He kissed me and I couldn't imagine ever being in the arms of another man.

"Well, then it's your lucky day because at the moment you have me…" I gestured to my naked body "…all of me."

He twisted the ring on my finger back and forth. "You don't want to be my wife?"

"Well honestly, it seems like a step down from the love of your life." My face distorted into a dramatic cringe. "Seriously, synonyms to wife can be things like old lady and the old ball and chain."

"True, but so is significant other, better half, soul mate, and *love of my life*."

He had such a gift for saying the right thing at the right time. "I'll marry you, Quinten Lucas Cohen, just tell me when and where. Look for me, I'll be the one in the white gown and veil."

"Cheeky little thing, aren't you?"

"Cheeky? Is my Latin lover turning into a British bloke? I'm good with either accent."

"You like my accent, huh?"

"Mmm, hmm." I nuzzled his neck. "Now, let's get you incognito again and check out the town folk and breathtaking scenery then we'll come back and throw together some grub."

"I'd tell you to lead the way but I'm pretty sure I'll be the one leading the way."

I fastened my bra and grabbed my pants. "How so?"

He stared at my capris as I zipped and buttoned them. "The thought of you sans panties under those is going to have me looking like a blind man with my long stick leading the way through the village."

His goofy comment caught me off guard, so my laugh came out as a snort eliciting a chuckle from him.

"Would you prefer I wear granny panties and a muumuu dress?"

"In public? Yes," he deadpanned.

THERE WAS GREAT climbing on both sides of the gorge. We planned on staying four days, so we opted to sleep in and climb in the afternoons. I had never climbed anywhere that even came close to Rodellar. It had everything: slabs, pinnacles, arches, and overhanging caves. It was all stamina climbing and Quinn was in climber's paradise. He knew in advance about the climbing—I had to confess that much ahead so he would pack his gear; and boy did he have a lot of gear. His gift to me, and all other female climbers we met, was his simple climbing attire: shorts and climbing shoes.

I opted for my prAna climbing knickers and a yoga top with crisscross racerback straps. I hadn't worn my climbing shoes in a while, and as I clipped them to my backpack, my feet started to hurt just thinking about being shoved into them. We finished gearing up and got ready to start our approach.

"Where's your helmet?" I asked him.

"At home. I didn't figure we were ice climbing."

"Helmets aren't just for ice climbing, you fool." I shook my head at him.

"I've never worn a helmet for sport climbing and look, I'm still here," he mocked.

"Whatever." I slung my backpack over my shoulder and started trekking up the trail to our first climb.

"You're not upset that I'm not wearing a helmet, are you?" he asked. His look was a little condescending, as if it would have been ridiculous to be concerned with his safety.

"Nope, it's your choice. Not everyone has a brain like mine to protect," I giggled.

"Ha ha, I'm sure you're right. If you sustained a head injury it could knock your IQ down to mine, then what would we be?"

"Two idiots in love," I quipped, grabbing his hand to stop him before stretching up to plant a kiss on his full red lips.

A while later we finished our approach, which was a feat all on its own.

"Looks like a nice one for you." Quinn squinted his eyes, looking up the massive limestone crag.

"You think? I don't know, but I'll give it a go."

Quinn climbed first, leading the route by attaching quickdraws to the bolted anchors up the face of the rock. After securing one quickdraw, he clipped the rope through and climbed to the next. After he made it to the top, I lowered him down and took my turn. I followed on the rope that he had secured all the way up the crag to a double anchor at the top. On my descent, I "cleaned up the route," essentially removing our equipment one clip at a time while I rappelleddown. When my feet reached the ground, he grabbed me and pulled me into him, kissing me so hard it felt like my teeth were cutting into my lips.

"Whoa, what was that for?" I managed between breaths.

"For bringing me here, for being so adventurous, and for looking like sex on a rope up there."

I laughed at his enthusiasm. "Down killer, you need to keep your head in the game. This isn't exactly child's play we're doing up here."

"No worries, I'd never let anything happen to you," he oozed with confidence.

We navigated our way to a nice pitch Quinn eyed after our first climb.

"Am I your first?" I questioned.

"First what?"

"Am I the first girl you've taken climbing?"

"Well, technically you're taking me climbing, but yes, you are the first girl I've climbed with." He grabbed his water taking a long gulp then wiped his mouth on his arm. "Most girls I've ... *been with* haven't had much interest in anything but—"

"Sex," I interrupted.

"I was going to say shopping and partying, but sex too, I suppose." He stopped and dropped his backpack. "This one ..." He scanned the huge arch over us.

"It looks like a good project."

"Project? A thousand dollars says I flash it." He checked his gear and tied in.

"A thousand dollars for making it to the top without coming off? A little steep, don't you think?"

"You'd better be talking about what I'm about to climb and not the wager, my billionaire beauty." He slapped me on the butt.

I checked his knot and he looked over my belay set up. I loved watching Quinn climb, and it wasn't just about his body. Although a video of him climbing without his shirt and sweat dripping off his taut muscles was my type of porn. It was his skill and ease of movement that mesmerized me the most. It was his happy, carefree attitude, as he made every move look so effortless. That was the Quinn I said "yes" to when he proposed.

"Belay?" Quinn asked as he chalked up.

"Belay on, climb on, my hot, sweaty, Latin lover."

He gave me a slight sideways glance, but I could see the smile on his face. Once he secured his first clip he started his small talk, which I noticed was his norm until he made it to the crux.

"How long has it been since you've climbed?" he hollered down.

"Maybe a year or so since I've climbed outdoors. Since then, I've occasionally gone to the climbing gym in Milwaukee with Mac and Evan."

Evan was a great climber and Mac never wanted to climb with me, but when Evan suggested it she acted like it was the best idea ever. She had yet to try anything outdoors, but I knew Evan would have her halfway up a mountain someday.

Quinn made the difficult route look easy. He had one more vertical clip before he reached the horizontal traverse across the top of the arch.

"Am I the first guy you've climbed with, other than Evan?" he yelled.

"Nope."

"Guy number one?" he questioned.

I don't know why I didn't just tell him Malcolm's name; guy number one sounded weird.

I gave Quinn more slack in the rope as he prepared to clip again.

"Yes, we climbed a lot before we got marri—" I about swallowed my tongue, I couldn't believe I let even part of the word slip out of my mouth.

That fraction of a moment in time changed everything, like lightning striking or pulling the trigger of a gun. There was no turning back and no time to react. The next thing I remembered was my whole body jerking off the ground as I braked the rope. A split second later an agonizingly painful cry escaped Quinn. My pulse raced from the flood of adrenaline through my veins.

WHEN A LEAD climber falls, the belayer pulls the rope into brake position, preventing any more rope from being fed to the climber. The climber falls until all the slack in the rope is gone. The force of the fall pulls the belayer off the ground a few feet when the climber's descent is stopped. Both the climber and belayer are supposed to keep their feet in front of them to keep their bodies from hitting the rock. I braked the rope and I kept my feet in front of me as my body lifted from the ground. Having followed protocol for belaying a lead climber, I was fine. Quinn was not.

He was an experienced climber, he knew how to fall properly. *What happened?* I released some of the tension on the rope until my feet reached the ground. The piercing anxiety strangled my heart. With each inch of movement, Quinn moaned in agony.

"Quinn?" My shaky voice broke as I called to him. He didn't answer.

"Quinn, can you hear me? Are you okay?" He still didn't answer. I could see one of his arms was wrapped over his stomach as the other held the rope. Tears blurred my vision. *No! No! No!*

"I'm going to slowly bring you down." I yelled. With trembling hands, I fed the rope an inch at a time. I had to dig deep to stay focused. He was injured but I had no idea to what extent. His inability to say anything left me feeling helpless and vulnerable.

Deep breath … I am peaceful, I am strong.

A few soft taps sounded next to me. Blood. Quinn's blood.

"Quinn!" I screamed as I fought to keep my nervous hands from releasing the rope too quickly. "Oh my God, Quinn!" I sobbed in aching desperation as I eased his limp body onto the ground. My body shook as I tried to assess his injuries.

His weak eyes found mine. The pain in them was unbearable. "Addy," he strained.

His left arm and complete left side of his body was bloodied.

"No, Quinn. You're go-going to be f-f-f-fine."

I grabbed a T-shirt out of my bag and my emergency kit. I dumped cayenne pepper all over his wounded areas. Cayenne pepper had a stabilizing effect on bleeding and aided in clotting. I had used it numerous times on my own cuts, including some that would have required stitches, and each time the bleeding slowed or stopped within minutes. Quinn's injuries were far worse than anything I had ever experienced, but I had to buy him some time. After I finished applying it externally, I added it to his water and made him drink a few swallows. He was weak and it was difficult to get it down but he managed.

"I love you … I love you so mu—much." Cradling his face in my hands, I sobbed.

Using a towel and all extra pieces of clothing we had in our packs, I covered him as best I could. Two other climbers made their way to us.

"Help, we need to get help right away!" I cried as they

approached.

"Quinn! Don't you dare close your eyes. Stay with me, babe, please!"

"We'll get help. There's no cell signal here but down near our camp area we have it," one of them explained.

Both guys looked to be in their twenties and I assumed they were experienced climbers, so when I saw the grave looks on their faces after looking over Quinn, I knew we didn't have much time.

I grabbed my phone out of my pack and searched for a signal even though I knew it was unlikely.

"Addy—"

Turning back around, I knelt beside him. "Shh, they're going to get help. You're going to be fine, okay, just stay awake," I begged through chattering teeth.

Please, God … I'll do anything.

He reached for my arm. "I love—"

"Don't … don't say it, you're not leaving me, do you understand?" I sobbed uncontrollably, clasping his hand and bringing it to my lips. I wasn't ready to say goodbye. "Never goodbye, remember, never goodbye."

He gave me a slow nod as he winced in pain. Every minute that passed felt like an eternity. I looked up at the massive rock formation and saw the spot where he hit. There was blood on the jagged edge of granite. Quinn was a skilled climber. I was certain he knew how to properly take a fall. So why did he not get his arms and legs in front of him?

In a place I wasn't ready to acknowledge, I knew why. He lost all concentration when I slipped up about my past.

I was the reason he didn't get clipped in.

I was the reason he fell.

I was the reason he was lying on the ground fighting for his life.

The tears wouldn't stop. "Quinn, I'm so sorry. I love you so much, please hold on." As I wiped my eyes and nose with the back of my hand, I tried to clear my throat. It was sore from my desperate pleas.

HE MOANED IN such pain it tore me up inside. I hated the sound of it, but I hated the silence that surrounded us even more. I was desperate to hear sirens from rescue vehicles or a helicopter nearing us, but we were enveloped in an eerie quietude of agony.

He kept one hand clutched to his stomach and reached for my arm with his other hand.

An indecipherable whisper squeezed through his throat.

"I can't understand you, but don't try and talk, babe, help will be here soon."

I held his hand and leaned into him as he insistently tried to say something again.

"Wh-wh-why?" he finally managed.

Why what?

My mind raced, grasping for an ounce of comprehension. I didn't know for sure what the question was, but I knew the answer had everything to do with me. I'd spent so much time protecting myself from my past I never considered the possibility that Quinn needed protection too. He had hurt me, more than once, but I always had the option to walk away.

Within a matter of seconds, I broke him emotionally and physically. I wondered if he would ever forgive me. I wondered if his family would forgive me. It really didn't matter; I knew I would never forgive myself.

All time was lost to my thoughts and concern for Quinn. I had no idea how long it took, but eventually the hum of a helicopter could be heard in the distance.

"Quinn?" I held his face in my hands.

It was still contorted into the most painful grimace, and his moans turned to screams when he tried to move.

"Quinn, open your eyes, they're coming. Do you hear that?"

He was leaving me and I was slipping away too.

Quinn didn't respond and then everything for me became a blurred line between my past and the present.

"MALCOLM! THE FIRE alarm, oh my God the house is on fire! I've got to go get—"

"No, Addy, you get out. I mean it, get out of the house right now!"

"Ma'am, can you tell us what happened? Did he fall all the way to the ground?"

"I'm coming with you, Malcolm."
"Addy, I said get out of the house. I'll go, you just get out!"

"Ma'am are you hurt? Is the blood on you yours or his? You need to come with us."

"Malcolm! Oh God, oh God … Malcolm, can you hear me? Hurry, you have to hurry!"

"His blood pressure's dropping. Start an IV."

"I'm coming back in, Malcolm, where are you? I can't see

anything. Ugh!" Cough "I can't breathe." Cough "Ma—" Cough "Mal—" Cough "...colm?" Cough. Cough. Cough.

"We need to transit to the nearest hospital or he's not going to make it."

"I'm sorry, sweetie, they're ... they're..." Sniffle, sniffle "...They didn't make it, they're gone."
Th-thump, th-thump, th-thump ...

TO BE CONTINUED ...

Acknowledgements

I owe an enormous debt of gratitude to my village. Without you, Addy and Quinn's story would not have come to fruition.

To my lifelong friend, Jyl, thank you for introducing me to the world of Adult Contemporary Romance Novels and encouraging me to turn my obsession into my passion.

To Dave, a special thank you for your "free" orthopedic and emergency medicine consults.

To my sister, Kambra, thank you for being my biggest cheerleader and my unofficial, underpaid, but hugely appreciated publicist. This smut's for you!

To my mom, thank you for critiquing the love scenes and making the grueling first edits, and for keeping an open mind and showing me how to do the same.

To my beta readers: Sherri, Tricia, Jyl, Leslie, and Kambra, your input and kind reviews have given me the confidence to keep writing.

To my editor, Max Dobson of the Polished Pen, thank you for turning my chicken scratches into a publishable novel. You've been a great mentor.

To Kiezha with Librum Artis, thank you for your patience with my re-edit after I decided my first book needed some (a lot) of changes to make it not so cringe-worthy.

To my three awesome boys, thank you for not killing each other over the past six months while I've been locked up writing, and for learning how to cook, clean, and navigate Netflix on your own.

Finally, to my amazing husband, thank you for getting up early and going to work everyday to pay the bills, while I sit in front of a computer and pursue my dreams.

You are a true friend, father, husband, and lover. Eternity will not be long enough to show you how honored I am that you chose me.

ALSO BY JEWEL E. ANN

Holding You Series
RELEASING ME

Jack and Jill Series
END OF DAY
MIDDLE OF KNIGHT
DAWN OF FOREVER

Standalone Novels
IDLE BLOOM
ONLY TRICK
UNDENIABLY YOU

jeweleann.com

ABOUT THE AUTHOR

Jewel is a free-spirited romance junkie with a quirky sense of humor.

With 10 years of flossing lectures under her belt, she took early retirement from her dental hygiene career to stay home with her three awesome boys and manage the family business.

After her best friend of nearly 30 years suggested a few books from the Contemporary Romance genre, Jewel was hooked. Devouring two and three books a week but still craving more, she decided to practice sustainable reading, AKA writing.

When she's not donning her cape and saving the planet one tree at a time, she enjoys yoga with friends, good food with family, rock climbing with her kids, watching How I Met Your Mother reruns, and of course...heart-wrenching, tear-jerking, panty-scorching novels.

Printed in Great Britain
by Amazon

21201045R00222